SHADOW OF THE WHITE BEAR

JW WEBB

Acknowledgement for:

John Jarrold, for editing

Roger Garland, the late Tolkien artist, for the illustrations

Ravven, for the cover design

Chris Kocher, for proofreading

Crystal Sarakas, for book design

Ansu map Illustration by Hanna Sandvig: www.bookcoverbakey.com

Ta Shen map illustration by Linda Garland

lakeside-gallery.com

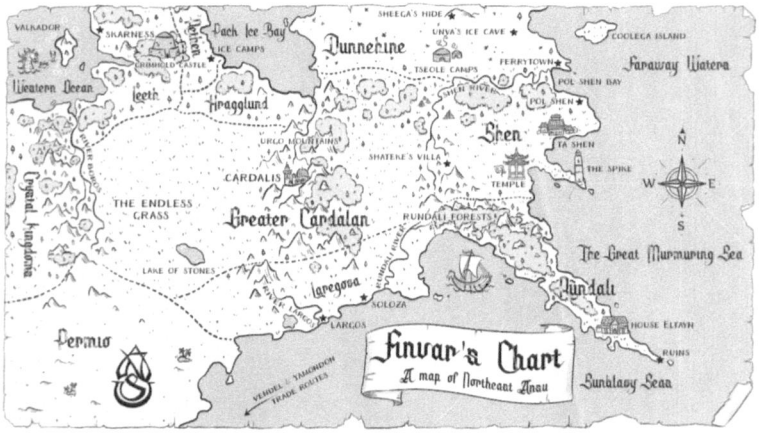

For Ravven,
A fabulous artist and wonderful person,
Thanks for your stunning covers and help over the years,
This one's for you, Ravv

Would you trade your soul to save your life?

The Crimson Lady knows that her soul may be the price she has to pay to get revenge.

If you enjoyed *Blood Feud,* you will love this new tale, *The Crimson Lady.* It's available free for newsletter members only. Don't miss out! Join our fun newsletter the JW Webb VIP Lounge. *Subscribe today!*

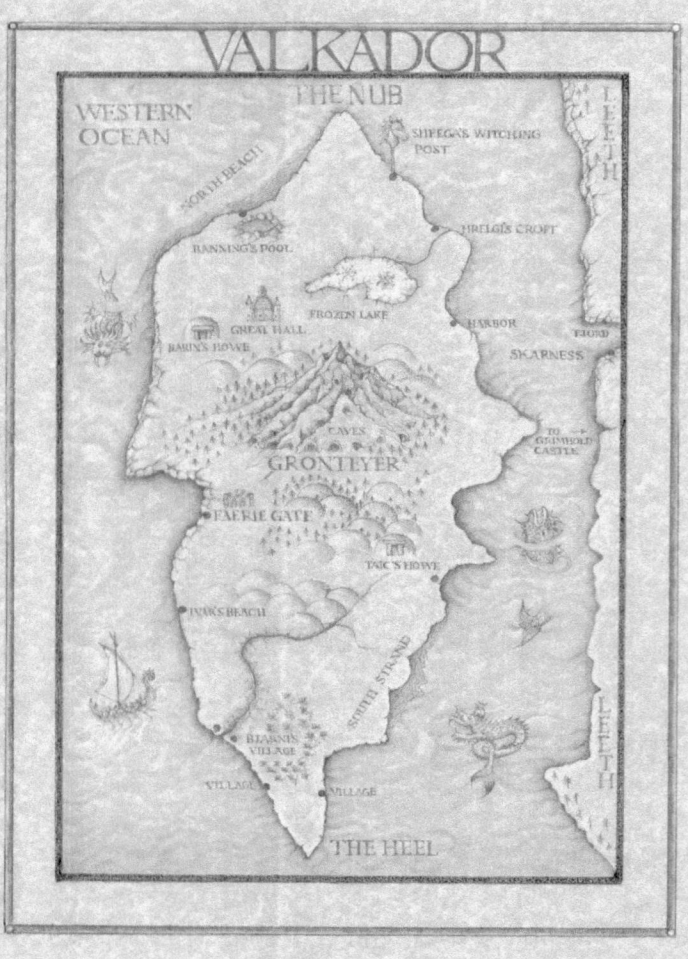

PART I

REFUGE

THE MESSAGE

IVAR KETILSSON WATCHED the flashing lights away in the distance. What was she up to today? He felt the familiar cold shiver creeping up his back when he thought about her. The witch some dared call Sheega, though most would never utter the name for fear of being cursed or, worse, hunted down by one of her creatures. They were always watching, listening in from the dark woods.

Another flash, brighter this time. He shielded his eyes from the glare. Was she hunting? It had to be her, or that ghastly elf creature who'd come from the sea. Crawled out of her mists.

The flash a third time, followed by a boom and the sound of feet approaching. Ivar stared north along the strand, as the cold brine washed his worn-out boots. He needed to get back; it would be dark soon. There was nowhere safe on the island after dark.

The sound of giant feet grew nearer. One of her sendings? Ivar had been on the mountain last week and had seen weird smoke rising from the hall, hardly visible at the far north end of Valkador. Sheega was conjuring another horror into the world.

The ground trembled. Ivar knew he should drop his catch and run. No cover here on the beach. Whoever this giant was, he'd soon spot Ivar.

But he didn't run. He stayed put, his fear matched by a hidden wonder, and a strange assurance. *He who comes has nothing to do with the witch.*

The wind—already strong—picked up around him, blowing spindrift and white spray across the empty beach. It howled in his ears like some hunting beast. To his left, the sea rose up in towering spume that crashed and thudded onto the shore.

Ivar was buffeted and battered, deafened and drenched. He kept his feet braced, leaning hard on his fish spear, his sharp hunter's eyes on the rocks at the top of the beach. The wind whirled. He saw a water spout dance along the ocean. Ivar's eyes followed it until the heavy thud and tremble brought his gaze back to the strand.

A figure was striding toward him. Huge and terrible, with eyes of blazing silver. Ivar felt his legs tremble as he gripped the spear. The giant approached him and towered over the spot where Ivar stood, too terrified to move.

"HE IS BACK. YOU MUST MAKE READY." The voice rose above the wind. It became the wind, controlling that gale, channeling the gusts out to sea where the water spout still danced and whirled like a writhing leviathan. Ivar stared up at the giant, feeling those terrible eyes burning inside his head. He guessed who it was that stood before him on the wind scourged beach.

Mighty Kullaan, you who own the wind.

The god stared down at Ivar for what seemed an age, but

must only have been seconds. Somehow, he found his voice and called up at the towering figure.

"What must I do?" Ivar's long hair tossed about his face. He couldn't hear his words, but had to show that he was ready for whatever must be done. Kullaan the Wind God was not one to defy.

"FIND JARAN SAERK BEFORE SHE DOES." The eyes blazed at him a moment longer, then the god turned away. Ivar watched Kullaan stride off into the waves, passing beyond the broken crag of rocks where he'd emerged minutes before.

The wind eased as the god departed from sight, a rack of storm clouds threatened squalls, and rain started studding the sand at his feet. The sea flattened out and a thin veil of blue cracked open the clouds above his head.

Jaran Saerk? The name meant little to him. Ivar, in his sixtieth year, recalled that brave Hrelgi's lost babe had been called Jaran. Could it be? He shook the spear skyward as a sudden hope and excitement filled his heart.

Jaran survived—Bera's child lived yet. And he was here! Why else would mighty Kullaan visit? And why would Sheega be active after so long? Jaran Hrelgisson would be nearing thirty winters. A warrior like Hrelgi, and wanting revenge. He'd come home to kill the witch.

Ivar felt younger than he had for years. He scooped up his net full of writhing mackerel and slung it over his back, the fish spear sloped across one shoulder. Ivar walked the beach, as dusk settled and rain soaked him. He didn't care. Three decades had passed since last he smiled with any mirth. He reached the village and saw Myra standing in the rain, her pale locks strewed across her face. His daughter had her fists thrust in her hips and looked cross.

Bjarni Orlsson exchanged a questioning look with his wife, as her father drained his soup bowl and belched enthusiastically. Old Ivar seemed uncommonly cheerful this evening, despite the foul weather and miserable catch. He'd been away all day, as was his wont. The old tracker harked back to the lost times before the witch. Ivar had been one of Jarle Hrund's thanes. A skilled hunter, he'd been up in the mountains when Sheega arrived and discovered the news on his return. A terrible time apparently. Bjarni hadn't been alive then, nor had Ivar's daughter, Myra, who he'd wedded last summer.

The village was all he'd ever known. Their drab, cold existence at the southern tip of Valkador. That and a terror of nightfall, and the creatures that sometimes wandered this far. Sheega's sendings, they said.

But the witch was far from here. It was twenty miles over the mountain to the great hall where Hrund had lived, before the foul murder that distant day.

Bjarni grinned as Ivar wiped his mouth and slammed the wooden bowl on table.

"We expected salmon, Father." Myra smiled at Bjarni, who knew she was only teasing. Ivar always promised salmon, but the fish were scarce. Too many bears up there where the forest met the mountain slopes.

"What's that?" Ivar glanced over at his daughter and then gazed hard at Bjarni, his clear blue eyes sparkling in a most unusual way. The village elder was well known for his gloomy manner and doom-speaking. Bjarni was curious about this sudden change.

"I'll cook the mackerel tomorrow," Myra said, showing no

hint of surprise at her father's spritely mood. "Hopefully the sun will show his face—been a miserable summer so far. Father, are you listening?"

He wasn't. Ivar looked to be in a dream. Myra rubbed her hands on her oiled-stained apron and looked at Bjarni. "Talk to him," she said. "I've the goat to milk and our children to muster for their supper and bed."

She gave Bjarni a frank expression and departed from the wattle hut. He heard her shouting the girls' names out there, as fresh rain assaulted the willow hut they called home.

Bjarni stoked the fire, his eyes flicking to where Ivar sat dreaming. "You seem content with yourself this evening," he said, taking seat on the bench and pouring a weak ale into his mug.

"I saw a thing," Ivar muttered.

"What kind of *thing*?'

Bjarni sipped and scratched an ear.

"Call it a visitation—the god Kullaan dropped by."

Bjarni snorted through his ale and tried to quell his mirth. "Kullaan Thunderer?" Bjarni had huge respect for Ivar but suspected he'd hit his head, or had eaten mushrooms perhaps.

"The same." Ivar caught his expression and his face turned sour. "You don't believe me."

"I'm just shocked," Bjarni said, placing his beer down carefully. He was intrigued, Ivar not being a man to fabricate wild notions. "Are you certain it was the Wind God, not a trick of the light? Or something *she* …?" He turned away, not wanting to go there.

"It was Tyho's terrible brother," Ivar said. "He spoke to me, boy. The god sought me on the beach and assailed me with His winds. Kullaan Thunderer spoke a name I haven't heard in nearly thirty years."

"What name?" Bjarni leaned in close. The hut seemed very quiet—even the fire had dwindled to embers, as though the flames were listening. Bjarni studied his father-in-law's hard features. He looked eager, charged by some hidden knowledge.

"Jaran *Saerk*." Ivar stared hard at Bjarni. "Kullaan has tasked me to find him."

"Who?" Myra's head had appeared through the entrance. She looked angry, flustered and tired. Bjarni waved her wait a moment. She entered with the girls. All three were soaked— his daughters giggling, their mother annoyed. "What nonsense is this?" Myra said, shaking the rain off her coat.

"Kullaan was here," Bjarni said quietly.

"The god, Kullaan?" Their youngest and brightest, Geda giggled.

"Shut up," Myra clipped her ear, but Ivar grinned at the girl, making her giggle again. Silfi started too, so Myra shouted them to go eat supper. They poked each other and ran through to the tiny kitchen.

Ivar chuckled, "I love those girls," he said, receiving a stern stare from Myra.

"What's wrong with you?" she said, before looking over at Bjarni, who shrugged in response.

"You had best tell your daughter," Bjarni said eventually, draining his beer mug and pouring more. Myra looked weary but resigned. She pulled up a stool by the fire.

"Go on," she said. "Tell me. You saw Kullaan ..."

"I did, and He saw me," Ivar said, his face serious again. "The Thunderer approached me on the beach while I was spearing fish. I saw a strange flash of lights somewhere north along the leeward shore. A waterspout. Knew something uncanny was about to happen. Next, I heard footsteps and feared it was one of her creatures. Instead, the Wind God was striding toward me."

"Why would Kullaan Thunderer pay you a visit?" By her tone, Bjarni could tell his wife was humoring the old man. Ivar clearly knew it too, but told her what the god had said as Bjarni poured him a brimming ale. Ivar sipped slowly and looked at his daughter.

"What are you going to do?" Myra asked him

"Set out for the mountains at sunup," Ivar said.

"I'll come with you," Bjarni said.

"You two have gone soft in the head." Myra wiped her brow. It was hot by the fireside, but she didn't complain. "It's not wise or safe to stray that far from the village. Not that you ever listen to my counsel, Father. But I'd sooner keep my husband around."

"We will talk about it in the morning," Ivar said. He drained his ale and left them for his cot in the room he shared with the girls.

"What do you think?" Bjarni asked her when Ivar's snores announced him done for the night.

Myra shrugged. "He saw something, that much is clear. An enchantment, perhaps? Though we've had no trouble from her for many years."

"It is strange—your father's not one to take on fancies."

"Let us see what morning brings," she smiled at him. "I'm for bed."

"I'll stay and sip for a while yet," Bjarni told her as she kissed him goodnight. He sat for a time dreamily watching the fire, before sleep eventually found him in his chair.

It was Geda that woke him still slumped there.

"What is it?" The fire was ashes, and bright sunshine filtered in through the doorway. Bjarni blinked—it wasn't normal for him to sleep past dawn, especially in the chair. "Well?" He stood and gripped Geda's shoulders.

"A ship," she said, excitedly. "Mother's with Silfi outside. Grandfather's there too."

"It cannot be," Bjarni stepped outside and poured an urn of seawater over his head. Refreshed, he walked through the village to their little harbor where he saw Myra, her father and some of the townsfolk gathered. All were staring north along the shore.

Myra turned as he drew near. She looked anxious, but excited too.

"A ship?" Bjarni asked, and then realized the other thing that had changed.

The mist has gone. Sheega's fret. He could see for miles along the rugged coast. A clear blue day with no fog or haze on the horizon. Away east were huge bluffs announcing the mainland and Leeth. It was the first time he'd seen them. Closer, yet still miles to the north, he saw a small vessel cutting through chop and making for the island. He watched until the ship disappeared behind the mountain's eastern shoulder.

"Her enchanted mist ..." Bjarni felt a rush of excitement. "First Kullaan and now this. "Perhaps she's ... gone."

"Don't say it." Myra covered his mouth. "She's always listening."

"But her mist has departed, Myra. The witch must be in trouble."

"Most likely causing the trouble, but something's amiss for sure."

"I'm leaving for the hills," Ivar told them as the entire townsfolk had arrived to stare.

"I'd sooner you didn't," Myra said nodding her head. She looked at Bjarni. "You had best go with, husband."

He gripped her hand and kissed the salty cheeks. "We won't linger," Bjarni told Myra. She nodded and turned away.

"Father—bring my husband home safely," Myra said.

"I will, I promise you," Ivar flashed her a wolfish grin and grabbed Bjarni's arm. "You ready, lad?"

"I will be after some breakfast," Bjarni grinned back.

FOUR HOURS LATER, BJARNI STOOD ON THE SOUTHERN slopes of Gronteyer, the wind buffeting his ears. He was smiling like a fool. So good to be up here, the furthest he'd ever strayed from their village. A few times as they'd climbed the long ridge and wended through the pines, he'd glanced back at the distant sparkle of ocean and the homestead huddled on the windward shore.

Myra would be busy mending nets and scolding the girls. Theirs was a good life, if poor. Something told Bjarni that was about to change.

"Where are we heading?" Bjarni shouted as the wind deafened him and stole his voice.

"Caves," Ivar yelled back. "Should reach 'em by dusk."

Bjarni didn't like the sound of that. Creeping inside caves was not for the careful. There were rumors of bears aplenty. But it wasn't natural beasts that concerned him. He had his bow and a plain wrought axe. Ivar had his fish spear and a flensing knife. These trusty tools wouldn't prove over-useful against the demons that might lurk in the dark holes deep inside Gronteyer.

There were so many stories about the other end of the island and what had occurred up there. Beyond the mountain, he'd never been. But Ivar had lived there back then.

They left the crest behind, and the southern slopes were lost to cloud. Ahead were thick pines marching up into the frost that mantled Gronteyer's twin peaks. The walk through the pine forest took several hours. They stopped once, Bjarni thinking he spied an owl flitting through trees. It struck him as strange, seeing the bird in daylight.

Ivar was true to his word. The sun was sinking over western water when they left the woods and entered a saddle of broken stone and deer tracks, which led up to a gray rise of flat- sided slabs. Bjarni saw the cave entrance and felt a shiver inside.

"Are we going in there?"

"Tomorrow." Ivar winked at him. "Even I'd not chance the caves this late in the day. Are you nervous?"

"I'm fine," Bjarni said, relieved they weren't camping in that cave tonight.

"Good. You should be—you're from warrior stock."

"I've never killed a man."

"Plenty of time," Ivar said. "And not a thing one seeks out lightly. This will do." He'd found a hollow a hundred yards from the cave mouth, almost hidden in the gloom. Bjarni gathered deadwood as his father-in-law struck flint to stone and made a spark.

That night, they sat talking, the low crackle of fire awarding sufficient warmth. Aside from the distant howl of wolf the night was clear. He saw an owl again, gliding low. Bjarni yawned at the flames.

"Sleepy?" A dozing Ivar opened an eye.

"Not really." Bjarni couldn't settle with that cave so close.

Ivar saw where his gaze went and grinned. "Sheega's not in there, boy. You worry too much."

"Your daughter would disagree," Bjarni said.

"Hah, so she would. Poor Myra frets enough for both of us."

"Aye, she does, and rightly so." He glanced at the cave again. "What happens next?"

"We sleep. Daylight will tell us what to do."

"I'm not for sleeping," Bjarni said. "I'd sooner you tell me about the man we're seeking."

"I don't know him," Ivar replied, evasively.

"You knew his father."

"That I did, and was proud to." Ivar's blue gaze misted over. "I never encountered a better warrior than Hrelgi Hrundsson."

"Killed by a bear." Bjarni gazed at the fire. "So strange a tale."

"Stranger than you think." Ivar glared at him. "It was no bear that did for Hrelgi. Rather, *he* was the bear. Cursed by the witch, after he alone dared challenge her. I was following the hunt from a safe distance. I remember that grim day like no other."

Bjarni was surprised to see the tears rimming Ivar's eyes.

"Erlund killed his brother," Ivar said. "At that time, we all thought it was a monster. A great white bear that had somehow roamed down from the frozen north. Swam the sea or else crossed from the mainland when it was frozen during winter's worst."

"Erlund killed his brother? This is news I haven't heard."

"We elders kept it from you, that dark day. Most of what

happened." Ivar sighed. "And few are left who remember what she did."

Bjarni shivered as he heard the owl calling out. Moments later, a second one answered. It seemed colder and darker than it had been. He should get more sticks to bank the fire.

"If Sheega killed Hrelgi, how is it that his son survived?"

"I do not know the answer to that, though I can guess," Ivar said. "When she came the witch brought others. Strangers, from—wherever she came from. Not all were her friends. It was though she was continuing some private quarrel. There was a man ..." His voice trailed off and he looked toward the cave.

Bjarni turned that way, and for the briefest instant thought he spied a figure standing there, his cloak and hood rimmed by moonlight before clouds stole the vision away. If Ivar had noticed the figure, he showed no sign. Bjarni willed it a trick of moonlight.

"There was a feast," Ivar said quietly. "I was one of the guards posted outside the halls, thus spared what happened. The thanes ..."

"Jarle Hrund?"

"Him too, before she killed him. And the thanes in the hall—they all ate of the bear's flesh without knowing it was Hrelgi. After that, many fled to Leeth, though others stayed and became her playthings—her favorite amongst these being Erlund, who'd killed his own brother. She made him a king in Leeth, I heard, before taking that elf for a lover."

"Do you remember the witch?" None in the village had ever encountered Sheega, or if they had, they'd not told their tale. Most, like Bjarni, had been born after Sheega's ill-fated arrival.

"I see her face every day," Ivar said. "It haunts me yet.

Beautiful, foreign. Her eyes were pale, blue—as were poor Hrelgi's, I recall. But slanted and cruel. She had—has—a raw, terrible presence. You wanted to please her. I remember feeling proud when she smiled at me one time. I would have done anything for her that day.

"I was very young," he added mournfully. "Think I'm done talking."

Bjarni let Ivar be and allowed his mind to wander. He closed his eyes, but kept opening them again, half-expecting to see a hooded figure over by the broken stone. He saw nothing and clouds hid the moon. He must have slept for a time.

When Bjarni woke, he found himself staring up into the eyes of a stranger. A hard-faced warrior, clad in gleaming mail, his fair hair wild, and a great axe hanging in a loop at his belt.

"Who are you?" Bjarni managed, still half-asleep and wishing he hadn't left his weapon against that tree.

"The one you've been looking for." The man smiled down at him. "My name is Jaran Hrelgisson. I've come home to kill the witch."

2

THE VILLAGE

SAVARNA WORKED AT THE CARCASS, slicing of chunks and draping them over the makeshift rods, as the fire blazed and cast long shadows across the cave walls. Jaran was out there keeping watch; her task was to get some food inside them. He'd felled the deer at dawn with a crafty throw from his knife, having crept close enough through the dense pine.

The strips were taking nicely. They hadn't eaten much since arriving on this island three days past. If *arrive* was the right way of describing what had happened.

And what had happened?

She still couldn't fully grasp what had occurred over the last few days. Savarna, despite being used to strange events, found her mind addled in a blur of confusion and worry. It seemed only a short time since she was staring at Rasnei's face, before that her quarrel with Vian during the brief but fraught stay in Ta Shen. The horror of her *Aikashi* fight with Scard still stained her. Even their fight and escape from Sheega's hide seemed only yesterday. So much had happened. Faerie, the journey with Rafin—*had that been real?* It must have been, for here they were in Valkador.

Or so it seemed. Savarna wasn't convinced. At least Jaran seemed happy, and she was grateful for that. And they were together. *Good.* What next?

Staying alive and keeping their whereabouts secret for two entire months seemed quite the task, even if this wasn't some new illusion created by Sheega. They had crashed through the back door from Faerie. Surely that would have sent red warning flares skyrocketing in Sheega's direction?

JARAN SAERK APPROACHING.

Savarna almost chuckled at the absurdity. Sheega would know they were here. It wouldn't be long before her creatures came crawling through these pine woods. The hell hounds, or perhaps another Stoon? Worse—a second changeling like Scard. She shuddered at the thought.

And she didn't like hiding like a frightened doe. Savarna was a huntress, not cornered game. Were it possible, Savarna would go visit that witch again to put an end to this business for once and all. But two moons needed to pass before that would be possible. Not only that—they needed Finvar Droll. Unva, the other witch, and the Tseole shaman had said all three of them were needed to kill Sheega.

And where was Finvar? Jaran had said he'd most likely turn up. Again, she hadn't held out to his optimism. Finvar could be lost, for all they knew. Dead as stones. Her nagging doubts weren't helpful. Annoyed with her mood, she turned the strips on the rods, pulled one slice off and stuffed it into her mouth. Good and crunchy—juicy, too. Outside the cave, she heard blackbirds calling and the soft tingle of rain on stone. Jaran should be back by now.

Damn this!

Savarna slid her scimitar out of the belt and went to stand at the cave entrance. The rain fell steadily, but she saw blue sky spreading in the south; the clouds were shifting at speed. *Where was he?*

Too many riddles and questions. Their being here in Valkador. Rune's sudden appearance. And, of course, he'd disappeared again. The one thing that hadn't surprised her. After their leaving the beach, the silver mystic said he needed to attend some complex issue involving Faerie and would return in due course.

Jaran seemed content with that. Savarna wasn't. What game was that creature playing? And where was Rafin the Dwarf? She didn't want to believe the nonsense about Rune living inside Rafin's head, but after passing through Faerie anything seemed possible.

Savarna harbored concerns that both Rafin and Rune were using Jaran for some dark purpose. Time would tell. They had two months to work it out. To survive. No point dwelling on these murky matters.

She stiffened, hearing voices close by. Gripping her scimitar in both hands, she stole carefully into the trees.

Savarna stopped abruptly, seeing Jaran seated on a rock, a gray-haired man crouched beside him and another younger one standing a few feet away, with arms folded.

What's this? Savarna walked in on the party and glared at Jaran. The older man crouching next to him leapt to his feet, and the other one's eyes widened in shock.

"You should have introduced us," Savarna said, smiling at the pair. The older one grinned back at her, having recovered smoothly from his initial shock. The younger looked alarmed.

Jaran turned and grinned up at her. "My countrymen, Ivar

Ketilsson and Bjarni Orlsson." He nodded toward each in turn.

"Happy to meet you." Savarna stowed the sword and folded her arms. She stared sideways at Jaran. "Breakfast is ready," she told him. "There won't be much, as I wasn't expecting company." She motioned that the two should come with them. This they did readily enough, though the young one, Bjarni, still looked worried.

"Savarna won't hurt you unless I ask her to," Jaran said to Bjarni, as Savarna turned away and walked briskly back to the cave.

"I like your hair," Ivar said as they entered inside. "Unusual color."

"Thank you," she replied, handing a slice of venison across. "Tell me one thing, will you? Is this really Valkador and not some lost corner of Faerie?"

"Faerie?" Bjarni looked at Ivar, who shrugged.

"Valkador it is," the lean, sharp-eyed oldster replied. Ivar seemed a durable, confident type. "Or always has been as far as legends speak."

"Then you are our Jarle?" Bjarni blurted the words out. He appeared in awe of Jaran and was over-shy, in her opinion, or maybe not that bright. A well-built, handsome lad, but with scant metal inside him.

"I am Hrund's grandson," Jaran nodded, chewing at the meat with his teeth. "I've come back to avenge the Jarle and his son—my father, Hrelgi."

"That won't prove easy," Ivar said.

"We're aware of that," Savarna said. She smiled at Bjarni, who dropped his gaze, his face flushing. Bjarni seemed much taken with watching her from the corner of his eyes. She pretended not to notice. "Hard or not," she added, "we've a witch to kill."

"But not today," Jaran said, grinning. "We have to hide out for two moons."

"Why so long?" Ivar asked, and then smiled as though he'd worked it out. "Omens and portents."

"Yes, and from all sorts of people," Jaran nodded. "We've had an interesting time getting here."

"You'll be safe in the village for a day or so," Ivar said, and she noted how Bjarni looked shocked hearing that.

"We'd sooner stay away, else we put you in danger," Savarna said, flashing Bjarni another smile, and meaning it this time. He grinned back, looking relieved.

"It's too late—you already have," Ivar said. He chewed on his meat for a moment and sighed. "Kullaan was here."

"The god?" Jaran looked surprised for the first time.

"Himself," Ivar said. "Told me to come find you. Yesterday. It's why we're here."

"Tyho's brother?" She looked at Jaran.

He nodded. "And just as perilous they say."

"Well, that's bloody marvelous," she said, standing up. "Why don't we rig up some flags and wave them on top of that mountain, while screaming out, '*Sheega, we're here!*'" She sat down again and grabbed the last piece of meat.

"She gets like this sometimes," Jaran told them as their guests stared at Savarna with open mouths. Ivar stifled a grin. "One of the reasons why I love her."

"We need to hold council in the village," Bjarni said, trying to insert himself into the conversation. "Let the other villages know."

"How many are you?" she asked him.

"Perhaps three hundred," Bjarni said. "Our village is small, but there are two other settlements at the southern tip of the island."

"How many fighters?" Jaran asked Ivar.

"I'd say about eighty strong lads—but none are warriors. Most are like young Bjarni here—honest fishermen, scared of their wives," Ivar said, and she noted how Bjarni scowled hearing that. "There haven't been any warriors on the island since the witch arrived."

"We have some training to do." Jaran grinned at Savarna, who failed to see what was funny.

"It will take more than four score brave lads to deal with witch-men, or worse," she said, but agreed that they might as well get started. Anything was better than hiding in a cave.

"We'll meet with your thanes and discuss our strategy," Jaran told Ivar. The old man replied that there were no thanes, only elders, and he was one of them.

"I didn't know we had a strategy," Savarna said later, as they walked through the pines toward the southern slopes of the twin-peaked mountain that she'd learnt was called Gronteyer—an odd-sounding name to her Rundali ears.

"I'm working on one," he responded wryly.

It wasn't long before Ivar pointed out the ribbon of huts strewn crooked down by the shore. He seemed proud of his village. Savarna pictured Stoon and Crane arriving with axes, then shut out the image. *That's not going to happen to these people.* She wouldn't allow it.

MYRA HAD FELT THE WORRY-WORM GROWING INSIDE HER all day. The girls had sensed their mother's mood and stayed clear. She'd been mending nets when she heard Bjarni's cheerful shout and rushed grinning to meet him.

Her grin fled her face, though, when she saw the huge blond fighting man and the exotic wild-eyed woman walking beside him. The man had an evil-looking axe hanging from his thick leather belt. The woman looked half savage, a feral creature with strange-colored eyes and vivid red hair. She seemed half animal and smiled a fierce greeting at Myra, who suppressed a shudder and hoped the girls weren't hovering close.

"Time to cook that mackerel, Myra," Bjarni said. "We've guests for supper tonight." Myra noticed with irritation how his eyes glanced admiringly at the redhead as he spoke.

"I was just finishing here," she said, grinning up at the huge blond and making sure Bjarni saw. "You, husband, can go see to the girls." Bjarni nodded and left them.

As dusk fell low, Myra took seat beside Savarna as Bjarni, with limited help from the two very excited girls, prepared the fish.

"It smells delicious," the woman called Savarna said.

"You're not from around here, are you?" Myra said after an awkward silence.

"I'm from Rundali."

"A hot, steamy land in the east," the big blond, who she'd learned from Ivar—unsurprisingly—was the mysterious Jaran Saerk. He seemed friendly and approachable for a legend, and he grinned at her. "She's half tiger," he added beaming at the girls, and receiving an elbow in his ribs from the woman.

The girls ran off, laughing and pretending to be frightened. Myra nodded at the odd couple's private joke. These people were strange but would hopefully be gone soon. *Either that or the witch will come here, and we're all be dead in a week.*

Though likely, that wasn't a cheerful thought, so she stowed it neatly away.

"How did you get here?" Myra asked them.

"It's hard to explain," Jaran Saerk said.

"A long story," Savarna added. Myra left that alone too.

"Have you seen a small fellow around?" Jaran Saerk asked Ivar, after a moment's silence. "Quick of eye, fast on his feet and deft of hand. Talks too much. He carries a short bow around with a sack full of arrows."

"You're our only visitors," Ivar said shaking his head. "There was a ship two days hence, after the mist departed."

"A ship? Where did it go?" The big blond looked intense, his easy manner replaced by a glint-eyed stare. Myra felt a stab of fear, thinking of her girls. They didn't know these people. Never mind what Kullaan had said to her father—if indeed that had been the Wind God, and not some sly fetch from the hall.

She saw how Ivar met Jaran Saerk's look with a steady gaze. "It was lost behind the hills," he said. "But appeared to be making for these shores at the north end of the island."

"Two days ago?"

"Yesterday morning," Ivar nodded.

"That had to be Fin," the blond warrior said. "Our friend," he added to Myra and Bjarni.

"You can't assume that," Savarna said, shaking her head. "More likely coincidence."

"The mist departs and a ship arrives here so soon?" Jaran said. "No one has sailed to Valkador except us, and your lost friend Carlo Sarfe. It's Finvar, I tell you."

Myra looked questioningly across at Bjarni, who shrugged.

"If that was your friend arriving, he's in direst peril," Ivar said. "That craft looked to be making for the only stone harbor on Valkador."

"Near the Great Hall?" Savarna asked.

Ivar nodded.

"How far are we from there?" Jaran asked, his pale eyes gleaming.

"Twenty miles," her father told them. "A hard hike across the mountain, and down through deeper woods than we walked today. That, or twice as far along the beach."

"If Finvar has survived this long, he should hold out for a time." Savarna placed a hand on her man's arm. She looked worried, Myra thought.

"Not if she's waiting for him," Jaran Saerk said. "And why wouldn't she be? Fin must have seen the island after the mist vanished and set sail, the daft fool."

"If anyone can outfox Sheega, it's Finvar," Savarna said. "Our friend has special talents," she told them.

"He's going to need them," Ivar said.

"When were you last there?" Savarna asked her father.

"It's been years," Ivar said, and Myra saw how his brows knitted and tough face was haunted by doubts.

"Father, you don't have to speak of those days," Myra said.

"I must," he told her. "But later, when everyone is here. Our Jarle needs to know who he's up against."

"He knows that well enough," Savarna said.

Our Jarle ... Myra looked at Jaran Saerk, who appeared lost in thought. Her gaze flicked across to Bjarni, who was nodding.

"You sure about this?" she asked Bjarni. "Jaran's a common enough name, though I've not heard of anyone called Saerk."

"Why else would Kullaan visit your father?" Bjarni asked. "This is Jaran Hrelgisson, Myra. Grandson of Jarle Hrund."

"You were the lost child." Myra gazed at Jaran Saerk in wonder. He said nothing. "We were told the stories—there was a rumor that Bera's son was stolen by a wight in the dark."

"That's not far from the truth," he said wryly. Then the big warrior grinned at her. "The fish is excellent."

Then his face became serious again and he added: "I'm going to settle matters here on this island, Myra Ivarsdottir. Free Valkador and its people. We have all suffered more than enough from that witch. Sheega will die soon. That much, I promise you."

"You'd better let the others know," Myra said to Bjarni, as Ivar started talking about the last time he'd visited the north end of the island.

"Asmund's on that, and Olof is already away south to inform the other villages," Bjarni told her. "We'll meet in council when they're back. Hold a Thing, like they used to in the old days."

Myra nodded, hiding her misgivings. "That is well." She reached across and touched the warrior's arm. He turned and looked at her. His eyes were kinder than she'd first thought. Hard, but not cruel. He looked sad, too. "I'm glad you're here, Jaran Hrelgisson," Myra told him.

"Jaran Hrelgisson was lost many years ago," he told her. "I am called Jaran *Saerk* these days." To her alarm, he tugged off his mail shirt and the leather one beneath and stood up, bare-chested before them.

Myra covered her mouth with a hand, Bjarni looked startled. Ivar smiled and nodded.

"There was a man who came here some years back," Ivar told

them. "Gorstein of Rethen. Somehow, he sailed through her mist and was beached on our shore. A canny sailor and fighting chief. I remember thinking there was something strange about the fellow. His eyes had a silvery look that didn't seem natural."

Myra wondered where her father was going with this.

"Gorstein mentioned a great fighter in a distant land who'd left Valkador and had made a name for himself in foreign wars. He called the man the Whitebear. Gorstein said he would return one day. It was strange—I went to bring him food the following morning, but both Gorstein and his damaged ship were gone. Perhaps five years ago. I'd almost forgotten."

"Did this Gorstein wear a hood, a dark coat?"

"Truly, I cannot remember much about him," Ivar said. "But it seems that he was right. You are the Whitebear, the hero Jaran Saerk."

"The Whitebear is another," Jaran Saerk said quietly. After that, the conversation turned to more immediate matters, and Myra found herself busy with the girls for the rest of that night.

SHEEGA WATCHED FROM AFAR AS THE TALL REEDS TOSSED their heads in the breeze, half-hiding the longship. They'd moored two days ago—the fools. She'd seen the vessel approach, and she and Ranning had watched it sail close by her quay.

Hard to miss. A sleek wooden craft with a red-and-white square-sail. Later that morning, her birds confirmed it was Finvar. He and some renegade Northmen were setting up camp a dozen miles to the south, near where her forests skirted the mountain, Gronteyer.

"He thinks I'm dead." Sheega smiled and gazed sidelong at Ranning, who stood rock-still beside her. "Because the mist has gone. A touch optimistic, even for one such as he."

"I'm surprised those men dared sail here," Ranning said.

"Finvar doubtless persuaded them."

"Aye, and he has Lofhi's charm."

"Finvar and his friends will lead us to Hrelgisson," Sheega said, as the wind picked up and blew hair across her face. She brushed it back, watching the tiny figures of the men in the camp they'd made, close to their half-hidden vessel.

"We should send Gorvaron down there." Ranning said. "Prove sporting to watch his first kills."

"I think not," she said. "Why flush out the prey when it will come to us soon enough, and with a bigger prize? Let them find Hrelgisson first. When they are all happily together, I'll unleash your latest spawn."

"You're cutting it fine."

"No, I'm not," she told him. "They're here too early. We have ample time. Hrelgisson will either come for me or lie low like a wastrel in the fells. If he hides, Gorvaron will flush him out. If he chooses to act sooner"—she smiled and rubbed her hands together—"then all the better. I'll prepare a far warmer welcome than he had in Dunnehine. The three of them united will be confident. They're young and over-proud. And there is Lofhi. He assured me that Finvar will have scant choice but to betray his friends."

"I'd sooner we hunt them out and deal with the pests," Ranning said. "Those three have uncommon luck for mortals, even with Lofhi controlling the thief. And there are the Traveler and Tyho to consider."

"We have the armies of Faerie to keep those two occupied. Unva might meddle, but she's out of her depth. Finvar will play into our hands. What choice does he have with Lofhi pulling his groin strings?" She laughed. "That leaves Hrelgisson and the girl. I'm going to prepare something special for Savarna," she licked her lips, picturing the *Aikashi* wench naked, lashed and writhing. She'd be screaming and begging as Sheega took leisure deciding her fate.

"Until then, I'll be watching their every move," Ranning said.

"No, you won't," she told him. "I've another task for you, lover. We need to know what Rune's up too. I don't sense that one's presence. He got them here but is far too slippery to stick around. Could be old Silver Hair's meddling in Faerie. That concerns me."

"You want me to return there?"

"I do," she said. "I need you to find Rune and kill him if you get a chance. That vile creature could undo me yet. Also, I would learn how Aldorian and the others fare."

"I'd sooner not greet the elf king again." Ranning's milky eyes flickered.

"Why would you need to?" Sheega said. "Spy on them and the trolls, but remain hidden."

"It's not easy to hide in Faerie," he said.

"You'll manage." She brushed his hand with hers. "Go back to the hall and await my return at dusk. I'll have need of your touch by then."

"What are you planning?" His eyes narrowed.

"A little visit to the camp." She smiled and he grinned back.

"I daresay they will enjoy that."

Ranning left without a sound. Sheega stood for a time

leaning on her rune staff. She saw a dozen or so Northmen below, their camp being well hidden by the reeds. Interestingly, she saw a woman among them. Sheega recognized the faint golden aura hovering over the woman and sensed that this was no normal girl. *The Vulkorye.* It had to be.

You're the one She's chosen to challenge me and protect Lofhi's fool.

Sheega smiled. It was time to discover more about this girl. She spoke the changing rune and clapped her hands, allowing her features break apart like exploding smoke, becoming a dark storm of black birds that circled, and then winged low to settle in the bushes by the campground.

Once they'd settled quiet, Sheega bid the birds begone. She became herself again, walking out into the glade having followed the girl, who had foolishly left the camp to fetch water.

A young woman, not overly pretty. Fair hair. Perhaps twenty, no older. The aura hovered over her. The mortals wouldn't see that, but it was a plain sight to Sheega.

This child has a power she cannot control or understand.

The girl had her back to her. She was scooping up water from the nearby stream. They were alone, the men's voices back in the camp were lost to the distant sounds of waves, and the reeds sighing in the wind. The girl filled her bucket.

"I came to say hello," Sheega said.

The girl froze. She turned slowly, and seeing Sheega standing there, dropped the bucket, allowing the contents empty and splash at her feet.

"That was clumsy." Sheega smiled at the girl, whose wide blue eyes were glaring back at her, and the small mouth struggling to reply. "Tell Finvar I'll expect you both to come visit me in the hall."

Sheega flashed the young woman a beautiful smile, before fading back into the trees. Once there, she shifted to bird form and, as dusk fell silent, flew back to the hall where Ranning stood waiting.

Morphing again, Sheega felt a flush of excitement and anticipation. The quickening had arrived.

The final dance.

3

FIRST BLOOD

RASNEI COVERED her ears as the cannon roared and flames shot out across the sky. Looking on, she saw the great fiery ball sail through the air and crash down on their riders, causing chaos and confusion in the ranks of the enemy.

The battle for Ta Shen had started, and the defenders had struck the first blow. Rasnei cheered, as did all the men gathered around her. General Matax ordered another shot and his cannon team made ready, their hard practice and drilling had resulted in a smooth swift action that was a pleasure to behold. The ball sailed through the summer sky, causing more mayhem in the riders out there. To her right, Vian stood with his arms folded, his face calm as he gazed down from walls.

The Cards were milling about down there like agitated insects. They hadn't expected the cannon—an oversight on Chulan's part. Her former magister should have warned his new masters about Ta Shen's formidable weapons.

At her signal, the cannon team loaded, made ready, and fired a third time. The boom and roar seemed even louder, sending doves skyward from the gardens behind her. The third missile proved enough for the Cards. As one, they turned their horses about and cantered back out of range.

It had just been a show of force, but the new Ran would know he wasn't taking this city without a long, hard fight. She watched as they reformed out of cannon range. Moments later a single rider trotted back toward the walls. Truggan nocked arrow to string, but Gurtei beside her bid him wait.

"Who is this bold fellow?" Rasnei asked Gurtei

"One of the sons, I'd guess," Gurtei said, hawking and spitting down over the wall. The rider reined in his horse and stared up at them. He wore dark ring mail and a conical helm, his mustached features and black hair visible.

"I've a message for you cowards!" the rider yelled up, his voice carrying easily on the wind. He appeared paunchy slouched in the saddle. Not their finest warrior, Rasnei guessed. But the Card sat his horse with arrogant confidence

"Speak it and be gone, knave!" Rasnei shouted back, leaning over the parapet walls. She saw Truggan ready his arrow. "Else we fill you with arrows."

"I've got a clean shot," Truggan told her.

"I want to hear what he says," Rasnei told the men, and Gurtei motioned to Truggan that he should relax.

The rider wheeled his horse about and shouted up again.

"I am Ran Casca," he yelled. "Your death! Your noisy toys won't save you, Shen bitch. I was going to be lenient—I am not my father. But you, empress, have just sealed your city's fate. We will break down your gates, proud Rasnei, storm your walls and put every one of your people to the sword."

"I'm not swayed by idle boasts," Rasnei yelled back. She saw Vian raise a quizzical brow. He was looking at her keenly. She flashed him a brave smile and looked down at the rider again. "I'd expect no less from a mangy cur that murdered his own father," she shouted. "At least Wolf Calla was a warrior—whereas you are a canker and slime, and your treachery will prove your bitter end."

The mustached face in the helmet reddened. "Lies are all you Shen are good for," Casca shouted. "We're done here." He pointed up at her and made a lewd gesture with his hand. "Enjoy your short reign, Empress. I will seek you out personally, and order my captains to hump your imperial arse bloody before I let you die." He tugged at his mount's reins, the horse reared and kicked out with its fore hooves. Then the animal circled and trotted back to his waiting camp.

"Please let me shoot that bastard," Roile said as he readied his bow next to Truggan, but she ignored his request.

"Leave him be—that one is rash," Rasnei said. "Casca's temper could play to our advantage."

"Or prove our ruin," Vian said, as he watched Casca rejoin the army and signal his riders depart for their camps. "They'll be like disturbed fire ants working day and night, building siege towers and ladders."

"Let them do their worst," Rasnei said, her face hot with anger.

Matax nodded viciously beside her. "I will cut out that serpent's liver for what he said to you, Empress."

"I'll enjoy watching that," she smiled back at him, before glancing down at her hands and noticing how they were shaking.

LATER IN HER CHAMBER, SHEN'S EMPRESS SURVEYED THE gardens below, as Vian stood by sipping wine, his face unreadable. Cicadas and crickets drummed the rhythm, as birds chirped a shrill chorus.

A beautiful afternoon. Rasnei watched as hummingbirds darted below, their tiny wings trapped the sun's rays and making each a green flash of light, as they hovered over the tall orchids and cannas ringing the largest of the famous koi ponds. She glimpsed the silver and golden fish gliding beneath that clear summer water.

I cannot allow this beauty to be lost.

Rasnei brushed hair back from her face as the warm breeze reached her. "Ta Shen will stand," the empress said without realizing she had spoken out loud.

"We can hold out for long months, perhaps. But not a year."

"What are you saying?"

"That I don't think this Casca is a quitter."

"Was I wrong to goad that monster?" She rounded on him, annoyed at his lack of support. "What do you think I should have done—smile meekly and order our guards to open the gates?"

"Hardly." He smiled at her sarcasm. With his customary coolness, Vian placed wine glass aside and walked up to stand beside her. He slid his hand into hers and leaned forward to place a kiss on her mouth. She pulled away but permitted him to try again.

"I thought you were magnificent this morning," Vian said. "But truth be told, a little hasty. The Cards were showing off, nothing more. The cannon surprised them, and your words shamed that young wolf. Casca has to prove himself. His brothers and captains will be watching him for errors. He won't—can't—stop until either he wins, or we kill him. We're in for a hard time."

"You said you wanted action," she smiled, as he stroked her hair. "At least Casca knows I'm not weak like Chulan."

"Hmm, perhaps Roile or Truggen should have shot him. That said, the other brothers might prove cleverer. Time will out. As for your Magister, I've cause to wonder where that one is lurking."

"Somewhere safe until the hard work's done," Rasnei said. "I suspect Chulan will show his hand if he senses we are vulnerable."

"Chulan troubles me," Vian said. "As does his man, Gujun. The Imperials from Pol Shen must still be around. I'll wager that Gujun the Slayer has them hidden close, while he and his master keep an eye on rash Casca's progress."

"We can't do anything about those two traitors at present, so why worry?" Rasnei said. "We need to make ready for their first proper attack instead. Do you think that will be tomorrow?"

"Could be tonight," Vian said. "But my hunch is they'll wait until their carpenters have constructed sufficient siege towers, ballistae and battering rams, to hit us with maximum impact. That gives us a week, perhaps ten days? The Cards have been idle with their siege preparation. But that's about to change."

"A week's waiting allows time for some fighting lessons," she smiled.

"The men are well trained and drilling hard. Matax is showing rare skill as a commander. His garrison adore him. Even Gurtei is winning them over with his rough jokes."

"I'm not talking about the men," Rasnei said. "Teach me how to use those swords you carry—the long chiang spear, too."

"I cannot do that in a week."

"I'm a fast learner."

"We'll try the knife," Vian said. "A smiling woman with a crafty dagger can oftimes get closer than a proud warrior with a chiang spear."

"Very well—the dagger it is."

He left the balcony, returning with something wrapped in a cloth.

"There is also this," Vian unwrapped the bundle carefully. Her eyes widened seeing his silver flute.

"You haven't played for so long."

"I've not been in the mood," he said. "But the flute has another use that I would show you."

Intrigued, Rasnei bid him do so.

Vian produced a small, pointed dart with black feathers from a bag tied neatly inside the bundle. He removed the flute's mouthpiece with a twist of his wrist and placed the dart inside the instrument. Then he covered the holes with his fingers, placed his lips over the flute, and blew. Rasnei heard a slight thud and turned, seeing the dart sticking in the door, an inch below the handle.

"The range isn't long," he told her. "Maybe fifteen feet. But the dart makes for a good surprise."

"I like it," she said. "Were you planning to use those darts on me back in Pol Shen?"

"Perhaps." He smiled. "The flute works as a dagger, too, if you twist the mouthpiece away like so." He showed her how, and she marveled at the thin sliver of needle-pointed steel. "It's yours, Rasnei." He sheathed the skinny blade again and handed her the instrument, plus the small bag of darts. Rasnei examined them and decided to try. She laughed when her dart struck the door in inch below Vian's.

"You're a natural," he said with a grin.

"But you might want to play," she said. "I can't take the flute."

"I'll never play again," he told her. "The music has left me, Rasnei. I doubt that it will ever return."

"Because of Savarna?"

"I'd sooner not talk about it."

"You will see her again—I do believe that, Vian. In this world or the next."

"Perhaps I will," he said, forcing a smile. He touched her arm and departed from the balcony, leaving Rasnei alone with her thoughts.

RAN CASCA WATCHED THE MEN SWEATING AND SAWING hard at the thick timbers. His father should have started this work weeks ago. They could be inside those walls by now. It would take long days to get the siege towers and other contraptions ready for use.

Casca had never given much thought to sieges. The Cardalan were horse warriors. Riders of renowned skill. That was honorable warfare. Instead, they would have to stand by and let the wooden machines do their work.

He'd ordered ballistae made, rigged, and tightened, and he sent a crew to quarry the stone in the hills. They'd departed with carts this afternoon to gather any sizable rocks they could find and dig up others. Casca would enjoy tossing stones over those high imperial walls.

He'd ordered the slain horses stacked in a pile close to the city. Once the ballistae were ready, he'd have the operators lob some rotting horse meat at the Shen. That should make them tingle nicely. Nothing weakens a city's morale like the diseases caused from decaying flesh.

The thought pleased Casca, as he dwelt on her arrogant words.

Their bitch empress.

A pampered, aloof ruler who saw herself suddenly as a warrior queen. Rasnei would come to regret her ill-spoken words this morning. Casca had lacked his father's obsessive loathing of the Shen. He'd found it amusing. But things had become personal.

He'd not mentioned the empress's words to his brothers. How she had mocked him after those fiery balls killed two score of his best riders and their mounts. Why hadn't Father warned them about the cannon? Or that snake Chulan's man? The killer, Gujun, would have known the cannons were there. What other tricks did those Shen have waiting?

That didn't much matter. Once they were ready, Casca was going to hit the Golden City with everything he had. Ten thousand men, aided by tall siege towers and iron-clawed battering rams, with the ballistae artillerymen sending a storm of missiles overhead. Day and night—they wouldn't stop until the gates were shattered or walls breached. It was only a matter of time.

"You've got three days," Casca shouted at the carpenters.

"It will take a week, Lord Ran," their ganger said.

"Three days," Casca told him. "Else I order you shoved in the first bucket and test-launched at those walls." The ganger's face blanched. Casca left them to their travail.

He walked through the camp, noticing how the men were glaring behind him as he passed. They weren't happy, his soldiers. The Shen had drawn first blood, and the only shaman they had was dead.

Bad omens.

Casca ignored the baleful stares. Omens didn't destroy cities. Steel and stone would, as would fire and fear. All were tools he intended to employ.

Casca joined his brothers inside the great tent. A fire was roaring despite the summer heat. Uzcara had arrived this morning and sat cross-legged, chewing at a haunch of steak.

"I heard it was a gang fuck, brother," Uzcara said, wiping grease from his mouth and spitting it in the straw. "Your army isn't happy."

"They're not paid to be happy," Casca said, glaring at his brother. The other three were playing dice out of earshot. None had looked up when Casca entered. "I didn't know you were back."

Casca wasn't overjoyed seeing his only surviving older brother in his camp. Like Daigar, Uzcara had little respect for Casca. That could prove problematic.

The youngsters, Calgara and Casla, were wet clay in his fists, and even Racara was manageable with careful handling. Uzcara was as belligerent as Genza was sly. Those two belonged in Cardalis. He'd stir things up, would Uz. Casca would have to watch his back until the fighting got underway.

"What news from our little brother?" Casca grabbed a chicken bone from a servant wench and chewed down. "I'll have wine, too," he shouted after her.

She had nice legs. He marked her for some play later.

"Genza's having trouble with his new shaman."

"The Vendeli? I thought the man was reliable?"

"He's rat-tricky, as they all are," Uzcara said. "But this Octaxa's proud and a warrior too. Seems our Genz upset him."

"You came all this way to tell me that?"

"I came to pay respects for our father. I was saddened to

hear of his tragic fall from that horse last month. I trust you gelded and quartered the stablemaster?

"His entire team," Casca said, his eyes hooded.

Uzcara stared hard at him. "You were over hasty, brother. Taking control of this camp."

"There was little choice," Casca said. "After father died, Caranax was content to mope and fuck around. Someone needed to act, Uz—else we spend the next year camped outside this city playing with our cocks."

"You killed Caranax and Daigar."

"Caranax deserved what he got."

"What about Dai? Did he deserve to get hacked down by your bribed guards?"

"Who's been talking of these matters?"

"News of kin-slaying and murder travels fast on the night winds, Casca. You are cursed by Kullaan for what you have done."

"It was necessary, I tell you. And Daigar should have listened to me. His temper got him killed."

"That may be so, but you have me to deal with now, *Ran*." Uzcara smiled. "I'm not planning on being murdered anytime soon."

"Doesn't Genza need you in Cardalis?"

"Genza can clean up his own shit—he invited trouble by involving the Vendeli. No, brother—I'm here for the spoils inside that city. When are we attacking?"

"As soon as those slug carpenters have our siege engines ready. You see—I've had to do everything around here."

Uzcara grinned at him and slapped his shoulder. "I've missed you, Cas—let's get drunk tonight."

So you can stab me in the back? Casca showed his lizard smile. "Sounds like a plan, Uz."

The girl arrived with his wine. He leaned back to get a better look at her legs. "Wait for me in my tent tonight," Casca told her. She nodded and left them.

"Well then, brother—what exactly did Genza do to piss off this Vendeli?"

4

RE-UNION

"She was here."

Finvar looked up, seeing Gunsala emerge through the reeds. Her hair was disheveled and tangled, and her face white with fear. He noticed the bucket swinging empty in her hands.

"You went to get water?"

"I saw your witch," Gunsala cast the bucket on the ground and squatted hunched with her hands covering her face. "We were stupid coming here, Finvar."

"But Jaran? The mist has gone," he said, feeling a wash of emotion. *Is Jaran dead? Did she banish her mists to lure them here?* "Are you sure it was her?"

"She spoke to me." Gunsala dropped her hands to her lap and stared at him. "I was confident we're going to win, Fin. Eager like you. I felt that we had things under control. But when I saw her face, those terrible mocking eyes." Gunsala shook her head. "I felt like a little girl again, scolded by a village elder."

Finvar saw Gunard and some of his men readying the camp for later. They couldn't stay here tonight. Not if Sheega was creeping about. He'd have a word with Gun and Tofei in a moment. *But first ...*

"What did she say to you?"

"She called me clumsy—I dropped the bucket." She stared at him and shrugged. "She said that she expected us to visit her in the hall. I'm scared, Finvar. I think we've been played for fools, and not only by that witch." Gunsala looked up, as though she feared Sheega was still watching them.

Finvar sighed and rubbed his tired eyes. "Nothing has changed," he told her. "We're here, and she knows. So what? We couldn't have reached the island without Sheega knowing. Jaran must be here, too—and Savarna, I'll warrant."

"Why do you still believe that?"

"Because Sheega would have told you if he was dead. She wants us to lead her to him, so she can kill us all together, and before the appointed time when she is vulnerable. That's two moons away. We've got to stay away from Jaran until then and somehow distract Sheega."

"How can we hope to do such a thing?"

"By taking her up on her offer." Finvar grinned at her. It was obvious, really.

"You are unhinged," Gunsala said.

"Often." He nodded. "But think about it, Gun. Lofhi will protect me in the short term—and if he doesn't, I have you, my shieldmaiden." He grinned at her, and she scowled back. "Sheega will not harm us until she can get Jaran. She'll be intrigued and want to probe us about him. Where he is on the island. That looks like wild country to the south, even her creatures might not be able find Jaran for some while. If we don't know where he is, we cannot tell her. It will give him time to prepare."

"You are deluded," Gunsala said. "She'll most likes kill us

both and stick our heads on poles, for your friend to collect on arrival."

"She might," Finvar said. "But I doubt it. Sheega revels in the game. That's why she didn't kill Savarna back in Dunnehine when she had the chance. She is like a cat who plays with her victims—it's her one weakness. I mean to exploit that, Gunsala. You don't have to accompany me."

"Of course I'm coming with you."

"It's better you don't, thinking about it," he urged her. "Sheega won't hurt me because Lofhi would intervene. You …"

"Have new skills."

"I thought you were afraid of her."

"I am," Gunsala said, nodding. "Terrified. But I'm also angry, and with myself. That witch surprised me and made me feel and look a fool. I'm not happy about that."

"Very well, then." Finvar gripped her hand. "Together we can foil Sheega if we keep our heads."

"That part might prove difficult."

"We can do this, you and I."

Gunsala awarded him a long hard look. "All right, I'm in. What about Gunard and his men, the ship? She could return tonight."

"I'll tell Tofei—he's shrewd enough to understand, and more adventurous than his father. That way, they can go search for Jaran and tell him we're here, while we keep the witch busy so she forgets about them. Sound like a plan?"

He grinned at her.

"A sketchy one." She grinned back.

They took what rest they could throughout that day. Finvar thought they'd be safe until dark.

After sunset, he deemed it time they got moving. Finvar

had a quiet word with Tofei while the rest played dice. He bid Gunard's son join them, which he did readily, his face calm but wary.

"We have to part company for a time," Finvar told him, and explained their plan. Tofei looked worried, but nodded.

"I know you two possess skills I could never understand," he said. "I'll tell Father that you must have made a head start. We'll sail south, find a new mooring and make for that mountain, see what's around. If we spot any settlements, we'll go and enquire about Jaran Hrelgisson."

"Good luck," Finvar told him, and turned away.

Finvar and Gunsala left Tofei and the camp without further ado and stole through the reeds toward the dark forest ahead. They walked throughout that night, as owls called out to each other, and beasts could be heard shuffling and snorting down in the deep places.

Dawn found them at the northern rim of the forest. Finvar saw a great lake sparkling pink before the sun's early glow. Beyond that were low bald hills, a building sat amidst the largest. A great wooden structure it appeared.

"That must be the Great Hall." Finvar gripped Gunsala's hand. "You ready?"

"No," she said, and they walked toward the glittering lake, the sun rising like pink-quartz and dazzling their eyes.

Jaran Saerk, the things I do for you.

JARAN STOOD BY THE SEA, ALLOWING THE SALT BREEZE TO sting his cheeks and the soft rain to dampen his hair. Two days had passed in the village. He was anxious to get moving, but Ivar's people wanted to help, and he needed to learn what he could about them and the island's terrain. *They are my people*, Jaran thought, feeling a flush of pride. It was his duty to protect them.

The folk from the other villages had arrived this morning. A shoddy group they appeared, though tough and hardy. The young men looked eager, their womenfolk and the oldsters more concerned. They'd even brought their children. Ivar explained that it wasn't safe to leave anyone behind, lest one of her creatures or maybe a bear or wolf was in the area.

"Mostly she's left us be," Ivar said, as the people gathered outside his fishing hut, crowding the beach where they were to hold the Thing, the name the islanders and most Northman used for social gatherings and important events. "Though this hasty coming-together might draw her attention," he added glumly.

"She'll know I'm here right enough," Jaran agreed. "But I'll be seeking to lead her on a merry dance."

"And I'll be coming with you, and young Bjarni," Ivar said. "You will need to find all the hiding places on the island. I know them better than that witch—she rarely leaves the hall."

Once the villagers had mingled and stood hustling together, Ivar went over to greet the two other elders. These three conferred for a time, as Jaran stood with Savarna and the woman, Myra. Savarna was stroking little Geda's hair. The girls seemed to like her.

Ivar came back. "I've told Torund and Haning everything I know. They agree we must help you any way we can."

"I appreciate that," Jaran said.

"Come, follow me, and we'll address them all." Jaran followed Ivar over to a hummock of dune that awarded good views of the village and beaches. The folk gathered closer. The rain had gotten heavier, but no one seemed to notice.

Ivar spoke for a time. Finally, he introduced Jaran and bid him say something. Jaran stood in silence for a moment, watching their faces. He saw Savarna; there were tears of pride rimming her eyes. He took a deep breath.

"You people don't know much about me," Jaran told the gathering. "Nor I you. And it must seem beyond strange, our being here." He glanced at Savarna again. Nobody spoke. He felt hair whip around his face as the wind grew stronger. Out to sea, a storm was mustering. He needed to make this quick, else everybody drown.

"I am your rightful Jarle," he said. "The grandson of Hrund—foully betrayed and murdered by the witch who stole his hall. My father, Hrelgi, was murdered too, the same dark day. I knew little of these matters until recently. Thus far, my time's been at the far side of the world, serving an empire in a foreign war. I had no idea how my own people were suffering back home in Valkador. Had I known, I would have returned sooner."

"You are here now," Myra said. "That is sufficient."

"It is most dangerous, your being here," one of the elders —Torund, Ivar told him— said, his gray brows knitting together. "She will get word. There are birds ..."

"I know this," Jaran said. "That's why I'm leaving this part of the island and taking refuge in the mountain slopes. A day approaches when the witch is vulnerable. I have been told on good authority that I can kill her after two moons have passed."

"That allows plenty of time for her to find you first," Torund said.

"True enough," Jaran said. "But this witch and I have met

before, and there is another—a friend who I have reason to believe is somewhere on this island. Savarna and I"—he motioned to her—"and this other fellow ... we three have defeated Sheega once, but we couldn't finish the business without returning here."

"What do you expect us to do?" the other elder, Haning, asked.

"Stay alive, look after everyone, and keep your wits sharp and weapons sharper. Are there any of the old thanes still living?"

"There is one fellow," Ivar said, "though he could be dead. I've not seen him in years."

"Stay away from that one," Torund said. "Svipdag is mad."

"He's sane enough, though dangerous," Ivar said. "Unpredictable. Svipdag was one of the few thanes that stayed around after Hrund died. One of the hunters who went after the bear. Hrelgi." He looked at Jaran, who nodded slowly.

One of my father's murderers, you mean.

Ivar caught his expression and continued in a softer voice. "Tortured by what had happened, Svipdag went berserk and made for the mountain caves. I saw him a few years ago while tracking bear sign."

"We need to find this Svipdag," Jaran said.

"Best you didn't," Torund said, and then ducked his head as the squall reached them.

An hour later, as the wind whistled and rain lashed the huts, Jaran sat cross-legged by the fire in Myra's dwelling. The other villagers had taken shelter where they could. They seemed excited, though a few were edgy and unsure. These had departed with Torund, chancing the storm as they left for their own homesteads at the southern edge of the island.

Jaran sipped an ale, courtesy of Ivar's seaweed brew. It was bitter, but not unpleasant. With them were Bjarni, his wife, and two of the younger men from the village. Asmund and Olof looked keen and strong. It was agreed that they would accompany Jaran and Savarna, as would Bjarni and Ivar, up into the mountainside.

Ivar had spent an hour telling Jaran and Savarna all he knew about what had happened back then.

"Those who could made for Gronteyer," he said. "For despite the grim cold, all present had such a dread of the hall that we braved the journey south. The sea was so rough we dared not take the coast route. A dozen souls perished on Gronteyer's slopes as the fell chill took them. We were without hope or leaders. Most the thanes had fled to Leeth in ships, with her tongue lashing them with curses.

"Sheega changed after Hrund and Hrelgi's murders. Before that, the witch had seemed a quiet and beautiful stranger, meek even—biding her time. Once she had the hall to herself, she turned terrible. We knew she would inflict all manner of cruelties and perversions on our people were we to linger near the hall. Thus, we fared south through winter's worst, stayed in the caves for many months, sharing our homes with bears and worse things—there were strange creatures that had arrived the same time as she did."

"I daresay there are still some up there," Myra cut in. She wasn't happy about them leaving.

Ivar looked at her and continued: "When winter abated, we fared to the deserted southern end of the island and made our homes as best we could, scratching a living from fish and whatever game we could source. Sometimes she would send things to fill our nights with horror, but mostly her cold gaze was far away. So it has been for almost thirty years." He sighed. "What a waste."

"Two moons, and that all changes," Jaran said.

"Do you honestly believe you can kill her?" Myra asked him.

"I do," Jaran said. "And I will—you have my promise. But first, Savarna and I must lie low. That witch will be searching for us with all her creatures. We've encountered some of those before. I'd sooner they not visit here. This is a big island, but we'll most likes have to keep moving and sleep with both eyes open."

"And we need to get moving right away," Savarna said, her eye catching Jaran's. "Don't want you good folk in any more danger than we've already placed you."

"We should go." Jaran nodded and looked at Ivar.

"This evening, after the storm's passed," the old man said.

"I'll prepare a meal," Myra said, and stood wiping her hands. "I'd not have you leave hungry." She looked at Bjarni. Jaran noted the wet glisten at the edge of her eye.

"Bjarni should stay here," Jaran said. "As should you other lads—Ivar alone can help us well enough."

"You think I cannot manage this village without the men." Myra gave him a frank look. "I do everything most days, so don't fuss about us needing looking after."

Bjarni gave her a grateful look.

Jaran nodded. "As you wish."

"They'll be others, too," young Asmund told him. "They'll join us near the mountain. We want to fight beside you, Jarle."

As dusk arrived and the storm clouds had departed for Leeth, Jaran walked the beach, the wind buffeting his ears. Ivar was readying supplies, and they'd eaten a full plate of fish chowder. Savarna was talking to Myra and her husband. They would be leaving soon. Jaran decided he needed a moment alone, a brisk walk by the churning rollers to clear his head.

I'm home.

But this place had never been his home. Jaran didn't know these people. He'd stood up on that dune telling them he was their Jarle, come home to put everything right.

I cannot let them down. This was no longer solely about his vengeance. And where was Fin? Jaran still believed he was here. Perhaps that was wishful thinking, but something inside told him he'd see his garrulous friend soon.

Fin is here, I know it.

Jaran walked north along the beach for long minutes, the shadow of huts dwindling behind. The air was so clear here. Fresh and clean, different by far than the moist swelter of southern Shen in summertime.

Ahead, a broad stream crashed down from the folds of a low hill, chiming through the shingle on the beach. This he waded and then stopped and stared out at the ocean. The setting sun flooded the beach with pinkish-gold as its rays pierced cloud wrack. He turned his gaze to the north, his keen eyes following the beach toward dark cliffs and the shadow of the mountain behind them, cloaked by the dense forest flanking, and marching up its glinting shoulders.

Jaran gazed that way for a time, allowing his mind to wander. He blinked, seeing movement. He saw it again—a flash of light and rumble of sound, as though a giant was striding toward him. At last, Jaran saw him. A giant indeed. A huge figure had rounded a corner of rock and gazed across at him with eyes that blazed like silver suns.

At first Jaran thought this was Tyho, but the giant—though similar—had a different look. He also had two hands, the right one gripping a huge, short-handled hammer. The god strode across the beach, a heavy spear gripped in his left fist. Jaran waited with folded arms, knowing that if the giant cast that spear, there was no way he could avoid its path.

"You are Kullaan," Jaran said, as the figure loomed close and stared down at him. Jaran braced his feet and ran a hand along Griner's haft. "I've heard you've been visiting these parts of late."

The giant stopped and thrust his spear butt deep into the sand. He glared down at Jaran with those silver eyes. Jaran met that stare, though his heart pumped like thunder in his chest.

"Are you ready for your greatest challenge, JARAN SAERK?" The voice boomed around his ears like thunderclaps. Jaran saw the clouds mustering out west, the sun having sunk below distant water. He needed to get back to the village. They'd be wondering where he was.

"I am ready," he shouted back at the figure. "I've kept your brother's axe well honed."

"That is good to HEAR," Kullaan leaned on his spear and shook the hammer, and the sky blasted thunder around his head. The terrible face studied Jaran. Again, he met that gaze as best he could. The god wore a long coat of ragged wool, his face was half-covered in tangled beard, and the hair was dark, wild and strewn, streaked with gray. He wore heavy boots and trousers, and a wide belt where he must keep that hammer stored. "MUCH depends on your SUCCESS."

"Why?" Jaran said, bracing as he saw the anger flash across the Sky God's features.

"YOU DARE QUESTION KULLAAN?"

"I do," Jaran said. "Your brother never fully explained why He gave me the axe. I've been warned by the dwarf who made it that Griner was cursed by Faerie and will turn on its wielder. Perhaps Tyho doesn't care what happens to His champion."

For a moment Jaran thought the god was going to fall upon him with the spear, or swat him like a bug with that terrible hammer. But Kullaan threw back His shaggy head and laughed, long and hard.

"You are BRAVE enough, mortal. I like THAT. We have OUR reasons for wanting you to win. They are not your concern. BUT I WILL TELL YOU THIS. Sheega was once the sorceress UNDEYNA and served the ENEMY of All WORLDS. She has much to pay for and deserves NO hiding place in this realm, or any other. Even so, it is her ALLIES who concern US most. The host of FAERIE. You killing Sheega on the appointed HOUR will enable us to deal with THEM."

"Why don't you do it yourself? You gods? Tyho, the Traveler—you're all in this together. This is your struggle as well as mine. How do I know you're any better than she is?"

"We CANNOT intervene without drawing attention to OURSELVES," Kullaan boomed, his eyes blazing angry again. "Have a CARE, lest I stamp on you and choose another for our WORK."

"I'm sorry, but you gods should explain yourselves better," Jaran said. "At least help me and my friends stay alive long enough to do your dirty work."

"I came to WARN you," Kullaan thundered. "There is ONE coming for you from the hall. GORVARON, he is called. A Witch-Guard like no other. Vile Ranning's last SPAWN has the strength of all the others COMBINED. You will have to tackle Gorvaron before you can reach Sheega. I wish you well with that. FAREWELL!"

Kullaan's eyes blazed silver fire. Jaran held that gaze until Kullaan nodded slowly. "You are a worthy CHAMPION, Jaran Saerk. And you are WRONG to believe we don't value courage in mortals. I cannot speak for the OTHERS. But KULLAAN of the WINDS will help you when HE can."

The giant god shouldered his spear, shook the hammer a last time and turned, striding back along the beach. Each step shook the rocks, even as fresh rain spat tiny holes on the sand. Jaran, shaken, turned and ran back to the village.

"WHERE'VE YOU BEEN?" SAVARNA LOOKED ANGRY.

"Having a conversation with Tyho's big brother," Jaran told her, as he joined Ivar and the others by Ivar's hut. Myra said the other villages had left, and there was a great deal of excitement about the new Jarle.

"They do believe in you," she told him. He nodded, feeling suddenly weary. "Look after my husband," she said in a softer voice meant only for his ears. "Bjarni is a good man."

Jaran replied that he would, and he waited as the other two men said their farewells to their womenfolk. Ivar stood with a bow across his shoulders and a skinny sword at his hip. He also carried his fish spear.

"I stole this sword from the hall," he said. "In the chaos after that feast. Kept it close ever since."

After parting, they took the rough track inland through marshes up into the lower hills. Ivar led the way, Savarna and Jaran behind him. The three younger men loped at the rear.

Bjarni had an axe, the other two carried bows and a knife each. It was a start.

"Are we making for the caves again?" Jaran asked Ivar as they reached the hills. It would be dark very soon.

"Different ones. Deeper. Gronteyer has many secrets. But tonight, we'll risk a camp in the woods."

"THEY DID *WHAT*?" GUNARD WAS FURIOUS WHEN HIS SON told him that Finvar and Gunsala had left after dark. "Our only chance of survival here is by staying together. Why didn't you wake me?"

Tofei muttered about Finvar being persuasive and offered vague excuses. It wasn't like Tofei to be hoodwinked by a glib tongue. Gunard knew something must have happened.

"He said Hrelgisson's in the mountains," Tofei explained lamely. "Seemed very confident."

"I'll not abandon our ship." Gunard said, thinking hard as the night deepened. "But I do see that we can't stay here. You're hiding something. But no matter—truth will out, and I'll not press you. But we are too damn close to that hall."

"What do you propose, Father?"

"That you, my son, climb the slopes of yonder peak and catch up with those two fools. They are your responsibility. The ship is mine, as are the men. We'll cast off at first light and make for the southern end of the island, hoping there's a safe place to beach or cast anchor thereabouts."

Tofei stared at him wild eyed. "They went in the other direction," he said after a moment.

"I know." Gunard grinned at him. "There's no helping those two. But I need eyes up there—a scout. The men are needed to help me sail that ship. You've the sharpest eyes amongst us, Tof. Can you promise me you'll stay alive long enough to join us, after you spied out the terrain for any sign of inhabitance and life? That way, we know what we are dealing with here?

"I can, Father. Thank you." Tofei's eyes were bright, and his young face flushed with pride.

"That's good," Gunard said, rolling into his blanket. "Best get some sleep before dawn comes, or that witch creeps up on us too soon."

5

SIGNALS AND WATCHTOWERS

Trisa stared through the thick, oily atmosphere, her face streaming with sweat and eyes smarting badly. They were elevated high above the jungle, but the mountain passes were behind them. A journey of two weeks had found Valgarn and her close to the Yamondon border. Even up here the heat was stifling. Trisa dreaded how bad it would be in the tangle of jungle below.

Despite her worries, the Vendeli had left them alone. The cruel-eyed leader, Utuxla, had watched her sometimes during the nights. His sly gaze chilled Trisa's spine. But Valgarn's proximity ensured she felt safe, though often she had to force herself be calm. That man would turn on them sometime. Perhaps on the way back, when they crossed from Yamondo. If they made it that far.

There were more immediate concerns. Valgarn had a king to kill. Trisa didn't know what to think about that, terrifying though it was. She knew little of these countries, Yamondo and Vendel. She'd read the histories as a girl in House Alatais, her family villa, close by the Rundali Mountains half a world away.

Both were hot southern lands with a long history of enmity and rivalry. The Vendeli were merchants and traders, but also raiders and warriors. They were a fierce seafaring nation but greedy, with ambitions for ever more land. She'd read how the Vendeli kings had always coveted the larger fertile regions of Yamondo across the central mountain ranges.

The maps showed Yamondo as a vast sprawling mass of jungle and wilderness. Those old charts had no clear borders. To the north, the jungle lands met a fuzz of brush, eventually drying out enough to merge with the Permio Desert—a vast, arid region filled with myth and rumor. Yamondo was rumored to have coasts both along a south shore and in the far west. There were no maps of these that she knew of.

The Yamondon kings ruled in Cantacari. The royal city was situated in the fertile eastern side of the country where jungle gave way to ordered fields, villages and townships with neat huts and stockades.

The current monarch, Ulani III, was said to dwell in a huge palace made of onyx and gold. She'd heard that Cantacari was one of the wonders of the world. The Yamondons were warrior-born, with both girls and boys taught basic weapon skills from an early age. Such was Trisa's limited knowledge of this part of the world.

They'd stopped for a light meal of figs and water. Utuxla's Sangala—the word roughly meant shaman-hunters in Vendelise—always kept their distance. Utuxla and had been joined by new warriors at Kulshana. His Sangala numbered twenty. Grim, hard looking men; she didn't like them, and caught nothing but contempt from their casual glances. At least Valgarn wasn't swayed. He ignored them, and Trisa followed his example.

They kept a steady pace across the rough lands, before reaching the thin Vendel jungle strip and climbing up into the misty heights where vulture and buzzard held domain. The trek had left them aching and weary. They'd eaten little. Trisa worried they'd fare worse as they neared the border.

Valgarn remained buoyant in mood. The Northman was enjoying this challenge. He sat and rubbed his knees as she stooped low beside him, her eyes on Utuxla, who she noted was watching them keenly.

"See how he looks at us," she whispered in Valgarn's ear. "We must be close to the frontier."

"That's good." Valgarn cast a lazy eye at Utuxla, who casually dropped his gaze. "I'm ready to leave this country."

"I don't expect Yamondo will prove any kinder," she said, and tensed as Utuxla approached them, a broad smile on his swarthy face.

"Can I help you?" Valgarn's fingers brushed his axe; his eyes gleamed like that freshly honed steel.

Utuxla's grin deepened in mock defiance. "This is where we part, Northman. We've entered the border regions. I have no desire to slay Yamondons until your task is done. After that, the reaping will be plentiful. My Sangala will set up camp close by that stream we passed half-hour ago. We will await your return there."

"How far to the frontier?" Valgarn asked, as Trisa avoided Utuxla's questing gaze.

"Two hours' descent, where jungle meets mountain," Utuxla said. "There are watchtowers, so you will need to be careful."

"You are sending us to our deaths," Trisa said, glaring at his smiling face.

"Probably." Utuxla stared hard at her. She shuddered—the man was unclean inside. She sensed the evil lurking deep within his soul. "I don't much care. If you fail, we'll find someone else. But if you succeed and bring Ulani's head in the sack for proof, all shall be well."

"Says you." Valgarn grinned viciously. "More likely you'll stab us when we're asleep and take the trophy yourself."

Utuxla's grin fled his mouth. "I'll happily kill you, Northman—but I'll make sure you're awake when it happens. Kill the king and come back with his head. You'll be well rewarded—your woman, too. That I swear."

Trisa could guess what that reward would be.

"You've rested," Utuxla said. "Best be on your way." He turned and left them.

"Ready?" Valgarn grinned at her. Trisa rose smoothly and started making her way down the steep, crooked track toward the hazy fuzz of green far below.

They reached the jungle an hour later, the sounds a wall that deafened her ears. Trisa wondered how Valgarn fared in his leathers and iron. The heat was stifling, the humidly unbearable, but he never complained. On the contrary, he seemed eager, strangely content.

The path dropped lower as the jungle swallowed them whole. She heard shrieks and howls, the sounds of birds squawking, and she saw flapping large wings in the tangle of vines and broad leaf above. There were all manner of creatures surrounded them. Trisa saw an ape once, a huge silver creature that stared as they passed, its eyes curious and watchful.

The track widened and leveled. They'd reached a gorge where the way met a rickety rope bridge spanning wide across.

Far below, a churn of brown water slugged and steamed. They reached the other side as quickly as possible. Trisa could hardly see ahead through the wall of green. She kept wiping the sweat from her eyes. Something bit her leg and she cried out. A large wasp—she flicked at it.

"You all right?" Valgarn looked worried.

"A sting—it's nothing."

"That gorge was probably the border," he said. "We should spy the watchtowers soon." They emerged ten minutes later. Two tall green towers stood barely visible through the gloom.

"What now?" Trisa looked at him. "Do we just keep walking?"

"Got a better plan?"

"I haven't."

"Doubt they'll shoot us before demanding who we are."

"I don't share your optimism." Trisa scratched her leg and wiped more sweat from her eyes.

"They're bound to be curious." He grinned at her. "Come on."

"You're enjoying this, aren't you?" She gripped his greasy hand in hers as they walked toward the towers.

Predictably, it wasn't long before an arrow thudded in the moist soil to the right of Valgarn's boot. He stopped, and she slammed hard against him. Valgarn grinned up at the closest tower. Trisa saw slits in the green-covered stone, perhaps thirty feet above.

"We're lost!" Valgarn yelled up. For answer, another arrow buzzed to her left. A third struck the path in front. Feigning boredom, Valgarn let go of her hand and folded his massive arms.

"You're crap shots," he called up. "Do we have to wait all day for one of you to hit us?"

Trisa felt a stab of fear as silence greeted them. Even the jungle noises died back, as though bird and beast were startled by his boldness. She gasped in relief hearing deep laughter trickling down from up there.

"You are a bold fellow for a trespasser. How is it you survived this far? Are you spies from Omala City sent by Tulomon Caze?"

"I don't know who that is," Valgarn said.

The laughter again, followed by a disturbance in the brush to her right. Another sound, closer still. Trisa started as a figure emerged to her left, appearing like a specter through the dense undergrowth.

"Valgarn," she nudged his arm. Other men appeared silently like wraiths, their dark sinewy arms holding bows. Soon they were surrounded.

"Bring those fools up here," the deep voice said. The silent warriors urged them to move ahead, prodding and pushing with their bows. Valgarn winked at Trisa as they were ushered toward a narrow door that had revealed itself in the base of the nearest tower. This they entered without a word.

A long, hard stair-spiral twisted up, eventually opening to a small round space with three large windows that awarded sweeping views above the jungle canopy twenty feet below. Trisa panted and rested after the steep climb. She took in deep breaths. Blue sky, no clouds. The air was almost clean up here.

A hard-faced, heavyset man sat on a whicker rocking chair. His ebony arms were corded with muscles, and she noticed the crisscross of scars covering his skin. His face was scarred too, but evenly across each cheek. Jagged red-blue marks. Trisa suspected these were brands, or badges of honor.

They stood pinned, Valgarn and she, the silent guard behind, filling the round room.

"Leave us," the leader said, his voice deep and authoritative. The guards departed without a sound. His dark eyes brushed over them. "I am Dolusa, Third Tarakai, and therefore the controller of the Eastern Sector," the leader said, as if they should know this already. "Tasked with the honor of keeping our country free of Vendeli filth."

"We are not Vendeli," Valgarn said.

Trisa gave him a sharp look. *Don't provoke him.*

Third Tarakai Dolusa didn't answer. He looked them over, his calm brown eyes studying them both with interest. First Valgarn, then her. Finally, he nodded.

"I could put you to cruel questioning," he said. "If you are Vendeli spies, you'll tell me everything. But I'd sooner not go there, yet."

"That's good to hear," Valgarn replied. "You might find our meat hard to chew on. I am Valgarn of—"

"—a Northman and a Rundali," Dolusa said, cutting in. "There is meaning in your being here. I've no doubt that the Vendeli are using you. That said, my uncle will be very intrigued by your arrival in Yamondo. We don't get many of your kind—neither Northmen nor Easterlings."

"How do you know of the Northmen?" Valgarn looked puzzled. Trisa worried that this *Tarakai*—the word loosely meant nobleborn chief, she recalled from somewhere—was playing games.

For answer, Dolusa smiled. "Are you hungry, or thirsty perhaps? The jungle is hard on those not used to its ways."

Trisa nodded as Valgarn's stomach rumbled beside her.

"Good. We'll eat and make ready. I myself will escort you, via carriage to Cantacari."

"Carriage?" Trisa couldn't help herself. "Through a jungle?"

"You were in Vendel, so I forgive your ignorance, Rundali," Dolusa said. "We Yamondons are civilized folk, unlike those two-headed snakes, the Ven. Our roads are without flaw and our famous carriages run throughout the land, crossing jungle, hill or desert, without pothole or blemish—as far as the Golt and Permio frontier regions. Even Dalcia in the far south. Yamondo, you'll learn, is a special country."

"Who is your uncle?" Trisa asked, as a nagging doubt tweaked her lip.

Dolusa's smile broadened as he looked at her with those shrewd brown eyes. "The one your man has come to kill, my dear. King Ulani III."

"He's crossed," Octaxa told the flickering face on the wall. "I've received the mind-flare from Utuxla. It is done. My second will stay put near the border and report back as soon as the Northman returns."

"That is well," the voice sounded bored. The face staring at him was blurry. Octaxa's far-vision wasn't working its best tonight. It was this cursed city. These filthy Cards, so distracting with their noise and stench.

Octaxa hated Cardalis and detested its current ruler—the self-titled *Ran* Genza. He'd endured the man's tempers one too many times. A change of direction was needed, else he'd kill Genza out of rage and ruin everything that they'd worked for.

Patience was needed to achieve their goals. Octaxa didn't want to be here any longer than was necessary. That said, he needed to watch Genza's every move and keep the great Yanturi in Omala City informed. That meant sending code words via express bird to the High Califez, Tulomon Caze—the Yanturi's mentor and chief administrator. Caze was also the head of the Vendeli army, and lord master of ships. The real power in Vendel. Octaxa was currently high in his favor and determined to stay there.

Tulomon Caze was not a patient man. Lately their conversations had proved vexing. Caze insisted the Yanturi wanted results too quickly. King Ulani dead. The trade routes opened for Vendeli use only. Caze had no idea how thick-skinned these Cardalan bastards were. Nor did he care. Results alone mattered. Octaxa had been working on both issues. He concentrated his mind, focused hard until the face on the wall became clearer.

"I have my Sangala awaiting the Northman's return," Octaxa said again. "With Ulani dead, Yamondo will be in turmoil. We can go after their coastal cities one at a time, as far south as Dalcia, while feigning false attack across the mountains toward Cantacari."

"Strategies are my affair, Octaxa." Caze's cold eyes narrowed. "Stick to your witch-doctoring. Leave the business of war to your Califez."

"As you wish, Exalted One." Octaxa watched as the face shimmered and flickered. So hard to keep the signal going.

"What of this Genza? The new Ran? Can he be trusted to deliver the promised trade routes to us?"

"Genza's unpredictable—we dare not trust him."

"What of the other Ran, the new leader in Shen?"

"Rumored as bad, or worse," Octaxa said. "Word has reached me that Casca killed two of the other brothers. Calla's whelps are hyenas tearing at each other's throats. They lack their father's discipline. We should place our trust elsewhere."

"Let me think on this."

"I've an idea, if you'll permit it."

"Go on—you've proved to be one of my shrewder servants in the past."

"We abandon Cardalan for Shen."

Harsh laughter reached him. "You've become soft, Octaxa. I never took you for a fool. Must be the air up there. The Shen are a cracking egg, the yoke spilling free."

"Mostly, yes." Octaxa held his nerve. "But I believe there is one among the Shen who can help us. We have but to wait a while."

"I'm listening." Caze's blurry face flickered again. "But I warn you, my patience is ebbing."

"Chulan, the former magister of Pol Shen, is a shrewd player. He wants Shen for himself and has thrown his lot in with the Cards."

"What is that to me?"

"Like myself, this Chulan has small love for the Cardalan rabble. But he needs them, at least in the short term. Casca's army has besieged the second city over there. The empress is within. Chulan has been promised both her and the city."

"This is not my concern. Again, you test my patience."

"The Cards will take the city," Octaxa persisted, knowing how he tempted disaster by upsetting this man. "But they are divided. The pups, Genza and Casca, will come to blows—I am certain of it. It's only a matter of time before the Cardalan Republic erupts in civil war. Chulan knows this, too, and is hiding out awaiting the outcome."

The eyes watched him with interest. Octaxa took that for a good sign.

"Ta Shen won't fall easily," he added, "but neither can it hold out indefinitely. Once the city tumbles, Chulan will need new allies to keep greedy Casca at bay. Ta Shen is rumored wealthy like no other city." He placed his hook carefully, knowing Caze to be a greedy man. "Why shouldn't the Vendeli benefit from that wealth?"

"You are proposing we help this renegade Shen against his own people, as well as the Cardalan army?"

"Eventually, perhaps. For the moment, I'm merely asking your permission to contact this Chulan. The man intrigues me. Exalted One, please believe me when I say I see an opportunity for Vendel here."

A slight nod. "Very well, seek him out with your magic-scrying—whatever you call it. Do so, quickly, and report back to me."

"Thank you, Exalted One, I shall begin the arrangements at once."

"Your scheme has piqued my interest, Octaxa. But have a care. Of far more pressing import is our business in Yamondo. Let me know when your man has Ulani's head safely stowed in that sack. The Yanturi will want to inspect it in person before he bids me finalize our plans for invasion." The face faded and vanished as the connection was lost.

Octaxa stared at the wall and let out a relieved sigh. *Time to implement.*

"Grodu!"

The huge warrior entered and bowed low.

"I'm sending you east to Shen. There's a man I need you to meet, eye to eye. I'll send spell-words ahead to ease your journey. Here are your instructions." He handed over a parchment of code he'd prepared earlier. "You can leave right away."

Grodu bowed low again and left the room. Octaxa's bodyguard was the only man he could trust entirely. Even Utuxla and the other Sangala would turn against him to save themselves. Grodu was wholly his. A slave from Golt who he'd purchased and freed from the fighting pits of Omala City. He'd taught the fighter how to read in both Vendeli and Yamondon lore codes.

RAN GENZA LEANED BACK IN HIS CHAIR AND TRIED TO ignore the man. Octaxa was a dripping tap, sapping a man's will like the infamous Shen water tortures. He'd grind anyone down in time.

"We need assurance that the trade routes will be protected, both at Largos and Shen," the Vendeli shaman was saying. "Our continued alliance depends on this."

Is that what this is—a fucking alliance?

Genza hawked and spat on the floor. "What would you have me do, shaman?" he said. "Work miracles? I've already given you my word."

"Your brother's recent violent actions in Shen have unnerved our ruler, the Yanturi. He doesn't want his best people caught in a Cardalan kin strife."

Of course, you've heard about that too …

Genza shivered. He hated shamans, and this man was worse than most he'd encountered. An oily adder. Dangerous and cunning. But regrettably, useful too. Genza needed Octaxa's special skills, at least until Ta Shen fell and he could stake his claim there, ensuring Casca and Racara didn't grab everything.

He blew out his cheeks and squeezed the goblet in his fist. "Casca's got a temper," Genza said. "He is much like my father. That's why you are better off with me. I like to think through my problems before I lash out with steel."

"Kin-murdering seems to follow a pattern in your family,"

the man said, his dark eyes glinting. "Your father killed his siblings, did he not?"

State your point, knucklehead.

"He did," Genza allowed, "and the old Ran too. I liked my grandsire, used to play on his lap. That's why I'm not mourning my late father. Shit happens—it's the world. Don't your highborn elite poison one another in Vendel?" he sneered at the proud warrior-priest watching him.

"We admire strength in Vendel. Intellect too."

"As do I." Genza relaxed into a lazy smile. "My impression was you southerners were as obnoxious as us." He barked a harsh laugh, and Octaxa showed the ghost of a grin. "The trade routes are yours alone, Vendeli. Again, I promise it. And I've sent my best Northman to help you against the Yamondons. I miss Valgarn's warm smile. What more can I do than that?"

"Send me east to watch events at Ta Shen and report back."

"So that you can serve my brother instead of me? I think not."

"I'll not serve Casca. You have my word of honor on that as Sangala chief. But I'll be of more use to you over there. Your ears and eyes in Shen. Your brother stands to gain everything when the Golden City falls. Judging by recent events, I doubt he's much for sharing all that gold."

"I'll think on this." Genza waved the man away. Octaxa dipped his head, inching a bow. And as he turned, Genza caught that ghost of a smile again.

There's more to this, for sure.

But it did make sense. He needed eyes over there, and Casca would get testy were he to make the long trip and visit the camp in person.

And these Vendeli needed a sensible ruler in charge of the trade routes. Casca would prove too volatile. If Octaxa let him down in Shen, Genza would seize all the Vendeli traders and their vessels in Largos and Soloza. He'd set fire to the trade agreement. As long as he held the coastal cities in Laregoza, Genza was winning this game. He smiled wolfishly and drained his goblet.

6

THE SECOND BLOW

VIAN WATCHED the ugly wooden towers roll and grind toward the city. There were twelve on the move, dragged by teams of horses. Doubtless more were being constructed in the camp. The Cards had also built three huge ballistae machines raised onto carts, supported by heavy oak wheels at each corner. The monsters stared across at him from half a mile away. The catapults were driven forward by mules, the men whipping the beasts. They looked sturdy, with the wheels' irksome creaking and rattling added to the ominous sight.

The Cardalan host rode behind, keeping their distance this time.

They'd stung Casca's pride a few days ago. Vian knew the new Ran would hurl everything at them. Ta Shen had no idea what was about to hit her. A city that had stood for two thousand years. Unassailed, never even threatened. The people were nervous, but the real terror hadn't sunk in yet.

That would come today, or tomorrow when those machines were set to work. Ta Shen's walls were strong. The city could hold out for long weeks—whatever they threw at her walls. But could the people? Unlikely. Vian had served briefly in foreign wars. He'd traveled as far as Yamondo and Golt, plying his trade as a mercenary in his youth. A young, keen student of war. A trait that he'd inherited from his great-grandfather, the illustrious adventurer Eltayn.

Vian knew these early days were crucial. What would be the Shen defenders' reaction to those first volleys of bone-crushing stone? The hideous rolling towers and screaming invaders? Fear or defiance—which would win?

Vian had to help. He cared little for Ta Shen's citizens, but Rasnei was his world. He had comrades here, too. Besides, those coarse thugs out there had no concept of beauty. Ta Shen would fall to flame and ruin. An ancient, beautiful city brought down by the wolves—savages who'd never appreciate what they'd taken. And not all Shen were weak. Vian wasn't about to abandon Gurtei and the Cutters, or the big warrior Lin Gu. They had all proved worthy companions.

He wiped sweat from his face and shielded his eyes from the sun. The carts were almost in range. They hadn't long to wait.

He'd failed with Savarna. Vian accepted that. It tore him open inside. But he'd made his choice, as had she. Their fates were sundered. Vian doubted he'd see her again, despite Rasnei's assurances.

I need a plan.

But the truth was Vian dared not call on his *Aikashi* yet. The two times he'd employed the dragon had worn him out, draining body and soul. His *Aikashi* was too strong. A tiger—however terrible—was easier to tame than a dragon. But Vian knew the dragon would be needed soon. It was a matter of timing. He dared not use his power before he had to. In his heart, Vian suspected the result would prove fatal.

The dragon would devour him, too.

The tension grew along the walls. He could see it in the faces of the helmeted guards leaning over and the colorful citizens gathered below.

General Matax was yelling orders from the barbican keep. Up there, Vian saw Lin Gu listening to Rasnei. Beside her stood the tall Northman Dorthar. The two big men towered over Rasnei's diminutive form, but she was pointing and demonstrating with her hands, while they listened attentively. On any other day, the sight of those two looming over her like gentle giants would amuse him. Not this morning.

He'd taken a walk along the walls to clear his head before the attack. Those soldiers he'd passed were on edge and quiet, their eyes bright with anticipation. Vian had smiled and saluted any who glanced his way.

Despite the show of force, Vian doubted Casca would attack immediately. He'd want to push all his pieces out, impressing his might on the trembling city. Launch a missile, maybe two. They'd attack at dawn, he suspected. *Unless provoked.*

He kept walking and thinking. A beautiful day, almost high summer.

Ta Shen must hold!

The thoughts kept jamming in his head.

What can I do?

Vian reached the east side of the city. Here the high walls looked over the smaller, harbor wall, the quiet sea glistening beyond, a greenish-blue serene sparkle that belonged to a happier day.

North, the range of hills they called the Long Ridge showed hazy gray amid the heat shimmer. Those hills would be crawling with Cards. Vian turned his gaze to the harbor.

Aside the fishers and shrimp boats, it was empty. The Shen weren't great sailors. If the city fell, it would be a panicked scramble resulting in those few craft sinking as the terrified people fled their city, clinging like rats to oar or sail.

They needed proper ships. Were it down to Vian, he would have grabbed those Vendeli traders before they set sail. *Insurance.* Too late.

He leaned on the Chiang spear. Vian had grown fond of the weapon lately, practicing intricate moves on the balcony at night while Rasnei slept. Restless and edgy, Vian had trouble sleeping these days. The twin Jians he'd polished and oiled his morning. He was poised like a dancer ready for the drama to start. They'd struck the first blow, but more would be needed.

The sound of someone approaching turned his head. Vian smiled, recognizing the slim form of the Laregozan girl Jilanna running toward him. She'd done well. Rasnei had softened toward her and was using her as a personal aide. She was bright and useful, without the simpering oiliness most Shen servants employed that the empress so detested.

Jilanna stopped to get her breath back. Her big brown eyes glistened with dread.

"What's the rush?" Vian smiled at her.

"The empress desires to know where you are."

"I'm here, as you see," he said. "Taking in the air. I required solitude before things got busy."

"They're about to attack."

"Tomorrow," Vian smiled at her. "Unless we can make it happen earlier."

"Why would we do that?"

"I don't like cringing," Vian said, receiving a blank expression.

"But the machines, the army—so many riders. Surely they must be ready?"

"The enemy wants to break our resolve," Vian told her. "The Cards will try something today, but the real attack will come in the morning. I expect they'll set up camp where they are tonight and get underway at dawn."

"Either way, you had best come with me," she said, and Vian complied readily, walking beside her back to the barbican. Approaching the high tower, he could see Rasnei looking out from the keep parapet. He waved a hand, but she didn't respond. Probably angry he'd left.

Jilanna was silent beside him, her dark eyes deeply troubled.

"You look good," Vian told her as they neared the barbican. "Happier than you did."

Before they reached the doors, she rounded on him. "Can we survive this, Lord Vian? Please be honest with me—you are wiser than anyone I know."

Vian rested his Chiang against the door. A guard watched him, but Vian waved at the man and he withdrew to the shadows. Vian gazed hard at Jilanna and gripped her shoulders, hugging her for a moment, wanting to banish her fears.

"Ultimately, no," Vian told her. "Ta Shen cannot hold out, unless something unexpected happens."

"But you have power—everyone talks about this."

"Limited. And there's a price for unleashing it," Vian said. "But yes, I'll do what I can, when the time is right. The best defense in the short term is courage. Whatever those turds throw at us, we must laugh back in their faces, Jilanna. Courage and fortitude. The odds are against us, the chance of victory sliver slim. But I've never been a gambler, so I don't subscribe to odds."

He pushed her away gently. Rasnei might get word or take his actions the wrong way. The last thing Vian needed was another quarrel.

"What does your heart believe?" Jilanna asked.

Vian sighed. The guard was staring at him. Rasnei would be anxious.

"That some of us will survive," he said, kissing her lightly. "This storm will pass, Jilanna. Everything does. There will be some left living to clean up the mess. Maybe write a song or two."

She said nothing but nodded. Vian motioned the guard allow them through inside the barbican. Once there, Vian took the stairs nimbly, the girl hurrying behind him.

Vian emerged to sunshine and Rasnei's tense expression.

"Where did you go?"

"For a walk."

"Again?"

"I like walking," Vian replied. "Helps me think."

Lin Gu bowed when he saw Vian, and Dorthar flashed him a grin. These two at least were ready for the fight. So was Matax, it appeared. The young general was immaculate today, with twin Jians polished and a small crossbow strapped to his belt, the bolts pushed into slots on either side. His eyes caught Vian's, and he nodded fiercely.

At a word from their empress, the others left the two lovers alone. Vian and Rasnei moved over to the south side of the barbican tower. The high keep's parapet commanded views right across to the distant woods shrouding the western horizon. The entire plain wedged between city and forests was covered in men, horses, and machinery. Their mounts trampled and stamped hoofs, as the riders jostled and quarreled for position.

"That's an ungainly rabble," Vian said.

"How many are out there, do you think?" Rasnei asked. She seemed calm; he was grateful for that.

"Ten thousand, maybe twelve."

"We have scarcely a fraction of that number—and they are veteran fighters."

Vian smiled at her. "Battles are like moods, Rasnei. They shift back and forth like quaking sands. Sudden events can alter everything. But sieges sap resolve like water leaking from a broken pail."

"What are you saying?"

"We drew first blood with the cannons," Vian said. "Why not follow up with something else? A second blow. Casca's enjoying showing off again. Seems to be a failing of his. We should exploit that. There's time, yet. I doubt he'll attack till morning, unless we can provoke him."

"We've already done that," she said. "It's why he's here and not idling in that camp. The old Ran, Calla, seemed content to bide his time."

"Casca's impatience could well prove his downfall," Vian said.

"I think that's highly unlikely in this instance."

"I've an idea." Vian smiled at her.

After he explained, Rasnei called Matax over. Vian asked the young general if the lone arbalest positioned up on the keep could reach the nearest siege tower. Matax thought it could.

"Another signal." Vian winked at Rasnei as they watched

Matax's men soak the huge projectile in oil and light the gauze, before firing the arrow from the large machine. "Casca won't be able to resist that." Vian grinned, seeing the flaming shaft arc high then dip, plummet down hard toward the distant siege towers.

"Load another one," Rasnei ordered as the arbalest's missile struck the corner of the closet tower and flames soared on impact. Vian saw tiny figures leap from the wooden structure. The second missile struck, and the flames grew higher.

"Enough," Vian said. "That should do the trick. I doubt Casca will delay further."

Casca watched the giant blazing arrows sliding down and striking the wooden siege tower, which collapsed in an arc of flame. Beside him, Uzcara chuckled. Casca knew his brothers were waiting for him to get it wrong again. The others refrained from jibes, but Uzcara seemed to delight in Casca's discomfort.

"I thought we were meant to use those towers against their walls, brother?" Uzcara said. "Instead, those Shen are marking them for target practice."

Casca had had enough. Plans had been to line everything up and terrify the foe by tossing some stones from the ballistae as a taster of what was to come. Let the terror take hold overnight, then bring the ram out at dawn and start the attack in earnest, while they were still filling their buckets with night soil.

Instead, the Shen had struck out again, before he'd made a move.

"Load those ballistae and pummel those walls!" Casca

roared at the artillery men gathered behind him. The three artillery captains snapped into action, ordering their launch teams line up and ready the missiles.

Casca watched with satisfaction as the first one cranked back on the ratchet. He counted to three and signaled. The ganger ordered fire. His team released the staying ropes, allowing the spoon-shaped cup swing forward at lurching speed, hurling a man-sized rock at the barbican walls.

The rock sailed through air and struck the wall a dozen feet below the keep parapet. The dull thud and dust explosion resulted in nothing. Casca saw the stone crack to powder as it slid down the walls, a mess of scree and pebbles settling close to the gates.

"Another!" Casca yelled across. "Get those towers moving!"

"I thought we were attacking in the morning?" Uzcara said, lazily.

Casca ignored him, turning his head to see the wooden attack towers grind forward, like drunken giants on creaking stilts.

"It starts now," he told Uzcara.

The brothers watched in silence as the siege towers rolled forward, swaying precariously on the iron wheels he'd had the blacksmiths forge. Eleven great platforms, each holding fifty men, inched their way closer to the walls.

Casca grinned and rubbed his hands at the sight. His joy proved short-lived. A sudden roar and blast of responding explosions stole Genza's smile, as he covered his ears from the racket.

The defenders had answered again. This time, cannon flame spouted forth from several places along the walls. A second tower was hit, the ball crashing clean through the center of the platform and shredding it in two. Men spilled like ants from a freshly disturbed nest.

A third tower was struck with flame, and to add insult, the next in line threw a wheel and tottered over, crashing into the fifth and causing it topple, too.

What a fucking mess.

Casca wiped sweat from his face. Uzcara was laughing out loud beside him.

Two more of the siege engines were struck by the giant arrows before Casca ordered them back, lest he lose the lot. He kept his temper in check and motioned the ram team forward. This would work. The rammers had arrived fresh from camp with their heavy burden. Two score strong men—protected by the shields of their fellows—carried the huge, logged fir tipped with riveted smelted iron.

At Casca's command, a score of riders made for the walls and sprayed arrows up at the keep parapet. The defenders answered, and several of Casca's riders fell from their horses. The ram cleared his ranks, the shield mass making it resemble a huge, crawling scaly insect.

A second group of riders drew near and loosed their shafts. Again, the Shen responded with crossbows. Casca saw two more warriors tumble.

The ram was getting close. He saw arrows striking the shields of the men protecting the bearers. Casca grinned. They'd break through those doors in no time. This would be over tonight.

Again, his smile was obliterated by a flash and boom, as a ball of fire struck the shield-shell covering the ram. That cannon blast killed twenty rammers, and the bodies of the shield bearers were strewn everywhere. To make things worse, the archers leaned down from the walls and sent volleys into the surviving men struggling to flee the carnage. They took their time aiming and loosing those bolts and shafts. Red-faced, Casca witnessed his ramming team perish to a man.

Beside him, slouched easy on his horse, Uzcara was laughing like a madman. Casca glared at his brother, guided his horse about and cantered back to the camp. Racara yelled the command, and the army turned and followed its leader.

"THAT WAS MOST ENTERTAINING, BROTHER," RAGAN Uzcara said, slurping wine at the camp. "I don't think you've thought this out properly. Aren't we meant to be the attacking force?"

Casca didn't respond. He'd been in a foul mood all evening. Seven siege towers had been destroyed, the ram abandoned outside the gates, and several hundred men had died for nothing. The Shen had struck the second blow, too. Casca felt determined there wouldn't be a third.

Uzcara smirked as Racara joined them. All the brothers were drunk. Young Calgara had passed out on the floor. Casca knew he wasn't popular. The captains were talking behind his back. Word was that he hadn't thought their strategies through. Or, worse, the new Ran was cursed for the black deeds he'd done. A *Kinslayer*. The gods of victory would abandon such a one. Casca feared a knife in his back more than ever tonight. He'd sleep with his armor on, eyes half open.

Damn those Shen.

It wasn't meant to be like this. He had the biggest army in the world. Twice, the knaves had foiled him. Perhaps Father had been right to take his time and break them slowly.

"Do we repeat the show tomorrow?" Uzcara grinned at him. Casca let go of his eating knife, else he stab out his brother's eyes.

He forced a smile. "I fucked up, underestimated them. That won't happen again."

"We need the shaman," Racara said.

"Fuck the shaman," Casca said, wiping his mouth. "I'm going to tear those walls down with my teeth, if all else fails. We had a bad start, lost a few men, nags and some lumber to flame and arrows. So it goes."

"A few *hundred* men," Uzcara glared at him, his dark eyes moody.

"We're ten thousand strong," Casca yelled in his ear, reaching for his eating knife again.

"Presently. I'm not sure they'll stick around, unless your luck changes," Uzcara said, watching the knife.

"What do you mean?" Casca stuck the knife in the table and scowled at his older brother. "Are you planning to lead a mutiny against me, Uzcara?"

"I won't need to," Uzcara said. "Genza will get word of this debacle. And those Shen have armies hiding close by, waiting. I saw soldiers creeping in the woods when I traveled here. They're biding their time. Everyone is watching you, Casca. Are you strong enough? Or have you taken on something you cannot handle?'

"We'll build more towers and soak them in water," Casca said. "Fell more trees for rams and train yet more fucking carriers and shield men."

"We'd do better to wait for their supplies to run dry," Racara said, gloomily.

"That could take years, brother."

"Not if we control the harbor," Uzcara said, leaning

forward.

Casca spat in the dirt. He was tired of Uzcara. "You haven't been here long, Uz, else you might have noticed that the harbor is also protected by a wall."

"Why not allow me take some men there and test the enemy's defenses on that side of the city? That way I don't have to watch you make a fool of yourself again."

"Do what you want," Casca spat on the table and stood, wobbling. He would retire to his cot soon, if he could find it.

"It was a good idea," Rasnei told him, as she and Vian stood on the balcony watching the flames dwindle on the ruined siege towers.

"It could have gone either way," Vian said, sipping his wine. "But I think Casca's in trouble. You know what these Cards are like. They don't respond well to failure, being used to winning. Ran Calla never lost a battle, they say. Casca's proving unlucky. I sense further unrest in that camp."

"Certainly, they are volatile enough." Rasnei kissed him and smiled. "You are my hero, Vian. Your cool thinking won the day for us. Moreover, I doubt they'll attack again for a week, perhaps longer."

"Aye," he said, his arm slipping around her shoulders. "But when they do, it will be terrible, Rasnei. Casca has been made to look a fool. If he survives his own brothers and captains, he'll stop at nothing to destroy us. And if they kill him, the next Ran will want to prove himself the better man. Either way, the Cards aren't quitting until Ta Shen falls."

"It's bought us more time."

"To do what? *Stew?* Idle away the hours in dread of a

storm we can't avoid? I'd sooner be fighting, Rasnei. We need an alternative plan, and ships to give us a way out of here. A chance for escape when those gates crumple, which they will.

"If Ta Shen falls, I'm staying put," she said. "Ships won't save all my citizens—so why should I be spared? This city is Shen's last bastion. I will not abandon my people. The game ends here, Vian. Please don't mention ships and ways out again."

"I'm only saying we lack any clear defensive strategy."

"I know, my love—but you have always urged me to be patient. Perhaps I've finally learned to listen." She kissed his cheek and left him standing clenching his fists.

What to do?

His love was being unrealistic speaking of patience and duty, instead of survival. Vian wouldn't wait day after day until the enemy finally got it right. It didn't matter who controlled that army. The Cardalan foe was here to stay. There had to be another way. Try as he might, Vian couldn't find a solution.

Damn you, Savarna—where are you? I cannot think straight these days.

Vian drank too much wine that night, fretting and brooding. He'd come up with a plan somehow. Perhaps he'd take Gurtei's advice and lead a sortie against their camp. One thing for sure: Vian wasn't waiting indefinitely. Action was required. Perhaps it was time to summon the dragon? Rasnei was asleep by the time he staggered to the bed.

7

AMIDST GRONTEYER

GUNSALA GRIPPED Finvar's hand tighter as they skirted the frozen lake, the ice glinting and dazzling her eyes. *Frozen*, yet it was summer in the land. Her power must be greatest here. Gunsala felt a shudder below. Why were they doing this? And why had she listened to Fin?

I am such a fool.

But it wasn't just Finvar's persuasions. Gunsala knew they couldn't avoid the witch. Sheega would hunt them down wherever they fled to on this island. Confronting her head-on —utter madness—seemed to her the only choice they had.

Play Sheega's game as long as they could. Fin was right— that trickster Lofhi wouldn't desert him. Not unless He had a good—or, more likely, bad—reason to do so. And she was there to make sure that didn't happen. The Goddess Elanion —or whoever that was on the strange beach—had given Gunsala powers, too. The shell she kept wrapped in her tunic. A pulsating abalone from Galenki. A distant world she'd somehow arrived in. The shell comforted her, though she had no notion how to use it.

But Gunsala had killed King Gorn, Sheega's brutal first-born son. A berserker feared by all, brought down by a young woman.

How had that happened?

A fog in her mind, like Galenki, the woman on that beach. Riddles and dreams, recurring echoes of something she didn't understand. Gunsala thought about that confrontation as she walked, her hand gripped tight in his.

She'd been carrying the unconscious Finvar. Gunsala remembered how light he had felt—no effort to hold him in her arms. King Gorn had blocked her way. A terrible figure with a sword in each hand, the castle Lofhi destroyed and crumbling behind him, and orange flames flickering in his eyes.

After that, things had become stranger, her memory murky. Gunsala recalled how an alien strength had taken over her fear. Gone was the dread, replaced by a heated rush of adrenaline and eagerness. A kind of strange joy, exultation, and strength. Wonderful, powerful strength. The next instant, she'd overcome the berserker king and slain him with his own swords.

I am Vulkorye.

But Gunsala didn't understand this new part of her, or know how she could summon that blissful strength again. Perhaps it has all been a dream, a memory distorted by the chaos and choking smoke? Maybe Lofhi had tricked her into believing she'd killed Gorn. Or, worse, this was Sheega's work, like the disappearing mist—all contrived to lure them over.

Away with these thoughts! She was part of this, whatever it was. Pattern. Thread. Destiny ...

Keep walking, don't think.

The lake fell away, as low hills cracked open to reveal a

winding path leading up to more woods and the smoky hall beyond.

They took the path tentatively. Finvar smiled at her, and Gunsala nodded back, her heart thudding in her chest. The air was cold, and the sky above bright and clear. She saw no clouds, and to the south, the lone twin peaks of the mountain sparkled purple and white in the sunlight.

It wasn't long before the turf roof of the Great Hall came into view. There was smoke trailing up into the blue. It looked peaceful. Tranquil. The only sounds were the distant murmur of waves grinding on shingle, and a lone eagle calling out as it circled up high in the wide, clear skies.

They rounded a corner and crested the hills. The hall stood waiting. A large wooden structure, solid and broad, the low turf roofs and firs corked with resin. Two ornately carved wooden doors were the only visible entrance. One was open, and a strange green light drifted out. A vapor or mist, it lifted and faded before her eyes.

"Are you ready for this?" Finvar asked as he squeezed her hand.

Gunsala nodded. Her tongue felt like a block of wood, making it hard to speak.

They walked slowly toward the hall. Gunsala's mind raced as she imagined shadows leaping out and falling upon them. All was calm. The wind had dropped, as though holding its breath. That ominous silence settled like carrion around them.

Gunsala saw the tall pole off to her right and shuddered. A fir had been stripped of bark and shaped. There were rune carvings cut into it, and black crow feathers were tarred up its length. At the top was a horse's skull, and the hollow eyes seemed to watch Gunsala with hostile disapproval.

She averted her gaze, kept walking toward the hall.

"I'm so glad you decided to come."

Gunsala crashed into Finvar's side as he slammed to a halt. The woman was seated on a flat rock some fifteen feet in front of the hall. She appeared young and very beautiful. Her pale blue eyes were kindly and wise. She wore her smile like other women sported jewelry. Her dress was blue, and it shimmered in the sunlight. The woman's feet were bare, and her long legs were ivory-white and flawless.

And there you are. Gunsala chewed her lip. No turning back now.

Sheega rose with a quicksilver grace and drifted toward them, her bare feet barely touching the frozen ground. Gunsala felt Finvar tense like a bowstring beside her. As the witch approached, Gunsala studied the perfect features: her oval face, the high cheekbones, and large, slanted, pale-blue eyes. The curled, rouged lips hinted every kind of pleasure and reward. And that full rich body, the firm breasts and perfect skin—the dress showing off every curve. Even her fingernails shone like diamonds. Sparkling rings with opals and pearls glittered on those long fingers. She seemed wise, patient. Gunsala felt ugly and rude, like an intruder who shouldn't be here.

"I never turn down an invitation," Finvar squeaked the words out beside her. She could feel him shaking. "Especially from a witch."

Gunsala saw a brief shadow like a bat's wing flitter in the woman's eyes. It left and she smiled again.

"A witch?" Sheega looked at Finvar for a moment and then turned her gaze on Gunsala. Her arms were folded, the long pale fingers brushing her chin. "You are much misinformed."

"You know who I am," Finvar said as they walked toward the woman. "Who watches over me."

"Of course, I do, Finvar Droll." Sheega smiled beautifully. "You are favored by the Trickster Himself, and protected by the brave Vulkorye walking beside you. This charming girl who thinks she loves you." Her eyes flashed at Gunsala. "You haven't learned how to use your power yet, have you, my dear?"

"I killed your son." Gunsala spat the words out and wished she hadn't.

But Sheega laughed, a hollow sound like ice crystals cracking.

"You did me a favor, sweetheart. Gorn was worse than useless, and thanks to his sad demise I know all about *you*."

"You know nothing about me."

Sheega's smile broadened. "But I do, my dear. More than you yourself can ever understand. Come now—you must be hungry after your many adventures. Let's go eat and sip honey wine. We've much to discuss."

"I'd sooner not be poisoned." Gunsala stood her ground.

"Poisoned?" The dark flicker showed in her eyes again. "I'm not going to poison you, Gunsala. You are my guests. Come, follow me. Don't be churlish, child."

"Is it too late to run?" Finvar whispered in her ear.

"I understand your reservations—of course I do," Sheega said. "Jaran Hrelgisson is your friend, Finvar. And you are loyal, which is an admirable trait in a mortal. But you've never heard my side of the story."

"You'll not win him around," Gunsala said.

"Am I going to have trouble with you?" The question was kindly and curious, like a wise patron addressing a delinquent infant. Gunsala didn't reply. Sheega smiled again as though it was a small matter. She rubbed her palms together. "Chilly out here. Come now, let's enjoy some warmth together by the fire."

"Where is Ranning?" Finvar asked suddenly.

"I don't know who that is," Sheega's eyes glinted sudden cold. She turned and beckoned them follow, drifting like blue wood smoke toward the hall.

Both doors were now open.

RANNING RAN HIS COOL HANDS THROUGH THE ROCK pool. The giant's shadow was reflected in the water.

"When can I hunt?" Gorvaron's voice grated like rusty iron sawing through badly knotted lumber.

"Tonight," Ranning turned and gazed up at the Witch-Man. "At dusk, you can leave this place. Make for the mountain, Gronteyer. Hrelgisson will be there. Find him and bring me his head."

"Only one man?"

"Do that, and you can return and kill anything that moves. But be on your guard. Hrelgisson is cunning and has aid from afar."

"I am Gorvaron," the giant boomed. "I would have revenge for the slaying of my kin."

"It is yours to take and with my blessing. Go, make ready. Your byrnie and mace await you. I've sown rune-spells into the steel. Tyho's axe, Griner, will not bite your flesh while those protect you."

"I need not your protection." Gorvaron loomed close, and the stench of his weed-breath had Ranning choking. "I will stamp on that bug and rip off his head."

"Even so, it is done," Ranning said. "Leave me, Gorvaron. I've a journey to undertake."

Gorvaron's bulk shifted away. Ranning turned and watched the huge figure of the witch-man shamble off toward the darkening hills. Another hour and dusk would be here. Sheega had told him about her visitors. For some reason he couldn't grasp, Ranning had felt a disquiet hearing mention of the girl, Gunsala. Some kind of foreboding surrounded that name.

He placed the premonition in the back of his mind. Ranning waded into the rock pool and spoke the charm rune. He reached down and strapped on his Faerie shoes that would allow him to travel the Chaos realms without detection. He had no desire to encounter Aldorian's people or, worse, the trolls. And that dwarf king, Rafin, would be looking for him.

He took to the water, swimming hard and fast like a quicksilver fish that cut through the waves and dived low, keeping the shore close to his right.

Ranning felt a strange sorrow as he swam. How he missed watery Telimantua and his kinfolk, the Faen. His grandfather, Sensuata, had been cruel to banish him all those years ago. Ranning had nothing left—just his hatred for the thieving mortals and a huge void that was his missing soul.

Faster than any shark, Ranning reached the sea cave by nightfall. The *Faerie Door,* the people of this island called it, without understanding why.

Ranning knew its real name. The cave was how he first came here, seeking the sorceress who called herself Sheega.

His head broke above the water's surface at the cave entrance. There he stood dripping for a time, his chest thudding. At last ready, Ranning hopped free of the brine and entered the tunnel. There were gleaming stripes of iridescent light twisting toward the middle distance. But Ranning knew the way, and the many traps and perils that he'd have to pass to reach the other side.

The lost door was barred and locked. Ranning found the chest he'd buried in sand and opened it, dressing quickly into the silver byrnie and cloak, and placing the winged power-helmet over his head. Finally, he reached for the crooked dagger and stowed it in his belt.

Then Ranning muttered the rune-codes and pressed hard against the door. It creaked open, slowly revealing a swirl of darkness and electric blue gas that reached out for him with whispery fingers.

He closed his eyes and jumped into that spidery noth-ingness ...

NIGHT FELL DEEP ON THE MOUNTAIN. TOFEI HEARD AN owl calling close by. He suppressed a shiver. It was cold up here above the timberline, the heather sighing in the night winds. The mountain's upper slopes reared to his right, a quarter moon coated silver along the ridges and crags. The glisten of snow and a diadem of stars added a surreal mood to the night.

Tofei was weary but kept moving. He dared not rest in this cold place, else he awaken stiff and useless. A deer track led up from the dark woods, winding across the heather. Tofei followed this until he reached the first crust of snow and then took another track that ran parallel, the vast shadow of the mountain looming sharp to his right.

Tofei walked until dawn. As the first warmth from the sun

seeped into his bones, he collapsed in the springy heather and slept for several hours.

He awoke hungry and afraid.

I shouldn't have fallen asleep.

Annoyed with himself, Tofei shook movement into his limbs. He started trotting along the deer track, heading east toward the rising sun. Another bright day promised good progress.

He reached a wide, flat overlook and crouched low. From there, Tofei had a clear view of the eastern side of the island and ocean beyond. The dark cliffs of Leeth reared in the distance, seeming almost in arms' reach. He marked the place where the cliffs parted like a missing tooth as the fjord leading to Skarness town, with Grimhold far beyond.

At last, Tofei saw what he'd been looking for: A ship catching waves, faring south hugging the island's shore, the red-and-white square sail trapping the sun. A brave sight that cheered his heart.

Tofei grinned in relief, knowing his father and the men had got away safely. He shifted his gaze south past the mountain's shoulder. That way, Tofei saw more forests. Deep pines, and beyond them were flat lands and thin strands of pale empty beach. He saw the gleaming ribbon of a river and what looked to be settlements at the far end of the island. Two clusters of what appeared to be squat buildings, and a rough-looking dock that might serve his father for a mooring. Beyond these, Valkador wedged to a sharp hooked point where shingle and rock met ocean.

Encouraged, Tofei trotted along a new deer track until the mountain slopes were behind him. He jumped down through a maze of boulders and heather-clad rocks. There were deer paths framed by furze and broom and willow, all leading to rough crags and dark hollows. He saw caves half-hidden as he trotted past. You could hide an army in here, Tofei thought.

It was mid-morning by the time he reached the southern woods. He was hungry and tired again. He had his spear ready in case a rabbit or deer should show.

Instead, it was an aging man with a bow who blocked his path.

I'm called Ivar Ketilsson," the oldster said. "Are you lost, boy?"

JARAN LOOKED UP AS IVAR APPEARED, A YOUNG, HARD-faced man carrying a spear walking beside him. They were seated around the campfire outside the deep caverns where Ivar had led them yesterday—a well-hidden spot high in the west shoulder of the mountains.

The caverns had been expansive and confusing, with many tunnels leading off in all directions. The brands they'd carried had dwindled before Jaran could discern where those crevices led. Deep into the mountain, he suspected. The realm of wolf and bear.

During that foray underground, Ivar had shown Jaran a hole where a spark of daylight peered down. The crack was wide enough to climb through, allowing a way up through twisted rock. They'd climbed this narrow chimney, emerging in sunshine on a ledge that overlooked the western side of the island, awarding views of the ocean and narrow beaches running north. From there, he glimpsed distant smoke, several miles away.

The Great Hall. It had to be.

They'd got back two hours ago. Ivar had said he wanted to

check the woods again. He'd returned with this fierce-eyed stranger.

Jaran studied the young man who Ivar introduced as Tofei from Leeth. The name seemed familiar. Jaran had assumed this was another villager who had made his way up here— there were four who joined them yesterday. But as he studied Tofei, he saw a marked difference in the way this man stood. He looked a doughty fighter. Useful. But where had he come from? The sight of Tofei pleased Jaran. This was no shy village lad. He held the spear with confidence, his face sharp and lean. He was strong and lithe, well put together.

"We meet again, Jaran Hrelgisson," the newcomer said and dipped his head in what might be a bow.

"Do I know you?" The boy did look familiar.

"We met on that other beach," Tofei said, his eyes shifting to Savarna and the others gathered around. "My father, his men. Before the honey-green ones came. We saw you kill Holtarn Erlundsson and feared we were next."

"You're Gunard's boy!" Jaran leaped to his feet and rushed over to embrace the startled Tofei. "I'm glad you're here, lad. How are you here? Where's your father?"

"Give him a bloody chance," Savarna said, holding back a laugh.

Tofei grinned at him. "Gunard's making for those villages. My father will try and find somewhere safe to moor."

"That will prove hard," Ivar said. "Windy and rough, that end of the island. Water's shallow, too. There are dangerous skerries hidden below the tides."

"Gunard's a canny sailor—he'll manage," Tofei said, his eyes still on Jaran.

"You were on that ship we saw," Savarna said.

"I suppose." he looked at her, clearly puzzled about who she was.

"Finvar?" Jaran gripped Tofei's shoulders until the man winced. He let go and stood back. "Is Finvar Droll with your father?"

"He was," Tofei said. "And Gunsala."

"Who's Gunsala?" Savarna looked at Jaran, but he hardly heard her.

Fin is here.

"He's on the ship—we have to go meet them." Jaran felt a surge of joy hearing of his friend's return, knowing that Finvar had survived and was here to help them kill the witch. *Destiny will win through.*

"Finvar's not with my father," Tofei said, leaning on his spear.

"Where is he? Take me there."

"They went to meet with the witch called Sheega."

Jaran felt his mouth slam shut. Silence and white faces surrounded him. There was a hush and sudden chill—even the fire died, as a cold blast of wind smothered the embers.

"What did you say?" Jaran glared at Tofei.

"Finvar and Gunsala, they went to the hall."

"Why would they do that?" Savarna rose and stared hard at Tofei, as Jaran stood shaking like a tree struck by lightning.

"To lead her on a false trail, I suspect. I've seen them do things, those two ..." Tofei shook his head, avoiding Jaran's bleak glare. "Both have special skills. Finvar woke me before leaving, the night before last. Gunsala said Sheega approached her close by our camp where we'd hidden the ship in reeds. She said Sheega invited them to join her at the hall. That I should not mention this to my father until morning, and then insist he took the ship south in search of you."

Jaran stared hard at the young warrior's face. "What special skills?" he asked eventually. *Fin came to help, and now he's caught in her nets. This is all my fault.*

"He is …" Tofei shook his head. "I don't know … *different*. But Gunsala—she killed the king."

"The king?" Savarna said "Erlund?"

"No. He died earlier. I mean King Gorn."

"Sheega's eldest son." Jaran nodded slowly. "That means there is only one brother left. Doubtless Valgarn Erlundsson is on his way here, too."

Tofei shrugged. "I know nothing of his whereabouts."

"Who is this person Gunsala, and how did she kill one of Sheega's terrible sons?" Savarna awarded Jaran a sideways glance.

Tofei looked uncomfortable. "She is Vulkorye," he muttered.

"What is that?" Savarna asked, and looked at Jaran again. He shrugged in response. The word was familiar. He'd heard it before but couldn't fathom where or when.

"They serve One Eye," Tofei said, looking off toward the caves.

"You're not making much sense," Savarna told him.

"He means old Oroonin, the god we Northmen call the Traveler," Ivar said, shaking his head. "First Kullaan, now the Traveler. I fear that we are caught in something far bigger than we first believed."

"And Tyho gave me this axe." Jaran's hands brushed Griner's steel. "Why would three of the northern gods care so much about the fate of a witch? And Rafin and Rune—they are part of this, too."

"Four gods," Tofei said quietly.

"What's that?" Savarna looked at him. Jaran noted the dread in his eyes—he'd seemed fearless a moment ago.

"Lofhi," Tofei muttered. "I saw the Sly One's red-eyed shadow rise from the pit in Grimhold."

"You were in Grimhold?" Jaran said.

Tofei nodded. "Finvar was captured by Gorn. His idea. They dragged him to Grimhold for torture and questioning. We followed. I thought we were all going to die, but …" He shook his head.

"Gone on," Savarna said, smiling at Tofei for the first time.

"We stole into the castle after dark when they were feasting," Tofei said. "Gunsala, she … Gorn had the prisoner tossed into a pit of snakes. The king was laughing when we broke into the hall. Next, thing, all manner of shit happened, and my head exploded with pain. I'd thought it was a lightning strike at the time. Didn't make sense. The castle was breaking apart before my eyes. I saw the shadow rising from the pit. It had Finvar's face and Lofhi's eyes. I ran, as did we all. Except Gunsala."

"The Vulkorye," Savarna said.

"Yes," he nodded. "She walked through the carnage of rubble and flames. Returned with your friend's unconscious body limp in her arms—how she carried him, I've no idea. But I saw Gorn follow and attack her with a sword in each hand. I wanted to run and help her, but there was no need. It happened so fast. Gunsala killed him in seconds, wrenching both swords from Gorn's grasp and then slicing them sideways through his neck. I'd never witnessed such a thing."

"I need to meet this woman," Savarna said to Jaran, a gold-flecked sparkle glinting in her eye.

"Tomorrow," he replied. "When we deal with Sheega in that hall."

"We can't go there, Jaran—time has to pass," Savarna said.

"That can't be helped. We cannot allow her to kill our friend. Can we …?" Jaran glared at her but knew she was right. Whatever Finvar was up to, he was on his own. Jaran's shoulder was still weak from his battle against her changeling. The gods alone knew what lay in waiting in that hall. He dipped his head in defeat. "Yet again, she mocks us."

"We must send forth the War Arrow," Ivar said, and they all looked at him.

"What's that?" Savarna asked.

"Jarle Hrund's arrow. A red shaft that was passed down from his ancestors. Any who touched it were pledged to the service of Valkador. I'm thinking you need help from Leeth and the other northern lands. The Northmen must rally."

"Against what—one witch?" Jaran glared at him. "Why would they care?"

Instead of answering, Ivar shook his head. "Cradon Iwey," he said eventually.

"What?" Jaran glared at the old hunter.

"The cave we call the Faerie Gate—that's how you got through her mists," Ivar said. Jaran had no idea where he was going with this.

"There was no cave," Savarna said, looking as puzzled as he felt. "We landed on the beach—at least I think that's what happened."

"They'll come from Cradon Iwey." Ivar's eyes seemed dreamy and lost. Jaran wondered if he'd found some mushrooms earlier.

"Who will come?" Savarna said, then stared hard at Jaran. "Oh, I see!"

He nodded slowly, understanding at last. "The elves and trolls—their armies will issue from Faerie. That cave must lead to the Worlds Gate where the great bell tolled. Sheega must be counting on Faerie help against the Traveler and Tyho. The pieces are coming together, it seems."

"We need Svipdag," Ivar said, chewing his moustache. "He alone knows what became of the War Arrow."

"The madman?" Savarna shook her head. "Why would he help us?"

"Svipdag will know," Ivar said.

Jaran turned as Bjarni approached. "I will fare to Leeth and ask for help," he said.

"No, you won't," Savarna replied.

"I'd sooner not have Myra on my back," Jaran added.

"We will go," Asmund said, and his friend Olof stepped forward, nodding.

"We need the War Arrow before anyone leaves this island," Ivar said. "You, Jarle, and this young warrior," he nodded at Tofei. "We three will take the caves and find Svipdag."

"You're not going anywhere without me," Savarna said.

"It's better you stay here," Ivar said, and Jaran saw her eyes glint angrily. "I mean no offense, woman," Ivar had caught her gaze too. "But Svipdag might take you for the witch. He is troubled by visions, and your sudden presence could well unhinge him. You have a wild look about you, if you'll forgive my saying so."

Savarna stared at Ivar for a moment before nodding. "If you say so."

"That's if we can find this hermit in the first place." Jaran smiled at her. "At least I can get my bearings in these caves. That might help us later."

"What about Finvar and Gunsala?" Tofei asked.

Jaran shook his head, unable to answer that.

"Finvar will survive, and I suspect your Vulkorye woman, too. This last gambit is just beginning," Savarna told Tofei. "Destiny says Jaran, Finvar and I will kill that witch. We must have faith that he'll pull through."

"Aye, the Norns spin faster than a man can read," Ivar said.

Savarna ignored that. "You three go find the crazy man, and do it quickly," she said. "I will keep a look out for ghost hounds, witch-men and changelings."

Jaran nodded. "In the morning then."

"At least allow me to go greet your father and his men," Bjarni said to Tofei. "Tell them where we are."

"Aye," Ivar nodded. "Those fighters are scant use to us on the beach."

8

SHEEGA'S STORY

SHEEGA STUDIED their faces behind her smile. The young, angry girl and the tortured man with the haunted eyes. *Enemies, and yet* ... They intrigued her. It took courage coming here. She'd seldom found that quality in mortals. They usually fell apart like warm, cracking clay in her hands.

Gunsala was scared, of that there was no doubt. She was changing. Developing into something new—morphing from grub to butterfly. A plain young woman who'd been gifted something she couldn't understand. The ancient honor being chosen as Vulkorye. The poor child had no idea how They were using her.

I am always portrayed as the bad one. Those two are no better.

Finvar avoided her gaze. He would be aware that she knew about Lofhi and would try his upmost to stay evasive. They were playing for time—that much was obvious. They'd either seen Hrelgisson or were aware that he's on the island.

I'll squeeze his location out of you.

There was no need to rush. They were here to keep her

distracted, while Hrelgisson lurked and skulked until the second moon. Two poor children doomed as sacrificial lambs.

You came too early, Jaran Hrelgisson. Your friends are mine, and Gorvaron will find you. You don't know it yet, but I have already won.

The fires crackled, Finvar fidgeted, and the girl gripped her wine glass as though she'd break it in two.

Relax, you pair," Sheega purred and showed them her warmest smile. "The honey wine is good—you should try it."

Finvar sipped carefully and nodded. "It is good," he said, wiping his mouth. "I expect you're wondering why we're here."

"There's plenty of time to discuss such nuances. I'm just happy you dropped by." She sipped her own glass, her eyes watching every nerve that twitched on their faces. "Before that, we should get to know each other better."

"Why?" Gunsala asked her. "We are hardly friends."

Sheega ignored the stupid comment. The girl was young and acting brash because she was afraid. Not her idea coming here, but his. Gunsala was loyal to Finvar. It was sweet. A pity she'd have to die. *But not yet.* With Ranning gone, this diversion was perfectly timed.

She rose like silk and walked to the doors, closing each one with a dull thud. "It gets chilly at night."

"We ..." Gunsala glanced at Finvar, who was watching Sheega, his dark eyes troubled.

"Are staying for a few days, yes?" Sheega asked.

Finvar's mouth hung open; Gunsala looked at him, her eyes glazed like an arrow-struck doe.

"I'll take that for a yes." Sheega walked across to the long table and poured herself another drink. "Silly things, you've hardly touched your wine. Drink it up, it's warming and will help you sleep. I can tell that you've been through a lot lately."

Finvar gulped the wine down and placed the glass on the table. He cleared his throat. "You know Jaran Saerk is going to kill you soon."

Sheega swilled the glass in her deft narrow fingers, her eyes watching the golden liquid. "I know that he thinks he is, your big friend." Her smile at the glass faded as she hurled it into the fire. She reached across, grabbing Finvar by the ear, twisting the golden rings and lifting him to his feet.

"I'm not going to let that happen," she hissed, squeezing the lobe before letting go of his ear. Finvar jumped back, his eyes wide and watering. "Speak to me like that again, boy, and I'll rip your fucking earrings off."

Finvar looked visibly shaken, and Gunsala stood glaring at her, with fists clenched at her sides. Sheega sighed and summoned patience. *Mortals ....*

"Oh, do sit," Sheega waved a dismissive hand. "I'm sorry, but I have a temper. You shouldn't test me so."

Finvar nodded and took his chair. Gunsala stood her ground. "Don't touch him again," she said.

Sheega smiled, as though it had all been a misunderstanding. She suggested they drink after refilling Finvar's glass. He drained it with a shaking hand, and she filled it again.

"How about you, Vulkorye? Are you not drinking tonight?" Gunsala tensed and her eyes widened in alarm. "Well of course I know about that, Gunsala. How else could you have killed my son? Gorn was the strongest of the three."

Gunsala's lips twitched. She looked at Finvar and took a sip of the wine, followed by a second. She sat, her expression grim, eyes dull and defeated.

Sheega smiled. "That's good—you're relaxing at last. I'm

happy. I need you to relax, because I want to tell you my story, so that you know the truth."

"The truth?" Finvar looked hard at her before dropping his gaze.

"Aye, Finvar the Droll—you haven't heard it yet."

GUNSALA FELT ANGER WASH THROUGH HER. THE WOMAN was seeping inside their heads, making them submissive, kneading their resistance like soft clay in her twisted claws. How could they hope to win here? Why had they come? *Foolishness.* She closed her eyes and summoned what courage she could find.

"Look at me." Sheega's voice reached inside her.

Without her realizing, Gunsala's eyes blinked open and were hooked by the woman's hypnotic gaze. Those pale blue orbs were haunting lamps that burnt her like invisible fire. It was though the witch could see deep into her soul. And perhaps she could, Gunsala thought. Her mind was a tangle of rage, loathing and dread. And something else … *admiration?*

The enchantress was terrible indeed, but also alluring. Despite how she fought against it, Gunsala felt herself wanting to believe what this spinner of lies was saying.

"I've always been misunderstood," Sheega told Finvar and Gunsala, as they sat by that roaring hearth. The heat in here was making Gunsala tired. The strong mead, which she'd tried so hard not to drink, was making her drowsy and calm. The danger surrounding them had seemed to fade. An illusion, she knew, but one she could no longer fight this evening.

"Even at the beginning," the witch continued, "the earliest days, I was left out."

"From what?" Finvar was an open ear. Gunsala feared she had lost him to the cruel charms of this sinister, beautiful woman.

"Everything, young Finvar," Sheega said, her voice soothing and plaintive. "*Everything.* I backed the wrong player and was misled. Even He wasn't twisted back then."

"The Traveler?"

Sheega laughed, a harsh sound that jarred the drowsiness from Gunsala's eyes. "Fuck, no. I've always hated that dry old stick. Meddling bastards, Him and His wife. You should know." Sheega's ice-blue chips glinted at Gunsala.

"I ... don't."

Sheega ignored her. "I'm talking about my oldest brother. The Firstborn. He was ... hmm." She licked her lips, and her eyes misted over. "Beautiful and magnificent. The strongest of us. I loved Him. It mattered not that Saan was drawn to the dark? I was, too, and to everything He put forth. The light is so predictable."

"The Shadowman." Finvar nodded slowly. "You served the Lord of Night. *Cul* Saan, they called him in the ancient texts. The dark spirit of Ptarni. He who was overcome during the last war of the gods."

"The Ptarni were dirt under my brother's finger nails," Sheega said. "Like myself, the Shadowman—as you call Him —was betrayed twice. The other group didn't play fair. We had to even things up, develop a certain ... bad attitude. Call it survival." She curled her lip and winked at them.

Gunsala was losing track. Sheega's words meant nothing to her. Fin seemed to understand, but Gunsala felt out of her depth and drowsy again. Predictably, the mead was affecting her as much as Sheega's soothing voice. Why had she partaken? *Stupid.*

Damn the heat in here. She forced her eyes open wider. *I will not be weak in front of her.*

"We fought back, yet again," Sheega said. "Raised some of the old crew to the cause."

"The Urgolais." Finvar nodded.

"Were part of it, yes." Sheega nodded. "But I always detested their creepy ways."

"Who are you?" Gunsala said, her mind racing as she struggled to keep up. "I heard a name like that mentioned somewhere before."

"I was Undeyna of the Shadows," Sheega told her. The witch's eyes had turned dreamy and sad, almost as though she was looking back at some distant memory. "And like my eldest brother, I too was beautiful. Dark and lustrous was my hair, pale and flawless this skin. Undeyna was tall and powerful. An enchantress wise in rune-craft and lore. Not that that ever did me any good. They all loved Simi. To Them, I was invisible."

"Who is that?" Gunsala wished she could recall more of what had happened over in Wynais.

You were a goddess.

"My sweet sister," Sheega smiled lovingly at her memories. "Beautiful, laughing Simiolanis—my twin. We two were the youngest children of the Weaver's First Born. Simi was golden-haired and radiant like the sun—that orb was fashioned in Her likeness. She represented the light, whereas I was the forgotten dark, her neglected shadow."

"You killed her," Gunsala said.

"Stabbed out her eyes," Sheega replied. "Simi had such lovely eyes." Her own eyes flashed with sudden anger. "I was provoked. Goaded. And Simi was such a flirt, she'd lie with anyone. I killed my sister and fled with my darling nightmare eldest brother. Together We plotted against Them. Father's favorites."

"Your kin, the old gods" Finvar said with a wry smile.

"The war was millennia long, but we lost yet again thanks to the intervention of a certain Aralais warlock and an obstinate mortal."

"The Crystal King." Finvar smiled again. "I've read about this."

"Yes," she said. "Him especially I blame. Corin an Fol was my guest in Darkvale for a time. He proved ungrateful company."

Gunsala was lost again, but at least she felt awake. And terrified. This was a goddess, or had been once. How could they hope to win against such a being? Suddenly she had a thought. *Your greatest enemy.* The woman on the beach.

"Who is the Emerald Queen?" Gunsala flashed a side glance at Finvar.

"You ask me that?" Sheega stared at her. "When She gave you a Galenki pulse-shell for protection against my talons?" She barked that harsh laugh again. Gone was the elegant beauty, replaced by a dark and creeping shadow. The sudden change was over before Gunsala's eyes could register it ever happening, and Sheega was all calm smiles again.

"The Mistress of the Trees," the witch said whimsically. "My big sister. Aloof Elanion, whose husband you call the Traveler." Sheega's eyes narrowed slyly. "They detest each other, those too. Long story. Elanion was the second oldest, therefore gifted this planet—Ansu—for Her domain. She loved Simi and hated me, especially after what happened. Elanion ruled over the Faen, the original occupants of Ansu. Related to the elves of Faerie but very much their own crew. The Faen existed

even before the pompous Aralais and resentful Urgolais arrived
in their space barges from afar to wage their dreadful wars.

"They came from space?" Finvar looked as confused as
Gunsala felt.

Sheega ignored him. Her eyes were far away.

"Ansu was my world, too, and I was happy to share—but
Big Sister wanted me out. But Elanion couldn't reach me in
Darkvale. In that enchanted forest I set traps and became her
opposite. Many of Elanion's people joined me there because of
their fear and loathing of humans. These became known as the
Dark Faen."

"I heard Undeyna perished when her master died." Finvar
arched his fingers and stared hard at Sheega. His voice seemed
different, the eyes glittered with a dull red sheen.

"Finvar?" Gunsala said. The shadow passed. Finvar looked
at her, his face blanched and eyes troubled.

That was Lofhi, wasn't it? Her eyes bore into Finvar's, and
he nodded slightly, reading her thoughts. Sheega had noticed
the change, too. She turned quiet, thoughtful.

"I barely survived," she said. "Had to flee to distant
Gwelan. Lick my wounds dry for several lifetimes. I returned
as Sheega the Ice Witch and settled in the east of this world. I
was happy there."

"Why did you come here, to Valkador?" Gunsala asked.

"Because I attract enemies like fucking flies," Sheega
said, her blue gaze flashing with irritation. "My old kin
wanted to make sure I couldn't settle anywhere in Their
corner of the universe. The Traveler guessed my identity but
couldn't act, as the Weaver, our dear father, had banned us
all from Ansu, after so many calamities. We, His first batch,
have always been a disappointment to the maker of the
universe. Part of the reason why He created a new team, and

you mortals—who for some reason dear Father seems to dote on. Hence using His low cunning, the Traveler stirred up the warlocks of Dunnehine, setting them against me. He didn't act alone."

Sheega stared hard at Finvar until he blinked. "You played a part in that, *Lofhi*." Sheega switched her gaze to the flickering shadows in the hall. "I know you're around, Trickster. Stop skulking in the fireplace."

Gunsala heard the sound of distant laughter, followed by Finvar choking.

"Is he here?" Gunsala asked Finvar.

He shook his head. "If he is, he's not letting me know."

"Well, isn't this nice," Sheega said, rubbing her long white fingers together. "You see, we three have much in common. We've all been treated badly by our peers."

Are you there?

Of course I am.

Why don't you help us?

Why the fuck should I? You got yourselves into this.

Finvar's eyes saw the shadowy shape appear like a blood stain at the edge of his vision. If Sheega had noticed, she didn't let on. Her slanted blue gaze looked dreamy, lost in her reminiscing. She was feigning weariness at the late hour.

Finvar stared at the blood stain shadow sliding along the wall. Almost it had a shape.

You're invested in my survival, Lofhi. You need to help us, lest she does something when we are asleep.

No answer. Finvar suppressed a yawn.

Sheega's eyes flicked across his. "Of course, you must be

tired, poor things. I suggest we resume this cheerful visit on the morrow. I'll have breakfast ready for you when you rise."

"Where do we sleep?" Gunsala looked around. There was nothing but shadows and smoke. The hall was a gloomy mass of emptiness.

"In the chamber I've set aside for you," Sheega smiled, and snapped her fingers.

"He seems to handle you very well," Sheega said to the spidery shadow sliding down the wall. A dark, rusty shape, it plopped like wet coal into the fire. The flames surged up greedily as that contact took on form. A small, shadowy, winged creature with red, glowing eyes leered back at her.

"I put a lot of work into Finvar," the bat-like creature said, its voice squeaky high, almost as grating as Gantallian's. "I'm proud of the boy."

"You lied," she said. "Finvar thinks you made him from spell runes. But rather, you stole the poor wretch as a boy." Sheega jabbed at the eyes with her fire poker. They vanished, reappearing at the other end of the fireplace—two dull red, blinking candles. "That small error might prove your undoing, Trickster."

"Finvar is mine." Lofhi sounded peeved. "He will kill Tyho's thug, despite not wanting to."

"You say."

"I DO say," the voice hissed at her. "He has no choice. One task, and he gets to be free of me, and survives you. That's a good deal, Deyna. He's sensible and won't let us down. With their champion knocked out, we can use Faerie's might to counter anything They send against us. Your kin and mine. Even Tyho and Kullaan, with the Traveler too, are no match for the trolls and elves and goblin forces combined."

"I wish that I could trust you, Lofhi."

"Don't be obtuse. Nobody trusts anybody," the voice sneered. "Saving humans, bless them. Look at those two hiding in the illusion you created—isn't it cute."

Sheega poked the fire again. "If you fail me, Lofhi, I'll find you wherever you lurk. You don't need another enemy."

"True," the red eyes flickered. "But neither do you, as I've said before. You're not who you were, Deyna. We two have everything to gain from this alliance. Leave Finvar to me, witch. That way I get to play with the girl, too, when he's not looking." The coal eyes flickered and went out as the shadow drifted up like smoke from the walls. Lofhi had gone.

Sheega stood. She felt old tonight. The two mortals were sleeping at the end of the hall, content inside the fabricated dream chamber she'd fashioned for them. She stared at them with a sour expression and felt a wash of sadness.

Oh, Simi ...

Why should they be happy and she not?

I should kill the girl.

But Sheega didn't want to, yet. Young Gunsala was Elanion's latest puppet. Her champion, as Jaran Hrelgisson was Tyho's and the Traveler's.

Two pawns. It would be so much better to turn Elanion's untrained tool against Her. Sheega's mind was too busy to rest. Lofhi was right—she needed any ally she could muster. Even him. She'd lost so much. Her powers were miniscule compared to those glorious times.

I am but a shadow of who I was.

Her fault. The Emerald Queen. Long had Elanion hunted Undeyna with the bow called Kerasheva, wounding her three times, until she slipped Her nets and fled in bat form to far-off Gwelan.

For a while, Sheega had hoped that they'd forgotten her. But the Traveler was always searching. Once he'd found her, it was no surprise His estranged wife would join the hunt.

Sheega walked out into the night, the wind whipping her long hair back and causing her cloak to flutter. She reached the beach and stood by Ranning's rock pool, seeing her face reflected in the moonlit water.

"You had better find that silver creep," Sheega said. Rune worried her, knowing he was out there somewhere, a hole in her plans.

But what could Rune do? Gorvaron would find Hrelgisson and stove his skull. They were fools coming here. Sheega had won—they'd realize that soon enough. The problem for her was that she couldn't convince herself it was true.

I must make ready.

Sheega's eyes smarted at the sharp inshore gale that was rising. She loved storms—they always improved her mood. Head clearer, she walked back and sat under her horsehead witching pole. Closing her eyes and concentrating, her dark mind drifted down ancient roads. She saw a beautiful face with hair of shining gold and green lovely eyes. The face crumpled and peeled apart like ancient parchment eaten by termites.

Simi, will you ever forgive me?

9

THE LOST LANES

RANNING MOVED AS SWIFTLY as he could through the twisting murky tunnel of caves, his fine-tuned ears pricked for any sounds. It was always dangerous in the Lost Lanes. The twisting confusion of tunneling pathways led between the worlds and issued out in many places, the Faerie Door known as Cradon Iwey being one.

Ranning knew the way through but was also aware of the many traps that could spring out at any time, cruelly snaring or even slaying the wayward traveler. He'd come prepared and kept his rune-code key safe in his fist. The other hand held his lantern, and a long Faen rune-dagger was strapped to his belt.

The hours had passed slowly since he'd entered within. It was warm and damp, but that meant little. A sudden cold draught could shiver his bones. There were tales about the Lost Lanes—dark, lonely stories of creatures and altered beings that roamed these places in creeping silence, or else called out in fell voices as they searched for fresh souls.

It was best to keep your mind neutral, else the stench of fear drew the dark things closer. Ranning focused and trotted through the gloom, stooping low as the cave ceiling pressed down on him. Sometimes the way through was quick, but on other occasions it took many hours, days even. This time was proving arduous.

He heard noises and the distant tolling of a bell.

The World Gate. He was getting close. He took a fork, following that until he saw two dark holes looming ahead. A choice of new tunnels.

Which one? Ranning chose the one on the left, as wind shrieked bitter chill from out of the other. He slowed to a walk. There were cracks in the sides of the tunnel here where greenish vapor seeped out. Ranning jumped past those, ensuring he didn't breathe in any of the foul stuff.

The sounds faded and disappeared, replaced by doleful silence and heavy, damp air. Perhaps he'd chosen badly and was lost down here. No point fretting about that. Time moved differently in these tunnels between realms. Ranning could walk in a circle for a week and yet still arrive before he left the island.

Ranning turned another corner. He halted, seeing distant golden eyes watching him from the gloom.

I know you.

Ranning smiled and walked forward slowly, the lantern raised and the dagger loose in his other hand. This was where Rune had been hiding all along. Made sense. The hairy lurker knew the lanes better than most.

"I see you, Yetain. You can't escape," Ranning called across, his voice muffled by the heavy air.

The golden eyes winked back at him and were gone. Ranning heard the awkward shuffle of heavy feet. He'd chosen the right path after all. He grinned, giving eager chase, and darted toward the spot where he'd seen the shadowy bulk of the creature called Rune.

RUNE HEARD RANNING CALL ACROSS TO HIM AND quickly murmured the code words, allowing his shaggy body to turn to liquid and merge with the tunnel walls, blending in like a dark, gooey stain of glistening slime. There, as rotting fungi, he waited until the hunter arrived.

The trap had worked. Rune had no power over Ranning directly, and should he attack the Faen would kill him. Rune knew how deadly this outcast from Telimantua was. A wanted renegade throughout the nine worlds and all five dimensions. Only Sheega was strong enough to hold her Faen lover in check. Luring Ranning down here was beyond risky.

But also necessary.

Rune had lingered in Valkador as long as he dared, masking his presence and listening to Sheega and her lover as they awaited Finvar and the girl. His enemies had been distracted by the new arrivals to the island.

That brief window of time had allowed Rune to slip away and reenter Cradon Iwey to wait for Ranning to come after him. He'd learned of the creature Gorvaron and needed to warn Jaran and Savarna. Rune also worried that Finvar would be in dire need. All three mortals were needed to destroy the witch. Jaran couldn't achieve that alone. Like the goddess he served, Rune dared not involve himself directly.

But help was needed, and knowing that, he'd left in a hurry.

I have to go back there.

But not alone. If Rune returned to Valkador, Sheega would sense it immediately. He would be worsted, trapped again or slain. Like his enemies, Rune needed help from the other realms. There was only one individual he could think of who might oblige, though he could well choose to kill Rune instead. They hadn't parted company in the best of spirits. He'd deal with that problem shortly. First, Rune needed to keep Ranning busy.

Rune knew the Lost Lanes better than most. His mind had often wandered here while his body was trapped in Sheega's nets. Adept code-master, he'd known about the hidden door on the island in the marshes. It had been his idea to guide Rafin and the mortals out that way, ensuring they got through Cradon Iwey safely via the express tubes—a secret he'd discovered during his sorry sojourn down here.

Footsteps approached.

Rune saw the glint of steel and lantern casting shifting shadows along the walls. He spoke the distraction code and cast his mind out, allowing an image of himself to manifest further along the tunnel. Ranning saw the image and took the bait. Rune waited until Ranning reached his mirage and then snapped the code doors, trapping his enemy inside, the tunneled walls closing behind him. In there, Ranning would wander for hours, possibly days until he found a safe way out. After that, he still had to find his way back to Sheega. That would prove no easy task. Ranning of Telimantua was neutered for the moment.

And Rune was safe from pursuit. It was time to implement the next phase. He dared not return to Valkador until the final moon had reached its zenith. She'd be wary, looking out for him. This was all about timing. Ironic that, considering time as a concept didn't exist down here. But out there in Valkador, six long weeks had to pass. That meant someone else had to help Jaran keep her busy. A recent companion who should prove willing for a price.

Besides, the dwarf was already invested in this.

Rune allowed his body manifest as he crawled out from the slimy walls. It was deathly still. He turned and entered the other tunnel leading up toward the World Gate and the distant tolling bell.

Once he arrived there, Rune changed himself into a shapeless zephyr and, undetected, drifted through Faerie's blue vastness, until he reached the huge stone doors guarding Swartzheim. Another spell-code cracked in his fist, and those doors opened. Rune entered like a chilling breeze and settled inside the Dwarf King's hall.

THE ASSEMBLED CROWD TOASTED HIM WITH ALE HORNS, the loud music blasting in his ear. Rafin smiled and fondled his youngest daughter's hair. It was good to be back in his halls with his people. Only his wife and brothers knew about Rafin's perilous journey into Faerie, and even they knew nothing of the time that had followed, his unplanned passage through to Ansu. The sharing of his identity with Rune— something Rafin didn't want to think about, as it still made no sense to his practical dwarf mind.

Had it even happened?

Rafin wasn't entirely certain. The whole adventure could have been induced by tainted Faerie air—the toxic remnant of some noxious spell gas left by an angry troll wench. He'd heard of such. But a dream? No. The experience had been real enough. He'd met good people out there. Had been involved. Pipe and ale. Laughter, swords. Proud towers, the sea. A hero. That woman's smile. It was hard to let go of the memories.

Rafin hid behind his own smiles, but deep inside he brooded and thought about the Northman and his tiger-woman. He'd liked them and hoped they lived yet. He'd enjoyed the mind-foggy sojourn through worlds, despite his initial outrage. But he'd come back empty-handed.

Rafin's memory was hazy as to why he'd even left. The thief Ranning had stolen something from him. He'd gone to Faerie to claim it back. *A byrnie.* That was it. One of his best steel jackets, he'd made for them. *Bastards.* Rafin's enemies the elves were involved, and in Faerie he'd seen their armies meet the trolls in parley and realized the threat.

He'd agreed reluctantly to allow Rune's mercurial mind to mingle with his own. Together, with Rune's navigation, they'd traveled through to Ansu—these days the realm of humans. Once there, Rafin had found himself involved in the start of a war between nations. Strangely, he'd been invested. He wondered how things went for the doomed city, Ta Shen. His mind tugged this way and pulled the other—the fresh pipe smoke and ale helped, but Rafin was restless.

I started something and left it unfinished.

He was angry, too. Rafin had been used, not only by his enemies, but by the strange being called Rune. An ancient, eccentric entity from the outer fringes of Faerie, Rune had climbed out of his mind without warning, leaving Rafin abandoned and confused and stumbling through dark tunnels until —by lucky chance—he found the doors leading into Swartzheim. His haphazard return had allowed him scant time to think through everything that had happened.

Rafin was a king here, and yet he'd been taken for a fool. He'd made a mail shirt, in good faith. They'd stolen it and bestowed it on a monster she'd conjured out from Yffarn. Sheega the witch, who was really someone else. The hero, Jaran Saerk, had killed her changeling outside Ta Shen. Rafin's stolen armor lay in tall grasses outside that city's walls.

Pah. I'm a damned fool.

Jaran Saerk. The legendary hero. Tyho had given Rafin's axe to Saerk, the weapon Lofhi cursed long ago. Griner would fall on its user, should enemies dwindle. That axe was tainted by Lofhi's evil and needed to drink often and deep. Jaran Saerk was in dire peril. Not that that was Rafin's affair, or at least shouldn't have been. But he'd liked Jaran and the wild-eyed feisty girl, Savarna. Truth was, he'd been bored here at home and had enjoyed his brief time in Ta Shen.

Dream or reality? You could never know for sure when Faerie was involved. Rafin ruffled his favorite daughter Drini's hair again. It was good to be back.

And yet …

Something was missing here. Events were stirring in the other realms. The elves and trolls had united to destroy the world of humans. The older races were resentful of the favors these clumsy newcomers had been gifted by the Weaver. The dwarf kings had played no part in these matters, staying aloof and proud in their halls, delighting with their smith-craft and riches.

But Rafin felt differently now that he was back. He hadn't had time for humans before, deeming them worthless and feeble. That opinion had changed. Dream or not, he still saw their faces. The other Northman, Dorthar, and the quiet and funny Lin Gu. Their proud empress, Rasnei Ti Ta Shen. And the half-human warrior called Vian, who shared his soul with a dragon, much like his sister, the tigress. Riddles and faces, they tormented him.

Rafin smoked hard and drank a dozen ales that night, his mind wandering down dark paths. The feasting ended late, and his people let him be. The children kissed their father goodnight. Gamalene, his wife of seventy years and third spouse in his life, was shrewd in her gaze as she took her seat next to him.

"You are much changed, husband," she said. "There is a shadow lying over you."

"Faerie always leaves a stain," Rafin said, stroking her amber-orange hair. "Truth was, I wasn't successful—the thieves got away and I've returned empty-handed."

"What of that? You have many coats of mail and delight in making more, and you, beloved, are generous in giving, too—unusual for our kind. But there is more. Things that you haven't told me."

"You are wise, as always, Gamalene. But I'll not discuss this further tonight."

Knowing him well, Gamalene left her husband alone with his thoughts.

The night deepened. Rafin sipped ale deep beneath the mountain, as the trench fires died low and shadows lengthened in the halls. He sat hunched and brooding in his carved chair surrounded by silence. He was almost nodding off when the familiar voice returned.

"Have you missed me?"

Rafin's eyes blinked opened.

What? He jumped to his feet, reaching for an eating knife and jabbing it into the air on either side of where he'd sat.

"I have not," he spat. "Where are you? Let me fill you with holes."

"You don't mean that." The voice was nearer and sounded disappointed.

"Why wouldn't I mean what I say?" Rafin hurled his ale mug at the direction from where the voice had come. "You played me for a fool, took me on a merry ride and abandoned me in the Lost Lanes."

"It was necessary."

Rafin's eyes focused on the dark mass taking form below. The shape grew and spread and congealed into a mass of oily silver fur and sprouting horns. Rune stood out before him, the golden eyes hypnotic as before. "Your participation is needed again," he said.

"Come closer, so I can hit you with something lethal," Rafin said, reaching over for his battle hammer.

Rune did nothing—merely stood there looming and watching Rafin calmly with those stormy golden eyes.

"I acted as I must, dwarf. I couldn't help you and the mortals and manage the portal. I knew you'd have the wit to get back here safely. I got you close. Those two would have fared badly in the express lanes without my escorting them through to Valkador."

Rafin stared at the huge, hairy creature for long minutes. Finally, he slumped back in his chair.

"You had better explain what it is you want," he said. "And you're not creeping back inside my head anytime soon. That upset me, and I haven't been able to think straight yet."

"We need your help again, Rafin," Rune said. "You are part of this ... *dance*. Your axe Griner, its connection with Tyho, the skill and knowledge—all are needed in the coming fight."

"We dwarves do not meddle with the gods or Faerie matters. Let Tyho and Kullaan sort their own shit out. I gave Griner to Tyho in good faith. Not my fault he allowed Lofhi to mess with the steel. This isn't my affair, Yetain. Bugger off."

"You don't mean that." Rune smiled sadly. "I've lived inside your head, remember. I know you better than most."

"Stop reminding me."

"Jaran Saerk will need you on his side."

"He has you, and the others."

"Who cannot help him directly. Ranning has created a giant kelp-man who is seeking the humans on the island. They cannot beat this Gorvaron without help. He is a more formidable foe than Sheega's original kelp-men and the changeling, Scard, combined. Jaran and his friends must be warned."

"Then warn them."

"I cannot return to Valkador until the second moon reaches its zenith. At that moment, I will be needed to keep the World Gate closed, as Faerie tries seeping through. It must be you, Rafin. There is no one else."

"Does it?" Rafin swung his hammer from fist to fist. "Why should I care? You're as bad as Ranning and his witch-queen. I feel sorry for that lad, Jaran, and his wild lassie. But it's not my fucking fight."

"We both know that it is," Rune smiled again. "And this is a war that will be fought on many levels. Even forgotten Swartzheim cannot be assured safety, as the gods too will get involved."

"We stayed away from the last war of the gods. That pretty much sorted itself out."

"This is different. The one I serve says it will be the final war."

"Not another *final* war," Rafin shook his head. "They always say that. Bollocks. You still serve Her? Hmm, and I thought She was lost to time and space. A victim of that last catastrophe."

"The Emerald Queen departed Ansu years ago, through necessity. But Elanion has returned in spirit. I am her agent here on Ansu. She it was who sent me to watch over Her ancient foe, the sorceress who calls herself Sheega. Alas, I failed and was caught and imprisoned by that one's mist-nets. But even Sheega couldn't watch me all the time. Hence, my mind escaped and found you wandering about angrily in Faerie. The rest you know."

"Your goddess has never been a friend of the dwarves," Rafin said. "Our people served Croagon, long ago, before the Golden Ones corrupted everything and ruined His trust."

"You are rambling, my friend," Rune said. "I cannot linger here discussing merry old times. I trapped spiteful Ranning in the Lost Lanes, so I have bought us some time. He will escape–of that I've no doubt. And sooner than most. I cannot linger hereabouts, as he will be vengeful."

"Where will you go?"

"Dunnehine, in Ansu—I'm a creature of the frozen north and can merge easily there."

"Why?"

"Because there remain a few talented individuals in Dunnehine who yet harbor a great loathing for Sheega. I will see you in time."

As he watched, Rune's body shimmered a paler silver and faded from view.

"I bid you farewell, Rafin the Smith. Know that for my part, I will always be your friend due to the time I shared inside your head. Do this last thing for me. Look out for Jaran Saerk and the other two. Get to them before Gorvaron does. Do that, and you might save us all."

Rune's essence flickered and vanished from the hall like a memory of wood smoke on a cold, misty morning.

Rafin downed his ale and sat back in his chair.

Fuck it.

He lit his pipe and puffed. Gamalene found him sleeping there in the morning.

"You're going back there, aren't you?" she asked, after he'd woken and drunk some ale.

"I am," Rafin said. "It's a long story."

"Then you had better start," she replied.

RANNING HAD REALIZED HIS MISTAKE AS SOON AS RUNE'S form faded. That creature had slippery powers he would never understand. Somehow his quarry had merged into solid rock and at the same time trapped Ranning, leading him into a dead end.

The walls had closed in on him from behind. At first, he'd worried he would be crushed to bloody pulp, but the walls remained. Ranning felt a flood of relief seeing a deep, dark crack led to further tunnels beyond, leading down in the opposite direction.

No choice but to follow.

Ranning's face burnt with rage as he squeezed his lean body through the gap. Once clear, he started loping toward the utter blackness. This would lead out somewhere: Galenki, Gwelan, Yffarn, or Faerie. Ansu—even back at Cradon Iwey if he was lucky.

It didn't matter. Time meant nothing here. Ranning could go for days without either food or water—his were a tough, forgotten people. The anger would fuel his strength. He would emerge to clear—or dirty— air, and the hunt would be on again. This time, the creature called Rune would suffer pain that no other being had endured throughout all nine worlds.

This Ranning swore to himself as he sped through the deepening dark.

I will be back.

10

THE LEOPARD KING

Trisa gazed out the window of the carriage at the fronds and leaves rushing past. She couldn't believe the speed of this contraption. The way was so smooth, as though they were sliding over a sea of black glass, the road gleaming like polished obsidian beneath the carriage wheels.

During that long ride, she felt no judder or jolt, nor were there sudden bends and curves to lurch the stomach. The jungle road ran arrow straight, cutting a broad swathe through the dense green of palms and shrubs and creeping vines that massed, reaching out like nodding armies preparing an attack on either side.

Despite everything, she'd kept her head. Valgarn sat opposite her, his calm eyes on the green blur of foliage. If he was troubled by their predicament, he didn't show it. If anything, the Northman looked grimly satisfied. As though this was all part of his plan.

They hadn't spoken, as the guards were seated beside them. Big, cruel-looking men, with scarred faces, ebony skin, and broad curved swords strapped at their sides. They wore gold bands on their sinewy arms, and studded earrings mixed with large hoops.

Valgarn retained his axe. The Tarakai Dolusa had remained civil. Even after he'd guessed their motives, Dolusa had been affable and had seen that they were well fed. Valgarn had torn into his fare, but Trisa had struggled to swallow, the fear of what awaited gripping her inside.

She turned her head from the jungle racing by. The carriage was driven by huge creatures with wide, flapping ears and spiraling tusks that sprouted either side of their heads. They bellowed fiercely at times and drummed the road with massive, round, thudding feet. She'd read of elephants as a child but never really believed in their existence.

Valgarn caught her gaze and winked. Trisa tried to smile back at him. She felt the sweat sliding down her face. Throughout that day, the carriage had rolled through the dense foliage, eventually emerging into a more open fertile region.

As night fell, she saw faint distant lights, reminding her of fireflies rising from summer pastures in her beloved Rundali. But these stayed put, clustering like a thousand glowworms along the rise and perimeter of an earth mound. The carriage tilted and turned toward the distant insect lamps.

As they drew nearer, and a horned white moon rose above the misty pastures, Trisa saw that these were lanterns on poles, and what had appeared to be a mound was, in fact, a large conical hill. She saw buildings clustered all around, and at the top a great round dome that glinted pale gold beneath the crescent moon.

Cantacari. They were here.

The carriage creaked for the first time as the elephants pulled them up the steep, winding lanes. They'd entered the city at speed. It was much bigger than first she'd thought. The great dome shimmered silvery-gold, as though resting on a cloud high above. The guards shuffled restlessly beside her. The carriage rattled and slowed. She could hear the great beasts stamping their feet.

"We've arrived," the one seated next to her said, as the carriage stopped smoothly and someone opened the door from outside. A tall, dark-eyed man in white robes smiled welcome. The guards nodded for them to climb out.

Dolusa stood with the newcomer, who was nodding his head repeatedly. This one turned to Trisa.

"You must be tired, poor girl," the white-robed man said. "It wasn't your idea coming here, but you don't complain." Trisa stared at him without responding, too startled to think. The man turned his smiling attention to Valgarn, who stood arms folded and eyes fierce with expectation. "Greetings Northman, you are welcome here. I am Jelagi Gur, the king's steward, and am charged with your welfare while you stay in Cantacari."

"Thank you," Trisa said, her eyes on Valgarn who grunted beside her.

"The king will doubtless summon you tomorrow," Dolusa said. "I will return when that happens to lead you to him. Enjoy your evening." He grinned and bowed. The Tarakai snapped his fingers and the guards followed him from sight, the carriage and elephants having departed already.

Smiling, Jelagi Gur led them into the massive structure that bulked ahead and above, its surface sparkling with the lanterns she'd spied from afar. High above, the golden dome crowned the white-washed mass of buildings they were entering.

"You are staying in the guest quarter," Jelagi Gur said.

"You will find food and wine—or ale, should you prefer." He grinned at Valgarn. "And there will be servants to satisfy any needs or questions." He led them through a long corridor where plants stood in ornate urns and fountains trickled with music and froth. Two doors opened on a spacious room, filled with lanterns and rich rugs carpeting the mosaic floors.

"Enjoy the night." Jelagi Gur bowed slightly and left them staring at each other.

Valgarn walked from room to room. The place was huge, and there were entire rooms devoted to bathing and other questionable pleasures. Trisa had never imagined such luxury. Valgarn's survey done, she followed him out to screen doors that opened on a wide balcony with stunning views of the lamplight city far below.

Valgarn grinned at her. "Beautiful, is it not?"

"What is going on here?" Trisa chewed her lip.

"I expect we'll find out in the morning," he said. "Fancy a drink?"

"Are you not worried for your life?" She stared hard at him, as he poured for both of them from the wine cask provided. She reached for her glass with a shaky hand. "Well...?"

"If they wanted us dead, it would have happened already," Valgarn said, draining his crystal glass and refilling it in one smooth motion. "This is sharp-tasting. Good, strong."

She sipped slowly. The wine was excellent and much stronger than she'd sampled before. "They'll probably interrogate us, perhaps torture us," she said. "This ... is but a ploy to trick us."

"I don't think so," Valgarn said. "These people seem very different from Octaxa's men. They are just as fierce and proud.

But these Yamondons have a noble air about them. I think the king wants to make up his own mind about us."

"An assassin sent to kill him?" Trisa snorted. The wine was very good. "Why would he not hesitate to put us both to cruel death?" Valgarn didn't reply. "What are you going to do?" Trisa asked him, draining her glass with shaky fingers. The wine had helped ease her worry but replaced it with exhaustion.

"Tell him everything." Valgarn grinned at her and reached for the bottle.

THE NEXT MORNING, AS TRISA STOOD WATCHING FROM the balcony, Valgarn appeared and said they had company. Both Jelagi Gur and Dolusa were there with three guards.

"Our king will speak to you in his gardens," Dolusa informed them with a half-smile. "We will escort you to the palace.

Dolusa and Jelagi Gur led the way out. The guards followed and flanked Valgarn and Trisa, who were taken through the many rooms and corridors of what appeared to be a huge mansion built on many floors.

They took the wide, sweeping stairways leading to and through more rooms, and finally they arrived at a set of heavy, gold-banded, wooden double doors. These were of a dark timber that reminded Trisa of the Rundal Forests near her ancient home. A place of dark rumor and enchantment.

The doors were carved with strange-looking animal symbols and looked very old. At the entrance stood a man of Valgarn's height, but more than half as broad again. This massive warrior leaned heavily on a broad spear. He wore a spotted kilt, and his naked chest and arms were latticed with a

crisscross of scars and welts. Trisa guessed he must be the
king's champion or bodyguard. He looked terrifying.

Tarakai Dolusa approached the motionless warrior alone.
"These are the guests my uncle asked for," he said.

The warrior stared at them for a moment before nodding
slowly. "Go, you two only." He pointed at Valgarn and Trisa.
She felt a stab of fear again, but Jelagi Gur beside her smiled
reassuringly.

"Storgo will lead you safely through the maze," he said
ominously, before turning and walking away. Dolusa flashed
them a grin and followed, his soldiers falling in behind.

The massive Storgo beckoned them through the doors and
closed them tight behind. "Who guards these doors while
you're with us?" Valgarn asked him.

"No one needs to," Storgo replied, his voice deep and
heavy. "To enter the palace gardens without a guide is
perilous."

Trisa awarded Valgarn a quizzical look. He shrugged, and
they stayed close behind Storgo as he led the way.

The maze Jelagi had mentioned turned out to be a
sprawling ornate mass of jungle-garden, accessed through
many different paths. As she walked, Trisa saw benches and
seats where people could rest; there were fountains chiming
and noisy birds singing everywhere.

They walked for several minutes following different paths.
Trisa stopped suddenly when a deep-throated, extended growl
issued from somewhere close by.

"What is that?" she asked Storgo.

"One of the king's pets," the warrior said, a half-grin on
his face. Trisa heard the growl again and shivered.

There was movement in the undergrowth off to her right.
Trisa grabbed Valgarn's arm and froze as a huge black cat

blocked their way. A panther—another animal she'd read about. Sleek and sinewy, it drew back its mouth and showed long, white fangs.

Valgarn reached for his axe, but Storgo stepped up. He spoke a word, and the animal slinked off into the undergrowth.

"Are we to be eaten?" Trisa said under her breath. Valgarn gripped her hand tightly, his eyes scanning the gardens they passed.

After what seemed an age, they emerged safely through the canopy to stand by a wide pool of glistening blue water. An ornately-carved pergola shaded a terrace with blue and gold mosaics surrounding the pool. Three seats were arrayed with views across the sparkling water.

"He will join you there." Storgo hinted they go take a chair and wait.

Relieved to be out of the maze, Trisa followed Valgarn to the chairs and took a seat beside him. To her right, the pool churned slightly, and she saw bubbles surfacing. More dangerous creatures lurked in there, she suspected. Trisa turned back and noticed Storgo had disappeared. She looked at Valgarn, her heart thudding in her chest.

"Have courage," he said, gripping her hands in his own. Trisa smiled back at him, masking her fear as best she could.

They waited for what seemed a long time, accompanied by the sounds of bubbling water and chirping birds. She worried that the panther would return, or maybe something worse. But, mercifully, the big cats stayed away.

"I trust you've been treated well by my servants and nephew?"

The booming, authoritative voice turned their heads. Trisa saw a broad-shouldered, heavily muscled man approach, a wolfish grin on his aquiline face. He wore a long tunic belted with gold, and on his feet were sandals strapped up to his knees. The hair was curly and ashy-gray; a short beard trimmed neatly was also peppered with gray, and forked to a fine point. His skin was paler than the other Yamondons she'd seen, though darker than her own honey brown. He sported a red scar on either side of his mouth, both curving up into the hairline brushing the sides of his eyes. The man looked as ferocious as Storgo, but far more intelligent.

They made to stand, but he bid them remain seated. This they did, and the smiling newcomer joined them by taking the remaining chair. He sat for a time staring at each of them. Trisa trembled under that gaze. His eyes were olive brown and shrewd. They shone with a wry humor.

At last, he nodded. "My nephew, the Third Tarakai has done well bringing you here. I am pleased."

"We—"

"—please remain silent," the ash-haired warrior said. "I wish to study your eyes and read what is inside them." He stared long and hard at Valgarn, who met his eyes without a blink.

"You, Northman, are a doughty warrior," the newcomer said. He switched his gaze to Trisa. She felt his eyes burning into hers. She wanted to turn away, avert her gaze, but she followed Valgarn's example, and instead stared back at him with unblinking eyes.

The Yamondon smiled and stood clapping his massive hands together. "You pass the test," he told them. "Valgarn Erlundsson and Trisa of House Alatais. You are welcome in my palace."

"You are the king." Trisa had spoken without thinking, but he smiled.

"I am Ulani III of the illustrious Baha Tribe. I have ruled this land for thirty-four years, twenty-five of which we have been at war."

"How do you know who we are?" Valgarn said.

King Ulani smiled again. "I've long suspected that serpent, Tulomon Caze, was planning an attack on my person. I was also made aware that the Vendeli have allied themselves with the upstart in Cardalis, who, so I heard, employs Northmen. It seemed logical they'd send one here. Your people have a reputation for thoroughness."

"His father, Ran Calla, employed us," Valgarn said. "That didn't go too well. I'm the only Northman serving under the new Ran Genza."

King Ulani laughed, a deep throaty chuckle that shocked Trisa. Was the king playing with them? Would he have Storgo return with the panther at any moment? But Ulani seemed genuinely amused by Valgarn's comments. His mirth was lost on her lover, too.

"What is funny?" Valgarn said employing his usual discretion.

"Northmen," Ulani said, "also, are reputed to be blunt. Honest. I like that."

"How is it that you know so much about Northmen?" Valgarn asked. "I'm not aware of any traveling this far—most of my kind have never heard of Yamondo."

Including you a month ago, Trisa's lip curled slightly. The king caught her expression and his smile deepened. He was sharp, this ruler. Didn't miss a thing.

"My namesake, Ulani the Great, ruled during the Crystal Wars. He wrote much in his diaries of the Northmen of that time. Indeed, his best friend was your ancestor, Barin of Valkador."

"You know of Valkador too?" Valgarn looked stunned. "My mother—"

"—is not to be crossed, yes I have heard stories," Ulani's face grew serious for the first time, and again his eyes studied them keenly. Trisa held back a shiver under that penetrating gaze. "I know who you are, Valgarn Erlundsson. That's partly why I wanted to look at your face. To decide whether this assassin was a mad dog or a warrior I could admire."

What do you see?" Valgarn met the king's gaze without a flinch.

"A man wrapped by darkness," Ulani said. "A terrible man, and a killer born. And *yet*—I see light in you, too. Your father wasn't evil, was he? Just weak and lost. Your mother though …"

"Has disowned me," Valgarn said. "I have no wish to encounter her again. I go my own way in this world."

"Working for a worm like Genza?" Ulani chuckled. "You could do better."

Valgarn shrugged. "It's the only offer I've had. But I will say this—I don't like the Cards, and I've little love for those Vendeli I've met."

Trisa coughed. The king looked at her. "Speak your mind, woman," he said.

She nodded, coughed again steadying her nerves. "How is it that you know all this, King Ulani? Even Genza knows very little about Valgarn's past."

Ulani gazed long into her eyes. Trisa didn't flinch, sensing this king despised weakness more than anything. He grinned and clapped his huge, scarred hands.

"You have a good woman here, Valgarn Erlundsson. She has both wit and courage."

"I know this," Valgarn added.

The king looked at Trisa again, his eyes were kinder this time. "Barin the Northman was a legendary voyager. He traveled here to Cantacari once after the Crystal Wars. Much is written in the royal archives beneath this palace about his and my ancestor's enduring friendship. Ever since that distant time, my people have kept a secret bond with the Northmen of Valkador."

"I know nothing of this," Valgarn said.

"You wouldn't," the king said. "When the sorceress who birthed you came to your island, we soon got word from a man who'd escaped her wrath and took to the wilds. Another wayfarer. A score of years ago, this Northman sent word via coded bird to my spymaster that a great calamity had fallen on the island Valkador. That his Jarle, Hrund, had been murdered by a witch, and the surviving son, Erlund, was betrothed to the killer. When I heard of the three new Northmen arriving in Cardalis last spring, I was intrigued."

"Your spies are watching Octaxa, even as he spies on you," Trisa said.

"I know little of Octaxa save that he is rumored a skilled warrior prince and shaman—more importantly, he is favored by Tulomon Caze. Caze is the real power in Vendel. A clever, most dangerous enemy whom I admire a great deal."

"Admire?" Valgarn blinked.

"Indeed so. Caze is both brave and industrious. He is also treacherous and twisted, as are all the Vendeli. I don't hold those traits against him. A man uses what tools he can employ."

"You said Valgarn was *part* of the reason why you wanted to see us?" Trisa said.

"Another name reached me," Ulani said. "Jaran *Saerk* is Barin's direct descendant via his nephew Taic. Both men heroes from the Crystal Wars. And the names Jaran and Saerk have been mentioned before, by the prophesies written by our sacred scholars."

"Jaran *Hrelgisson* is a renegade from Valkador and an enemy of my father's kingdom, Leeth," Valgarn said, his face turning grim. "My brother has vowed to deal with him."

"Your brother is dead," King Ulani said, and Trisa noted how quiet things had become.

"Holtarn, yes."

"Gorn, too," Ulani's hard eyes were on Valgarn.

What's this?

Trisa paled as Valgarn stood angrily, his hand pointing at the king. "If you are lying to me, king, I'll kill you here and damn the consequences. How can this be?"

"Sit." Ulani met his rage without flinching.

Valgarn glared at him and sat again. "What has happened?" he asked, looking at Trisa.

"King Gorn of Leeth was killed by a woman," Ulani said. "News reached my most trusted man in the north. He sent word to me."

"How is that possible?" Valgarn said. "Gorn was the strongest among us." He stared hard at Trisa, his face red with fury. "I don't understand what has happened. How it is you know all this, king—despite your assurances that Valkador is your country's friend."

"Who was the Northman who sent original word of Sheega?" Trisa asked, wanting to step in before Valgarn did anything rash.

"His name was Svipdag," Ulani said. "One of Jarle Hrund's trusted men. A traveler who spent some months in our land. That was years ago—I don't know what happened to him."

"But you know of my brother's murder," Valgarn stared at the king. "Are you a sorcerer as well as a king?"

Ulani's eyes narrowed angrily, and Trisa worried they'd be killed at any moment. But the king nodded slowly.

"I understand your anger and confusion. Do not speak of such things in my presence again. We of Yamondo despise the dark arts employed by our enemies. We are a warrior race, unlike the Ven, who deal in all manner of vile necromancy and black magic. There are good fighters among them, and cunning foes like Tulomon Caze, but even men like him have no honor. Do not speak of this again."

"I meant no offence," Valgarn said. "But how do you know about Gorn?"

"Our man in Cardalis got word soon after you left."

"Who is he?"

"One of Tulomon Caze's most trusted people. I've good cause to believe he is currently assigned to the Sangala chief —Octaxa, whom you mentioned. The man's a former gladiator from Omala City, now a double spy in my pay. You will meet with Grodu on your return there," King Ulani said.

"You're not going to kill us?" Valgarn said.

"I've considered it, but I wanted to meet you first. Now that I have, I can see a way of helping us both. We have a mutual enemy."

"My enemy is Jaran Saerk," Valgarn said. "My brother swore to kill him. If Gorn's dead, that duty falls on me. And yet, you say he's a descendent of your ancestors' friend.

Perhaps you'd sooner help my foe, do Hrelgisson a favor by killing me today."

"I do not know this Hrelgisson, though I assume he's the Jaran Saerk our scholars mentioned in their prophetic texts. Those ancient writings also refer to a warrior they call the Whitebear, that has some connection with Barin, your island's first Jarle. My renowned ancestor's dearest friend. And are you not too a descendant of Barin, through your father's line?"

"I know little of the history of Valkador," Valgarn said, as Trisa watched him carefully, her breath having slowed finally. "The island's people kept themselves hidden while we three grew up. Mother told us nothing of the past. She was more interested in what was happening in the east lands."

"You mean to send us back to Vendel." Trisa felt the fear returning.

"To Cardalis." The king smiled at her. "But not via Vendel —I value my new friends. There is a longer safer way back that would serve you better."

"What about Utuxla?" Valgarn asked. "He and his Sangala henchmen await our return with your head tied in a sack at the border." Trisa winced at his directness, but Ulani roared with laughter.

"You, Northman, would not make a counselor. But do not fret, you and your woman. We will send word of your failure and execution. I'm always having trouble with pirates in the far southern coast of my land. It's cold down there. I'll order the prompt execution of a corsair captive held at the ruby coast. Their faces are pale like yours, Northman. That should convince their Yanturi. The fool's not known for his wit. Caze will see through it, but that cannot be helped."

"Ran Genza won't be happy," Valgarn said.

"Hmm, well, that Cardalan oaf will soon have bigger problems, I suspect."

"You want Valgarn to kill Genza?" Trisa interrupted, as the sudden chill of fear stabbed her belly like an ice dagger deep inside.

Ulani smiled warmly at her. "You're almost right, but I don't care much about this Cardalan upstart. I believe his shallow schemes will unravel soon enough, without our help. No, my dear. I want your man to kill Tulomon Caze."

"I thought you said I wasn't going back to Vendel?"

"You're not." The king grinned at Valgarn, whose face was reddening again. "We have heard rumors that Tulomon Caze is meeting his man Octaxa and another in distant Laregoza."

"Why would he go there?"

"Because Caze has it on good authority that Vendel has been promised the spoils of Ta Shen when that city falls."

"By Genza?" Trisa asked, as Valgarn blinked beside her.

"Not him, the Shen conniver called Chulan."

11

THE FIGHT AT THE HARBOR

VIAN WOKE to the urgent sound of bells tolling in the city below. He rose quickly, as Rasnei stirred from her sleep beside him.

"What is it?" Her eyes were half-open.

"I'll go see." Vian wrapped a robe around his shoulders and went out onto the balcony. He could see men rushing around in the gardens below. Soldiers. "What's happening?" Vian shouted down.

An officer looked up with an anxious face. "Lord Vian, wake the empress—we are under attack!"

Vian noticed the direction his men were heading. "The harbor?"

"Yes, a large force is attacking the Sea Gates. We are on our way there."

"I'll join you," Vian called out, before returning inside. Rasnei stood in her robe, her dark eyes kohl-stained and large with worry.

"The harbor is under attack," Vian said. "Someone in that Card army's using their wits."

"Will the Sea Gate hold?" She looked sleepy, not fully comprehending.

"It has to," Vian said. "I'm on my way there."

"Vian." She clutched his arm with white fingers.

He smiled, kissed her mouth and broke away gently. "You had best send word to Gurt and Matax, if they don't already know. And tell them to make sure the outer wall is ready for an attack. This could be a ruse to draw our attention from the main gates."

Rasnei nodded. "I thought we'd have a week at least before …" He nodded and kissed her again. "Be careful, my love," she told him.

"I will." Vian dressed quickly into his fighting gear and grabbing his twin Jians and the long Chiang spear. "Keep that flute close by," he said before leaving their chambers.

Vian ran through the palace and down the stairs, his eyes noting the rushed movements and worried faces he encountered inside the palace. There were soldiers and servants on the move everywhere. He almost crashed into big Dorthar outside the gardens.

"You've heard." Dorthar's blue eyes were wild. He held his axe and was clad head to foot in mail and iron. Vian was pleased to see him.

"The Sea Gate," Vian said, as they rushed through the open Harbor Gate and entered the docks and town beyond. Vian heard shouting and the heavy boom of what could only be a battle ram thudding against the distant gates.

"Matax is there," Dorthar yelled in his ear.

"Good."

They sped through the narrow harbor lanes until the Sea Gate loomed ahead, surrounded by the dark shadow of wall. Vian saw Matax on the parapet, a score of men surrounding him, their armor and conical helms glinting in the half-light. Dorthar followed him close behind, as Vian skipped the stairs two at a time.

Matax nodded. "They came in the small hours," he said breathlessly. "Fortunately, our Harbor Guards were vigilant and got word to me right away."

"How many?" Vian asked, as he looked down over the wall. Hard to see clearly. There were dark figures on horses milling around down there, covering the road and pastures flanking it. More riders waited in the shadows near the woods. Vian's immediate concern was the mound of heavy shields covering the men below, as those they protected swung the ram to and fro. Their archers wouldn't pierce that shield roof. "A hundred? More?"

"Hard to say, but I don't think it's a large force." Matax glared at him.

Vian nodded, wincing as the ram struck the gates again. "Be light soon," he said, looking down. "Those gates won't hold out indefinitely."

"I expect they've brought ladders, too," the deep voice came from behind him. Vian turned and saw Lin Gu standing with his Jians held ready.

"Glad you're here," Vian said.

"I wouldn't miss this." Lin Gu grinned back at him.

Matax ordered another volley of arrows spray the shield mound below.

"That's not working," Vian said, as Matax shot him a wild glance.

"What are you suggesting?" Dorthar said beside him. "A melee? Some close-quarter axe work?" He grinned nastily.

Vian nodded. "We need to take out those rammers before the main army arrives. Judging by their noise this is only a small force. I fear a distraction, and that Casca will be sending his main host against our front door at sun-up."

"We cannot emerge through those gates while they are ramming them," Matax said.

"Ropes?" Lin Gu suggested.

"There should be plenty in the quays," Dorthar said. Matax nodded and yelled for some men to run and source ropes. Vian saw a dozen soldiers make for the harborside quays.

"I'd not send my soldiers to their death without leading them myself," Matax said, tightening the chin strap on his helmet. "You will have to cover us."

"You, general, need to stay here," Vian told him. "You're needed on these walls, and those men are your archers. I'm going down soon as the ropes arrive."

"I'll be coming with you," Lin Gu said.

"And me," Dorthar added with a grin.

The ram struck again, but Matax bid the archers hold off rather than waste more arrows. It was getting light. Vian could see the dark line of road angling up toward the shadow of the Long Ridge. He heard the surge of ocean flanking its side and glimpsed waves combing the banks.

He could see the enemy more clearly. *A hundred—no more.* This had to be a diverting skirmish. Vian looked for a leader and noticed two figures seated on horses at the head of the main troop, a way back from the rammers and their protectors. Vian saw ladder bearers emerge through those gathered and press toward the walls.

"We need those ropes," he yelled.

A familiar voice shouted back. "Try this."

Vian grinned when he recognized Roile and Truggan

among the soldiers clambering up onto the parapet. Roile tossed a thick coil of rope at Vian's feet.

"Where's Gurtei?" Vian asked the former Cutters.

"At the barbican, watching the main gates," Truggan said.

"Good," Vian said. "We're going down." He beckoned to the big Shen and Northman standing beside him.

"We'll come too." Roile flashed him a glare.

The ram struck again, harder this time. Vian feared the gates would buckle at that force. He could see the distant officers pointing and yelling. Further up, the ladders had arrived and the men were hoisting them up to land on the walls. Matax yelled, and a squad of spear-carriers ran that way at his command.

"Keep us covered," Vian said to Matax, as he looped the rope over the parapet wall and slid down, using the Chiang spear as an anchor for his body, his legs gripping the rope for breaks. He saw other ropes descending and trailing beside him, and heard Dorthar yell. Vian landed and rolled, dancing back onto his feet with the Chiang held forward and ready.

The Cardalan shieldmen saw Vian and the others jumping from the base of the walls. He heard a shout and glimpsed one of the officers pointing at him, before guiding his horse down the slope toward them, a score of riders following behind.

Matax yelled from above, and a volley of arrows sprayed the attacking Cards, leaving Vian and his volunteers time to run across and strike at the vulnerable shield-bearers.

Vian saw the officer was cantering at speed. They hadn't much time. He ducked below a desperate swipe from a shield-bearer.

Vian swung the Chiang wide and hewed the legs from under his attacker. The man fell. He swung again, slicing a second shield-bearers' belly open and quickly stepping in to skewer a third. He heard Dorthar yelling obscenities to his right, the heavy axe hewing helms and splintering shields.

Lin Gu was at his left striking out with his Jians, stabbing at legs and torsos—any flesh he could find. Vian noticed Roile had his bow aimed low, doubtless awaiting sly shots.

They cut in with precision working as a team. The shield-bearers crumpled and fled, leaving the huge ram and its wielders exposed. They were unarmed and pleaded for mercy. They were out of luck. Vian fell upon them, killing all six men with swift clean swipes from his Chiang, the long weapon trailing crimson.

"We've got company," Dorthar shouted in his ear, as he dispatched a wounded screaming shield-bearer sprawling in the dirt.

Vian turned and saw the young Card officer had arrived with a score of horsemen. Matax ordered another volley fire down. Arrows struck the enemy riders. Vian saw a dozen tumble from their horses. The remainder of the horsemen were upon them, the curved swords swinging out as they yelled in fury.

Vian braced, leveled the Chiang as the riders crashed into them.

"We need to kill that bastard," Dorthar yelled, pointing at the leader. He blocked a downward thrust with his axe, trapped the Card's scimitar and forced him forward, while Lin Gu skewered him with a lunge from a Jian.

Vian dived low under the horse's feet, rolling, slicing up, jabbing whenever he could. He cleared some space and tossed the Chiang aside. This was Jian work. Behind him, the sun was rising over water. Vian feared the main gates would be under attack.

"We need to finish here," he said, slicing through a horse's girth. Its rider tumbled, and he deftly employed his Jian to cut the man's throat as he landed.

The officer was upon him next—a proud-looking rider in glittering mail and fur, a conical horsehair crested helm half covered his features. The long spear he held jabbed out at Vian's helmeted face.

"Shen bastard," the officer spat down at Vian, as he readied his spear for another lunge. "I am Racara, son of Calla the Great. I'm going to kill your women and children and everyone in that fucking city!" He urged his mount forward and stabbed down at Vian viciously. A skillful strike, fast and clean.

Vian danced to his right as the spear struck the soil. Close by, the enemy riders and his comrades were locked in bloody confusion. Vian heard screams, glimpsed horses collapsing, saw blood spraying everywhere.

Racara pulled his spear free and jabbed down at Vian again, leaning forward in his saddle.

Vian knocked the weapon aside with one Jian while sweeping the second high in an arc. A crafty side cut scored a line along the rider's calf, cutting through the coarse leather boots, biting into the flesh within.

Racara flailed and kicked out at Vian's face as his spear thrust went wide. His balance lost, the Cardalan leader turned in his saddle, scrambling for his scimitar.

Vian leaped up and got a foot in the vacant stirrup.

Jostling for balance, Racara dropped the spear and sliced across with the scimitar.

Vian was quicker, bringing the Jian hilt up hard into the Card's chin, knocking him from his horse. Racara tried to rise, but Lin Gu emerged from the mayhem and jabbed down hard with a Jian.

The big Shen stood over the screaming Racara. Lin Gu grinned across at Vian as he worked his Jian through Racara's exposed neck, freeing the head and hoisting it high.

"Your leader is dog meat!" Lin Gu swung the head high, before tossing it at the remaining riders. They had backed off, seeing their leader killed. They circled and milled around like cattle at market.

Vian saw the other officer signaling from the rise and yelling. *That must be another son.*

"Gates!" he yelled up at the helmets looking down from above.

"Arrows!" Dorthar's voice boomed beside him.

Vian watched warily as the rest of the attackers urged their horses at speed toward them. He heard the grind of steel and wood behind, turned and saw the gates creak open.

"Time we left." Dorthar grinned at him, his hairy face and horned helmet covered in blood. Vian and the others sped through the crack, as Matax ordered yet more arrows fired across at the new arrivals.

As Vian got through the gates, he looked back to see the second officer urge his mount into the mangle of bodies; his men were firing arrows at the defenders above.

The gates creaked shut, a dozen men pushing hard. Vian stood there, shaking with exertion while regaining his breath.

"That felt good," Dorthar said. "Are we all …?"

"They have Trug." Roile emerged, his expression even grimmer than usual.

The gates were barred and barricaded with carts that some of the soldiers had brought up from the quayside. Vian took stock and loped up to the parapet, where he joined Matax and gazed down at the mess of corpses strewn below. The officer had retreated out of bow shot, his men on horseback surrounding him in a circle.

Vian's heart sank when he saw that they'd captured Truggan and dragged him away. He stood with his arms clenched by his sides, a ring of riders surrounding him. They were playing, jabbing out and poking his flesh with their spears. One got in close and knocked Truggan to the dirt with the butt of his weapon.

Vian watched on as they expertly looped a rope around Truggen's neck and started dragging his body towards the spot where the officer waited. This one sat his horse coolly. Vian saw him signal they released the prisoner. The Card leader guided his beast toward Truggan casually, a long, gold-hilted scimitar glittering in his gloved hand.

The rider stopped short and turned his head to see if they were watching. He smiled seeing Matax's men lining the walls. The ladder squad had dispatched the attackers further along the wall, but not without casualties.

"This will be the fate of all of you." The officer's clear, mocking voice reached them easily. "I am Uzcara, eldest living son of Calla the Great. You killed my favorite brother. Your suffering will be long, Shen. It starts with this one!"

Uzcara swung the scimitar in a glittering arc.

Vian yelled for a bow, as he watched them dismount and kick Truggen to the ground before spreading his arms and legs wide and tugging off his mail shirt.

Uzcara dismounted elegantly. He watched on as they stripped Truggan. Uzcara grinned across at them as he drew a curved dagger in his other hand and held it high. He walked up bidding his men back away. Vian watched as the Cardalan Ragan leaned over the prone Truggan. The sun was bright and the sea shimmering. Funny how he noticed such things at times like this. The Card lowered he knife.

Damn you, Uzcara.

Vian closed his eyes.

He heard a bowstring snap to his left, saw the arrow soar, arc high and fall. A brave, impossible shot. The shaft pierced Truggen's left eye as he looked up at his tormentor, even as Uzcara's knife cut deep into his belly. Vian saw Roile sob as he cast the bow aside and turned away.

Vian watched Uzcara cut open Truggen's corpse and remove his throbbing heart. Another archer fired, but the arrow fell short and Matax bid them stop. The Ragan held Truggen's heart high and shook it, spilling blood. Then he tore into it with his teeth and tossed it on the soil and stamped down hard. Rage sated, Uzcara showed them his back, mounting up on his horse again and trotting over to where his riders waited.

Then Uzcara turned his horse about before he reached his men. He held his arms out wide as though daring them to risk another arrow. The distance was too far. Uzcara pointed at the spot where Vian stood beside Matax and the others.

"I am coming for you, Red Hair!" Uzcara yelled.

"I will kill you when you do," Vian shouted back. Uzcara circled his horse and bid his men follow him back up the rise. The immediate danger had passed. But even as he studied the mess below, Vian heard the sound he'd been dreading. The main gates were under attack. Gurtei would need them up there.

The real fight for Ta Shen was finally under away.

"LOOKS LIKE THEIR ATTACK FAILED," THE OFFICER SAID AS he sat his horse in the shadow of willows beside Gujun. Unlike the other Imperial officer he'd worked with, Goi Stagan was both competent and observant. Gujun almost liked the man.

"They'll make some noise at the main gates," Gujun said. "These Cards aren't used to having their arses kicked."

"You think we can beat them?"

"I know we can," Gujun said. "We have a strong ally called time."

"What about the Vendeli? I heard the new Ran in Cardalis has made a bargain of sorts."

"Bargains can be broken," Gujun said. "Don't worry about the Vendeli, Stagan. Those corsairs might yet prove an asset rather than enemy."

"What have you heard, Slayer?"

"That changes are underway," Gujun replied evasively. "These Cards are not subtle men. They will throw everything at the walls of our Golden City. We'll bide our time, until I get clearance from Chulan."

"It is not easy hiding five thousand men in woods so close to the enemy camp."

"I'm certain you will manage," Gujun said, showing his half-smile. "You've done well thus far. What of those hopeless stragglers from Pol Shen?"

"Some sixty survivors joined us." Goi Stagan shook his head. "All that's left of Pol Shen Garrison. A waste. Goi Ban—"

"—was a useless turd," Gujun cut in. "He lost an entire fucking army through desertion and incompetence. I expect more soldiers will join us when they realize Goi Stagan is a man they can follow. Our number will swell, General, be certain of this."

Stagan shrugged. "It won't make much difference. Pol Shen Imperials were seldom seen at the front."

"Whereas your people are battle-hardened veterans," Gujun said.

"True, but I wish we had Northmen with us. That said, we are ready to deal with this Cardalan scourge. I would prefer to attack soonest, Slayer."

"They are yet too strong," Gujun said. "Let them lose a few thousand to Ta Shen's cannons and archers. They're good at dying, these Cards. Besides, we need the fools to get into the city and do the grunt work for us. Once they've mopped up Rasnei's people, we can follow behind and send their filthy souls to Yffarn. Chulan will rule in the Golden City before this summer ends."

The general looked at him for a moment, his eyes unhappy. "The empress ..."

"Rasnei Ti Ca Shen chose her path when she fled the Imperial Capital," Gujun told him. "Romantic as that flight was, the girl is not strong enough to rule the new Shen. We need a stalwart and artful leader. Forget Rasnei and her valiant defenders. The new emperor, Chulan, will reward his victorious general well."

"And you leaving us again, so soon?"

"In the morning. Chulan has a task for me."

"We'll see you on your return." Goi Stagan guided his horse about without further word and cantered back into the denser woods behind. Gujun stayed put and watched the Cardalan army for a time, as they milled like freshly disturbed ants spilling out from their nest in front of the high walls.

You're not going to win this war.

Satisfied all was as planned, he bid his horse walk on.

Gujun rode casually along the wooded crest of the Long

Ridge, stopping occasionally to watch the scene playing outside the city. He heard the roar of cannons firing, and smiled. The Cards were wasting another day, but sooner or later they'd break through those gates, or else scale the walls. It was a shame. Gujun admired Rasnei, and the man he knew as her lover. He hoped that Vian died an honorable death.

I'll kill you, if I can reach you before they do. It's not personal, Rundali. I have to back the winning side.

Gujun left the sorry scene behind and cantered along the ridge, until he reached the other forest that lay shrouded in the hills a few miles west of the Cardalan camp. Amongst these denser willows, by a large, slow-flowing stream, the Shen veterans from the River Wars were camped. They'd arrived a few days ago from the western mountains. Gujun had caught up with them yesterday.

A message via bird had reached him on arrival. Chulan was making new friends, it seemed. Gujun was required to greet them in distant Laregoza.

THAT EVENING, CASCA WAS JOINED BY HIS BROTHERS again. They were angry and vengeful, but this time the wrath was directed at Uzcara. Casca enjoyed the reprieve. Another frustrating day had led to more burning siege towers and broken ladders. At least they'd reached the city walls this time. They'd even killed a score of defenders in a brief skirmish, before the ladders were cast down and his men trapped on the walls, butchered.

They'd poured bubbling oil on those still trying to clamber up from below. That had brought a swift halt to their only achievement since renewing the offensive. But nobody was blaming Casca this evening. Uzcara was feared. Were that not the case, one of his younger brothers would have demanded retribution.

Casca reveled at the change of heart in his army. The soldiers had lost their thinly masked contempt of the Ran. They were vengeful, too. One of Calla's sons was dead. Racara had always been popular with the fighters. And the murderous Shen were laughing at them from those walls. They'd heard how the bastards had butchered Racara outside the city harbor where Uzcara had attacked early this morning.

An attack that hadn't been authorized by the new Ran.

"You fucked up, brother," Casca said, twirling the knife around his fingers. "Now Racara is dead, too. Like me—you're a brother slayer."

"I am nothing like you," Uzcara hissed back at him, his eyes flashed to the younger brothers. No support there. Casla and Calgara backed their Ran this time.

"Your stupidity got him killed," Casca twisted the knife as he released his smile.

"Racara got himself killed," Uzcara said. "He charged without waiting for the rest of us, underestimated their counterattack."

"Five men, I heard," Casca said, twirling the knife again. "Against a hundred. You managed to kill one fellow, maybe a few on the walls. I think you should go back to Cardalis, Uzcara. We don't need that kind of help."

"At least I did something." Uzcara screwed up his eyes. "We almost broke through those gates. If it wasn't for their …" he shook his head in disgust. "We were nearly done—the city could have been ours. It was bad luck. Racara should have waited."

"I heard he was the only one to use his initiative," Calgara said. "Rac saw the scum climb down those ropes and was on them right away. You stayed put, brother, didn't want to help out."

"Shut up, Calgara—you weren't fucking there."

"We've heard from plenty that were," Casca said. "And don't bother going back for the ram. They poured oil on that too and torched the area this afternoon."

"We were unlucky."

"Racara was unlucky," Casca said. "I'll have to give that city to one of these lads now." He winked at Casla and Calgara, who grinned back.

"Not while I'm breathing," Uzcara said.

"You might not be breathing for long," Casca said. He glared at his brother, neither dropping their gaze. The younger Ragans looked anxious. Eventually, Casca laughed. "I don't blame you, Uz," he said. "Racara was always headstrong. He assumed all these Shen were cowards, but it seems they have some fighters worth killing."

"I marked a face," Uzcara said. "One of Rac's killers. A redhead. Good with a sword. I saw him again on the walls before we left. He'd removed his helm and his hair blazed like fire. I'll know him next time we meet, the moment before I scoop out his guts with this knife." He held up the blood-stained weapon.

"Do we resume in the morning?" young Casla asked, the tension having passed for the moment.

"We hit them with everything we've got," Calgara said.

"That won't achieve much without more siege towers or ladders," Uzcara snorted. "Ours seem to have a habit of breaking apart."

"We'll have more in a few days," Casca said. "Stronger ones. I flayed the carpenter's ganger. The new team are working day and night. We'll have more ballistae too, and plenty of stones to toss at them.

"So far, it's been a warmup. But I mean business henceforth. I'll order the men take their ease tomorrow and prepare. We four can toast poor Racara while we set fire to his flesh. His pyre should focus everyone's anger for the next day. By then, we'll have some new machinery and can resume our assault at a quicker pace."

"It won't work. We are beating our heads against the stone," Uzcara said. "We need to try something new."

"You did that last night, and without consulting me properly," Casca told him. "We'll attack the harbor again, but I want to hit those main gates, and walls surrounding the day after tomorrow. This time we won't stop at dusk," he vowed. "This time we'll keep going all bloody night and into the next day, until we either scale those walls or break through their gates."

RASNEI STOOD ON THE BATTLEMENTS, THE WIND buffeting her hair. With her were General Matax and Gurtei. Vian stood to her right, his left eye pressed against the spyglass. Two days had passed since the last attack. They'd replenished the oil cauldrons, and primed and reloaded the cannons with the few balls left. The same for the scorpions and trebuchets. All the machinery ready to fire from the walls.

How they fared today was crucial. Rasnei knew that because they'd seen the enemy camp empty its belly onto the plain. So many men. She'd watched early that morning as an unusually cold wind had whipped the gonfalons high above her head.

She'd seen the riders in their thousands heading out: captains, their artillerymen leading slaves dragging more huge ballistae—Rasnei counted four this time. They were bigger and would fire from a greater distance. There would be damage. People would die today, citizens as well as soldiers. Her soberest moment was when the siege engines came rolling out pulled by teams of horse and men, twelve great towers of wood.

How can we hold back this storm?

Vian smiled at her as he passed the glass to Matax. "Going to be a busy day," he said as the enemy filled the plain below and beyond. Rasnei saw four captains ride forward and thrust the butts of their spears down into the earth.

"The Ragans," Gurtei spat over the wall. He'd posted Roile and the remaining Cutters at the Sea Gate, as doubtless they'd be attacking there again too. Probably today, after testing the main wall and gates. Roile seemed attached the Sea Gate after seeing his friend fall.

Matax had a squad posted there, and a team of runners ready to deliver errands and messages between, and along the walls. The main gates and barbican would take the brunt. The east stretch of wall would get the main assault from ladders.

From the high barbican's tower, Rasnei could see all along her walls. The men waited there in their freshly polished mail, armed with long Chiang or halberds and spikes. Some carried scythes hanging from chains, and other traditional Shen weapons.

She noticed a few women were among them, most carrying bows but a few gripping Chiang spears. Rasnei felt a flood of pride flush her face. These were her people, rising to the challenge. The old fools she'd found on entering this city were either dead or in hiding. The real people of Ta Shen left wouldn't let her down. Her Golden City would sell itself dear.

"Three rams," Gurtei said. "Think they mean business this time. See how they're throwing water on the roofs."

"They meant business before, and failed," Matax said, looking at Rasnei, his young face red with pride. She smiled back at him.

"We killed a Ragan," Vian said. "This is the first real test. Yesterday, the brothers were quarreling and their men unhappy, after Calla's … accident. Casca was struggling to hold the rabble together. This morning, that's no longer the case. They are united in their loathing of us."

"We'll hold them off, whatever they do," Rasnei said, annoyed that Vian was casting dispersions.

He caught her gaze and nodded. "That we will. But this fight won't be over this evening. Those bastards won't quit. We need to stagger the defense," he said to Gurtei and Matax. "Not everybody should be fighting at the same time. Stamina and courage will pay dividends. And we'll need a squad of volunteers to rush to any trouble spots—say, fifty men. The best fighters we have."

"I'll arrange it," Matax said. "And I'll lead those men myself." He left them, as did Gurtei, and for a short while, as the enemy got ready, Rasnei stood alone with Vian, her hand inside his.

"You shouldn't order my generals around," she told him, squeezing his fingers.

Vian smiled. "An old habit, I'm sorry."

"Hmm, you don't look sorry. And when did you last command an army?"

"In Yamondo," he said, surprising her. "Five years ago, when I served as a mercenary for a short time. The king there noted my skill as a commander, even though I was very young and a foreigner. Ulani rewarded me well."

"There is so much about you I still don't know."

"I hardly recall it myself, Rasnei. Seems a lifetime ago, events happening to someone else. Hazy, carefree days spent journeying and plying my trade as a fighting man, before I returned to Rundali to discover my house burnt to ashes and family butchered, or captured by slavers. Since that day, the time has passed more swiftly."

He kissed her.

"I'm both happy and sorry you are here with me, Vian," Rasnei said, watching as the siege engines formed a ragged line in front of the horde gathering behind the four Ragans.

"*Sorry*, why?"

"Because of Savarna—of all the things you've sacrificed for me. Your old enemy." She smiled.

"I wouldn't be anywhere else," Vian told her. "I struggled for a time with that, and seeing her here almost broke my resolve. But Savarna's destiny lies with Jaran Saerk, a world away. Mine is to die defending you, if there is no way I can persuade you to leave this city."

"No, Vian," she said, a tear moistening her eye. "You will survive this. I have dreamt it." She turned her head as Gurtei ambled over.

"They're on the move," he said, pointing.

"How are Roile and your lads at the harbor?" Rasnei asked him

"Ready to kill."

Rasnei watched the four commanders split and return through the ranks. They left the spears standing tall in the soil. She noticed one of them order a large group of riders follow him, and these cantered off bunching close as they flanked to the north.

"That'll all be Uzcara making for the Sea Gate," Vian said. "I'd best go and greet him. We two have unfinished business, and I've cause to believe the fighting will prove fiercest there."

"I'd sooner you stayed beside me," Rasnei told him.

"I know," he kissed her a final time. "I'll check back once I see how things are holding at that end." He turned and left without further word.

"We can hold these walls, Empress," Gurtei said. "I am confident of this."

Rasnei smiled at him, her heart warmed again and face flushed with pride. "General Gurtei," she said. "With men like you and your Cutters, Dorthar and Matax, big Lin Gu, and mysterious Vian of House Eltayn ... with such warriors, how can we fail?"

As soon as she'd spoken, a great shout went out from the horde gathered on the plain. The siege engines started rolling forward, and the horsemen lined up for attack. The ladder-bearers were already marching for the walls, flanked by hundreds of crossbowmen, their triangular weapons raised at the defenders on the battlements.

"And so the first real battle begins," Gurtei said beside her.

GORVARON

SAVARNA WASHED her face in the cold stream. It was a clear bright morning, and chilly considering it was high summer. The caves were shrouded behind her, and the vast shadow of the mountain called Gronteyer seemed to watch her every move.

They'd all left. Jaran and Ivar had departed with the young warrior, Tofei, while villagers Asmund and Olof had joined Bjarni, and they were heading for the southern shore to greet Tofei's father.

Bjarni hadn't wanted to leave Savarna on her own. She'd smiled at the lad and told him not to worry. Truth was, she didn't want anyone around besides Jaran. The quiet space finally allowed her time to think. She hadn't had that leisure since first they arrived on this island. And Savarna needed to work a way out of their problem, else Jaran do something rash. Two months was a very long time with that witch breathing down your neck.

They had come here too early. Their mysterious ally, Rune, had miscalculated. But what else could he have done? She had no idea. Worry and dread wouldn't save them from Sheega. Preparation and planning might. And there had been scant choice. It wasn't though they could have waited in Faerie for the right moment to jump through the—whatever it was they'd travelled through—and attack Sheega at the precise preordained moment.

They were stuck here until this was resolved. Sooner or later, Sheega would be sending something bad to scour this mountainside. Perhaps she had already? Old Ivar seemed sensible, but Savarna failed to see how finding some deranged survivor from the pre-Sheega days, lurking crazed in a cave, who might or might not have Hrund's signal arrow. *Probably won't*. That might—again probably wouldn't—help rally more Northmen to Jaran's cause. And all that achieved inside two months? Absurd.

The War Arrow venture seemed fruitless to her. But Ivar believed it worth the try, and he knew this island better than anyone—so Myra had told her in the village. Who was Savarna to argue?

And the gods were lurking close. She could feel Their presence like shifting clouds in the skies. They too, were waiting an outcome here. Not a good thing, in her opinion. Savarna felt certain that Kullaan and His dreadful brother—whatever They were up too—wouldn't ditch Jaran before he'd served Their awful purpose.

Her task was to ensure he stayed alive during and after the final confrontation with the witch. Finvar worried her, too, trapped in her hall. So close, and yet helpless. Savarna pushed the nagging thoughts away. It was pointless fretting about things that she couldn't control.

Since leaving Ta Shen, her mind had been a maze of confusion and frustration—since she'd first met Jaran in

Dunnehine, if she was honest with herself. She could hardly picture Vian's face these days. Her twin was lost to her forever, fighting a terrible foe at the far side of the world. She had made her choice, as had Vian. Dark-eyed Rasnei had won.

I need a walk.

Savarna wrung water from her hair with strong fingers and dressed quickly, her skin covered in goosebumps. She scooped up her scimitar and walked briskly back to the cave. Earlier, Ivar had led Jaran and Tofei up into the woods. He'd said the main cave system was higher on the mountain. That the one down here wasn't connected. He also insisted they'd be back before dark. She'd replied that they had better be.

But Savarna was content to be alone this morning. Ivar and the others had spent most of yesterday afternoon and evening talking about Valkador's past, the coming of the witch, how those who could had fled to the desolate southern end of the island. The cruel fate of Jarl Hrund and his first wife. And Hrelgi, their first-born son. Jaran had pressed the old islander in every detail. The intense discussion made her head spin.

Savarna glimpsed inside the cave, not wanting to lurk there. Instead, she took to strolling in the sunshine, following a deer track up through the winding woods. She smiled— walking and thinking worked well together, especially in bright sunshine.

For over an hour, she hiked and climbed until the woods thinned and parted, awarding panoramic views of the southern end of the island. Ahead, the slopes of Gronteyer were carpeted with purple heather and yellow gorse, both sighing in the wind. An eagle soared high above. The bird made her sad, thinking of Fin.

She sat for a time in the spring of heather, brown arms

folded, the curved sword strapped at her side. From that high place, Savarna watched the eagle soar and thought of Fin again and how he fared. The girl, Gunsala, and who she really was. It was hard to be despondent on a day like this, with the chilly wind in her face and bright blue skies overhead.

She smiled in the sunshine, allowing her busy mind calm and settle. This was meant to be. *It's our destiny.* Why buck against it? They would prevail, the three of them. Jaran would kill Sheega. They had only to endure until the appropriate time. She closed her eyes and slowed her breath.

Let go, allow the mind to range free and answers will come.

Savarna remembered how Vian had tried to teach her meditation—something he'd learned in his far-ranging days. The ability to relax inside one's own head. She'd never mastered it like Vian had. He'd been a natural. Savarna was always too restless and got bored quickly.

I am a creature comprising claw and tooth.

But the *Aikashi* inside her was silent—had been since that dreadful day when she'd chewed upon the changeling's flesh. She didn't want to think about that.

She watched the eagle again until it faded off in the blue. Rested, she stood and turned her gaze to view the south end of the island. Savarna saw the tangle of pines she'd left behind, marching in dense green ranks down toward the brown stubble of hills below. Beyond those, Savarna saw the sparkle of the river that fed out to Myra's village.

She followed its meandering path to the west shore. It was hazy, but she could make out the huts and animal fences of their homes. There were two other settlements further south. Her eyes glimpsed one and followed the beaches until she saw the island's southern shores meet, in a sharp, curved point shaped like a fishhook where the sea foamed white and frothy.

The leeward coast fanned up from there to the third village, barely visible. Beyond that was a beach of sorts, running pale and empty for several miles. Savarna saw the ship resting by that shore. Even from this distance she could make out its red-and-white striped square sail rippling in the breeze.

Content with her survey, Savarna moved on, strolling through the heather until she reached a high ledge of stone. From there, she saw more cave entrances half-hidden in the jumble of rocks above. Savarna suspected these were the ones that Ivar had been talking about. She had no wish to enter them, so she walked for another hour as the sun climbed overhead. Gronteyer's upper slopes were steeper here; she saw snow glinting in the sunlight. Eventually, Savarna reached another spot awarding wide views of the southwestern side of the island.

This shore looked more rugged, with huge breakers crashing against cliffs to her right and far below. She could make out a bay of sorts, curving round and hemmed by craggy cliffs. There was a thicker haze rising from there. For a moment, she thought it was smoke from a settlement Ivar hadn't mentioned. But no, this was different. Savarna sensed something strange about the smoky haze surrounding that part of the bay. As she gazed down, she felt that eyes were on her. A voice spoke inside her head.

Beware of Cradon Iwey.

"What?" she said angrily, convinced she was being scrutinized. "Who's out there?" Savarna looked around, her hand on the sword. An echo answered her.

Who's out there … out there … there …

Savarna turned away in disgust, her earlier calm replaced by anxiousness. She should get back in case anyone had returned. She shouldn't have left their camp unguarded for so long. It was already late afternoon. But there was something tugging her gaze toward that bay and the fuzz of haze, rising like smoke from its center. She looked harder.

There is something watching me.

Savarna turned slowly and gazed higher up the mountain where the snow met heather and rock. Up there, she saw a flat ridge of stone butting out a hundred feet above where she stood. A figure stood upon that slab. A giant, he appeared, and seemed to be looking for something. She saw that he carried a club. The sun caught his skin as he moved, and she felt a shiver, seeing the familiar sheen of greenish honey-gold. The giant had long, shaggy hair and what appeared to be a short horn protruding from his forehead. Hard to be sure at this distance.

A witch-man?

It had to be. But much bigger, and for a moment she wandered if Kullaan had returned to the island. But the longer she stared, the more certain Savarna became. Up there was a giant witch-man searching for Jaran and herself. On closer inspection, he looked much like Stoon and Crane—only this fiend was three times the size.

He is searching and knows I'm here. Savarna ducked low behind a rock as the hideous horned head turned in her direction. Savarna sensed an awful power in that gaze, even from this distance.

She didn't move and kept her mind calm. She'd killed Crane, and they'd done for Stoon. She would not give in to fear, else this new one sense her presence. For a long time, the giant stood gazing out, the club slung across a massive shoulder. Eventually, he jumped back from the high rock and vanished from view.

Savarna didn't hesitate, but sped through the heather as

fast as she could. She entered the deep woods and ran down the steep slopes like a woman possessed until she almost crashed into Bjarni Orlsson at the camp.

"You're back already," she said, catching her breath.

"Asmund and Olof went on ahead." Bjarni smiled. "It made more sense for one of us to return here, in case you needed help."

"Thanks," she said wryly. "But it will take more than your fucking help to deal with what's coming our way."

IVAR HELD THE BURNING BRANCH HIGH ABOVE HIS HEAD. "Almost there," he told them. Jaran was stooped low beside young Tofei. They'd walked for what seemed like hours through a labyrinthine mass of caverns, which had cut deeper and deeper inside the mountain.

You could hide an army in here, Jaran had thought, as he'd followed Ivar's flaming brand through the gloom. He guessed it was afternoon by the time they reached a corner where a tube of light showed a crack. Closer inspection revealed a narrow crevice twisting up to daylight high above.

"Ready for a climb?" Ivar grinned at them in the murk.

"After you," Jaran replied. He grabbed Griner in one hand, else it snag on the rock.

The crack was funneled and angled, the rocks sharp and scraping. Bigger than his companions, Jaran had to force his body up and almost got stuck three times. Tofei climbed behind him, Ivar already nearing the surface above. Jaran was impressed with the older man's agility and toughness. Ivar Ketilsson was goat-agile—all sinew, wire and gristle.

With a last push, Jaran heaved himself clear of the crevice, his head emerging out into bright sunlight that dazzled him. Jaran rolled free of the crack and allowed his eyes readjust. He sat cross-legged on a broad swathe of flat, lichen-covered rock. Tofei jumped alongside and crouched low. Ivar stood close by looking out.

"Where now?" Jaran asked, stowing Griner back in its loop.

"We wait," Ivar said. "Svipdag will come to us once he knows we're here."

"How will he know we are here?" Tofei asked, but Ivar didn't reply.

Jaran blinked in the sun. Eyes recovered, he walked over to the edge of the rock and gazed out.

"A fine view," Jaran said. "We must have journeyed through the heart of the mountain."

"Gronteyer holds many secrets," Ivar said. "I discovered the North Seat—as we call this lookout ledge—by accident while caving as a boy."

"We?" Jaran looked down at the distant woods and what lay beyond. The view was impressive—he could see the entire northern half of the island.

"Svipdag and I."

"I see the hall." Jaran pointed and felt a tingle up his spine. He could make out the wooden structure he'd seen with Rune and Savarna, the thin smoke rising. To its right, a lake glittered silver, as though it were covered in ice, unlikely as that was in summer. Beyond that, the island formed a blunt point at its northern tip.

Across the channel of water to the right, he glimpsed the rearing cliffs of Leeth, marching north and fading in the haze. Jaran thought of Sheriff Doggan, who'd perished in Skarness when the witch-men came. The sheriff had helped them and paid the highest price. Another soul to avenge. Doggan's village was up there somewhere, lost amidst those bluffs. Jaran chewed his lip. The wind stung his face, and his fine hair blew in his eyes. He pushed it away, his mood darkening.

"Finvar is down there." Jaran looked at Tofei, who nodded. Jaran felt a sudden urge to jump off the ledge, Griner in hands, and run down through those woods. He'd reach that hall by dusk and put an end to this. It took all his willpower to turn away. When he did, he blinked in surprise.

A stranger was watching him in silence, standing beside Ivar and Tofei. Ivar was grinning, but Tofei looked edgy.

"You are the one the eagles speak of." The stranger's voice was crackling-rough, as though he hadn't used it for some time.

"And you must be Svipdag," Jaran said. He saw Ivar nod slowly, and then returned his gaze to the gaunt looking scarecrow of a man, staring intently at him with cynical blue eyes. "Ivar, here, says that you can help us."

"Nobody can help you, as long as you wield that." The wastrel gestured to Griner, looped at Jaran's waste.

"You fear my axe?"

"I can guess where it came from," Svipdag said. "Like you, it stinks of Faerie corruption."

"I thought you said this man would be useful to us." Jaran glanced at Ivar. "I think your friend has spent too much time on his own. If he keeps jabbering and staring at me, I might have to hit him with the axe he admires so much." He flashed Svipdag a testing grin.

Svipdag's eyes remained hostile. The newcomer stared at Jaran without blinking. His face was craggy and pitted, and the long straggle of hair and wispy beard were almost white. Svipdag's fingers were filthy, the nails broken and black. A miserable wastrel indeed. A scavenger of birds' eggs and carrion, most likely. Jaran tapped Griner's steel and winked at him, gauging a reaction.

"This is Jaran Hrelgisson," Ivar confirmed. Jaran noted how Tofei looked afraid of Svipdag—doubtless believing the wretch cursed by something that could spread to him.

"I know who he is," Svipdag said. "The silver-furred creeper got inside my head, told me that Hrund's heir would return on the darkest day."

"It's bright and sunny this afternoon," Jaran said tartly, not liking this Svipdag overmuch.

"You can't kill her." Svipdag glared at him.

"I mean to try."

"Sheega is no worse than the others."

"What others?" Jaran wondered if they'd been sensible coming up here. Perhaps this woeful creature served Sheega and had tricked Ivar into trusting him. "I know only of the witch called Sheega and her sendings?" *Are you one too?*

"The vengeful gods who are using you to destroy their ancient enemy."

"I think we're wasting our time here," Jaran said to Ivar. "This wit-starved cretin doesn't appear the helpful kind."

The hoarse croak of laugher caught Jaran off guard.

"Helpful?" Svipdag laughed. "Why should I be helpful? I've only stayed alive this long because she thinks I'm howling-mad. If you'd seen what I have, boy, you wouldn't be so fucking judgmental."

"That may be so," Jaran said. "And you'd best run and hide again, matey, because I'm here to stir up the shit right across this island."

"We need the War Arrow," Ivar said to Svipdag, his eyes on Jaran. "Don't tell me you've lost it."

Svipdag spat at Jaran's feet. "The War Arrow," he said, still looking at Jaran.

"Why we came here," Jaran said. "Ivar said you'd oblige."

Svipdag's lopsided smile returned. He rubbed a grubby ear with a finger. "Follow me," he said eventually. Jaran glanced questioningly at Ivar, who grinned back as though this was a good sign.

"That young pup can stay here," Svipdag pointed at Tofei, who still looked on edge.

"That's fine by me," Tofei said.

"Keep a lookout," Jaran told him.

Svipdag hopped off into the rocks behind them without waiting to see if they followed. Ivar sprang after him, and Jaran, scowling, clambered behind. They climbed over and squeezed through a mass of strewn, jagged lichen-covered boulders, leading up to yet another cave, high above. This was a broad windy, scooped-out cavern, hidden from without by a shoulder of rock. On entering, Jaran saw a makeshift camp, the low-burning fire, and the bed made of heather and thatch.

He also saw a sword and shield resting against the cave wall. They were clean, freshly oiled and looked in good repair, which surprised him. Past Svipdag's makeshift camp, at the rear of the cave, was a mass of clutter and items strewn in a pile, half-visible in that gloom. Svipdag dived into the pile and started rummaging through all manner of gubbins. Jaran was amazed to see artifacts from Shen among the mess of broken pots and pieces.

Svipdag saw his look and smirked a grin. "I wasn't always as I appear to you, laddie," he said, his grubby hands poring through the stuff. "I traveled far in my youth, sailed the distant seas before she came here and fucked everything up."

"You were one of my grandfather's thanes."

"I was, in my prime. But a sailor before that. As an adventurer, I ranged far in my longship. I had a crew of twenty men. Hrund wanted me to seek wide for news of our people who had fared to other lands in days gone by. During that voyage, I sailed further than any Northman has since the time of the Whitebear himself."

Jaran felt a shiver hearing that name mentioned. Svipdag continued talking excitedly, as though he was pleased he still could. Ivar watched from outside, as Jaran listened to the ceaseless reminiscing of Svipdag's glorious past.

"I traveled as far as Yamondo," he said. "Met the king of that jungle land. Fine warrior. A descendant of the same King Ulani who was the Whitebear's friend during the old struggles."

"You don't say." Jaran hoped he'd find the arrow soon. This was beyond tedious.

"I do, and you should bloody well listen and quit being churlish." Svipdag glared at him for a moment before continuing his rummaging through the heap. "Here it is."

Svipdag tugged a sharp-looking metal object free of the tangle and tossed it at Jaran. He caught the arrow deftly and examined it. It was made of iron and short in length, no more than a foot. Thick and heavy, almost an inch in diameter, the point and steel feathered end wider. The arrow was stained a deep red, the color of freshly spilled blood.

"The War Arrow," Ivar said in relief from the cavern entrance. "I thought you'd have it."

"Of course I kept it," Svipdag said. "The legends always said it would be needed again."

"Well, thanks." Jaran stared at him in the gloom. "You're welcome to join us back at our camp," he added reluctantly, trying to be reasonable. "We'll have food of sorts."

"I'll stay put," Svipdag said. "Don't want to get involved in your heroics, boy. Might prove hazardous. Besides, the colossal ugliness I saw earlier was making for the south side of the island."

"What are you talking about?" Jaran wanted to hit him again.

"Gorvaron," Svipdag chuckled, catching his eye. "He's Ranning's new gift to Sheega. Like the others that hell-spawn brought out from the sea. But Gorvaron is bigger."

"How do you know this?" Ivar said.

"The fucking eagles told me," Svipdag laughed again, and Jaran barely refrained from braining him. He left the cave without looking back.

"We need to get back to the camp fast," Jaran said to Ivar outside. They'd left the grinning Svipdag in his lair.

"Do you think he's lying?" Jaran asked as they clambered back down to the North Seat. He hoped it was so. Jaran couldn't bear the thought of a giant witch-man like Stoon crashing through the trees and seeing Savarna all alone. Like him, she was worn out by their earlier struggles and needed rest from fighting.

"Svipdag doesn't lie," Ivar said. "But often his words are cryptic and have different meanings."

"I should have brained that stick of bones while I had the chance," Jaran said, as they joined Tofei. "Don't ask," he told Gunard's son, handing him the War Arrow. "Is there another way back?" Jaran asked Ivar.

"If we climb higher above these rocks and trudge through the snow for an hour, curving west below Gronteyer's peak. That way, we'll cross to the south side and drop into the woods. It's harder on the foot, but shorter as the eagle soars."

"Don't mention eagles again." Jaran glared at him and started making for the round boulders above.

I CAN SMELL YOU.

Gorvaron had sensed the woman's presence somewhere below. A strange scent, as though she wasn't wholly human. There was something in that smell he didn't recognize. Gorvaron detected a smoldering anger in this prey. He grinned. It didn't matter. He would tear her open, rip out whatever the strangeness was from her belly.

They were close, his prey. *Time to devour.* Gorvaron licked his lips and felt his nostrils flare wide, as he sniffed for the stink of fear below. Nothing reached him—the woman must have got away. She wouldn't get far. He jumped down from the flat rock where he'd stopped to survey this part of the island. Below him nestled a pine forest broken by rocks and hills. Gorvaron made for the needle trees with urgent strides, his sinewy massive legs carrying him down there at speed.

As he strode through the woods, Gorvaron swung his heavy iron club lazily, hitting trees and laying them low, crashing noisily and without care through the pines.

He was happy today, alive and free. Unleashed to avenge his weaker, smaller kinfolk who had been killed by these enemies. Ranning had told Gorvaron all about Stoon and the others, how they had been overcome by nefarious spell craft from the warrior shaman and half-human woman lurking below. There was a third one, but the sorceress was dealing with him. Shame—Gorvaron had wanted to destroy them all.

Ranning said this axe warrior, Jaran Hrelgisson, had special powers, and the weapon he carried was stolen from

Faerie. That Gorvaron must be wary of tricks. These renegades were more dangerous than the bugs they appeared. But Gorvaron didn't care. He would use the man's Faerie axe to cut out a blood eagle on his back, after he had stunned him flat with his club.

"You are my strongest champion," Ranning had told him, after they'd arrived in Valkador. "You serve the high sorceress Sheega and myself, and stand to gain much by succeeding where your brothers failed."

Gorvaron didn't know where he'd come from originally. A vague memory recalled a distant sea-locked rocky land where his people, the Cragga, had ruled from hills and hurled great stones at each other from their lofty crags. He remembered that misty place. Vaguely recalling an invasion and war. The enemy that came out from under the sea. He'd been imprisoned wrongly in Telimantua. For what had seemed an eternity, Gorvaron had been trapped down there in the silence and the dark cold. Forgotten. He'd been a creature of stones. One of the lost Cragga, trapped in deep watery nets where no light ever filtered. Punished for crimes he hadn't committed. Or if he had, there was no mention of what they had been.

Who was I? Ranning had hinted at the answer.

The water-Faen had stolen inside the Sea God's halls and freed him with rune codes, shrinking and squeezing Gorvaron's essence inside the kelp spell-pod that had allowed both Ranning—disguised as a silvery fish—and his freed prisoner to escape the dreary fathomless halls of deepest Telimantua.

"You were of the mighty race of Cragga," Ranning had explained during that long voyage up to the surface. "A by-blow of legendary Fol. He was one of several giants who dwelt

in the misty western promontory named after him, back when
Faerie ruled all of green Ansu, long ago.

"You and your lost kin were betrayed, Gorvaron. As we
all were back then," Ranning had explained. "The sly gods
tricked us, and the vile maggoty human spawn were
awarded our domains, because they were easy to control.
Whereas we ancient folk have always been difficult in Their
eyes.

"Sensuata killed your kin, though some Cragga escaped to
Urdheim. The Sea God slew Fol and punished you wrongly, as
He has me, his daughter's son, ever since that dark time. The
High Gods are our enemies, Gorvaron—all save the greatest
one who is no more.

"But take heart, for I have saved you and made you even
stronger than Fol was back in those glorious days. By fusing
your giant bones with my kelp-craft, involving the pods that I
used to bring your half-brothers to life.

"You are Gorvaron the Cragga, whose people came from
the forgotten kingdom Kernowan, as Fol was called in those
days. Only a small part of that region remains as Fol. Most
was lost below the rising seas, when greedy Sensuata sent His
briny host upon you."

"Are you not also of Telimantua?" Gorvaron had asked, as
they reached Ranning's rock pool and climbed free, arriving
on the empty beach in Valkador. Gorvaron had gazed at the
sky and rocks in wonder and joy.

"I was the bastard son of Queen Rann," His rescuer had
said. "She was one of Sensuata's many daughters. My grandfather has no love for me. I was treated more cruelly by Sensuata
than even you can imagine. Again, I blame the mortals."

"Then I will avenge you, too," Gorvaron had told him.

All this Gorvaron had processed in his heavy mind, and he

learned more still from the needle-eyed sorceress who dwelt with Ranning in the hall.

A great wrong had been committed on both his person and race. Humans were responsible, they had told him. Therefore, humans would pay.

Gorvaron reached a break in the woods. He saw a whisper of smoke rising from below and grinned. *Time to kill.* Gorvaron swung the tree-thick club into his hairy palms and roared fury out from his lungs before charging headlong down onto the trees surrounding the smoke trail.

SAVARNA HAD HEARD A HORRIBLE ROAR AND WASTED NO time. She'd already sent Bjarni back to meet Gunard and warn them about the giant. She'd left the fire crackling to lure the creature down here, knowing he'd find it anyway. Next, she had to get clear and reach Jaran before he returned. She ran through the trees, heading west toward the sun that was arcing for the distant water beyond the island. Evening was drawing nigh. She heard the roar again, and the sound of wood ripping, trees breaking asunder. He must be in the camp. The fiend would doubtless seek her in the cave, expecting her to be cowering in there.

You're out of luck, shithead.

Savarna would return with Jaran and the other two, and they would trap the giant inside, set light to the cave with furze and bracken, and somehow block the entrance. Savarna had planned the whole thing. She cleared the tree line and grinned in happy relief hearing a voice she knew and loved call across to her.

Savarna looked up. Jaran was zigzagging toward her down

through the mountain heather. The other two were running behind him. Savarna ran to greet them.

She crashed into Jaran's arms, the wind sighing through the heather all around them. They embraced. He hugged her close. She broke free, wiping her mouth.

"There is a big—"

"I know, Svipdag saw it."

"It's fucking huge, Jaran," she panted. "I left it down in the camp—we can trap it in the cave if we hurry."

Ivar and Tofei had joined them. Neither looked overly enthusiastic about her idea.

"Best we stay clear," Ivar said, leaning on his spear.

"Aye." Tofei nodded. "Our men carry bows among them. Better we wait and attack it together."

"Go fetch them—and you, Ivar," Jaran said to the two men. "Savarna and I will keep this sending of hers occupied until you come back with Gunard's archers. Don't fret—we've met these things before."

"This one's three times the size," Savarna said, nodding. "We need to hurry, else it leaves the cave and comes after us."

Tofei had already left sprinting off through the trees. Ivar remained and stared hard at them for a moment. "Are you two sure about this?"

"You cannot run or hide from witch-men," Savarna told him. "But they can be killed, however big, and we're the proof of that."

"I hope that you are right." Ivar nodded and left them for the trees below, following the deer track that Tofei had taken.

Savarna and Jaran reached the area of the cave. She saw trees had been uprooted and the fire was stamped out. "It must still be inside the cave," she whispered. "We need to trap it in there."

"How do you propose to do that?" The bemused expression left his face when a deafening roar blasted through the trees behind them. "Too late. We have company."

Savarna turned, slid the scimitar free and gripped it hard in both hands.

The ground thudded as the monstrosity crashed upon them from the rocks above.

End of Part One

PART II

DARK ROADS

UNLIKELY ALLIES

RUNE RODE the ice drift through the frozen creek as electric-purple skies flickered above his head. Behind him, the phenomena that men called the Giants' Dance swelled and shifted, the clouds flooding crimson through green and blue, like vast curtains rippling in a breeze.

Rune hadn't much time. The mortals would need him back on the island. He hoped Rafin would help. The time he'd spent in the dwarf king's head had given Rune a new respect and fondness for a people he'd always disliked. Rafin could make a difference, should he choose to assist and stem the rising tide of evil on that island.

Rune hated that he'd had to depart Valkador as soon as Jaran Saerk arrived, leaving their champion vulnerable. But needs must. There were things he had to do.

The warmongers of Faerie were coming, and the World Fabric almost at breaking point.

He dared not allow Aldorian and the others break through, until Jaran could act against Sheega. Faerie intervention would tip things in her favor—even Tyho Himself

couldn't stop a joint assault by elf and troll. Faerie's advance
must be checked. It was all down to precise timing, and
Rune's time was running out—yet there was still ample for
Sheega to set traps for the avenger.

That said, this wasn't just about shielding Jaran Saerk and
his friends from Faerie's vengeful denizens. Neither was it
because the Guardian had tasked him to help Her gain back
the planet She'd been gifted by the Weaver in the earliest of
days. Rune had long held Elanion's trust, but the Goddess
hadn't intervened when Sheega destroyed his people. Like the
other deities—the Emerald Queen had done nothing. Rune
couldn't forgive Her for that.

Tyho and the Traveler were useful as allies, but far too sly
and dangerous to trust. They had their own reasons for
wanting Sheega out of the way. Rune knew any assistance
from either would prove costly. Rafin had made the axe Griner
with honest intentions. Lofhi had stolen it from Tyho and
carved the malicious runes along its surface, before giving it
back. Rune feared that weapon would strike down its user
once he'd done the War God's bidding. The gods were best left
alone. This was down to three mortals and a little help from a
lost ancient being with a grudge. Sheega must pay for what
she did when first she arrived in Dunnehine. The massacre of
his kinfolk.

The creek ended in a wall of solid ice. Rune shuffled off
his barge and clawed his way up the crevasse, emerging on an
ice hill with expanding views of the terrain to the south. He
saw where the pack ice broke and merged into mud-colored
tundra. Beyond that, the smudge of dark hinting pine forests
and his destination.

The frozen wastes had ever been the home of Rune's
wandering people. The solitary Yetain had roamed the Ice

Wastes for millennia. Wise in lore, they kept to themselves and shunned their cousins from the other Faerie realms. The haughty Elves always mocked the Yetain, the trolls hunted them for sport when they could—no friendship there.

A few of his people had journeyed south during the reign of the golden Aralais, and later, during the devastating Crystal Wars. Most, Rune amongst them, had remained in their habitual ice, content to ride out any storm. But he had ruefully learned there were some blights even the careful Yetain couldn't avoid.

The most devastating of these came with the sudden arrival of Sheega.

Rune soon discovered that this new threat was none other than the fleeing spirit of a dark, damaged soul—Undeyna, Queen of Night. One of the high gods who had sided with the Great Enemy during the Crystal Wars.

Part of Undeyna's essence had survived and morphed into the witch Sheega. Her vengeful malice swept through their land, enslaving those Yetain she didn't burn alive. This scion of Undeyna greedily seized control of Dunnehine. After breaking the rival warlocks' scattered resistance, the witch persuaded them to help her, feigning friendship, as some among them had followed the Shadowman and His dark queen during the days before the fall of Gol. Therefore, Sheega had known she could use the warlocks and bend their wills. The Yetain were more stubborn, so had to perish. Moreover, Rune's kin were a strain of the Faen people who had always served her greatest enemy, Elanion, The Emerald Queen.

The Yetain were destroyed. Rune's people, driven into the black, frozen waters, or caged and cruelly slain by fire. A scant few escaped. Rune had been young, away ranging the south-lands for knowledge, arriving back after the event. He'd evaded Sheega's trawling spell-nets for a long age. The former Witch-Queen eventually caught him when she moved to Valkador, having fallen out with the warlocks in Dunnehine again.

Rune vowed that those lesser sorcerers would answer for their actions too. Many of Dunnehine's warlocks had perished over the long years, but a few lived yet. The Vagrant, the Siren, and Blue Culmeni were names he loathed almost as much as Sheega. But not all the warlocks had been hostile.

There was one amongst them who had proved an ally. Unva had harbored Rune from Sheega's questing Hell-Hounds —the huge, rending red-eared dogs from Yffarn she'd sent to feed upon his people. The yellow-eyed Wolf Witch had her reasons for sheltering Rune. A seeress, shapeshifter and sorceress of skill, Unva's pride and ego had been badly damaged after her own personal fallout with the all-powerful Sheega. The two had been lovers for a time. That hadn't gone well.

If Unva yet lived, she would help him.

However slim, that was a chance he couldn't afford to miss.

Intent with purpose, Rune journeyed south across the snow at great speed with the wind-driven code-skis lashed to his hairy feet. Soon he had cleared the ice lands and entered the sprawling, bleak, pine-studded terrain of southern Dunnehine. Rune knew the way.

Two days passed, and he stood by her cave.

Empty. Had been for weeks. Unva had gone.

THE SKY SHIMMERED AND MERGED WITH A DEEPER GRAY, as the sonorous tolling of the Bell echoed around her head. Unva saw the armies massing at the World Gate, like myriad insects swarming, lining the cracks, waiting to explode out and fall upon the hapless victims on the other side.

Unva had scant love for Faerie. It was beyond risky, her coming here. Yet she knew the way through, as Sheega had showed her long ago. The Lost Lanes led out to hidden places throughout the nine worlds. Some to Galenki, others opened on tortured Gwelan, one or two led down to Yffarn—the darkest roads from which no one had returned to tell the tale.

The lane she'd chosen had been lined with eye-tricky lanterns. Work of the elves—their sentinels would sense her presence but would also be occupied with the coming invasion. Unva knew that weeks had to pass in Ansu before the Faerie horde could cross. But that meant little here. The World Gate was already weakening. Aldorian could bend time, allowing their assault plans to move forward. The elves, trolls and their allies could force their way through at any moment.

She'd not lingered at that terrible place, but had fled at speed into the nearest lane—a side cut she knew would eventually take her out to Galenki. Once out of sight, Unva had risked a little light. She'd shifted from wolf form to that of the young woman she'd once resembled. A vanity, but one that she cherished. Unva navigated the lanes with her memory as the winking lanterns followed her like restless, whispering guides coldly observing her passage from behind. She paid them scant heed.

After what seemed an age, she reached a corner she knew. A crossroads with a single lantern swinging from a chain, creaking and swaying as though buffeted by a sudden gale.

That false wind ruffled Unva's hair. She knew the crossroads were the most hazardous places in Faerie. Dark beings dwelt where the lanes meet. A wrong step or hasty word could get you spell-blasted to oblivion, or else melt the flesh like liquid and steal the soul from within.

Courage was the sharpest tool. She dared not hesitate here. The lantern crumpled to spangle dust. Unva chose the left lane. She heard the hostile wind-carried voices following behind.

You were trying to trick me, but you failed.

The way led up, twisting and tight. At times, Unva needed to squeeze her body through the tightest gaps. At last, she heard the sound she'd been hoping for. The sigh and surge of distant waves. The atmosphere had dampened. Unva shifted back to wolf form and loped toward the crack of daylight widening in the distance. She reached the cave entrance, made to leap across to the rocks washed by dark water.

Valkador—she'd made it through.

Unva leaped, but even as she jumped, something hard hit her flank. She cried out in pain, her wolf voice yelping. She fell badly, but the quickly mouthed spell had her on her feet again.

"I'm ready for you, Sheega!" The wolf form had left her before Unva realized she was standing alone at the cave entrance, the wild wet wind stinging her face.

"That's good to hear."

The voice came from behind her. Unva turned slowly. A short, sturdy individual watched her, leaning heavily on a crooked stave, its length carved with runes. Unva studied his gnarly features and realized this was no mortal, but rather dwarf out of Swartzheim. Clad in glistening black armor, he was smoking a pipe, his metal-wrapped arms folded neatly. An axe and hammer hung from his broad, brass-studded belt.

"Name's Rafin," the dwarf said. "I saw you in the lanes and assumed you no casual wanderer."

"Why would a dwarf seek access to Valkador?"

"Same reason as you—to help Jaran Saerk kill a witch."

NOT ONLY WAS THIS ONE BIGGER—HE WAS QUICK.

Savarna's scimitar was knocked free from her grasp as she dived for cover, the bushes ripping and branches flying around her face. She blinked, rolling on instinct before the giant's boot thudded down on the spot where she lay.

Savarna heard Jaran shout. She saw the boot sliding, scraping through the brambles. The thing couldn't see her, covered as he was by the thorny thicket. She raised herself on her toes and elbows, forcing her battered body backward, deeper into the thicket. She heard Jaran yell again, closer this time. The boots had withdrawn. Savarna heard a deep, snarling grunt and the clash of steel on wood.

Savarna pulled herself free of the briar and struggled to her feet. She saw Jaran circling, the axe Griner gripped in both hands. His face was streaming with blood. He must have fallen but seemed hale. He was goading the monster, who had its back to her.

The witch-man looked like Stoon and Crane, but almost three times the size. The brute had a single curved horn protruding out from its shelf-heavy brow. Savarna slowed her breath and kept her eyes on Jaran's movements. If he'd seen her, he showed no sign. Jaran had his back to the cave as the giant crouched, the tree-thick club resting in his filthy-looking claws. The sending seemed in no hurry to end this game.

She caught Jaran's eye. She had to do something to distract the witch-man. She looked about and saw the scimitar lying forgotten several yards distant. Jaran saw where she was looking and nodded. He spat up at the giant and swung Griner out in a wild arc, yelling and making as much noise as he could.

Savarna ran forward and scooped up the scimitar. The horned witch-man knocked aside Jaran's strike with casual disdain. He stepped forward, his club still resting idle in his shovel hands. Savarna approached him from behind. She focused on those sinewy, hairy calves and swung as hard as she could. The steel bounced off the witch-man's leg, as though it were made of wood. The shock numbed her arm, and she dropped the weapon again.

The horror had turned at last and gazed down at her with contempt and loathing. Savarna choked as the rancid odor of his breath stuck in her throat. He smiled, swinging the club toward her.

She backed off, leaving the scimitar abandoned. She glimpsed Jaran readying Griner for another swing.

"Run, Savarna," he shouted across to her. "It's going to take more than average steel to kill this one." He swung across at the witch-man's lower back, a blow that would have severed a Northman's backbone.

The giant turned with alarming speed and trapped Griner's beak with his club. He wrenched down hard, forcing Jaran to let go of the axe, else his arm snap in two. The giant grinned. Savarna saw him kick out with a massive boot, catching her lover in the midriff. Jaran's body sailed into the cave entrance. The giant followed, taking its time and savoring the moment.

Savarna saw Jaran stagger to his feet, blood covering his face. She ran forward and retrieved the sword a second time. This time she launched her body at the sending's legs and stabbed down hard. The scimitar snapped on impact, but she'd scored a thin line of blood on the creature's leg. It felt like a victory of sorts.

The giant turned to face her again, and she saw Jaran stumble out of the cave.

"Run!" he yelled across to her, as he crouched low and rested his hands on the axe again.

"I'm staying," she shouted back at him, her eyes on the huge figure striding toward her. The face was much like Stoon's, but a curling horn sprouted out between the dense brow and deep-socketed eyes. Its skin was the familiar greenish leathery texture, mixed with honey gold. The eyes were milky white.

Savarna backed away slowly.

"You are one big, ugly fucker," she said before turning to run for cover again. She didn't get far, his boot lashing out and sending her sprawling on her face.

"Bitch," she heard the giant's heavy voice like thunder erupting inside her ears. "I'll tear you open for that, after I sate my loins inside you."

The giant laughed, raised a boot again. She was too exhausted to roll. She braced, heard Jaran yell something, and blinked as Griner flew through the air and banged off the witch-man's steel-clad back. Savarna blinked again as she heard an explosion, and a bright blue light shattered the steel vest the giant wore.

Distracted and shaken, but the flesh untouched, the

witch-man roared, a deafening sound like an erupting iron-smelting furnace belching flame. It turned, staggered, steadied itself, roared again and chased Jaran back inside the cave. He was trapped there without Griner to protect him. Tyho's axe lay in the sun close to the broken shards of her scimitar and the witch-man's sizzling mangled mail.

The giant blocked the cave entrance and turned to face Savarna again. "You should run," it said with that thick metallic voice. "You won't get far, but I will enjoy chasing you."

"You're too slow and fat," she yelled back.

This time the giant belched at her in fury, his voice causing the bushes to shudder as though a man was trapped inside shaking them.

"I am Gorvaron," the monster shouted at her. "Your death!" He swung the club from fist to fist. She heard Jaran shouting, tried to yell back but screamed instead as some invisible force struck her face. A flash of violent blue, accompanied by an echoing thud sent Savarna flying backward, arms flailing as she crashed into the tangle of brambles for a second time.

Another blast ripped through her ears, followed by a third. Savarna heard the crashing of heavy feet and saw smoke rising from the cave entrance.

Jaran?

She pulled her body free from the briars, her arms and face torn and bleeding.

"Jaran!" The cave entrance had vanished, as had her lover and the witch-man, Gorvaron. She heard distant shouts and a familiar gruff voice cursing in a strange language, but the sounds faded. Savarna wiped blood from her face and saw that a young woman stood before her, garbed in homespun wool tunic and trousers, her hair long and tawny, the eyes sheened with an odd yellowy hue.

Savarna coughed and wiped more blood from her face. The woman was smiling at her. She looked strangely familiar, despite Savarna never having seen her like before. *Sheega?* No this was another.

"Who are you?" It was all she could manage. She felt badly shaken and bruised all over. But that was the worst of it. Where was Jaran? Had her lover survived that blast?

"You are safe for now," the young woman said, folding her arms. Her voice was familiar, too, and Savarna registered those oddly familiar yellow eyes.

"Should I know you?"

"We have met, Savarna."

She remembered a shabby old woman. *But surely …* "You're the peddler woman with the playing cards in Ferrytown."

"I am Unva," the young woman replied with a nod. Savarna marked how ageless her gaze appeared. "And we're here to help you two."

"We?"

Savarna heard a gruff laugh and someone swearing. She turned to see Jaran striding through the woods with a short stocky man beside him. She recognized Rafin by his black armor, shaggy hair and forked beard.

"You!" She giggled like a drunk woman feeling giddy with joy. "Jaran …?"

"I primed our hero before this canny-wee-lass blasted the cave entrance," Rafin the Smith said. "Jaran and me took to hectic running and climbing free, up out through the nose of a blowhole."

"Where is ...?" She looked around her head throbbing, feeling a cloud smother her happiness.

"Gone." Jaran smiled at her and stumbled across, pulling her hard against him. They kissed, and she heard Rafin grunting. She pulled free from her lover and grinned at the dwarf king.

"You're back," she said, as tears welled at the corner of her eyes. "It's good to see you, master dwarf."

"Well, for my part, I wasn't planning on that," the dwarf said. "Your furry friend—after fucking with my head—had the gall to drop by in Swartzheim, visit uninvited and ask another favor."

"Rune is back in Faerie?" Jaran asked beside her.

"Was," Rafin said, rubbing his eyes. He turned his attention to the woods below. "About time your reinforcements showed up."

Rafin nodded at the men approaching. She saw Tofei leading a small knot of warriors up toward them, accompanied by Bjarni, Asmund and more young men from the villages. Ivar appeared beside them, fish spear in hands. His eyes were on the damage.

"That troll must have been big," the oldster said.

"Gorvaron is no troll," the strange-eyed woman, Unva, said. "Would that he were."

She turned to Savarna again. She was smallish in build, her young face tanned and pretty. Nothing like the hag Savarna remembered. The only thing remarkable was the color of those eyes—a haunting pale yellow. She hadn't noticed them back at Ferrytown.

"You did well," Unva told Savarna. "That encounter could have gone either way. Guileful Ranning sowed a lot of resentment into that creature. And Gorvaron has cause to hate. He was kin to the giants who once roamed the far west, beyond the Crystal Kingdoms. A race like so many, overcome by treachery and time."

"Where has Gorvaron gone?" Jaran looked about, as though he was ready for a rematch.

"Wandering the fells, angry and lost. I sowed confusion in that blast spell," Unva said. "And Griner will have shaken him. A shame you didn't puncture the skin. The ill runes on that axe would have destroyed him."

"It was a good throw," Jaran said.

Unva raised a brow. "You need to try harder, hero. But we've a little time. Gorvaron will be wandering dazed and witless on the mountain for a while. But he will be back, and more hateful and dangerous than before. Worse—*she* will know I'm here."

"Why are you helping us?" Savarna asked, as Tofei and the other men filed wide-eyed into the clearing. An older man stood close to Tofei—his father, Gunard, fresh from his ship at the shore. Gunard, like the rest of the Northmen, gazed with slack jaw at the damage.

"Did the witch-man … do that?" Tofei's stunned eyes were on the blasted cave. No one responded.

Savarna's gaze held Unva's. "Are you and this dwarf in league with Rune?"

"We share a certain loathing for the one currently residing in his father's hall," Unva smiled at Jaran, who grunted. "It's in all of our interests to see Sheega fall."

"It is," Rafin nodded his head. "But speaking purely for myself, I'm here to shove this hammer half up Ranning's slimy arsehole."

"You're here because of Faerie," Jaran said to Unva, who smiled wryly.

"Of course, I am," she said. "It's no longer just about you, Jaran Saerk."

"I don't think it ever was," he replied.

"That doesn't matter," Savarna said. "It's time to fight back, while we have the advantage. At least we can hunt and kill her creatures, if we can't get to her."

Unva's smile faded from her lips. "Not yet, Savarna, though the time approaches swiftly. For the moment, we must take to the caves. Gorvaron will return in a day or so, and she'll doubtless send other creatures out, too. We must lay low until he can act."

"Who?" Savarna looked at Jaran, who shrugged in response.

"Your crafty friend Finvar, of course," Unva said. "The hawk must fly—else the flame shreds his wings to cinders."

"What?" Savarna's head ached badly. She felt giddy from the fight and couldn't grasp what was happening here.

She saw Ivar appear, leaning heavily on his fish spear. She hadn't noticed the old hunter leaving, but his wiry face was sheened with sweat, and he was panting from exertion. "That giant thing's out there on the heather—I've just seen it."

"Time to go," Jaran said. "We'll follow your lead, Ivar. You know the caves better than anyone."

"Actually, that's not true," said a new voice. Savarna turned to see a ragged, shaggy-haired figure standing beneath the trees. He leaned on a long spear, and he had a round shield and heavy axe slung across his back.

"Svipdag! You decided to join us after all," Ivar sounded excited.

"I hate missing out," the greybeard said. "You'd all best follow me."

THE MESSAGE

TULOMON CAZE STOOD at the prow of the saffron-colored dhow, as the waves parted below and warm wind whipped his long oily hair. Vendel's High Califez was happy. Affairs were proceeding well, after what had been a difficult month.

The war with Yamondo was taking its toll. The Yanturi wanted results that his war council, the Califezai, Tulomon's spies and military administrators had failed to deliver. Even a man of his exalted rank couldn't expect to keep his head, should things stay as they are. It was vexing. A lesser man would crumble.

Tulomon Caze was no craven. He enjoyed the challenge and had thrived in Omala where lesser men failed. And he'd found a new diversion offering fresh hope. A shift in his focus that—if played well—could impress his impetuous young ruler and alter everything in Vendel's favor. And more importantly, his own.

The Sangala, Octaxa, had promised this new alliance would pay dividends. The warrior-priest's head was on the block if it didn't. But Tulomon Caze knew Octaxa well enough to trust his canny instincts. That confidence in the Sangala chief had resulted in Caze boarding the ship back at Kulshana. It was years since last he'd traveled the ocean. Tulomon Caze had liked to sail often as a young man, but such leisures were rare these days for one as busy as himself. The price of power had its subtle chokeholds. Caze was working on that too.

Octaxa's second had informed him they would reach the Laregozan shore before dusk. Caze had studied Utuxla's hard-eyed face when he'd summoned him for reports. The man was trustworthy, a devout Sangala. And ambitious, he suspected. Should Octaxa fail him, this one could be useful as a replacement. The warrior-priests of Vendel all possessed knowledge of spell-weaving, though Octaxa was more gifted than most. The Sangala couldn't be bought with coin like other men. But Tulomon Caze knew subtler ways of persuasion. It was the reason why he controlled things in Vendel.

Caze had explained to his young ruler how impressed he was with Octaxa's scheme. With his permission, the Sangala leader had sent his servant east to meet the Shen called Chulan. That easterner had sent word directly to the Yanturi that Shen was eager for an alliance that would serve Vendel well, and that their recent ally, the Cardalan Republic, was not only untrustworthy, but about to implode. Caze had made sure that note never reached his ruler. This achievement had to be seen as his victory. It was enough that the council in Omala City supported the concept, the Yanturi included.

Meanwhile, let the courtiers in Omala fret about Ulani's next move. A fruitless exercise. There was only one way to defeat Yamondo and that was to starve its trade ports. Caze sensed a fresh opportunity over in Shen. It was why he'd ordered Octaxa's Sangala down from the mountains where they'd been lurking to escort him personally to Laregoza, where they would meet in secret with Chulan's man. No reason them remaining there, as Genza's Northman was most likely dead.

Octaxa had ensured Caze that Genza would suspect nothing. The Ran had promised Vendel full docking rights in Largos and Soloza. The Sangala chief's dhow would be safe there, and Tulomon Caze could take his ease in the famed Soloza brothels. There was no need to rush this. Caze had suggested Soloza and Octaxa had arranged suitable lodging for their stay.

His company would arrive guised as wealthy merchants. Caze had brought his spies, who would merge with the Laregozans and Cardalan soldiers stationed there. They would trade and barter goods to add authenticity. Caze would meet the Shen's contact and listen to the man's proposal, while taking time to weigh the matters up in his mind.

"High Califez, forgive me." The deep voice had him turning slowly. Utuxla stood arrow straight, his hawk-eyed shaven-headed features keen and scarred hands resting on his three-feathered spell-spear.

"What is it, Sangala?" Caze stared hard at the man until Utuxla averted his gaze. You couldn't show weakness to these people.

"A hunch, Exalted One—a shadow moves inside my heart."

"Out with it." Caze knew this man was up to something. Utuxla was sharp, that much was clear. But it was wise to trust the warnings of the Sangala. The warrior priests of Vendel knew things even he could never grasp.

"There is danger in Soloza," Utuxla's dark eyes were shining like black jewels.

"There is danger everywhere," Caze said, turning away to watch the ocean. Such a pretty day. He wouldn't allow this man to spoil the moment. "Be more specific, Sangala. Are you worried about this Shen? Your master says Chulan is sensible."

"Indeed no—the Shen need us, High Califez. My concern is for your person. I see a darkness surrounding you. A shadow that comes from the west but will find you in the east."

"Go on …" Caze turned and stared hard at Utuxla, his mood darkening.

"The Northman Genza sent to kill Ulani."

"Is dead."

"I believe he yet lives, Exalted One."

"And how would you know that?" Caze suppressed the shiver he felt inside.

"It is the Northman's shadow I see looming over you. I suspect Ulani spared him on condition that he kills you."

"From Cantacari?" Caze laughed humorlessly. "The journey would take him weeks, unless he returned to Kulshana. Your people are guarding that port."

"I realize that, Exalted One, but still I fear you are in peril."

"I have you to watch over me." Tulomon snapped his fingers dismissing the man. Utuxla saluted and left him be.

The man was trying to unnerve him. But why? Even the feared Sangala daren't mess with Tulomon Caze. The Northman Genza sent was dead or being tortured. Ulani's spies could not have known about this. The notion was absurd. But what was Utuxla up to?

Tulomon Caze stared at a train of dolphins dancing off to their side. The sight would have given him pleasure a few moments ago.

Chulan gazed up from his papers. "Do you know the quickest way to Soloza?"

"The forests and river," Gujun said with a shrug.

"There are high passes through the mountains behind us. You can access the Rundali River north of the forests. That will save getting entangled in …" Chulan shrugged. There were stories he'd heard about Rundal Woods. He didn't believe them, but why take the chance? "The Cards have rafts on that river. I suggest you commandeer one after dark, drift down to the coast. A journey of three weeks, no longer."

"I could have been halfway there, if your men hadn't intercepted my journey at the last village I passed. This diversion has cost me time. Stagan will need my help assessing progress in Ta Shen."

"Goi Stagan can handle that. He has only to watch and report back to me, via pigeon. Those inane Cards will take weeks to break Ta Shen, perhaps months. We have ample time, and I need you primed and ready for when you meet the Vendeli."

"That's not the reason you wanted me to stop by."

"You are correct." Chulan folded his papers neatly and threaded his long fingers, forming an arch. He forced a smile. "I'm sending someone with you."

"I work alone," Gujun's eyes narrowed.

Chulan's smile faded. He snapped his fingers. A servant appeared hovering by the door. Gujun's dark eyes flashed that way and said nothing.

"Go fetch our guest," Chulan said. The servant vanished and returned moments later with a huge shaven-headed warrior. Grodu had arrived two days earlier. Chulan's smile broadened as he saw a flicker of surprise flash across Gujun's eyes.

"This is Grodu," Chulan said as the newcomer bowed stiffly. "He originates from Golt, apparently, a land of mystery far beyond even Yamondo. Have you heard of Golt, Slayer?"

"No," Gujun shook his head, his eyes locked on the warrior. Grodu stood well over six feet tall and was very broad. He wore riding leathers over mail. His heavyset face was scarred, and half his left ear was missing. A former slave and gladiator freed by his Vendeli master. Gujun seemed tiny beside him.

"Grodu will be your companion on your journey to Soloza," Chulan said, still staring at Gujun. "I suggest you two get to know each other."

Gujun's hard eyes flicked up at the big man standing beside him. His lips quivered slightly. *He doesn't like this.* Chulan enjoyed seeing the discomfort in his man. Gujun had become overimportant of late.

"I travel alone," Gujun said again, this time to Grodu. The bigger man didn't respond.

"Grodu serves our new friends." Chulan slid his fingers apart and drummed them on the table. "He is Octaxa's personal bodyguard, and his presence here is a measure of the Vendeli shaman's trust. Grodu will introduce you to his masters when you arrive in Laregoza."

"I said—"

"—I know what you said, Slayer," Chulan snapped, losing what little patience he possessed today. His soldiers had found Gujun grooming his horse outside a tavern. They'd ordered he divert northwest and receive fresh orders from Chulan. He hadn't taken kindly to their tone, resulting in two dead and a third left broken on the road.

Chulan had chosen to ignore the incident, blaming his soldiers for fumbling. That said, Gujun was getting out of hand. First killing Goi Ban the Pol Shen garrison leader, and now this. The man was a low-born knave who had no respect for his betters.

His patience mastered, Chulan held up his hands and smiled again. "Ah, this is foolishness, Gujun. The Vendeli won't let you near Tulomon Caze unless Grodu is with you. You know how paranoid those southerners are about assassins, and poison."

Gujun stared back at him with flat eyes.

"Indulge me," Chulan said, rubbing his moustache. "You stand to gain much, remember."

"And I will hold you to that," Gujun said, glancing up at the scarred warrior looming beside him.

That's if I don't dispose of you first. Chulan masked his annoyance with a brisk nod. "Get some rest, both of you. I've fresh horses and pack mules for your journey over the mountains."

"Which road led you here?" Gujun asked Grodu.

"I came from Cardalis," Grodu replied. "Took the highway to the Shen River, crossed by barge and made my way here."

"What's your message to these Vendeli?" Gujun asked Chulan.

"It's all here." Chulan rolled his papers between deft fingers and sealed them with hot wax from the tablet on his desk. "This letter must be delivered personally to either Octaxa or Tulomon Caze himself."

Gujun nodded, and the big former slave bowed again. "Leave me to my thoughts, gentlemen," Chulan said. "I have much to ponder." Grodu turned and left, but Gujun lingered.

"If he slows me down, I'll cut his throat," Gujun said, after the Vendeli shaman's man had left for the gardens.

"I'd sooner you didn't," Chulan said and gazed out the window, until Gujun took the hint and left him alone.

The next morning, he watched the two mount their horses and ride out from the villa. Gujun seemed in better spirits. "You sit that nag like a sack of shit," he'd told Grodu, as his bulky companion slunk low in the saddle.

Don't you dare let me down, Slayer.

Grodu had assured him that Octaxa was keen to make this new alliance work. Genza believed the Vendeli were in his pocket. He was a fool and would pay a heavy price for that delusion.

Utuxla closed his eyes and focused on his breath, staying in rhythm with the swaying hammock that cocooned his body. He allowed his sharp thoughts to rise above the creaking pitch and fall of the dhow's stormy passage. There were things he needed to tell his leader. He spoke the words, summoned the vision.

Octaxa's face appeared, blurry at first but then clearer. The eyes shined back at him inside his head. They looked angry and resentful.

You've been quiet of late. Should I suspect your loyalty?

The voice was cold and echoed in his head.

None are more loyal than your Sangala, of whom I am second only to you.

The High Califez is a persuasive man—he could have turned you against me.

Utuxla opened his eyes and rolled free of the hammock.

He saw his master's visage rippling like wet, crumpled parchment on the cabin lining.

"There's a twist in this game," Utuxla said to the face on the wall.

You are being evasive—you failed me in Yamondo. Why not admit to it?

"You ordered me back from my station," Utuxla said. "I would have preferred to stay and see the task through. Ulani played us. He knew the Yanturi was up to something and spared the Northman, who he will use against us."

How do you know this?

"I have dreamed of the Northman's ugly face," Utuxla said. "I saw his shadow rise over Tulomon Caze, meaning the High Califez is in trouble."

And you informed Caze?

"I mentioned it, yes."

The Yamondon must have spies working in Caze's camp. I will consult with him and we will discuss this when you arrive here in Laregoza.

"Anything I can do before that? It's boring on this ship."

We can't have you bored, Utuxla. That won't do. I suggest you Fargaze, find your friend, the Northman, discover his whereabouts—let proud Valgarn know we're expecting him to join us in the east.

The sound of soft laughter trailed off as Octaxa's image faded from the wall.

Utuxla stared into space for a few moments, summoning calm. He felt angry, used. Octaxa had criticized him and questioned his loyalty. An insult. The Sangala were nothing without their honor. Octaxa had spent too much time in Cardalan. Their treacherous ways were affecting him. Perhaps

Tulomon Caze would prove a better master. The Califez had hinted as much with his eyes this afternoon.

Utuxla forced a smile. Octaxa was afraid of him growing too strong. The Sangala had killed their leaders before, when they sensed weakness and indecision. He would have to be on his guard when he reached the mainland. But before that, there were interesting notions to explore here.

Utuxla swung back into his hammock and closed his eyes again. He focused a second time that night, allowing his mind slip out of the ship like liquid and glide as a night bird skimming dark waters. Seeking with his third eye, searching the lands beyond his country. It took most of that night, but eventually Utuxla found what he sought.

TRISA COULDN'T SLEEP. HER BODY WAS WEARY AND aching, but her mind was alert with thoughts darting back and forth. Beside her, Valgarn's warm bulk rose and fell in heavy sleep. The camp was silent. A wisp of smoke spiraled up from the dying embers of the fire. Beyond that and all around lay the vastness of the Permio Desert. Even as she gazed out that way, the wind whipped sand into her eyes until she shuffled free of their blankets and stood with her back to the sudden gale, the tangled locks whipping around her face.

The Yamondon sentry on watch saw her and nodded. Trisa waved back at him, and he turned away again.

Something's wrong.

Trisa felt like she was being watched by someone else. A hard-familiar face with dark eyes was mocking her. *Utuxla.* She turned and, the wind smote her face again, the sand stinging her eyes. There was no one out there. By her feet,

Valgarn rolled in his sleep. He stirred, blinked, and stared up at her. *My imagination …*

"What are you doing?" He shook himself and jumped to his feet, standing beside her.

"I can't sleep," she told him, as Valgarn pulled her close with an arm. "I'm restless."

"I can help you with that," he smiled and squeezed her hand. "Give you something else to think about, and help you rest afterwards."

"Not tonight." She stared into his eyes. Valgarn nodded slowly, the smile fading from his lips.

"What's wrong?"

"Something's out there—I can sense it," she told him. "Some ill spirit hunts us. I think Utuxla knows we're here."

"Nah, that's daft, lass. It's most likely this place. The wind here makes strange noises." Valgarn gazed over at the Yamondon guard. The man was hunched low with his back to them, the tip of a spear showing over his cloaked shoulder. "You worry too much," Valgarn ruffled her hair. "We are far from Vendel with Tarakai Dolusa and twenty of his best men accompanying us. King Ulani was most generous allowing his favorite nephew join us for part of the journey."

"The king doubtless has his reasons," she said. They'd left Cantacari a week ago, after staying in the city for only a few days. Ulani's people had treated them with kindness—she hadn't wanted to leave. The Yamondons were a beautiful and noble race, those she'd seen. Trisa had felt safe there.

But Dolusa had appeared at sunup on the last day and informed them that he'd been tasked with helping them return to Cardalan, as he knew the caravan routes through Southern Permio, a land rumored as hostile as Vendel. A journey of several weeks that would mean hedging the borders of mysterious Golt and crossing a sizeable chunk of the vast Permian desert. A direction, Dolusa had assured them, that no Vendeli would suspect.

Ulani had sent a badly mangled head of a captive southern sailor with the message back to the watchtowers. The man had fair hair and must have come from the north, she assumed. He hadn't resembled Valgarn, but it was hard to tell after what they had done to his face, poor fellow. Dolusa had assured them there would be no response from the enemy.

Valgarn stroked her hair. "It's all right. A strange place—we are near Golt. There are stories of that land, are there not?"

"There are," she said. "Though not much is known for certain. A land of demons, I've heard. Shadowy folk."

"And I've heard the same said about Rundali." He smiled again.

Trisa grinned back at him. He liked to tease her about her country.

"You are right, my love—I'm being foolish," she said. "Let's get warm again." Trisa gripped his hand and made to kneel. She stopped when the shrill sound of what could have been a howl or scream rose above the dirge of the desert wind. She saw the guard stand bolt upright. He was staring at something off in the scrub, the short Yamondon stabbing spear gripped tightly in both hands.

"That was no beast I'm familiar with," Valgarn said. "Wait here—I'll go see."

"I'm coming with you."

The guard saw them and pointed in the other direction with his spear. "Hyena?" Valgarn yelled at him. The man didn't respond. Trisa noted how shaken he looked.

Movement to her right, she saw Tarakai Dolusa appear, his face bleary with sleep. Dolusa snapped at the guard, and he and two others left the makeshift camp behind and walked briskly out into the night.

Trisa shivered as the desert wind whipped cold around them. Above her head, the stars studded the void like a billion accusing eyes. They reached a flat area where the gray shapes of brush shivered in the wind. She saw something flesh-colored tangled amidst that thorny scrub.

"Is that an animal?" Dolusa asked the guard. The man shook his head, seemingly unable to speak.

Dolusa and Valgarn walked closer warily, while Trisa hung back with the guard. "What did you see?" she asked the man. He looked at her and shook his head. Though she was afraid, Trisa felt anger too. *They cannot reach us here.* But her instinct told her that was a lie. Someone had sent them a message. She walked up behind Valgarn, who was standing gazing down at the sight, his expression somber.

Trisa took in what he surveyed, and her heart thudded in her chest. A Yamondon soldier, one of Tarakai Dolusa's chosen men. His throat was ripped open, leaking blood. His eyes were gone, with two red feathers were protruding from the empty sockets. A third feather had been used to slice open the man's belly. Trisa gagged at the smell. She turned away, and for the briefest instant saw a face staring at her out of the night. She swallowed a scream and almost lost her balance.

Trisa stumbled into Valgarn, who stood rock-still beside her. No one spoke for a few moments. It was Tarakai Dolusa who moved first, kneeling down and tugging the bloodstained feathers out of the dead man's eye sockets.

"Bagelzei." He turned and looked up at them, his handsome face was stiff with rage. "My cousin's eldest. Who has done this to him?"

"I think that we all know the answer to that," Valgarn said, looking at Trisa. "My woman sensed someone was hunting, using spell-craft. The Rundali have a nose for such horrors."

Dolusa looked at her. "Well …?"

"It was Utuxla," she told the Tarakai and her lover. "The Vendeli have found us."

"We'd best get moving," Valgarn said. He turned to Dolusa. "Take that poor lad back to Yamondo. You need not risk more of your men. It's me that Utuxla and his filth are after."

"You don't understand, Northman," Tarakai Dolusa said. "That boy was my cousin's son. This is personal. I won't rest until we find this culprit and rip out his heart."

"Utuxla is at the watchtowers waiting for me," Valgarn said. I don't know how he reached us here, but going back there to ask him is not an option."

"Utuxla is on a ship bound for Laregoza, the same one we voyaged in last month." Trisa spoke without registering her words. The men looked at her.

"How is it that you know this?" Valgarn said. Behind him, the first gray of dawn hinted daylight's arrival. It would be warm soon—she was grateful for that much.

"I saw his face," Trisa said, shaking her head. She felt giddy, weak. "Utuxla." She almost spat the word out, looking up at Valgarn, who gripped her hand tight in his. "It was but a fleeting glance, but his isn't a face I'd forget. When I looked at …" she hinted the corpse. "The Vendeli was staring back at me, and he was laughing. Though he vanished almost imme-diately, I recognized the cabin from that time I had entered to look at his maps."

"Your woman has the magic in her." Dolusa looked at her bleakly, his dark eyes haunted. Trisa recalled how his king had informed them that Yamondons had scant love for sorcery.

"I … just … see things, sometimes," she said.

"You've never mentioned this before." Valgarn stared at her, his features hard, eyes cold and quizzical.

"False fancies are not a suitable trait for a slave," she replied.

Valgarn's eyes softened, looking ashamed. "You are no slave, Trisa."

"If this Sangala filth can reach us here, what else can we expect from him?" Tarakai Dolusa looked miserable having asked himself the question. "I need this murderer in reach, Northman. Not on a ship plying the oceans. What good is he to me there?"

"Utuxla will be in reach," Valgarn said. "Of my axe—that I swear to you, Yamondon.

"Your axe may find this coward," Tarakai Dolusa said. "But my spear will skin his hide, while he begs for death."

"How many days to Cardalis?" Valgarn asked him as Trisa walked back with them to the camp, her head shrouded in gloom. The Tarakai's men had dug a shallow grave for their companion. The mood in the camp was bleak as they quietly readied for early departure.

"We're not going to Cardalis," Dolusa said.

"Your king said that was my destination."

"My uncle was fond of Bagelzei," Dolusa said. "Ulani will happily sanction this change of plan, when he hears. As for that, I'm sending a man back to Cantacari. I can't spare anyone, but the king needs to know one of his beloved Baha is dead."

"I don't understand why we're changing our plans,"

Valgarn said. "I need to convince that turd Genza that the Vendel have deserted him for Shen. He might be interested to hear that. He could even prove helpful for a change."

"We're going to Largos," Dolusa said, ignoring his protestations. "We'll find Utuxla there, and Tulomon Caze. That, or in Soloza further along the coast. If Utuxla's on board a ship, that can only mean he was ordered to abandon his post at the border for something more important. There are only two men who could enable this, saving the spoilt idle turd in Omala City. Either Octaxa the Sangala leader or—I suspect more likely—Tulomon Caze himself has ordered Utuxla join them in Laregoza."

"How far is that?" Trisa asked, as Valgarn's face looked bleak.

"A shorter trip than Cardalis would be." Dolusa grinned for the first time that morning. "And on roads I've traveled before. We fare east over the dunes, crossing the edges of the Permio Desert, north of my country. I vaguely recall the route —it was years back.

"There's a small oasis in the border region known as the Brushlands. Permian camel traders stop there to conduct business. If we are fortunate, we can trade our horses or purchase some of their humped beasts to speed up our journey to the coast. It's roughly a hundred miles to the sea, as I remember. Across that deep sand, camels will serve us better. Once there, we can cross into Laregoza and make for Largos, and Soloza beyond. We can also send word to Genza or alert his soldiers of Vendeli treachery."

"And then the killing starts," Valgarn said, smiling again.

Utuxla opened his eyes, allowing his shivering body ease back in the hammock. He was soaked from the exertion. The creature he'd summoned had had its price. The djinn always did. But they also always came when the Sangala reached out. This one had been hungry. He'd wanted to know the Northman's whereabouts so he could intercept Valgarn, having suspected the fool would return to the east lands. The djinn had demanded a blood sacrifice for that knowledge. Now his enemy would know Utuxla was on his trail. No matter.

He'd seen the Rundali girl through the djinn's yellow eyes, as the demon feasted on that soldier's soul. They were in Permio, near Golt, and were taking the land route back to Cardalis. The long road avoided his country. That made sense. Perhaps Ulani had messages for Genza in that city. He should inform Octaxa right away, but he was too weary.

And Octaxa had offended him earlier. He was far away, which would mean more mind-work. Tulomon Caze was in the next cabin. Sensing his opportunity, Utuxla rose from his hammock with a grin.

FLIGHT

GUNSALA WOKE TO PALE NOTHINGNESS. She saw neither wall or ceiling, and no smoke rose from last night's fire. She was cold, her body naked. Worse, she was alone. She heard a soft sound. It could have been laughter, or maybe it was footsteps approaching. Hard to tell. Everywhere was a blue shimmering haze.

"Can you comprehend real power?"

Sheega's voice reached her like steam clinging to her nostrils. Gunsala looked around, saw nothing at first until a vague shape emerged from the blue emptiness, becoming a woman. A beautiful, tall lady. The sleek, smoky-black hair coiffed back in a cluster of tiny diamonds, the long silver-black dress shimmering with pearls. She walked with cat-like grace, her visage filling Gunsala's head, draped in a smile that traveled before her.

"Well ... *can you?*"

"Where is Finvar?" She barely heard her own voice. A mouse squeak compared to the mellifluous tones of the beauty walking slowly toward her.

"You can't trust that one, Gunsala." The woman approached, standing tall. Willow supple, Sheega stood over her, taking in her nakedness with keen, interested eyes. "Finvar will betray you." Her tongue slid out, wetting the pouting lips.

Gunsala blushed, tried to shuffle away. Sheega's smile deepened seeing that. "You're shy, I like that. Quite pretty, too, for a human wench. You could learn so much from me! I could make you a queen, Gunsala. A proper queen, not a Vulkorye husk. Would you like that?"

"Where is Fin?" She rose to her knees and glared at the witch, trying hard to see a flaw in her beauty.

"This is how I used to look," Sheega said, noticing her gaze and stroking her body with ice white fingers, the nails polished crimson, filed to sharp points. "Have you ever seen such beauty?"

"I prefer real beauty rather than a conjuror's tricks."

"Conjuror? Is that what you think I am? A mere deceiver and trickster? Some spiteful sprite who steals children after dark? Hmm, perhaps I am." A quirky smile flicked across her lips. A fleeting moment later her eyes darkened, and mouth turned cruel. "Foolish girl."

A hand struck Gunsala's face, knocking her back sprawling, followed by a sharp kick in her ribs that made her cry out.

Gunsala rolled into a ball, sucking in air. "What do you want from me, witch?"

"You are looking at the goddess Undeyna!" Sheega's face turned crueler than before. "I could flay your plump mortal flesh from your bones with the hint of a smile. I could fill your mouth with excrement, bitch. Reach inside you and smother your pathetic little human soul, pack it off in parcels to Yffarn."

"Then why don't you fucking do it?" Gunsala found her feet and lurched at the tall woman, a sudden strength and rage fueling her from inside.

Sheega's dark eyes widened in shock before she swiftly recovered her repose. She stepped back, smiled again. "You have courage, Gunsala. I see why She chose you, my enemy."

"She—"

"—will desert you, little fool," Sheega's eyes narrowed dangerously. But this time there was no malice or scorn. Instead, the woman looked sad, as though the Norns had dealt her an ill hand. It was she who had been wronged. "The gods have always used mortals for Their menial work—it passes the time. At least I was honest by admitting I didn't like your species. She. Her sly husband. The newcomers. My kin. They're all hypocrites, Gunsala. The Emerald Queen will use you, just like Lofhi is using Finvar. You can't win here, child. *Shame*, but there you are."

A sharp pain jabbed into Gunsala's eyes. She screamed and covered her face, feeling hot tears welling. The pain vanished. She blinked them open and saw Finvar seated beside her on a bench. The hall stretched empty and quiet beyond and off to the sides. The fire trenches glowed with crimson. It was warm, and she saw the soft settle of snowflakes drifting outside the great doors.

"You were dreaming," Finvar said. He looked spritely and clear-eyed, as though he'd slept well and long. "Crying out in your sleep."

Gunsala was relieved to see her clothes folded neatly on the bench. She rolled free of the blanket and dressed quickly, looking around in case someone was watching.

"She's not here." Finvar smiled at her. His eyes looked bigger than normal. Gunsala worried that the witch had drugged him with something. "You should relax." The smile deepened, his hand reached toward her and stroked her face. She felt a sudden shiver at that touch.

"Finvar, you—"

"Relax, I said," the other hand shot down and slid up inside her skirt, reaching. She started in alarm, noticing how his eyes had shifted to a blazing red.

She kicked out at Lofhi and stood up. The red eyes smoldered. Finvar-Lofhi leered at her and rocked back and forth on his bench. Gunsala clenched her fists at her side and was about to strike him when his mouth twisted horribly and he made a pathetic mewling noise. The eyes were brown again. Her Fin was back. He looked ashamed and confused.

"It's me," he said lamely, as though convincing himself.

Gunsala unclenched her fists as she slunk exhausted on to the bench beside him.

"Lofhi's gone, Gun," he said, his eyes haunted. "Sheega, too, for the moment. We are alone."

"Are you sure?"

"Yes," he said, and reached across grasping her arms. "You are in great danger here, Gunsala."

"We are both in direst peril," she snapped.

"Not so." He looked anxious. "There isn't much time, so please listen."

"Go on."

"I can hold *him* back for a time," he said. "Lofhi thinks he has me sold—but I'm not the quitting type. They both need me, and I can play hard to get. But you ..."

"Are here to protect you."

"I know—and you will. But first you need to escape her claws."

"I'm not leaving you. We agreed, and I'm the Vulkorye,

remember. Our best chance of foiling them both is working together."

"And they know that," he said, squeezing her arm. "That's why you've got to get away. They'll work on you day and night until you can't resist. You're strong, my love—Vulkorye strong. But you need to save that strength until after the next moon."

"I'm not leaving you here with her."

"It's our only gambit," he said. "Sheega's' up to something new. I can sense it. Ranning isn't here, but something bad's coming. You need to warn Jaran, else the big daft lump gets overexcited and attacks too early."

"Together, we are stronger."

"I know, *I know*." He smiled at her. "But I cannot stand what Lofhi does to me. What he'll make me do to you. I can play his game better if I know you're out of danger. Do this for me, Gun. Find Jaran, tell him I've got it covered at this end of the island, and he has to keep out of sight."

"It's two months, Finvar."

"Six weeks by my last reckoning." He grinned at her. "I can handle Lofhi, and she won't mess with me without upsetting him. Do you see what I'm saying?"

"My task is to protect you."

"And you will, as we approach the final moon. Save your strength for then. As for this moment. Go! The way is clear—I saw with Lofhi's eyes when he was here. They are both gone, but she will return ere nightfall, and I've a hunch she won't be alone. Flee, my love, while you have this chance."

"I hate this."

"Me, too," he squeezed her arm again. "I'll tell Sheega we argued—it's not a lie, so she'll believe me, knowing Lofhi was here." He reached forward, kissing her lips. She responded, but he pushed her away. "You need to go, Gunsala, else it's too late."

"Damn you." She stood and turned to gaze at the distant doors, standing wide open. The snow was swirling in from outside. *Summer, and it's snowing,* a small part of her mind registered.

"Please," Finvar said.

She nodded, wiped the trace of a tear from her angry face and left him without looking back.

"Find my big pal!" Finvar called after her, as Gunsala reached the doors and stepped outside. A swirl of white blinded her, and snowflakes dampened her cheeks. She saw the frozen lake and dark woods beyond; the heavy structure of buildings loomed behind her. She turned toward the woods and started running as the cold bit into her. Gunsala reached the first trees as the sound of wolves echoed down the valley.

SHEEGA SCRAPED HER FINGERNAILS ALONG THE SURFACE of the copper mirror. Inside, the goblin Gantallion covered his ears and stuck out his tongue.

Stop that!

"Why?" she purred, scraping again, playfully this time.

Because it puts my teeth on edge.

"You don't have any teeth." Sheega stopped scraping and drummed her fingers on the mirror, making the surface wobble.

I've one or two left, Gantallian sulked. *What do want from me?*

"News."

Don't have any.

"Where is Ranning?"

Don't know, don't much care.

"You're proving more tiresome than usual. I thought you liked it here."

I liked it the way it was. That's about to change.

"Is it? I wonder why." Sheega smiled and resumed her scraping.

Bitch-Queen, you know why. Gantallian covered his ears again.

"I don't know what you're talking about."

Yes, you do, you've opened the doorway to Yffarn, and big shit's about to happen.

"Oh, that." Sheega pouted her bottom lip and flicked the mirror, causing a hollow, twanging sound. "*Faerie*, not Yffarn—though that is an interesting idea. And you're from Faerie, imp, so you should be excited. You'll get to see some of your family again."

I don't like any of them.

"That's understandable," she said. "Now, Gantallian, stop your prattle. I need you to be useful, else I toss you into that lake."

You wouldn't do that to me.

"Wouldn't I? You've been scant help of late, and this incessant sulking is getting on my nerves. Shut up and get scrying. I need to know where Hrelgisson is hiding, and why Gorvaron hasn't brought me his head yet. And where the fuck is Rune? So tired of that meddling fur-sack. I always loathed the Yetain."

Isn't that why your dogs ate most of them? Those you didn't burn.

"Get some work done, goblin. I want results when I return."

Where are you going? Gantallian's golden eyes sparkled interest.

"Out for a stroll."

You just got back from one.

"This time I'm going somewhere different." Sheega pinged the mirror one last time and turned away, making for the door leading through to the main hall.

Where? The squeaky voice followed her out.

Damn you. She turned, glared back at the leering face in the mirror. "To Cradon Iwey," she said. "Happy now?"

Gantallian's eyes bulged golden, and he crept back inside the mirror, as though his face had been stung by hornets. Sheega grinned wolfishly and left the mirror chamber behind.

She wrapped her cloak around her shoulders and made for the doors, forcing them wide open and crunching her boots on the snow. She thought about calling in on the lovers, hidden in their screen at the far end of the hall. She'd seen Finvar reading something by the fire. He'd looked up as she passed, but her mind had been on other things. Gunsala was doubtless still recovering from Sheega's amusing visit inside her nightmare.

She forgot the pair for the moment as she stepped out into the winter cold, the snowflakes dusting her hood and cloaked shoulders. Shrouded in dark thoughts, Sheega walked down to the lake, the surface glittering up at her, its sheen mirroring the half-moon framed by stars above.

Six weeks—time was passing. Too quickly, and yet not nearly fast enough. It depended how you measured these things.

She missed Ranning and was irritated by his absence, having expected his return a week ago. And when she gazed up at that accusing dagger moon, Sheega felt a cold dread chip deep inside her skin. Her enemy was watching from Galenki.

You're out there somewhere—I can feel you, Elanion.

She shuddered, turned away and took the stony path toward the shadow of the mountain, passing by her hall, the ancient howe behind and entering the shroud of woods beyond. She heard wolf voices calling out to her.

Ahead, Gronteyer's nearest peak sparkled in the sun. It was summer there, a scant ten miles south and yet beyond her domain. There were spirits upon Gronteyer that protected its flanks and the woods surrounding, and the rest of the island beyond. She'd seldom ventured there. The dead Jarles, including Hrund—and probably Erlund, too—would be stirring inside that mountain. She'd defeated Barin, but the others were still there, including Taic, the Whitebear's troublesome nephew.

She would stay clear of the mountain. That was Gorvaron's task. *Flush them out.* She reached the remote beach, the shingle chiming under her feet. As she walked, the climate changed, her snowscape faded like dreams at dawn. She tossed aside her cloak and tugged off her boots, walking the beach naked, the warm sun tickling her skin.

Sheega strolled along the beach for hours, until the sun slipped down toward the sea. Out there, she saw clouds mustering and knew a storm was coming. She hadn't much time, as she needed to harness that power.

She reached a point where the shoreline cut away, a deep bay showing beyond, the water choppy and blue. Sheega stepped into that brine. She took a deep breath and plunged her lean body into the chop. She swam over to the dark rocks in the bay's midst with bold even strokes. She reached the cave mouth and clambered inside, squatted soaking and dripping on a flat rock. Behind her the sun had turned crimson and was falling from the sky.

Cradon Iwey at dusk.

The Faerie Gate, Hrund had called it. His people never went there. But Sheega was no stranger to this place, having first entered the island from here long ago.

She gazed long into that dark hole, before turning and watching the storm clouds swallow the sun before it met the distant water. Sheega entered the cave and made for the place where she'd hidden her darkest secrets. She scraped away slime and snails, and cranked open the trunk. Her corpse-summoning runes glittered inside. She couldn't wait on Ranning or his creature, and Faerie was taking too long. It was time for her to act alone. After all, no one else was completely on your side.

Sheega grabbed the rune necklace and slipped it over her head. Next, she retrieved the damaged shawl and sandals. The shawl would hide her form, the sandals grant her speed of foot. She walked deeper into the gloom, the cave closing in around her. Beyond lay a crooked line where the bay water was sucked into a crack.

Sheega reached the fissure and squeezed through. She gripped the runes and uttered her mind-spell three times. Sometimes you had to take the fight to the enemy, rather than wait for their vassal to come to you.

THE SHORELINE CHIMED AS ELANION'S BARE FEET brushed over the sand. Above her head, both moons shimmered, the larger one glowing red, the other pale yellow. She walked, her mind reaching, calling out a name, as a shadow settled on her heart.

Deyna knows I'm on to her.

Guised as a tall woman with long golden braids, Elanion stood and gazed out at the purple ocean, watching as the seas gathered their swell, bunching tight and exploding as the huge figure emerged.

A giant, corded with muscle and terrible of face. He strode fiercely toward the beach where she stood, stopped there, with gnarled fists thrust on hips, glaring down at her with shifting mercurial eyes.

"WHY HAVE YOU WOKEN ME, SISTER? I'VE BEEN LONG AT PEACE."

"I need your council, younger brother. A new Dance has begun."

"WHAT IS THAT TO ME? WE WERE BANISHED—YOU SHOULD TAKE HEED."

"That's easy for you to say, whose domain can cross through many waters throughout all worlds. Ansu is MY planet, gifted to me alone. I want it back."

"WHY SO? THERE ARE MUCH BETTER PLACES, AND I THOUGHT YOU LIKED IT HERE ON GALENKI?"

"I tolerate it here—needs must. But that's not important. I've found Undeyna hiding on MY planet."

"YOU NEED TO LET THAT GO."

"I can't. And she's with your daughter's brat. The skinny thieving whelp you banished. They've summoned Faerie, Sensuata. You know what that means?"

"WAR … *AGAIN.*"

"And one that could well destroy *MY* Ansu—Tyho and Kullaan are blunt thugs, brother, my husband can't be trusted

—as you well know—and Faerie will stop at nothing to reclaim its world."

"I THOUGHT IT WAS YOUR WORLD?"

"We shared Ansu. I was the Guardian, the Faen were loyal, but the other races turned sour."

"AND RANNING IS INVOLVED? LET ME THINK ON THIS."

"Another matter, which concerns Gol."

"I SUNK THAT LAND."

"Carlo Sarfe the lost voyager is sailing there—they have my bow, Kerasheva. That weapon will enable his ship sail back through time. If that coincides with Faerie and Undeyna, and they hear about it in Graywash Hall—even our Father won't be able to contain the rupture in the cosmos. Don't say I didn't warn you."

Elanion turned away and walked back to the distant white tower. By the time she reached her gardens, the Sea God had gone.

She walked through her maze of glowing lilies, their faces turning and smiling at her passing as she ordered her mind. Next, her birds came and spoke to her. She glanced up at the throbbing sky and felt a sudden shudder. The birds became her three daughters, the Norns. They lifted and flew away.

Mother, she is here, Vervandi called out in warning, before becoming a butterfly and vanishing above.

"I know," Elanion said. She turned slowly, gazed at the dark-haired woman seated neatly on her bench.

"This is bold, even for you, Deyna."

"I've nothing to fear, Elanion," the dark-haired woman smiled up at her. "Your magic bow is lost at sea with the mortals who stole it."

"It was a gift."

"You still trust those cretins? How quaint."

"You wouldn't understand, Deyna. Your shallow mind is too damaged, my dear."

"And who's responsible for that, big sister? Always you picked on me."

"And on each occasion, you deserved it. You ... killed Simiolanis."

"Again, it comes back to that ... *accident*."

"You alone of our Kin have murdered one of Our own."

"Aren't you leaving someone out?"

"Saan is gone, as is His stain. One good result from that last war. But some of His dregs still linger. I'm tasking myself to mop them up, every last drop. You are no longer a goddess, Deyna. Your strength has dwindled, Ice Witch."

"As has yours, Elanion of the Forests. If I were you, I'd stay put here in Galenki."

"You dare threaten me?"

"Take it as a warning that things are about to get rough."

As the woman watched, her visitor faded, shimmered and was gone. Sad-eyed, she walked over to the bench and took her seat gazing out at the waves. She felt a tear trace her cheek.

Undeyna, I'm sorry I failed you, child. And what she'd said was right, *I am not whom I was.* Here is but a shadow, a creature of dreams and memory. Elanion closed her eyes, allowing her magical mind to travel back to that glorious time before Old Night's stain had blighted them all.

SHEEGA WAS ELATED. SHE LEFT THE CAVE BEHIND, AS HER mind raced back inside her body. She swam back to the beach with her treasures. She'd put the necklace to use again tomorrow. Once on dry land, she walked beneath heavy cloud, the rain spitting on her flesh. Sheega scooped up her cloak and boots, and took the long walk back to her witching pole, the rime-covered fields and lake glittering with early dark.

The storm arrived and spilled its fury upon her. Sheega laughed as lightning spears struck the lake, cracking ice and flashing into the ocean beyond. She had called out her greatest foe. Elanion must answer. The final game had started, and old scores would be settled at last.

Yffarn take them all!

Sheega tossed her cloak aside again and let the storm's wrath lash her body with rain and icy hail. She laughed, giddy with electric joy, as power flooded her body. Looking up, she saw figures gazing balefully down at her from the dark clouds. Kullaan and Tyho were abroad tonight.

"Your time is coming, too!" Sheega yelled up at the faces that flickered and dwindled in the shifting dark. "Damn you all—Undeyna the Dark Queen is back!" She tugged a crooked dagger free from the earth by her feet, a tool stored there for sacrifice.

With one hand gripping the horse-head pole, the other clutching the knife, Sheega-Undeyna stabbed down into her left wrist and laughed before drinking deeply of the blood flowing out. She would use the blood and rune-necklace to raise the corpses she'd hidden beneath the lake.

This ends next moon.

The storm subsided. The shadows fled. Weary, Sheega again, she stumbled back to the hall. The man Finvar was there, but his woman had gone.

THE FIRST BREACH

VIAN WATCHED the rider wheel his horse around and point accusingly up at the walls. The Ragan was a skilled horseman, and his antics had been entertaining them for several minutes.

"Arrogant bastard." Roile hawked and spat in the mud.

"Confident," Vian replied, watching as Uzcara thrust his spear into the dirt and reached up with both mailed hands, adjusting his conical helm. He tugged to pull down the mask to hide his features. A metal wolf face glared up at them. "This brother will prove more dangerous than Racara," Vian added, sensing the challenge.

Uzcara's men were lined in three ranks ahead of the woods and out of bow range. Almost a repeat of the other day. But Vian knew Uzcara wouldn't fall for the same ploy as had the other Ragan.

Apart from Daigar—fortunately dead—Uzcara was rumored the best warrior from the wolf pack. The Northman, Dorthar had told him he'd seen Uzcara kill men at the river as though he was harvesting wheat. Vian adjusted his Jian, leaned on his spear, and hummed.

"I wish he'd stop buggering about and attack," the lean Cutter grumbled.

"He's teasing us," Vian said and turned, hearing shouts and the boom of cannon. "Looks like it's heating up at the Main Gates. Want to go check, see how Gurt and Matax are doing?"

"I'm staying put until that fucker's short a head." Roile spat again. He had his bow resting. He'd tried a few shots at Uzcara, but the rider never stayed put for more than a second. Three times they'd watched him ride in close, wheel his horse around and urge it gallop back toward his men.

"Guess I'd better send someone," Vian said. He beckoned a young officer, one of the three Matax had ordered to join them, together with two hundred men—all tasked with holding the Sea Gate and harbor beyond.

The officer sidled up to Vian. Young and eager, his face was hidden by the wide conical helmet, but nervous—maybe even a little terrified, judging by his eyes.

"I didn't catch your name," Vian said to the officer.

"Cul Baja, Harbor Defense Second Team Captain, sir."

"Relax, Cul Baja." Vian smiled, and saw Roile shaking his head in disgust. "Cul's a rank is it not?"

"It is, general sir," the officer stiffened, his thin moustache bristling like reeds. "Below Goi or General, and Mid Quarn, but above Dazer, and Qil."

"Good to know." Vian noticed that Uzcara had stopped his posturing and rejoined his men.

"About bloody time," Roile muttered.

Vian nodded. "Cul Baja, I need you to take a man and report our situation to General Matax. Tell him Uzcara's going to keep us busy here for a good while."

"Sir!" The young Cul dipped his helmet, yelled at a

Chiang soldier, and bid the man follow him at speed from the wall.

"That daft fucker needs to calm down," Roile said, watching the two soldiers leave.

"He'll settle once the fighting starts," Vian said, looking along the walls at the men Matax had placed under him. Most were youngsters, a few veterans that might have seen fighting at the River, though he doubted more than a dozen.

"That or die." Roile caught his glance and looked at the soldiers. "Poor bastards, they're shitting themselves," he said.

"Aye." Vian wiped sweat from his face and loosened his helmet strap, where it was catching below his chin. "We need this to start." Another blast from the cannon, and distant shouts. They waited, as across the city the sound of booms and thuds announced the Cards were unleashing their ballistae. Vian saw a cloud of smoke rising and suspected a direct hit on the walls.

Another twenty minutes passed. Uzcara sat his horse, the men bunched behind him. Vian saw him lean back and reach for the bow stored in his saddle. He knocked arrow to string and pulled back.

"Here we go," Roile spat. Vian watched the arrow arc high and sail across toward them, landing with a clatter on the parapet.

A sweating Cul Baja emerged from the gate stairs, his face red and bulging under his helmet. Vian almost smiled at the sight.

"They're attacking," he said very loudly.

"Yes," Vian said, as the Cardalan horsemen started shouting their challenges. The Cul heard that, and his face went white.

"The wall." He wiped sweat from his eyes. "They're hitting

it with large stones. I told General Matax ... we'd be hard pressed ..." He jumped slightly when the sound of horses galloping turned his head again. The Cards were moving at last.

"Well done," Vian said, glancing over the walls and seeing the enemy leaving the hill and woods, their steads galloping down toward them. "Are your men ready to kill these pests, Cul Baja?"

"They are, sir!"

"It doesn't fucking look like it to me," Roile muttered beside him. But the Cutter turned and grinned at the terrified Cul and the Chiang soldier standing beside him. "Now boys, watch and learn from a true master of the art of butchery." Roile leveled his bow, nocked arrow, pulled and loosed, in one fluid movement. The arrow arced high and fell. A man screamed among the attackers and pitched from his horse. Roile nocked and loosed again, and a second rider tumbled. More arrows whistled out from either side of where Vian stood.

Uzcara shouted orders, and a group of riders broke off galloping close and hurling weighted nets up at the walls. Most fell away, but some gripped and stayed put.

"Cut those fucking ladders!" Roile yelled, across at the nearest men and they rushed to respond, their Jian blades and oblong shields clanging.

"Gurtei should promote you," Vian said wryly, as Roile leaned forward and shot one of the riders through the throat after he'd jumped from his horse and started clambering, arm over arm up the wall. The Card pitched backward and crashed into the man below him.

"Arrows, boys!" Vian shouted, as he aimed the bow he'd grabbed from the armory and loosed, skewering the man leading the ladder crew. He heard bowstrings twang close by and ducked as a storm of shafts shot out from the walls. The Cardalan riders broke apart and most the arrows missed, though some struck horse or rider.

"Don't waste shafts," Vian said angrily.

"They're gaining a foothold," Roile said, dropping his bow and reaching for his Jian. "I'll deal with it." He rushed over to where a score of Cards had clambered free of two of the rope ladders and were jumping down onto the wall.

Vian saw Cul Baja standing with a Jian in his hand, his eyes wide with terror. "Go help him, man," Vian shouted. The Cul blinked and ran to help Roile, a dozen men following behind.

Vian shot two more climbers with his bow before tossing the weapon aside. He reached for the Chiang spear he'd stood close by.

"Come on, Uzcara," Vian yelled down at the wolf mask surrounded by his men, milling below as the ladders filled with crawlers. "How many men do I have to butcher before you get your fat arse off that horse?"

"I'm coming, red hair!" The Ragan's voice reached him as Vian crashed into the nearest attacker and swept low with his Chiang.

Rasnei winced as she saw the boulder strike her walls, a hundred yards from where she stood beside the big Northman, Dorthar, on the Barbican parapet. The massive rock struck the wall halfway up, sending a cloud of dust into the sky. She saw men tossed skyward from that collision, as shattered stone crumbled and splintered with impact.

"We need to do something about those machines," Dorthar grunted, as they watched a second missile wending over. That one fell short. But the ballistae were lined up with teams of tiny figures working, scurrying about like disturbed ants. The cannons had struck the big machines twice but failed to do lasting damage. Matax had ordered them hold back, as cannonballs were running short and not to be wasted.

"What are you suggesting, Northman?" Rasnei gazed at the scar-faced fighter. She liked Dorthar and wished she'd known more of her auxiliaries back in Pol Shen.

"A night raid—destroy them," he replied.

"Vian counseled against that."

Dorthar shrugged. "Aye, Light of the Sky. And he was right to. It's risky, but ..." He blew out his cheeks and wiped his nose. "Those fucking rocks will play havoc with your walls, if we allow them to continue for days on end. Err ... sorry," he added, ashamed that he'd utter profanity in front of his empress.

Rasnei raised a brow. "I've heard worse," she said. This was a good man, almost as big and terrible as Jaran Saerk. But friendlier of face and solid company, especially while she was missing Vian, and the tension inside her reaching bursting point.

The burly Northman had assigned himself as her personal bodyguard after talking to her lover. Vian had liked the idea. Dorthar was Sapphire Guard, after all—one of the few still living. They'd always been her loyalist defenders. Shen had sold the Northmen short. Rasnei intended to address that issue, if they ever got through this. She'd told Dorthar as much, as they stood together that morning watching the assault begin.

She heard Gurtei shouting near where the ballistae were

attacking the walls. The former Cutter had a squad of men clearing stone and rubble along there. The archers were busy, too, cutting down any Card who dared get too close.

The ram teams were waiting in the center, as were the commanders, the Ragans—three distant figures in bright-colored cloaks. They wore helmets with mesh visors covering their faces, but Rasnei had guessed the middle, heaviest-set rider was the new Ran, Casca. The two flanking him were lean and younger-looking. Those two sat upright in their saddles, while Casca was slouched idle, as though bored.

"May the Shadowman take you," Rasnei muttered under her breath.

"I hate Cards." Dorthar nodded, hearing her. "Murderous bastards, but they are good fighters. Thing is, Shining One"—he flashed her an ugly grin—"they're natural horse warriors, but not experienced in this kind of warfare."

"That won't matter if our walls collapse, or those rams break through our gates."

"Light of the Stars, that's my point." He grinned again.

"For fuck's sake, call me Rasnei," she said, and laughed seeing his face blanche in shock. "I'll speak to the others when we get a chance, Dorthar. I agree with you, watching the walls crumble isn't our best plan."

Another boulder whistled past as she spoke. This one was nearer; it missed the walls and crashed into the streets below. "Hope that didn't hit the Violet Girl," the Northman said gloomily. They watched as more rocks sailed across, causing a deal of damage along the walls. Rasnei noticed carts being wheeled off into the distance behind the machines.

"Off to get more ammunition from the quarries they dug," Dorthar said. "'Spect they'll try the rams next."

Even as he spoke, she saw the battering-ram teams

surrounding the huge timbers start hauling on their chains and marching forward. One of the younger Ragans, the one on the right, broke away, riding south at speed toward where the worst wall damage had been afflicted.

"Young Casla wants a piece of the action," the hoarse croak came from behind her. Rasnei turned and saw a panting Gurtei join them.

"How do you know that's Casla?" Rasnei said, smiling a tense greeting as he stood beside her.

"Studs on his cloak." Gurtei grinned at her. "Calgara has stripes, the new Ran circles. Rafin the dwarf told me, before he ... hmm. Departed." Gurtei squinted out at the plain.

"I miss Rafin," Dorthar said, and grinned as a big newcomer appeared from the stairwell. "Lin Gu, have you been sleeping?"

"Sharpening my swords," the big Shen said. "Waiting for their attack, but they are lazy, these Cards."

"We need to stop those rams," Gurtei said. "Flaming arrows won't do much, as they soaked the shield-roofs protecting them."

"A sortie?" Dorthar grinned.

"Bugger that." Gurtei shook his head.

"It worked for Vian and us lads at the Sea Gate."

"We dare not risk that again," Gurtei said, catching Rasnei's worried glance. "Vian's fine," he added. "They haven't started attacking the Sea Gate yet. Some young Cul reported to me a few moments back." Rasnei nodded, feeling a flush of relief. "The Rundali says he'll be stuck there for a while," Gurtei informed her.

"Vian's got the toughest job," Dorthar said. "That Uzcara's a wily bastard." His eyes shifted to the south. "Where's that one going?"

Rasnei saw that the Ragan who'd broken away from his brothers was leading a troop of fifty-odd riders toward the wall two hundred yards south of where they stood.

Gurtei rammed his spyglass into an eye. He grunted in disapproval. "That pup's keen. His men are carrying weighted rope ladders, I'll need to send Matax's thug squad to intercept them."

"I will join them," Lin Gu said, hefting a heavy Chiang and leaving without further word, the two Jian blades clanking as he walked.

"Good man, that one, for a Shen," Dorthar said. "Err … apologies, no offense, Ras, hmm."

"Go with your friends if you'd prefer," Rasnei said to the red-faced Dorthar, as Gurtei vanished behind Lin Gu.

"My place is with you … Rasnei, empress," he pronounced her name awkwardly. A half-mile out, the great rams were creaking toward them. They had twenty minutes, perhaps less. She heard Gurtei and Matax yelling, and saw soldiers running to protect the spot where Casla was leading his riders, the huge Lin Gu running behind to catch them up.

Rasnei gripped Dorthar's arm as adrenaline tweaked her belly. "Thank you, Northman," she said. "Aside from Vian and Jaran Saerk, I cannot think of a better man to have by my side."

Dorthar's ugly, bearded face cracked open with a grin. "I'll die for you happily, Rasnei," he said. "Can't say I felt that way during the river skirmishes."

"I cannot blame you for that," she said. "I listened to weasels like Chulan and Soma Ghee for far too long."

"They were your advisers." He looked at her strangely for a moment.

"What is it?"

"Vian …" Dorthar shook his head. "He's …"

"*Different* …?" She smiled at him. The rams were nearer—they had ten minutes at most.

"I'm glad he's here," Dorthar said eventually. "But I wish Jaran Saerk was, too."

"You were his friend at the front?"

"Not really," Dorthar said. "Saerk didn't have any friends. We called him the Whitebear after the tattooed scar on his chest. Most lads found him standoffish and proud, aloof. We all respected Saerk, though. I was in awe of him, truth be told. I've never seen a man fight like the berserker Jaran Saerk, save perhaps that creature who came to kill him."

"Scard the Changeling." Rasnei nodded and shuddered. She thought of Savarna, the tiger incident, and closed that horror from her mind. *Where were they now?* It was no longer her concern.

Gurtei reappeared with a score of men wearing thick leather gauntlets, bearing heavy-looking urns brimming with bubbling oil. Two others appeared behind them, carrying a long tube with a flanged, tapering muzzle. The thing resembled a cannon but was smaller and much thinner.

"Matax's engineers fished this relic out from the back of the armory," Gurtei said.

"A mini-cannon?"

"Sort of, yes. A *firelock,* Matax called it," he told her. "There are more down there, and his lads are working on them, as they're in bad shape, the functions having rusted for years. They only found the things by chance while fetching the last cannonballs. Takes two men, empress. One fires over the other's shoulder. They're getting set up now."

She watched as the two readied the long tube and the loader shoved a small, roundish ball down its length. He crouched low. The gunner—Gurtei called the other one that —looked down the length of the weapon, adjusting and squinting. He stood close behind the loader as the other man shuffled and grumbled, the long iron tube resting on his right shoulder. Rasnei didn't hold out much hope.

The nearest ram crew were within arrowshot, but Gurtei gave the order to wait. The wooden, shell-covered ram was hauled forward into place.

Gurtei ordered the men to ready the oil. Rasnei looked down, saw the ram-head swing back, then forward. She heard a dull thud. The ram was pulled back to swing again, but a sudden blast deafened her ears and flames and wisps of smoke shot out from the firelock. Rasnei gasped, seeing it had punctured a foot-wide hole in the ram-shield roof. She heard yells and a scream, and she saw men running away, these brought down by quick-acting archers.

"Good work!" Gurtei slapped the gunner's back. "Load another."

Three more shots and the rammers gave up, running back to join their comrades in the other teams. The archers raked them from behind, only half dozen made it back there. The ram shield lay in pieces, smoke was rising as the first flames caught hold.

"They dipped the balls in saltpeter and sulphur." Gurtei grinned. "We weren't sure if it would work."

"Best get the other ones working and bring them up soonest," Dorthar said. "Here comes the main event." He pointed across to where Casca could be seen yelling and waving his horsemen forward into position

Rasnei was about to respond when she heard the clash of steel to the south.

"They've breached the wall!" Gurtei said. "Fucking Casla!"

"Lin Gu will deal with him," Dorthar said to Rasnei, chewing his moustache.

"I certainly hope so," she replied.

Ragan Casla was grinning like a lynx as he gripped the rope ladder and climbed, his agile body lifting him easily and feet braced, walking up the wall. Several men had fallen past him, pierced by arrows or screaming as the bubbling oil devoured their flesh.

Casla paid them no heed. This was to be his victory, the moment when he became the greatest warrior of the age. Daigar was gone, Uzcara getting old and past his best, and Casca running to fat. That left Calgara and himself, the youngest and most passionate of the Ragans. They'd drawn straws over this attack. He'd won, and with Casca's blessing had led his troop across to storm the walls, a quarter-mile south of the barbican where they'd been damaged by the ballistae.

A man screamed and fell toward him, his head half hanging off. Casla ducked and swung out with his ladder, and the body fell past and thudded onto the bloody ground, joining the score of corpses down there.

Another ten feet or so to climb. A helmeted Shen appeared above the ladder and started sawing at the rope. Casla spat the dagger from his mouth, caught it deftly with his left hand and tossed it up. The knife struck the Shen's eye, and he disappeared.

Casla reached the top and swung his body over the parapet. Men yelled and rushed at him as his warriors followed behind, jumping free of their ladders and gripping their curved swords.

A Chiang spearman swung his heavy weapon at Casla. The young Ragan laughed and ducked low beneath that strike. He skipped forward, cutting up with his scimitar and slicing open the man's groin. He slung the round shield over his other hand and yelled for his men to follow.

The Shen were pressing against them. Casla was outnumbered, but that didn't matter. These were feeble fighters. He'd killed four and was dispatching a fifth when a huge shaven-pated warrior with a long pigtail stepped out in front of him. This one wore no helmet and was smiling grimly.

"Time to die, Card." The Shen swung his Chiang.

"I'm Ragan Casla, and you're a fucking corpse." Casla ducked out of range of that swing and ran in fast, the scimitar cutting out.

The big warrior blocked his slice with a confident ease Casla hadn't expected. He struck out again and jumped back, as his second swing was blocked and the heavy Chiang sailed across to strike his head.

Casla ducked as the spear sliced air over his head. Out the corner of his eye, he saw his men being pushed back as the Shen had rallied around this big warrior. *Must be some kind of chieftain. Got to kill this bastard quickly.*

Casla raised his shield, knocking the Chiang aside and stabbed below with his scimitar. The man blocked with his Chiang shaft, but the impact cut deep into the wood. The Shen tossed the weapon aside, stepped back two paces, and reached back behind his head to grab two Jian swords.

Casla swung out and charged, his shield crashing into the Shen's midriff. The warrior danced aside and stabbed out at him. Casla swallowed a scream as pain shot up his leg. He glanced down—his left calf was bleeding badly. He stabbed at the big Shen's face, felt a jolt and then stared in disbelief at the narrow sword sticking in his gut.

"You should never have come here," the big Shen said, stabbing him again. Casla spewed blood as the Shen picked him up like a rag doll and tossed him over the wall.

MATAX HAD WITNESSED THE WHOLE FIGHT. HE'D YELLED for his men leave room as Lin Gu had pushed through, after killing a half-dozen Cards who'd jumped down form the damaged section of wall.

A messy fight, they'd been hard-pressed, but the young Ragan had left himself exposed. That was when Matax saw the magic happen. Lin Gu transformed from a slow-moving, clumsy giant to a lightning-quick, deadly dancer. Never had he witnessed such sword and Chiang work.

The Card attack had crumbled when those few still living saw their leader tossed like garbage from the walls. They'd turned to flee but Matax had led the charge, taking them from behind and killing the lot. Danger averted for the moment, he'd yelled for carpenters to come and shore up the hole in the wall.

17

DEEPWATER EDGE

JARAN GRIPPED Savarna's hands as she walked beside him, crouching low as the cavern roof shrunk and sides funneled. "How far?" Jaran asked the shadow in front.

"He says we're nearly there." Ivar's uneven teeth grinned back at him, the torchlight blinking on his craggy features. They'd been walking for hours, it seemed, down and deeper inside the honeycomb comprising Gronteyer's heart. The labyrinth of caves and tunnels had far surpassed anything Jaran had imagined. They were deep within a water-carved maze the size of Ta Shen, perhaps bigger. Svipdag had told them that they'd only skimmed the outside when they'd taken that earlier journey to find him in his cavern.

"They say giant worms bored beneath the mountain," Ivar had said, as they'd trudged through the damp dripping tunnels. "In an age before man."

"Let's hope there are none down here," Savarna had replied beside him. Jaran had been worried about her—she'd looked ashen faced and tired, after her ordeal with the giant Gorvaron. She didn't seem herself of late. He wondered if she was thinking about Vian. She hadn't mentioned her brother for some time.

The men walked behind him in single file. Tofei and Asmund had stayed behind at the entrance, helping Unva and Rafin attend to what they'd called a "sealing rune" that would hide them from Sheega and her creatures, at least for the time being.

Seeing Unva the wolf-witch had unnerved Jaran, despite Rafin assuring him the yellow-eyed plotter was on their side. Who else was out there? Tyho and Kullaan, no doubt. Faerie? On its way. And the Traveler—where was he?

Jaran worried about Finvar, and he blamed Rune for bringing them back here too early. The accusation wasn't fair. Rune had helped them more than anyone, but Jaran didn't want to wait, hiding like a trapped rabbit in a snare.

Six weeks might as well be a year, lurking in a cave. There had to be something they could do. Gunard led the men behind him. He'd tasked his son with protecting Asmund while he fared through Leeth with the War Arrow. Another mistake? Jaran had no love for Leeth. Why should they rally to his cause? Both Gunard and Ivar had insisted that they would. Gorn was dead. Valgarn the only of her sons living, but Gunard said there'd been no news of his whereabouts. Jaran suspected that would change.

The ceiling lifted. He felt a welcome draught of cold air and grinned as the rock roof allowed him to stand fully erect for the first time in an hour.

"We're here." Jaran heard Svipdag's gruff tones from some-where ahead. He didn't know how to take the old warrior recluse. That man had a shifty, nasty look to his eyes—but Ivar trusted him, and that would have to do. Jaran worried that

Svipdag was half-mad and would lead them to Sheega—whether by mishap or design.

One thought troubled him more than any other. Why wasn't Sheega here, in these caves? She must know about them. And her Hide in Dunnehine must have resembled this before she'd started work on the tunnels. Something, perhaps someone was keeping Sheega away from Gronteyer, else she'd be waiting to pounce, and with whatever Yffarn-spawn creatures she'd raised too. Gorvaron was Ranning's creature, so what was the Ice Witch up to?

Nothing good. He fingered Griner and ground his teeth together.

He stopped walking hearing Savarna gasp beside him as they reached a wide crevice, opening into a large area of free-flowing air. They'd entered a vast cavern, the biggest one yet. He heard water tingling ahead. He gripped Savarna's hand tighter as the hairs on the small of his neck tingled.

"How are you feeling?" he asked her.

"Better." She smiled up at him. "Dreamy, tired, but stronger. What a place! Is that a lake?" Ivor's torchlight revealed a glimmer of water below where they stood. The old hunter had stopped and stood beside Svipdag's shadow. The two were waiting for the rest to join them.

Jaran heard Gunard grunt behind him. "Regret joining our cause?" Jaran turned and smiled at the old thane.

"I've never been happier," Gunard said, as his men loomed into view, joining Jaran and Savarna as they shuffled up beside their two guides. Svipdag was leaning on his spear, as Ivar held the torch out moving it from left to right. The flame was almost done, but neither man seemed worried.

"This is Deepwater," Svipdag grunted.

"That's original." Jaran glanced sideways at Savarna, who appeared lost in thought.

"It's bottomless," Svipdag continued. "And best avoided, as the water is icy to touch."

"Bottomless …?" Jaran said, unimpressed. Both the oldsters turned to look at him.

"Aye, Jaran Hrelgisson, do you doubt my word?" Svipdag's eyes glinted in the torchlight.

Jaran shrugged, and the old warrior turned away.

Ivar grinned at him. "The water's above sea level," he said. "But not much. Svipdag tried swimming it once, didn't you?" Svipdag grunted. "He says it leads down through holes, and out to the wide cavern the old ones used to call Cradon Iwey."

"Don't mention that place," Svipdag snapped at Ivar and seemed edgy.

"I've heard that name somewhere before," Jaran said.

"Faerie Gate, we call it," Ivar said, ignoring Svipdag's glare. "It's where she came from, and others, more recently." His sharp eyes hinted at Jaran and Savarna.

"Be silent, Ivar," Svipdag said. "Your wagging tongue might see us dead. There are …" He shook his head. "Follow me," he beckoned. "There is a narrow track to the right of the water. The Edge, I call it. It leads to a waterfall. Our cavern lies behind that screen."

Jaran gripped Savarna's hand again as they followed the taciturn Svipdag and cheerful Ivar, with Gunard and company following behind. They reached the rim of the pool, the silent water expanding, dark and deep off to their right, and ahead as far as Jaran could see through that gloom.

The Edge was a rough ledge, a narrow shelf chiseled out from the cave wall, the water lapping against it. Jaran felt that icy damp seep through his boots and tingle his toes. He shivered. There was something sinister about that bitter, wet touch. Savarna slipped once. He caught her and hoisted her up before she hit the pool.

"We had best stay out of that," Jaran said. She nodded and smiled thanks.

After long minutes, they heard the distant rumble of cascading water. Jaran glimpsed a filigree of light spearing down from somewhere lost above. He suspected there must be another blowhole or crevice up there, the water rushing down.

"Time to get wet." Ivar grinned back at them as they reached the deafening surge of rainbow water. "Don't fret, 'tis good, honest rainwater trapped and stored from high above."

"I'll have to take your word for that," Jaran said, eyeing the waterfall warily. Svipdag had already vanished beyond. Ivar followed and disappeared beneath the waterfall. Jaran looked at Savarna.

"Ready?"

"On three," she said, grinning.

"One, two …" They hit the water running.

"You pair of buggers better get going," Rafin said to the young men fretting at the cave mouth. "Me and this wolf lass have things squared away nicely."

"Jaran said for us to stay and assist you," the fierce-eyed Tofei said. Rafin liked this lad. Bright, promising for a mortal, and a proper Northman to boot. He reminded him of a young Dorthar, though comelier and without the scars. The other lad wasn't so inspiring. Young Asmund looked out of his depth. *And they trusted you with the War Arrow? Hmm, we'll see.*

"Do as Rafin says," the woman rasped beside him. "You

cannot help us here, and she will be sniffing us out soon enough. Best you hurry back to that craft and get sailing."

Tofei nodded, tight-lipped. "As you wish, lady." He turned to his pale-faced companion. "You fit, Islander?"

"Yes." Asmund nodded. Rafin noticed how he squeezed the red War Arrow in his left hand, as though he meant to snap it in two.

"Be careful with that thing," Rafin said. "Break it, and no one will come."

"Bring back many fighting men," Unva added and turned away. "Gives them something to do," she said to Rafin, who waved his hand as the two young men departed, Tofei leading the way back down through the woods.

"You shouldn't be so cynical."

"That handsome one called me a lady," Unva snorted.

"Boy's deluded," Rafin told her, and she clipped his ear with a finger. Rafin grinned. "It's been a long time, Wolf Child."

"Not long enough," she said, but the smile gave her away. "How is the wonderful Gamalene?"

"Angry with me, as usual."

"That's understandable," Unva said. "A fine woman you have there. Too good for you. But dwarf wives have ever been superior to their husbands. All you oafs talk about is smoking and counting gold, brewing more ale."

"What else is there?"

She cuffed his ear again. Rafin took the hint and left to squat on the ridge above the cave mouth. A clear, bright day, a skylark warbling above in the blue. Rafin lit his pipe and leaned back, drawing in a deep breath and blowing out three perfect circles. "I'm for having a nap, lass," he said. "Shout if you need anything?"

"Stay alert, you slug," she yelled up to him. "No napping." Rafin feigned a snore. He closed one eye, allowing the other scan the hillside and woods below. He wouldn't worry about Gorvaron sneaking up on him. Giants weren't the subtle type.

After half an hour smoking and idling, Rafin got curious as to how the woman was getting on. He jumped back down and saw her crouched at the entrance with a stem of rosemary and sage in either hand.

"You bring those weeds from Faerie?"

"My cave at Dunnehine," she said. "My travel bag is Faerie-proof, as well as watertight." She flashed him a lovely smile. "Nearly done—just the sealing runes and we should be good to join them at the Deepwater Edge."

"How long will they hold."

"Against Sheega's mind bolts?" Unva shrugged. "A week, ten days? Long enough for Svipdag to help me with the next task."

"That old wastrel tosser? I thought there was something canny about him."

"Svipdag has some spell knowledge," Unva said. "I saw it in his eyes, the moment he appeared from in there." She hinted the cavern. "I'm curious as to where he got it from. The man's traveled far, I'd guess."

"I'm sure you'll squeeze that out of the poor fellow."

She waved her hands about, the torched herbs trailing smoke. Rafin sneezed as the strong tang of rosemary got up his nose. "That should work," Unva said, hushing him as he snorted a second time.

"What are you hoping to achieve with this Svipdag character?"

Unva turned and grinned at him. "The Final Moon," she

said showing those lovely teeth again. "We need to bring it forward in time, shrink six weeks into two."

"I'm sorry I asked." Rafin scratched his head and relit his pipe.

SHEEGA FELT HER HAND STING AS IT STRUCK HIS FACE. Finvar hit the floor and banged his head. She kicked him as he tried to rise and stamped down on his head, causing his nose to crack against the floor and blood ooze onto her rug. He tried to speak, but she stamped again. He lay still until, weary, she stepped back and allowed the wretch recover to his knees.

Finvar rocked back and forth and stared at her in moody silence.

"Is that it—*she's gone?* You're not saying more?"

"I don't know the reason." Finvar spat blood from his mouth. She kicked him again, this time in the belly, causing him to double up. "We argued, and she was angry. She left. That's it."

"Think you can play your stupid games with me, Hawk-spittle? *Do you?*" A third kick sent him sprawling again.

I wish you wouldn't do that.

The voice came from above her head. Sheega glanced up and saw blazing ruby eyes gazing down at her.

"You need to talk to your scion, Lofhi—else I cut out his eyes and remove his tongue for starters. To sate my growing irritation. Gunsala was *my* guest."

Aye, well, shit happens, the voice above her head said. *Not Finvar's fault. Boy's in love, therefore stupid as a troll in water. And that wench is headstrong, has a mind of her own.*

"That's the point, isn't it, Trickster? Gunsala's feeble girly mind isn't her own. She's acting on Elanion's orders. I needed her contained here, Lofhi. Or better, dead. Instead, she's out there searching for Hrelgisson."

Ranning's sulking giant can eat Gunsala, for all I care, the coaly voice said. Her eyes glanced across to the prone figure bleeding on the floor. Sheega pulled a hot poker from the fire and walked towards him.

"She's a Vulkorye, however stupid," she hissed at the eyes smoking above the rafters. "This shithead needs to start talking and tell me where she's gone."

He doesn't know where she's gone—does he? Roaming the island, no doubt, like a moon-gazey heifer. What's the matter with you, Deyna? Are you cranky because wayward Ranning left you to dry up inside? I could oblige there, use Fin's throbbing yardstick to sate your need.

The laughter had her turning and hurling the poker up at the smoke congealing above her head. The rod stuck in a beam and quivered.

That was unnecessary. I was trying to be helpful.

"Fuck you, Lofhi."

You only have to ask.

Sheega turned and glared at Finvar again. "You had better start telling me where your wench went. You might think he'll protect you from me, but I can still hurt you."

Which also hurts me.

"Then you get it out of him, Lofhi. I'm away walking."

Lots of walkies today. Go quell that restlessness and cool off. Me and young Finvar will happily stoke your fires when you return.

Sheega ignored the laughter; her eyes were still on Finvar. He sat cross-legged and stared over at her, mouth and nose bleeding, a faint smile in his eyes.

"You want me to hurt you, don't you?"

"Lofhi might not like that."

"Perhaps I don't care what Lofhi likes." Sheega stared up at the rafters, but the red eyes had vanished. "Get your wits together, Hawk-man. I'll expect prompt answers when I return. Or else Lofhi and all of Yffarn won't be able to stop me cutting you open from gizzard to groin."

She turned, leaving him staring after her, and departed the hall with a swirl of her cloak. Outside, dusk had filled the sky. She walked briskly down the lakeshore and sat for a time on the hard, cold ground. She swayed back and forth, as she pushed back her hood and ran long fingers through her wind-swept hair.

They were all conspiring against her. Her enemies and their pawns, the mortals. She needed new allies. Aside from Garrosk and the few witch-men who'd survived Dunnehine. She only had Gantallian. *Not much help there.* But Valkador held a few secrets. The island hated Sheega, and she was blocked from straying near Gronteyer, lest the vengeful ghosts find her again—as they had before after Hrund and Hrelgi's murder. Cradon Iwey alone was safe. She'd dare not venture deep inside those caves. Even her sorcery held no traction there.

Hrelgisson was hiding deep inside that mountain. That red-haired bitch Savarna, too. Protected by the ghosts of his ancestors and the island itself. Unva was there, too. The sly vixen had got through Faerie without her knowing. Obviously she'd had help. *The Traveler?* Perhaps even one of the Brothers. Sheega felt a stab of fear. Was Tyho near? She'd heard Kullaan's mighty tread coming from the far side of the mountain a few days back. *If only I had my old strength.* But she would soon, once their champion was dead. *Hah! I have only to wait a little longer.* But the waiting was so annoying.

Sheega needed Ranning in more ways than one. His creature was missing. Gorvaron seemed as unreliable as his brothers, however much bigger he was. And Unva had shored up the caves with a blocking rune, so she couldn't even glimpse inside. Sheega would shatter those codes, but that would take time when she could be doing something more fun, like grilling Finvar Droll over the stoked fire.

What also worried Sheega was what else Unva planned next, and who had put her up to this in the first place? She didn't have to get involved but must have sensed a chance to get at Sheega before she came for her, the bitch.

I need to think clearly.

She'd been wrong to goad Lofhi, even though he'd angered her. That artful godling hated his brothers and the Traveler more than anyone, *even her.* But Lofhi's temper, when roused, was worse that Sheega's. She'd been overzealous with Finvar. Lofhi hadn't seemed to mind her beating him, but if she had taken it further …?

I have to find another way.

Gunsala had acted like Savarna before her. Both young women had slipped Sheega's nets. Was she losing her touch? *I've never been stronger.* Sheega knew that wasn't true, but saying it made her feel better.

She left the lake behind as clouds mustered in the west. She walked toward the distant surge of ocean. Not her usual path. This time, Sheega took the woods to the spot where Hrelgi's deserted cottage sparkled in moonlight.

She walked close and saw the face in the window framed by moonlight. "So that's where you're hiding, Bera? You can't save him from me." The face faded and was gone. Sheega walked on. *Another ghost waiting hungrily for me to cross.*

But not all the spirits were enemies. Some were her slaves. The dozen or so cravens who had ridden out with Erlund on that fateful day. The hunters of the Whitebear. Those thanes who'd helped their leader bring Hrelgi low and had stabbed their cold spears into his hide, as Erlund took his brother's head for a trophy.

They were cursed and trapped, and for a long time had been forgotten—by her included. A few had escaped to Leeth and beyond. She knew one lost soul was hiding in Gronteyer. A harmless, mad fool. She'd allowed Svipdag be, knowing that it would be risky for her to seek him out directly.

But most of Erlund's proud young warriors were still where she had left them, as insurance. *It pays to plan ahead.* She walked the beach, passing her witching pole, and making for the dull point the Islanders had called the Nub. From that bleak headland, she gazed for long moments out at the far-ranging line of cliffs that marked Leeth in the distance.

I need new allies.

Faerie was close. She could feel its presence in the atmosphere and glimpse their eldritch narrow faces with her witch sight, as their armies gathered and swarmed against the World Gate, waiting for the lost bell to toll one final time. But Sheega couldn't help with that, else the gods pounce on her. Those allies would have to wait. Slaves could be useful in the meantime.

Mind working fast, Sheega returned to the lake, as the night deepened and wolf voices called out from the forest. She wondered if Unva was with them, but put aside spiteful thoughts, lest her concentration lapse.

Sheega gazed down at her boots. She mouthed a spell-rune

and watched as spikes broke out through the soles, allowing her walk out onto the lake.

She walked as the moon waxed white and gibbous above. Time was passing—so swiftly, far too slow. How she envied Faerie. Aldorian and his kin had no fear of time. A concept they couldn't comprehend. The Faerie realms existed beyond time's narrow confines. The trick was allowing Aldorian and his troll allies through when that time was on her side.

Sheega stopped at the middle of the lake and traced a line on the ice with a razor-sharp fingernail. A crack appeared. She saw dead faces gazing up at her. She unclipped the broach from her gown, and let it drop into the ice crack. Naked, she watched as the dead eyes cracked open all at once and a skeletal hand closed over the sinking broach.

"You poor souls have suffered long enough," Sheega said. "Rise up and join me! I will free you when your last task is complete." The glazed eyes stared up at her, scanning her body, drinking in the naked flesh.

"Rise up, I say. Come to your queen! Share my bed, as your master once did. Each of you in turn, or all at once. Come, guard me from my foe."

You bewitched us, tricked us.

The briny voices drifted up through the ice.

"Alas, yes, and I regret that." She saw them wriggle beneath the ice, like white bloated maggoty worms, rising up. "But let me make amends tonight. Repay you—as I did Erlund, your Jarle."

King Erlund has crossed—we felt the shadow of his passing.

"Again, regrettable. What choice had I? He was weak and failed me. You have much to gain by serving me again. The vengeful ghosts of your island hate you as much as me, for murdering your Jarle's favorite son."

That was your doing.

Sheega saw the faint shape of a man floating across the ice toward where she stood. She waited. Others drifted up like heavy steam, joining him.

"Yes, it was—but does that matter? You are trapped for eternity under that ice, unless you give me reason to free your souls. I promise I shall, if you help me one last time, and guard the hall from my enemies."

The shadowy misty vapors surrounded her. Their icy breath soaked her skin. She saw the dead swell and ebb in lust.

"You shall have everything you desire," Sheega told them. "I will make you warm again, inside. You'll be men, as you once were. *Warriors.* Come, return with me to the Great Hall and claim your reward." She turned and scooped up her cloak, crossing the ice swiftly without checking if they followed.

"You could have intervened earlier," Finvar muttered, as he hunched painfully by the fire, the crackle of flame smarting his eyes.

I wanted to see what you did, how you'd stand up to her.

"She could have killed me with that fucking poker."

Well, I would have stopped that, wouldn't I?

"Would you? Maybe you don't care? And don't give me that 'when you suffer, I suffer, too.' We both know that's bollocks. And you most likely enjoy the pain."

I sense a certain attitude this evening.

"You think?"

Gunsala let you down. I know it's sad. Women always do that. We have each other, though.

"Go away."

Nope, I'm staying put until she returns. I want to hear what your plans are. How you're going to implement them. Perhaps you sent Gunsala out to stab Hrelgisson? That would have been my suggestion. That way you needn't do your own wetwork. And she's a Vulkorye, albeit an inexperienced one. Those violent wenches don't mind who they kill. Trust me, I know.

"I'd sooner not trust you."

Don't be peevish. You need to do something that convinces her you're onboard. I'll help you when I can, but Tyho and the other bastards will be after me, and Sheega—if you stall. It's up to you to kill your big friend. Simple task. Do that and you're free. Forever. That's a long time.

"I said I would."

Ah, yes—but I think you're having second thoughts. I need to be confident of your loyalty to our noble cause. Can you imagine what would happen if you let me—or her—down, Finvar?

"It wouldn't be pleasant."

Pain and punishment beyond the confines of your weak, mortal shell. But have a cheer—I know you're my boy. Oh, look, she's back—and she's brought some fishy corpses to join the party.

18

THE SECOND BREACH

Vian cursed as he witnessed the massacre. Cul Baja's men were being cut to pieces. A dozen lay hacked or dying and the wall was breached in two places.

Roile was there, the young Cul screaming hatred beside him, tears blurring his face. Uzcara had gained the wall with two score of his men. He'd jumped down after swinging free of the rope ladder and had started hacking and slicing through the Shen defense, as though he was harvesting wheat.

Vian yelled. He couldn't get over there, as the second breach had spilled men toward the spot where he stood, bow in hand again, loosing shafts and dodging arrows fired at him. For the second time in minutes, he tossed his bow aside. The nearest came running at him, scimitars swinging over their heads. Vian summoned calm. He couldn't help Roile or the young Cul. That was down to them. Frustration wouldn't help today. Breathe … slow and steady. *Relax, let it find you.* He slid the Jian blades free from their harness.

The first Card leaped at him, his scimitar arcing across at Vian's neck.

Vian danced to his left, skewered the man, piercing his mesh mail below the armpit. He screamed and fell away. A second Card swung in, stabbing up and hard.

Vian blocked with a downward slam of one Jian and sliced up with the other, cutting through the Card's neck and lower face as his chain visor fell away. Vian jumped over him and scissor-sliced with both swords, decapitating the man behind and slicing the next one's neck, causing him to fall and quiver like a hooked-dry fish on his comrade's corpse.

A spear jabbed at him.

Vian blocked, spun around stabbed out. Another man fell. He could hardly see, or hear their screams. He felt at ease, in the moment—the dance of death upon him. He smiled, moving forward, Jians sliding, cutting, stabbing out. The clashing song of steel. Men yelled and tumbled, weapons jabbed out at him. Vian knocked them aside, moved forward again. *Lunge, stab, hew, slice.*

And kill! He stopped, panting, saw the corpses piled around him. *How many?* He couldn't count.

"Roile!" Vian's voice was hoarse, and his vision blurred by the sweat streaming down his face. He unbuckled his helmet and tossed it away, allowing his hair spill free and catch the sun. The fighting had congealed into a mass of bodies thrust close, as more Cards had leaped over the wall, hearing Uzcara's shouts. The Shen defenders had rallied, bunching over and forcing them back.

Vian glimpsed Roile cutting out with his sword.

"Roile!"

"Need help here!" the man yelled back, as Vian vaulted over the slain and ran to assist him. He crashed into the back of two Cards as they pressed against Roile, slicing through one's hamstrings and stabbing the other in the thigh. They fell. Vian dispatched them with a backward slice.

"We can't hold—these twats are useless," Roile yelled in his ear. He sliced across, cutting away a man's face and taking half his helmet, denting his curved sword badly in the process.

"Run!" Vian shouted back.

"What?" Roile glared at him, wild-eyed.

"Get help, and another sword—looks like you've broken that one." Vian jammed a thrust from a spearman. He slammed his shoulder into the enemy, while Roile kicked out at his groin. The spearman lurched forward, Vian sliced down and the head rolled away. "Go!" He yelled at Roile, who nodded and made to run back to the stairs.

"Stay alive!" Roile yelled back before vanishing beneath the arch.

Vian cut and sliced, stepped forward, stabbed again. The sweat was running down his face, and he kept blinking it out of his eyes. Cards surrounded him—Vian could see the Shen were crumbling again, damn them. This time would prove disastrous, as more Cards clambered down from the ladders and soon outnumbered the defenders.

"Uzcara!" Vian yelled the name as he jumped forward, slicing across with one Jian and out with the other, taking three Cards and dispatching a fourth with a lethal backwards strike.

"Let me through," he heard someone shout. *Uzcara?* Vian sliced again. This time they jumped back out of reach, parting to allow someone through. Uzcara strode out to greet him, a heavy tulwar in one hand and iron buckler gripped in the other.

"Here you are," Uzcara's metal wolf face stared at him. Time froze and the Cards watched as Vian felt the sweat drip down from his face, puddling the stone at his feet. "Racara was my favorite brother."

Vian slowed his breath again, lowering the Jian blades. Uzcara's men were holding back—he was grateful for that. Despite their faults, these Cards believed in honor on the battlefield.

"Have you nothing to say before I cut out your heart?"

Vian smiled. "I have no words for cowards who hide their faces from me." He folded his arms, the Jian slanting out like giant scissors. Uzcara didn't respond, but he passed his buckler to a man behind him and slid a hand beneath his helm. He unbuckled the helmet and tossed that and the visor aside. Vian saw a hard face, half-moon scar under the left eye, a second one through the lower lip. Black, oily hair and thick brows. Dark, cruel eyes. A battle-captain in his prime.

"That's better," Vian said. "Now I know how ugly you are." He shifted sideways as the tulwar swung out at him with dazzling speed, its thick, curved blade trapping the sun.

Vian danced the other way as Uzcara swung again, yelling expletives and spitting. The man tossed the small shield across to his Ragan. Uzcara caught it deftly with his right hand, the tulwar still swinging in the left.

Vian jumped back out of reach, allowing Uzcara to move forward again. "I have him, boys," he told his men. He grinned across at Vian and started swinging the heavy blade in rhythmic circlers. "Can you guess what I'm going to do to you, Red Hair?"

Vian stepped back again, playing for time. The longer he could make this encounter last, the more chance the Shen would rally and Roile would return with help. Providing there was help to be found. But it was fruitless dwelling on that.

Strange how the mind works at moments like this. He smiled at Uzcara, stepping back again.

Uzcara grinned back at him. "Why not run?" he taunted, switching hands, the tulwar to his right, shield across to his left, faster than the eye could follow, then back again.

Vian glanced along the wall, feigning boredom. He saw Cul Baja, his face bloody and eyes wild, hair loose and helmet missing. There were twenty or so Chiang men bunched beside him. Like the enemy, they were awaiting this outcome.

I need to impress those poor lads. Vian lowered the Jian slowly and took a deep breath. Uzcara held his arms out wide, leaving his broad chest open, as though inviting Vian to attack. Vian held still.

"Fuck this," Uzcara spat. "I've had more trouble with wagon wenches." He jumped forward with a viscous yell, slicing across with the heavy blade, while slamming the buckler hard at Vian's face.

Vian jumped back again. This time he answered with his Jian, slicing across and down with even strikes.

Uzcara deflected one with the buckler, the other with his sword. He rammed his body into Vian, shoved the iron shield up at Vian again.

Vian twisted, sliced up close, sawing through the narrow gap showing between Uzcara's gauntlet and mail shirt. The cut ran deep, severing Uzcara's right hand. He blinked in surprise at the blood spurting from his arm.

No craven, Uzcara swung at him with the tulwar. His men were yelling, about to rush Vian, seeing their Ragan hurt. Uzcara mouthed a curse and slipped in his own blood. He staggered, slipped again and fell face-first on the stone. The Cards surrounded him. A half-dozen leaped across at Vian, their eyes wild behind the mesh visors.

Vian retreated until his back was against the gatehouse wall. They surrounded him, a dozen or more. Three had spears. He nodded and readied the Jians.

I'm sorry, Rasnei. Vian closed his eyes.

Shouting, new voices from behind. Men screaming. Vian opened his eyes and saw the Cards had left him as arrows were raining down on them from the distant walls. He glimpsed Matax up there with the huge Shen, Lin Gu. The Cards were in turmoil. Cul Baja had rallied his men, and they were falling on the confused foe.

A Card officer yelled, and his men dragged the unconscious Ragan and pitched his body over the wall, where other men caught him below. The remainder ran to follow, but Matax's archers punctured them from above.

Vian ran forward, killing and maiming with his Jians, as the last of the Cards fell back and jumped free of the walls. A few gained their horses and got away, including the knot that had gathered around Uzcara's body. These carried him off out of bowshot.

Vian helped the newly confident Cul Baja clear the wall of enemies, as Matax's archers took out any Cards in range. A good number had made it back to the woods and sat their horses in a circle, as some men attended the prone Ragan.

Vian saw Matax gazing down at him. He waved thanks. The general waved back and ordered his men away. Lin Gu stood for a time before nodding and turning away. Vian wiped sweat and blood from his face. He felt his legs buckle beneath him.

"We beat them." He glanced up to see Cul Baja grinning down at him.

"You did well," Vian told the Cul, as his heart thudded in his chest.

"You killed Uzcara," Cul Baja said. "And these others, so many. You are a legend ..."

"Bought us some time, here at the harbor," Vian said, as weariness washed over him. It had been too close. Was he losing his knack? Uzcara had nearly defeated him. It was the Ragan's overconfidence that had allowed Vian get that close and score the winning blow. But he should have followed up with a final strike. Ragan Uzcara would be back. Even missing a hand, he was a foe to be wary of.

Vian felt giddy, sick. He closed his eyes for a time, as the voices and movement stilled on the walls. He could hear the Cards yelling, the sound of hoofbeats cantering off. *I'm so tired.* He blinked and saw Cul Baja leaning over him with a flask of cool water.

"Thanks," Vian said, and drank deeply. He felt revived by the water but still weary. "You did well, Cul Baja, your men too. I'm proud of you all."

"We defeated them," the young Cul said as Vian drained the flask.

"They'll be back," Vian said. "I hurt Uzcara badly. But his pride will cause him more pain than that missing hand. He'll stop at nothing next time."

"THREE AND A HALF RAGANS LEFT, AND THAT'S COUNTING the one in Cardalis," Gurtei said with a grin, as Roile informed him what had happened at the Sea Gate. They'd watched from the barbican as Uzcara's riders had carried their leader over to a cart where his body was lain. Gurtei had seen Casca ride over and gaze down at his brother. The last remaining Ragan, Calgara, had stayed and sat his horse glaring up at the walls.

"What will they do next?" Lin Gun asked him. The three of them held command of the high keep, while Dorthar had accompanied the empress to ensure she got some rest. The exhausted Vian had joined them in the palace, as the immediate danger had passed.

"They'll rally and start over," Gurtei said, noting how the ballistae had been pulled back out of cannon range. The walls had been pummeled, but apart from the one breach—stemmed by Lin Gu and Matax's melee—the Cards had failed to make a sizeable dent.

"Casca needs a victory," Gurtei said. "His men will lose spirit else. Both Racara and Casla were popular. Uzcara being wounded leaves just the Ran, and Calgara, the youngest and least experienced Ragan."

Matax joined them and stood gazing at the enemy.

"I thought you were taking a break, general—you look like you need one," Gurtei said. "We've got things covered, here."

"I can sleep standing up," Matax said, shaking his head. "Casca will hit us with everything, and before this day is over. Uzcara's men will have told him what happened at the Sea Gate. Lucky you warned me in time," he said to Roile, who shrugged. "That could have gone badly for us."

"What are they doing?" Lin Gun said, pointing.

Gurtei blinked and gazed out. "They're withdrawing." He couldn't believe his eyes. The entire Card army had started moving back across the plain, leaving the deserted machines and rams abandoned as they marched or rode back to their camp.

"Perhaps Uzcara's dead," Matax said, blowing out air.

"They're up to something," Roile said, hawking and spitting blood over the parapet wall.

HIS ARMY HAVING WITHDRAWN, CASCA STARED DOWN AT his brother and tried not to smirk. "First Racara, now you. Oh, and fucking Casla got himself killed, too, while you were absent, brother. It seems like I'll have to do everything myself. Shame, about your injury, Uz. I know you preferred the feel of your left hand."

Uzcara glared up at him, trying to speak.

"You're angry—that's good," Casca continued. "Rest some, get your strength back. After that, you can ride back west and join Genza. He'll find something for you to do, a job suitable for redundant cripples."

"Fuck you, Casca," Uzcara spat back.

Casca smiled and left Uzcara with the field physicians. He walked out and watched the camp settle for evening, strolling through the tents and campfires as men gazed up at him. He spoke to a few, ensuring the captains knew what to expect.

Casca was happy today. Uzcara was neutered and one thing less to worry about. Better, he'd heard from Genza, receiving a coded bird this afternoon. The Vendeli were sending ships and men, his brother wrote. The shaman, Octaxa, had told Genza that they'd set sail from Soloza a week earlier and should be here in a matter of days. It was all the encouragement he'd needed to change his plans.

No need to rush things, as those ships would blockade the harbor and they could squeeze the enemy from both directions. Of course, if Uzcara had worked harder and not got himself crippled, the harbor could be theirs today. But aside

Calgara—and he was easy to handle—Casca had none left to challenge him. That was reassuring, and he was happy to let things take their course.

The ballistae and rams had failed so far. The walls were too damn thick, the city proving more resilient than he'd expected. They would be pleased with themselves, those Shen. They had done well so far.

That was about to change.

He waited until dusk and watched the men prepare.

Calgara's big chance.

He'd promised the boy he would have that city all for himself. He hadn't told him about the letter from Genza. Calgara was all fired up about his brothers. A night raid would achieve one of two things: Breach the walls by morning, or lose him his little brother. Either option worked for Casca.

Night fell deep and black around him. The cicadas drummed in the fields where he sat his horse, a score of riders attending his needs.

Calgara approached from the camp, and behind him rode his company. One thousand riders, chosen by the boy's captains. Volunteers who wanted to avenge Casla and Racara, and the insult done to Uzcara. The same men who had been secretly criticizing his methods, Casca assumed.

"You came to see me off." Calgara grinned at him as he reined in next to Casca. "Are you sure you don't want to be part of this glory, Casca? That city will fall tonight."

"Well, if so, send someone back with a Shen wench. I'll come and congratulate you, once I've finished with her. Off you go, little brother. Ta Shen's yours for the taking. Happy hunting."

Calgara flashed him another grin beneath his helmet. He ordered his three hundred volunteers muffle their horses' hoofs as they rode out across the plain, armor hidden by dark cloaks, one rider in twenty carrying a rope ladder. Casca watched them fade from view. It was Calgara's chance to shine. Either that or get himself killed.

The Ran sat his horse and waited as a servant brought him grog. Quiet night.

Here we go! Casca clapped, seeing the flare shoot out and pierce the dark. The Shen would be caught like bugs in a jar.

RASNEI WIPED SLEEP FROM HER EYES. NOLENZES HAD woken her, as she'd told him to if the situation were to change. She'd left Vian asleep in the palace rooms. He wouldn't be happy about that when he stirred, but he'd been exhausted when she'd caught up with him after the struggle at the Sea Gate. He'd wounded Uzcara, the most feared of the Ragans. And another brother was dead, thanks to the remarkable feats of Lin Gu—a man the whole city was talking about. Matax had reported that news back to her. Lin Gu had almost single-handedly seen off the attack when Casla's raiders breached the hole in the wall.

She'd been well pleased, and even happier discovering Vian was unhurt. She'd slept well, until Nolenzes' soft touch shook her shoulder.

"They're back," he'd said. She hadn't hesitated.

The gonfalons flapped high above Rasnei's scarf-wrapped head, as the clash of steel reached her from further along the wall. The night attack—though unexpected—had failed to achieve the surprise the Cards had hoped for. Gurtei had been vigilant, his guards taking double stag all along the walls. He said it was Roile who'd convinced him they were up to something and would be back sooner than expected.

For once, she was grateful to the surly Cutter. She'd thanked Roile, and he'd been quite taken with that. Matax appeared beside her.

"Did they breach?"

"Ladders again, empress," he nodded. "A large troop must have returned secretly soon after that withdrawal. Gurt's men didn't notice them until that flare went up—by that time, the night raiders were already scaling the walls. Same place as yesterday. Good that you were vigilant." He nodded to Gurtei.

"How many?" Rasnei asked.

"Hard to say, but they're eager, and our men are hard-pressed pushing them back."

"Is it worth a sortie from the gates?" Roile suggested. "Get them from behind, those who haven't climbed yet."

"Too risky," Gurtei said. "We have our best fighters there, among them Lin Gu and Dorthar."

"I thought that Northman was assigned to you, empress," Matax said.

"He was off-duty drinking in the Violet Girl at the time the flare was spotted," Gurtei said.

"Drinking? It's past midnight," Rasnei said, feeling angry that Dorthar had sloped off. She'd assumed he'd be here, or else waiting for her at the palace when she'd left.

"He's a Northman," Gurtei said with a shrug. "I ordered the taverns stay open for night watch, providing food and sustenance. A break from the walls, with orders of prompt flogging should anyone get drunk."

"I need to see what's happening," Rasnei said. "It's useless standing here in the dark."

"I'm on my way back there," Matax said. "I'll send swift word, once I see what's happening."

Matax vanished below, and Rasnei leaned out over the parapet trying to see. There were shouts and the clash of steel, but the moon was hidden by cloud, making it hard to mark how many enemies were out there.

Was this a night raid or full-on attack?

Gurtei saw her expression and smiled reassuringly. "I think it's the young Ragan, Calgara," he said. "Can't see Casca attacking after dark. He's probably sent that boy with some hotheads to avenge his brother. Hopefully Lin Gu will send Calgara to join them in Yffarn."

"Let us hope so indeed," Rasnei replied with a nod.

19

BENEATH THE MOON

GUNSALA CLEARED the woods as the questing moon rode out from dark clouds. It was warmer, remarkably so. She felt hot in her wool coat and heavy boots, the clothes Sheega had left for her after their first night. Gunsala had half-expected them to vanish or evaporate from her body like poisonous vapor once she cleared the witch's realm. Surely this gush of warmth must mean she was out of Sheega's reach, at least for the moment.

It would be dark soon. The wolves would gather, and goodness knows what else was out there. Sendings seeking her? Sheega's witch-men? She'd heard grunting and scrapings and seen shadows during her brief time at the hall. Nothing tangible. Finvar had told her all about the creature Stoon. There were others on this island—had to be. Hopefully not hunting her.

As Gunsala walked, she thought about when she had first seen Finvar. She'd been hunted then, too. *But I was the prey that time. Today, I'm a Vulkorye. My destiny is to save him, save them all.* She picked up her pace, fresh urgency driving her faster.

Then why are you running away? The accusing voice in her head demanded. She ignored the warrior inside her. Sometimes you had to retreat, so that you could advance in a different direction. Or be like a willow in a rainstorm, bend and give—survive the blow.

But how could they hope to survive? She broke into a trot, her strong legs pushing her forward.

Close by, the shoulder of the mountain loomed dark. To her north, she could see the moonlight shimmering on distant waves. *Which way to go?* Where were Gunard and the others? She guessed there were homesteads at the far end of the island. But how to get there, and at night? Dare she chance the mountain slopes, hoping for shelter, perhaps a cave? It was that or walk the beaches for hours, exposed and with no shelter.

Gunsala recalled when they'd skirted the island from above, as Finvar flew her to distant Wynais. That seemed like months ago. She'd glimpsed dark cliffs before Sheega's fret had swallowed them. Gunsala guessed that they must have been on the western side of the island where the seas surged rougher than the rolling fields and fertile regions on the leeward coast.

She chose the mountain, her sturdy legs carrying her up through more trees and beyond, to where a wide swath of purple heather and yellow furze sighed in warming winds. She felt her hair lift, and the last evening sun smiled on her skin. Summer was back. That gave her hope. If the seasons could defeat the Ice Witch, then so could they. Smiling, Gunsala turned and gazed back through the woods.

Silence. No wolf howls. No pursuit. Perhaps Sheega hadn't

returned to the hall? She daren't think about Finvar waiting alone for that terrible woman.

You'd better not hurt him, witch.

Gunsala forced that image away. *Keep moving.* To mope about her decision was pointless and weak. It wouldn't help her man. *I'll find your hero, Fin.* But where to start looking?

As night fell, she noticed the gibbous moon following her as it rose up behind the trees to her left. Six weeks. How could they possibly hold out that long? And yet her Vulkorye instinct had sensed something in Sheega that she hadn't expected. The witch was getting desperate. Time was running short, and her enemies were still at large.

The gods were stirring, Tyho and His brother—she no longer felt the terror thinking about those two. She was Elanion's champion. Chosen by the Emerald Queen to stop the witch, allow Finvar to thwart the evil Lofhi, and his friend to kill Sheega. Everything was linked, the moon told her as his white face watched her progress alone on that mountain.

She sought shelter when dark clouds stole the moon, and a colder breeze turned her face around. Gunsala crawled into a dense fold of bracken where a shoulder of the mountain rose up from a long, climbing valley.

Exhausted, she dozed for a time. Waking with a start as the moon remerged from cloud, she heard the shuffling of heavy feet. Something very large was abroad in the night.

She missed her sword, hidden somewhere in Sheega's hall. Gunsala kept still and silent, the heavy tread passing close to where she rested and faded off down the valley. She crawled free of the bracken and peeped out in the moonlight. Night had settled deep and dark.

She almost jumped when a voice called out of the dark. A heavy, angry roar. Almost like a bear, and yet sounding more human. There it was again, and this time the wolves joined in, howling and barking down in the distant woods, as though they were scared of this stomping night ganger.

Gunsala looked down the valley, her eyes making out movement. The creature was crashing through undergrowth hidden by trees. She watched for several minutes until she saw the figure framed by moonlight. A giant. He was swaying as though drunk and bore a huge tree trunk that must serve as a club. He was walking toward the distant woods, those she'd cleared yesterday.

One of Sheega's creatures, no doubt about that. Perhaps half a mile away and moving off. But what if it came back? Found her tracks or took the scent? She dared not lie here any longer, taking that chance.

Nor did she want to. The Vulkorye inside Gunsala surged with anger. That part of her wanted to run down and confront the monster. She quelled her rage and channeled it into climbing swiftly out of her shelter and running, half-hopping, through the springing heather, hare-nimble and fast.

She reached a ridge of rock and clambered over. Gunsala was out of sight and well above the place where she'd rested. She gazed down from that ridge. The giant had gone, and the wolf voices grown still. The moon was over water, having left her behind. She had reached that part of the mountain where heather met splintered gray rock.

Cooler up here. She would have been cold if her body hadn't adjusted to Sheega's ice. Instead, she felt invigorated, strong, her body eager to move forward. She walked carefully at first, waiting until enough moonlight allowed her to climb higher on the mountain. Gunsala walked until the pre-dawn glow raised the gray cliffs of Leeth in the east. They looked so close—she felt like she could fly there, drift over. That made her think of Finvar again.

Keep moving, don't mope.

Gunsala felt a wash of weariness sweep through her, as the first morning sun warmed her body. She was high on the mountain. There were eagles circling to her right, and beyond them the ocean marched in glittering sparkles into the west.

Though eager to keep going, Gunsala climbed higher until she saw a ledge of rock where she could rest her body, just for a short time. Out of the wind, she lay nestled against sun-warmed stone as the island revealed itself below.

She hadn't meant to sleep, but when her eyes blinked open, Gunsala knew it was already afternoon. She'd quelled the rising panic as she stood and commenced jumping and stretching, warming her sleepy body. *Why did you allow me to sleep that long?* she asked the Vulkorye inside her.

Gunsala climbed out from the ledge and took the stiffer slopes up, as the high winds strengthened and tugged at her hair. Above, another ridge led across to a summit, its tip rimed with a crust of snow. She could see the second peak shrouded in its shadow. Real snow that, she thought. Not of the witch's design.

She was glad of her woolen clothes as she reached the ridge and walked precariously along toward the nearest crusty summit. That took her an hour, and it was almost evening by the time she crested the final ridge. There she stood for a long time, the wind in her hair, eagles gliding below. The clouds sliding over distant waves, casting shadow on the blue. The island called Valkador stretched like a tangled ribbon below and beyond.

She took in the sight, her keen eyes studying the terrain, near and far. To the east, the cliffs of Leeth gleamed in the sunshine like neat gray teeth. She saw the fjord where Skarness lay, scarce a dozen miles distant. Nothing on the water. She looked back north at the haze surrounding Sheega's hall, the ice-covered lake and the dark woods surrounding them. She thought of Finvar again and drove the worry from her mind.

Gunsala turned away, gazing over the mountain's northern flanks past the second peak. She saw tangled woods and heather, the odd stream cutting ribbons down through. She followed the island's coastline, clearly visible from way up here.

Valkador appeared cut like a rough diamond, wider in the center where the mountain reared tall, and tapering off to points at either end. She gazed south and saw where the sea met the island's southern point in a crash of hooked spume. Gunsala descried the studded squares of what must be villages or settlements. Closer, far below, and to her right, a deep bay glistened in sunlight. Gunsala's eyes were drawn to the center of that bay. She sensed a power reaching out from something hidden down there. She sensed danger, too.

I need to get moving.

She left the peak and started trotting as best she could down through the twist of rock and snow-crusted scree. There were more trees far below, and what looked like cave entrances where deer tracks cut sideways. Gunsala had nearly reached the woods when she heard distant voices carried up on the wind.

She squatted, shielded her eyes, and looked. Finally, she spotted two men walking briskly down toward the far woods. Past that, she saw Gunard's ship and felt a surge of joy. The red-and-white sail was neatly furled. Gunard must be with Jaran Saerk. She returned her gaze to the walkers and recognized one of the men by the way he held his head. Even at this far distance, she could see Tofei, Gunard's headstrong son. She watched as he and the other one vanished into the trees. Her gaze filtered back to the ship. She could see no one there. Close to shore, the ship bobbed and dipped in sparkle.

Gunsala made for the spot where she'd seen Tofei. She stopped in alarm when a short, stocky, black-clad figure blocked her path with steel arms folded, a face covered by spiky beard.

"You're a comely looking lassie, I must say." The voice was deep and gruff. "Is it wise to be out wandering Gronteyer alone?"

"Who are you, short fellow?"

The man was stunted, yet broad. On closer inspection, she saw that he wore a black ringmail suit with a hammer and double-headed axe hanging from his studded belt. An odd sight. The little man's steel arms were wrapped tight across his ample chest. He chewed at a pipe, his face a bristly tangle of hair and beard, both the color of rust.

"I'm Rafin the Smith," the man spat his pipe into a fist and flashed her a grin. "And who may you be, sunny lass?"

"What kind of creature are you, one of hers?"

"I find that very insulting. Were you a man, or warrior, I would hit you with my axe."

"I am woman and a warrior, and you would miss."

His eyes widened in surprise. She heard another voice, a woman's shout from somewhere hidden below.

"What's happening up there, dwarf?"

"I've met a new friend," Rafin answered, turning his head. Gunsala heard a distant curse. "Shall I ask her to join us for supper?"

"You're a dwarf?"

"No, I'm a fucking giant. *Please* ..."

"From Faerie ..." Gunsala chewed her lip.

"Again, no ... And I'm tired of these insults. I'm a king in Swartzheim. That's where the dwarves live, my dear. Not Faerie. Saying that offends me."

"I don't care," Gunsala replied. "I'm in a hurry. You had better fight me or get out my way, if you can't help me."

"I'd prefer an explanation of why you are running around on this mountainside like a love starved wood nymph?"

"I'm looking for Jaran Saerk," Gunsala said. "My ... *friend* needs to know where he is, so that ..."

"He can help him kill Sheega?"

"You're not one of her ... creatures?"

"I'm charmed, really I am. You, wench, have a tongue crueler than the elf maidens."

"I'm Gunsala," she said, deeming this strange little man was not her foe, at least not at the moment. "Why are you here, dwarf?"

"That's a long story, and best told by a fire with sizzling meat. Are you hungry?"

Gunsala's stomach answered for her. The dwarf grinned. "Come on, fierce Gunsala, there's someone else you need to meet. I suggest you show more respect in her presence—she's not as gentle as I."

Unva looked up as the dwarf appeared from the brush, a young and fierce-looking woman close behind him. "Who is that?" She stared hard at the girl, who met her gaze with steady blue eyes. Blonde, quite comely. Something unusual about her.

"An ungrateful waif I found wandering the mountain,"

Rafin shoved his pipe back in his mouth. "Meet Gunsala. She's a charm." He nudged the girl's arm. "This here is Unva, and she might not like you."

"What's that to me?" The girl's big eyes flashed at her.

"You're an angry little one, aren't you?" Unva walked across and reached out, stroking the girl's hair. She glared back but didn't move. "You have courage for a mortal. I see a rare strength in you, something *familiar*." The woman said nothing but looked edgy, uncertain. "Well, it seems we are not enemies, at least. Come share our fire and a some coney Rafin caught. It's nearly cooked, and we're almost finished here. You're lucky you've found us in time."

"She's looking for the big lad—says she's a friend of his friend."

"Lucky again." Unva smiled at her. "Come, let's eat. We can't linger here much longer—it isn't safe, and I've things to do elsewhere. Once you've filled your stomach, Gunsala, you can tell me how Finvar is holding out."

"How do you know about Fin?" The girl's face blanched white. She reached down for a weapon that wasn't there. "Are you …?"

"I'm not Sheega, *no*. I suspect you realize that, as I can smell her odor about you. Did you leave your lover at the great hall?"

"What?"

"Eat," Unva said, turning away and walking to where the fire roasted hot flesh. "It will be evening soon. We need to be gone before nightfall."

"Gone where?" the girl said, crouching by the fire and stuffing hot rabbit into her mouth.

"Tough little thing, isn't she?" Unva said to Rafin, as she watched the girl tear at the meat.

"Where is Jaran Saerk?" Gunsala asked between mouthfuls.

"In there." Unva hinted the cave entrance, and the girl's eyes flicked that way.

"I need to—"

"—I know, and you will shortly. We're heading that way next."

"I saw Tofei with another man," she said. "His father ..."

"With Saerk and Savarna."

"Who's that?"

Rafin snorted and coughed. "I cannot wait for you to find that out," he said, his eyes sparkling.

"It's done," Unva said, as she emerged from the sheet of waterfall, her tawny hair dripping, and the steel-clad Rafin hopping out beside her, his beard and hair drenched. Savarna saw another figure emerge. A girl, perhaps twenty. Fair-haired, with a determined look on her eyes.

"This is Gunsala," Rafin caught Savarna's eye and nodded at the girl beside him. The girl, Gunsala, glanced her way. She smiled after a brief hesitation, lost for words. Jaran loomed out from the cavern gloom and stared at the girl.

Her eyes widened. "You're him." She nodded, seemingly pleased with herself.

Savarna's brows crinkled with curiosity. *Who was this?*

"Am I?" Jaran looked sideways at Savarna, as Unva busied herself with preparations by the veil of water. She was muttering obscenities, and Rafin stood beside her adding encouragement. *What were they up to?* Funny how those two seemed to get on so well together. Savarna's eyes flicked back to the woman.

"Were you looking for Jaran?" Savarna asked her. She suspected this to be a village girl, though a tough-looking one who must have sought them out, and instead found Unva and Rafin at the cave entrance. If so, she was lucky—that giant would be back soon. The girl had been spared from a horrible fate.

"Gunsala!"

Savarna's head turned in shock. The thane, Gunard, stood behind them, having appeared with Ivar and the others after they'd been exploring the tunnels behind the waterfall, old Svipdag having explained there was another way out.

The girl's face spilt open in a wide grin. "I saw Tofei," she said, "making for your ship."

"They are taking the War Arrow to Leeth," Gunard said. "This is Gunsala," he said to Jaran, his eyes meaningful and large.

"You're …" Jaran stared hard at her.

"She's Finvar's girl," Savarna said with a smile.

"And you must be the woman he mentioned," the girl nodded looking at her hair. "The *tiger*, he called you."

Savarna raised a brow but didn't respond.

"Where is our friend?" Jaran asked Gunsala, his eyes hard.

"With the witch in her hall."

"Jaran's hall," Savarna corrected.

"We have to get him out," Jaran said.

"I think not." Unva looked up from her study of the runes she'd gathered from somewhere.

"He's my—"

"—friend. Yes, Jaran Saerk I know, and Finvar's doing what good friends do by looking out for you. Shut up and listen to this girl, who … I can sense knows much more than her pretty little face reveals."

Gunsala shot Unva a wild stare and nodded.

"Finvar wanted me to find you, Jaran Saerk," Gunsala told him. "He says that you must hold out here and stay your distance. That way, he can keep the witch busy—he has special—"

"—we know about the flying thing," Savarna interrupted.

"I don't mean that," Gunsala said, staring at her. "Finvar … Fin has … *is* …" She shook her head. "He wants you to know he's got things covered at the hall. He begged me to leave, as she would use me against him, *them*. I didn't want to." She looked at Savarna again. "And there's Lofhi." Gunsala said.

Unva's head shot up again hearing that name. "Is Lofhi here?" she asked the girl.

"Sometimes," she said. "It's complicated. Finvar …" Savarna watched as Gunsala looked at Jaran, who in turn glanced across at Unva. There was something about this girl, Savarna thought. A presence—some kind of power hidden in that plain country face. Not *Aikashi*, but similar. How intriguing.

"That it is," Unva agreed, waving a dismissive hand. "And about to get worse. Gunsala, you need to tell these good people everything you know about your … friend's condition, and what's happening at the hall."

"What about you—aren't you helping us?" Savarna asked Unva.

"Yes, but I can't do that here, Savarna. The caves are secure for a week, or more if we are lucky. It's a stopgap to give us time for the next, far harder task."

"And what is that?" Jaran asked her, his eyes still on Gunsala.

"I have to enter Cradon Iwey and pull forward the moon," Unva told him.

"You know you shouldn't ask her anything witchy," Rafin said. "Suffice to say I'm going with her."

"You two …?" Savarna crinkled her nose and looked strangely at Rafin.

"Are old acquaintances," Rafin said, rather stiffly. He turned to Jaran. "Right, now then, big lad, while Wolf-Girly's getting her spells ready—let's you and I discuss battle strategy. How many fighters have we with us, and what's your plan of attack?"

Savarna almost burst out laughing when she saw the bland expression on her lover's face.

RUNE GLIDED DOWN ONTO THE LOWERED DRAWBRIDGE AS the lightning-blue castle flickered and faded above and ahead. To move through Faerie takes many skills. Not only do you need the correct rune-keys, or codes, you have to be silent, and you have to be swift. Even so, he was nearly caught.

After failing to find Unva, Rune had re-entered his old realm, journeying down through the far paths and old forgotten ways beyond the Lost Lanes. That way, he'd steer clear of Ranning, who would be vengeful and searching for him, if he hadn't already found a way out.

Rune's diversion took him perilously close to the World Gate. He'd shrank his form to that of a zephyr, a silent and shapeless drift of smoke. Even in such a guise, there were those here who would mark his passage.

The Djinn and other demons would scent him out. Rune had moved quickly, hearing the bell toll and acting on a strange impulse, as he was determined to make this dangerous crossing worthwhile. He'd stopped by at Aelfheim and stole inside Aldorian's dreamy castle. There was one he could trust, for they had shared something long ago. Aldorian's warriors were gone, massing at the gate with their enemies the trolls.

The elf women had remained, as they had little interest in the wars of their people, and preferred intrigue and their many twisted pleasures. Rune crossed the drawbridge, as the electric smoke rose from the chiming mist-wrapped moat. He drifted up the shifting stairs, ignoring the faces following him along the walls.

He reached her chamber, the door opened, and blue steam vented out, half-blinding him for the briefest moment. He entered as a soft voice reached him from the far side of the chamber.

She was seated idly on a velvet divan that rippled like breeze-kissed water. Her long, golden locks flowed down past her shoulder and small breasts, covering most of her body. She wore a long, violet dress studded with tiny jewels, which shifted color and gleamed like glowworms in summertime. Her smile was faintly amused, the eyes colder than the northern wastes that had once been his home.

"You dare visit us after all this time, like a thief in the murk light?" The smile shifted as the pale lips curved in mock anger.

"Coristain, you know the reason I could never return. Small love has your brother for my person."

"Had you been my champion, you would have braved his anger," the elf maiden said, her voice soft as silk, yet barbed with hidden menace. "You are not without power, Rune. Instead, you have left me to fade, all my joy spent in a world that shrinks." Her shifting, cloudy eyes drifted over him, stripping his disguise. "Ours was a happy time, albeit too short."

"It wasn't me that finished that," Rune said, his eyes on the door moving behind him. "Your sisters?" He knew she was seldom alone.

"Go, Jalayse, Corwinna! Leave me to my ... *diversion*." The door shut behind him. Rune turned to face the beautiful creature poised lazily on the divan. She shifted her legs, and he caught the long, graceful shape of her—the curve of her perfect face, the playful cruelty in her smile. She smiled at him, reminiscing.

"I'm happy to see you, Rune, really I am–strangely. It seems just yesterday when you were gifted to me by my sweet brother the king. It was after the filthy trolls had hunted down your people in a raid, no?"

Rune nodded. That had been Sheega's doing too.

"You, Yetain, were a novelty to assuage poor Coristain's boredom." She smiled, moving her legs slightly again. He tried not to look. Rune had been captured and sold by the trolls in a trade with their enemy the elves. The elves had scant interest in the Yetain and Aldorian bid him go, but his beautiful sister was curious.

"I saved you, did I not?" Her smile was a cat-cruel tease.

"You did, but you had your price." Coristain had persuaded her brother the king to allow the young Yetain stay with her for a time.

"But you learned so much, about everything ..." Coristain pouted her lips and shifted on the couch. Wise as her brother in Faerie lore, they had become lovers. For Rune, those had been the happiest memories. For Coristain, it was a mild diversion—no more.

"You were my only friend and helped me when the elf

lords sought new sport."

"It was fun until we were caught. Do you recall Aldorian's anger when he discovered us at play that day?" She chuckled cruelly. "My brother deemed you Yetain much like any other beasts in Faerie. Aldorian considered it beyond perverse indeed, that his sister had chosen such a one for her lover. You were lucky to escape back to Dunnehine. I helped with that, too, as I recall."

It was true, Coristain's code keys had saved him.

"I always loved you."

"Love? Don't be foolish." She clapped her hands softly spraying silver moths into the air that chimed and winked down at him. "Love is but a human fancy, a false flicker in a fading febrile glow. Love is a lie, Rune." she said softly. "But I missed your touch, our intricate moments. You should have tried harder."

"I did, but you weren't overfriendly." Despite the danger, he'd returned several times, but her ardor had grown cold and she'd bid him leave else she alerts her brother. That had been so long ago, the years couldn't be measured in numbers. But here in Faerie, it could have happened yesterday. She looked the same: ageless, enticing, beautiful and cruel. An enemy, a lover, his councilor, torturer and dearest friend.

"I need your help again, Coristain."

Her laughter was a ripple that tingled along the shifting walls. Rune felt his fur shimmer in response. She leaned back on the divan, taking a suggestive repose. "I cannot recall you ever being so bold. Are you a warrior these days, Yetain? Have you come to ravage my person?" She hoisted her dress with a finger, allowing him take in her legs and what lay between.

Rune resisted the trap. He saw silver-blue moths floating in the air above her head. Spies that would report his presence to Aldorian with a raise of her brow. "We haven't time," he said.

"*Time*?" Coristain smiled. "Did you learn nothing while you stayed with me? Time, like love, is a false concept, used by the gods for their own purposes, and so they can handle the lesser creatures among the nine worlds."

"And yet it is *time* that will prove the ruin of Aelfheim."

"How so?' Her cloudy eyes darkened to purple, and she sat taller, her pale features stern. "Are you testing my patience? Be wary, lest I grow tired of your presence, Yetain—you who have neglected me so."

"Your brother must be stopped."

"Aldorian does as he pleases, his lords the same."

"Ansu is no longer their home," Rune told her. "Returning there will bring down the wrath of the high gods."

"Who are always wrathful." Her smile turned playful. "Come, Rune, take seat beside me. I'm intrigued by your intensity—you were always such a nervous, clumsy creature. I saw you as my pet, something I could play with, who pleasured me with a passion I never received from siblings, or the lords—though they tried. Do you know how many lovers I've had?"

"You're changing the subject."

"Several trolls among them, two yellow djinn, a goblin lord. Even an *Aikashi* once—that was most interesting." She beckoned him over with a long, white finger. He tried to hold back, but elf women were hard to refuse. Rune took seat beside her, and she pressed her soft, cool body against him, the blue skin shifting under her gossamer-thin spider-silk dress. She kissed him, and his form shifted to that of a tall young man from the world of men. "Hmm, still special. Come, the bed awaits."

"Coristain, there is no time for this." Rune stood shaking off her charm. "I need your help, lest your wrathful brother destroys the fragile glue that holds the nine worlds together."

Anger clouded her face, but Coristain nodded. "Very well, I shall listen, as such purpose and intensity demand a hearing."

"Thank you," Rune said. "It's simply this. I need you to shatter the truce between the elves and trolls. Sow discord into the mix."

"And why would I do that?" The smile hinted curiosity and wickedness.

"Because if Aldorian breaks through the World Door and attacks Ansu, it will result in the end of Faerie. Time may not matter here, but it rules the nine worlds outside. The Weaver allowed Faerie to reside beyond those earthly constraints, on the condition its denizens stay well away, leave his new preferred children to thrive. The odd glimmer or seep-through would go unnoticed. But an army of elves and trolls ..."

"You are of Faerie, too." Her lips pouted. Rune noted they were moist. "And yet you champion mankind, the clumsy, blind usurper of beauty and wisdom."

"Ansu is Elanion's realm," Rune said. "Exiled, the Emerald Queen has tasked me with protecting it. I am the key master, the rune-coder. I learned much from you, Coristain, but more from Her. If Aldorian and Rumgorz lead their armies into Ansu, everything is for nothing, and all will be lost. Believe me, this is no game."

The elf maiden's mercurial eyes flickered over him, the ghost of a smile hinting a thousand different things.

"I'll see what I can do," Coristain said eventually. "In the meantime ..."

DEVIOUS ALLIES AND TREACHEROUS FRIENDS

GUJUN SAT on the rail as the barge drifted south along the wide, meandering river. It was hot and steamy, both banks shimmering in heat haze and flies buzzed around his face. He swatted them away lazily and resumed his casual study of his companion. Grodu seemed at ease on the river, steering their barge. A massive, silent man, his eyes on the water's churning path.

The Rundali River was a fat, curving snake, the color of wet mud. There were crocodiles and other dangerous beasts in the oily water. He'd seen triangular heads rise up, watching them pass. The banks were lined with reeds heavy with bird noises. The dark smudge of Rundal Woods could be seen in the distance, ranging toward the mountains in the northeast. They'd reached the marshes above the river's swampy delta.

Grodu handled the craft well enough. The Vendeli's messenger had proved an easy companion. He hardly spoke and was a gifted hunter, providing fresh meat on most evenings during their journey. Gujun had been impressed with his weaponry. Grodu had brought with him a short, stabbing spear; two thick-bladed, leaf-shaped swords; a small, round shield; and the bow, with its quiver brimming with arrows. He had a number of throwing knives stowed in his saddle. Bigger than the kind Gujun used, but one glance told him they were razor-sharp. He shifted his gaze when he heard a snort, turned and saw the horses tethered behind them on the barge. Occasionally, one got restless—but mostly they stayed quiet.

A week had passed since the two had left Shateke's Villa. *Soon to be mine,* Gujun smiled faintly at the thought. Property, wealth, and a life of ease. Not bad for a former cutpurse and guttersnipe.

Gujun had been born in the harbor slums, cast out as a boy by his impoverished father who couldn't afford to feed another child. He'd grubbed for rotten food on the middens outside Pol Shen, fighting the other waifs who lived and died in the squalor. He'd returned one day and killed his father. Forgiveness wasn't part of Gujun's plan. Neither was trust.

Grodu glanced at him and turned away. The man was probing him, weighing up if this was an enemy sitting in the sunshine. Gujun smiled, allowing his hand to brush the cool water as his mind wondered easy. A blue dart flew past, and he watched the bird settle on a weed-laden branch protruding from the nearest bank.

"Rundali kingfisher."

Gujun looked up surprised. "You are an admirer of birds?"

"All creatures." The hugely muscled former gladiator glanced across at him as he deftly worked the rudder, guiding the square, flat barge through the sludge of weed and bubbles. "All life is precious. So is beauty."

"That's poetic for a fighting man and a hired killer." Gujun smiled faintly. The kingfisher darted away again, vanishing into the reeds.

"I am not my profession."

"Of course you are."

Grodu held his gaze and smiled, glancing over at the banks passing slowly. "You won't goad me into an argument, Shen. I've met far worse men than you."

"I doubt that." Gujun was surprised to hear himself chuckle. "But do tell me about them."

Grodu looked at him for a moment before returning his gaze to the river. "We'll reach the coast by nightfall," he said.

"That soon?"

"We are close. See how the river widens. And I can smell salt in the air."

"I hadn't noticed." Gujun crinkled his nose, sniffed. "I was too busy admiring your kingfisher."

"Be careful when you meet the Vendeli."

"I am always careful," Gujun said. "Why would you care?"

Again, the short shrug. Grodu turned away. Gujun was intrigued. It was though the big thug wanted to warn him but couldn't bring himself to do so. This Grodu had a depth to him Gujun hadn't expected. The man was intelligent, not just a killer. He wondered how much Grodu knew about his masters' affairs.

"A Sangala will greet us when we arrive at the ferry dock. It's a few hours ride from the river delta to Soloza. Octaxa has a villa near there and will expect us not to tarry."

"Sangala?"

"One of his people. Priest-warriors." By the curl of his lip and dour expression, Gujun could tell Grodu didn't approve of these Sangala.

"In my experience, priests and warriors don't mix well."

"These are different," Grodu said. "Zealots, vicious killers. Cruel, hard men."

"Then I should get on fine with them."

"We'll see." Grodu glanced at him again, before turning away. "We'll reach the river wharfs by dark. You had better get ready, Shen."

"I'm always ready," Gujun said, the faint smile fading from his lips.

It was dusk when the dhow moored at the busy quayside in warm Soloza. Tulomon Caze ordered his gilded trunk and carriage carried across before anyone disembarked. Hawk-faced Octaxa greeted him at the closest harbor tavern, as slaves struggled with his goods. Utuxla and the other Sangala watched on, keeping an aloof distance.

"The Shen?" Caze gave Octaxa a hard glance, noticing how the man dropped his gaze more slowly than he should have. *I'll have to watch you, Sangala.*

"On his way, excellency," Octaxa said. "Chulan sent his best man with my servant, Grodu. They should be here soon. Grodu sent bird this morning that his barge was nearing the delta."

"Good," Caze said, glancing over to make sure the slaves and dockers didn't damage his goods. "I want to see the color of these Shen."

"They are subtle men, High Califez, unlike this Cardalan rabble." Octaxa kept his voice low. The dockers and their gangers were all Laregozan, but Caze's people had informed him that Cardalan soldiers were posted at the fort nearby.

"You're certain their Ran knows nothing of our visit."

"Genza hasn't a clue," Octaxa said. "The new Ran thinks that he's a clever man. Truth is, they're all stupid."

"But not the Shen."

"I believe not, High Califez."

"That's good," Tulomon Caze said. "I cannot abide stupidity. You'd best show me this villa you've purchased, so I can get settled. I'm looking forward to a few weeks' rest by the warm waters."

Octaxa smiled. "Everything is ready for your inspection. There are male retainers and female slaves for your pleasures. There is a clay heated mineral pool and cool verandah awarding wide views of this magnificent coastline. Built by the old Laregozans, before the Ptarni invasions over a thousand years ago. An articulate people, the servants inform me. The villa's cut high into the rocks."

"What of our fleet?" Caze stared hard at the smiling shaman. He didn't like the Sangala, never had. But the Yanturi had always prized them as his best warriors, which of course they were.

"They are close by and will set out at your word, after we meet with Chulan's man."

"How many ships?"

"Seven, my own vessel among them," Octaxa replied. "With your permission, excellency, I mean to travel with them to Shen."

Caze nodded. "Makes sense. You've done well arranging this, Octaxa. The Yanturi is intrigued by these Shen. The thought of exotic eastern riches has piqued his curiosity further. You're expecting no problems on arrival in their city?"

"None are anticipated, High Califez. Chulan's last letter stated he would soon be journeying to Ta Shen himself and would arrange everything and greet us there. His army is close to the city, waiting for him to join them. When his scouts spy our ships, the Shen will open the harbor gates, allowing us into the city."

"Their empress is that trusting?"

"She won't know," Octaxa smiled. "Chulan means to usurp her, with our—and the Cardalan Republic's—help. Allow the Cards gain the city, while his army follows after."

"A traitor?" Caze chewed his lip. "Won't he betray us too, Sangala—once this Chulan is the new ruler?"

"I believe not, High Califez. Chulan's clever. He knows that the trade routes are key to our mutual wealth. Shen stands to gain much, as do we. Chulan has also promised to send us Shen engineers and saltpeter alchemists to aid in the war against Ulani."

"Hmm." Tulomon Caze saw one of the slaves stumble with a chest full of gold, dropping it onto the stone wharf. The lid skewed open, and coins spilled out. Were that fellow Vendeli, Caze would have had the man gelded on the spot. Instead, he averted his gaze and made a mental note to ensure his retainer count those coins, lest any had vanished with slippery fingers. "How far?" he asked, allowing his irritation to pass.

"A mile, no more." Octaxa beamed annoyingly. They were proud of their teeth, the Sangala. "I have your carriage ready and have ordered the house servants prepare a scented bath for your arrival."

"You've surpassed yourself, Octaxa." Tulomon Caze flashed the tall warrior-priest a rare smile. "I shall not forget such thoughtfulness." *If you prove a disappointment, I'll cut that smile from your mouth with a rusty dagger, Sangala chief or not.*

A RAINY SUMMER'S DAY IN CARDALIS. DRANAN'S FACE made Genza miserable.

"What's the matter?" Genza snapped at his captain, irritated by his shifting eyes and fidgeting. "You suspect the Vendeli are hoodwinking me, yes?"

"I believe that they are all treacherous serpents, my Ran." Dranan dared to stare back at him.

Genza slid his tongue along his bottom lip and made a sucking noise. "We know this, Captain Dranan. I expect more from you than ... *suspicions*. I need proof, man!"

"You shall have it, my Ran," Dranan said. He'd been one of Calla's best officers. *Father liked this turd, so I'd best give Dranan a while yet to prove himself, before I replace him.*

"Tell me what you know."

"Octaxa has ships moored outside Soloza harbor."

"Doubtless awaiting mooring space—Soloza's a busy port."

"I've good reason to believe that's not the case, great Ran. My coast-watchers sent birds informing me these craft were in Largos a few days back, where they picked up Octaxa and several of his warrior-shaman. My spies heard mention of a Tulomon Caze, and a bargain to be made with the Shen."

"A bargain ... with the fucking Shen?" Genza snorted derision through his nose.

Dranan looked pained, but continued. "One of my people heard Vendeli sailors speaking in a tavern in Largos. They were drunk and mentioned that Octaxa's second was accompanying this Caze—he's some important official from Omala City—to Soloza to meet with a Shen leader. The fools were well into their cups, talking too much."

Genza stroked his chin. *Could it be true?* "That *is* curious." He rubbed his chubby fingers on his gown, glancing at the rain outside. "Tulomon Caze is the Vendeli spymaster. The High Califez, they call him. Unlike you, Dranan, he's highly effective, from what I've heard. If your people have got this wrong, I shall have their entrails pulled out through their nostrils."

"The man who sent word to me was emphatic, my Ran. And the soldiers he'd questioned in Largos harbor were certain Octaxa was up to something."

"Doesn't make much sense," Genza said. "The Shen are finished. We are the power in this world. Why would the Vendeli betray my trust?"

Well, I never trusted those fuckers and for good reason.

"The name Chulan was mentioned," Dranan said. "There's to be a meeting in Soloza, where they'll take this Caze. A villa on the cliffs. You bought it for Octaxa, Ran, as an act of generosity and good faith."

"I did?" *Fuck* ... "Send a troop there immediately and confiscate it! And you had best ride to Soloza immediately, captain. I want these treacherous snakes dealt with."

"Great Ran." Dranan bowed.

"No, no, fuck. *Wait.* Ride to Largos first, *yes?* Get the facts straight, and alert Talimi Garrison to send a troop to Soloza, led by yourself. Do that first, yes?" Dranan nodded. "Good man. I don't want that oily shaman bastard slipping our nets, captain. And do be careful on arrival at that villa. Octaxa will most likely know you're coming. You know what these shaman are like."

"Yes, Ran."

"He's worse than most." Genza stood up, wiping sweat from his face. "After that's resolved, send a messenger to my brother in Shen. Let Ran Casca know the Vendeli are not to be trusted."

"It shall be done, Ran."

"Good. *Bugger off.*"

THE MOTION MADE TRISA WEARY. SHE DIDN'T MUCH CARE for these bad-tempered beasts. They'd traded their fast Yamondon horses for the ungainly creatures back at the last oasis. The camels were horrible things, in her opinion, but they had bought them time. They'd left the desert behind and reached the coast. The ocean stretched out ahead, sleek and blue—the morning sun glinting off its waters. The sight made her happy, as did the man beside her.

Valgarn grinned as he reined up alongside. She knew he'd missed seeing the sea.

"How far to the border?" Valgarn asked Dolusa, as he passed over a water gourd.

The Tarakai smiled wryly. "We crossed that two days ago," he said. "We're in Laregoza, my friends, and should make Largos by tomorrow evening. Once there, we can trade these ungainly beasts for fresh horses."

"I'd best ride ahead before we reach that city," Valgarn said. "Those Cards won't take kindly to you boys appearing outside the city gates." He winked at Trisa. "Perhaps we'll catch up with Utuxla there?"

GUJUN STUDIED THE AQUILINE FEATURES OF THE MAN seated across from him at the table at an expansive villa carved high on a rock, with stunning views out to sea and along the cliffs. He'd arrived with the taciturn Grodu late last night, after being met—as his companion had said they would be—by a Sangala, a hooded rider wrapped in a cloak. This warrior-priest had looked Gujun up and down before bidding them follow him along the coast road to Soloza.

Gujun had noted how Grodu had looked tense in the presence of the man. There was history here, Gujun thought. *Hatred.* Octaxa, the Sangala's hawk-faced master, had greeted Gujun politely enough, bidding Grodu depart and leave them to speak alone. The brief introduction was long enough for Gujun to decide he didn't much care for the Vendeli he'd met. Octaxa's men had ordered servants to escort Gujun to a room where he could rest and take his leisure. They'd left him alone for the next day. Gujun had enjoyed the freedom, walking out on the cliffs, the sea wind in his hair and waves crashing below. A beautiful place that inspired a longing for more travel he hadn't recognized in himself before.

The curt summons had come that evening. He and Grodu were to attend Tulomon Caze in person.

The Vendeli High Califez—their spymaster and enforcer. Tulomon Caze, they'd informed him, was not a man to cross. Gujun believed it, casually staring at the aquiline, deeply tanned face and those dark, penetrating eyes. Lean and sharp, like all these Vendeli appeared. Cold. Hard-eyed and clearly cunning. A dangerous man. That was to be expected.

Gujun smiled. He knew they were all watching him keenly.

Tulomon Caze was seated at the head of the long table, wrapped in a scarlet robe lined with gold thread trimmings. He wore pointed shoes of curious design. The Sangala—Gujun counted twelve—were seated around the table in their brown desert cloaks and burnooses. Their leader, the shaman Octaxa, with his moon and stars cloak, stood by the door with sinewy, gold-banded arms folded—as though listening for signals from outside. Grodu stood beside him, face blank. Once or twice, Gujun caught his eye. Grodu looked worried, and Gujun suspected all was not as it should be here.

Octaxa remained quietly aloof, as did his proud Sangala. Tulomon Caze alone addressed Gujun, as he sat hemmed by Vendeli, a cold-eyed Sangala at either side. Gujun had his swords and the hidden knives. If prompted, he'd kill most of them before they took him.

"Chulan is a wise man, I hear?" The voice was sonorous and deep. It resonated power.

"He is," Gujun nodded slightly, masking a smile at the anger flashing through the man's eyes. *This one is used to obedience.*

"And has much to offer Vendel, and its Yanturi?"

"Magister Chulan has assured me that you will prosper by our alliance," Gujun said, bored with the subject. He wanted to explore this country. It looked so beautiful. He'd never traveled outside Shen before.

"How can this Chulan of yours be sure the truculent Cards will oblige him?"

"A matter of timing," Gujun said, scratching an ear. "I'm sure you know we have troops watching the city. Once the Cards break through, we'll be behind them. Shen soldiers will greet your ships in Ta Shen harbor. Not Cards."

"You intend to be there in person?"

"I am Shen."

Caze nodded slowly. "Good. You seem trustworthy, if over-bold. Octaxa tells me this Genza is a fool and has good reason to believe the other Ran in Shen is no wiser. I don't like doing business with fools. Mistakes happen. Misunderstandings. You take my meaning?"

Gujun nodded.

"Good. Return to your master and inform him the Vendeli will do as he asks, on his assured guaranty of half that legendary city's plunder being handed over to Vendel."

"Our ships are ready leave at my signal," Octaxa added, after being prompted by Caze.

"Let's hope your Magister Chulan doesn't disappoint us," Tulomon Caze said. "A man who usurps his ruler might not prove the most loyal ally."

"Chulan is a practical man," Gujun said, his eyes holding the other man's gaze. Again, he saw the irritation and hostility, and he found it amusing. "You needn't be concerned," he continued, daring a smile. "We Shen will have beacons lit along the coast to alert your ships, should the impetuous Cards fail to break through Ta Shen's defenses before you arrive."

"You think the city will fall soon?" Tulomon Caze steepled his fingers and stared hard at Gujun.

"If it hasn't already," Gujun replied, matching that gaze without a blink.

"That would mean Cardalan victory, a waste of our time and energies."

Gujun shrugged. "You had best get sailing, hadn't you?"

THEY HATED HIM. THAT MUCH WAS OBVIOUS. THE Sangala were silently hostile toward Gujun after their leader departed with Tulomon Caze. Caze had returned to his rooms, but Octaxa had signaled his fleet set sail, he'd already left to join them in his skiff. Tulomon Caze and half the Sangala were to stay behind. Gujun suspected that was to placate the Cards, lest Genza get word of their plans. But why was Caze staying? Not his concern.

A hard-looking Sangala blocked his way when he returned to the room they'd given him.

"You're leaving at dawn." It wasn't a question.

Gujun looked at the man and made to push through, but a spear blocked his way.

"I'm Utuxla," the warrior said. "A leader among the Sangala. I don't like you, Shen. You have an arrogance I find objectionable, especially for a messenger and servant."

"I'm not a servant," Gujun said. "And if you don't move right away, my knife will sever the artery in your groin."

Utuxla glanced down and paled, seeing the slim blade pressed against his leg. He stood aside, eyes blazing. Gujun walked on.

"You are a fool to make an enemy of me, little Shen. I am Utuxla, and I do not forget."

Gujun turned and looked at him. "That's good, Vendeli. Because neither do I."

THE FOLLOWING MORNING, HE WAS ON THE ROAD EARLY, the sunrise blazing fire in the east. He hadn't got far before he saw a man standing beside his horse, a spear in one hand at a place where the road forked into two directions. At first, he thought it was Utuxla come to accost him. He was almost disappointed when he rode closer and recognized Grodu.

"I thought you'd be gone." Gujun reined in sharply, seeing Octaxa's man standing in the pre-dawn glow. Grodu stood with his spear in one hand, the horse cropping grass beside him. "The fleet has left."

"Seven dhows hardly comprise a fleet," Grodu said with something that seemed like contempt. "My journey lies in the opposite direction."

"Octaxa is sending you to Cardalis, to appease Genza?"

"So he thinks ... yes. But I'm riding to Largos to meet with someone else."

Gujun caught the faint trace of a smile on Grodu's lips. "You hate your Vendeli masters, do you not? And I thought Octaxa had saved you from the fighting pits?"

"He did, after Caze's men put me there in the first place. I have always served Ulani of Yamondo. I was his contact in Omala. A high honor. That king will be very interested in what's occurring in the east lands."

"Why are you telling me this? We are not friends."

"Perhaps we can be allies. I noted your distaste for the Vendeli. And you spoke well at that meeting with Caze—I liked that. You're clever, but you sell yourself short, killer."

"I do?" Gujun barked a laugh. "I think you should place your trust elsewhere. Stick to your birdwatching, big man."

Grodu waved a dismissive hand. "We part company, Shen. Know that I wish you well, and I believe you to be better than most men, not worse."

"Is your king as honorable as he sounds?"

"Ulani is not my king," Grodu said. "My country has no king. But King Ulani saved my life when I was a boy. I love him like an uncle. He is the greatest warrior of this age."

"Perhaps I'll seek him out," Gujun said. "When I tire of Chulan and these Vendeli."

"Tire of them you will, and quickly. I will put in a good word for you in Cantacari. I like you, Gujun the Slayer. Farewell!"

Grodu swung up into his saddle, the weapons bristling

around him. He flashed Gujun a grin and urged his horse forward, taking the lane that led down to the docks, the city, and the glimmering ocean beyond.

Gujun sat his horse and watched Grodu until horse and rider vanished behind a rise. The man had said he liked him. *You're the closest thing I have to a friend.* Gujun laughed at himself. *I'm getting sentimental.* It must be this western air. He sniffed, at last noticing the salt.

"Ya!" Gujun bid his horse canter the other way, taking the road that led back to the river where he'd take a barge and return to notify Chulan of what had transpired.

21

CRADON IWEY

TOFEI glanced up as Asmund caught his arm. They tied off at the quay, having sailed the islander's father's skiff across from Valkador. The two of them had made for Skarness, having discussed this with Ivar and Jaran Saerk.

"Do you see him?" Asmund's face looked pale. They hadn't expected anyone to be here.

"Aye," Tofei replied, feeling a shudder. A shabby-looking figure was watching them from the deserted town. An old man, tall and stooping. The features were hidden beneath a floppy hat. Tofei chewed his beard. *Appearances deceive.* This could be a spirit left behind, or worse—a sending from that witch. Tofei knew that the honey-green killers had murdered everyone in Skarness, leaving a town of ghosts. He feared that this creature was one of them.

"Ignore him," he replied, after mouthing a protection rune.

"Hard to do that," Asmund said. "He's walking this way."

Tofei cursed and jumped from the skiff, his companion joining him, the red War Arrow concealed in his cloak. The old man stood at the end of the dock, leaning on what looked to be a broken spear shaft.

"You had best let us pass, old fellow," Tofei said, walking briskly toward the stooped stranger. "We mean you no harm, but we'll not tarry—so leave us be."

Tofei caught the gleam of an eye beneath that hat. "Young Tofei, you have your father, Gunard's mettle. That pleases me. Good men are hard to find these days." The voice was gravelly and rough.

"He knows you?" Asmund whispered from behind.

Tofei felt the small hairs tingle up his neck. "Who are you that knows our names—my father and I?" He made to pass, but the oldster blocked his way.

"A wayfarer, that's all. But a wise one who would help you with your task."

"How so?" Tofei waved his hand, bidding Asmund stay back. He stared hard at the old man. "I cannot see your face, old one. Why do you hide it from us? And I care not for the sound of your voice. You have the stench of gallows about your person."

The glimmer of a silvery eye glared back at him. "Have a care. You shouldn't tempt my wrath. For the moment, I am you friend. That can change like wind over water. Be patient instead, and listen."

"Speak if you must, but quickly," Tofei said, holding his nerve. "We cannot linger here."

The old man nodded. "Mine is the voice that gives your dreams clarity," he said—and as he spoke, the words seemed to take on shapes and form. Tofei imagined that he saw vague runes drifting out from the hood like tendrils of smoke."

Tofei heard Asmund curse behind him. "He's a sorcerer."

"I am the strength inside the wind," the voice deepened. "The cold is within me, and without me. And yet I blaze!"

The words contained a power Tofei couldn't comprehend. *Are we being bewitched here?* He felt his skin tingle and eyes water.

"Who are you?" Tofei forced the words out. His mouth was dry, making it hard to speak.

The silver eye locked onto his own, the hint of a smile showed beneath the hat brim's shadow. "The time is almost upon us, Tofei Gunardsson." The eye shifted to his companion, and Tofei felt a flood of relief when that chill gaze left him.

"Young Asmund, I see good things in you. Your task is waiting. Cross the fjord, head north. Seek out Sherriff Doggan's village. That one will help you find others. Every warrior must rally to the hero's cause. Do not tarry! Return you must, within a moon. Else your efforts prove futile."

Tofei heard a splash in the water behind him. He turned to look. The sound of a large fish jumping, or something falling from the dock? He heard Asmund gasp. The old stranger had gone, leaving a wisp of smoke that drifted up into the atmosphere. Tofei watched it fade and disappear. He wiped sweat from his brow and glanced at his friend.

"This is a bad place." Asmund looked terrified. He was hesitating, as though about to return to his father's skiff.

"Come on," Tofei said. "We knew it wouldn't be easy."

"But that—"

"Wants to help us, or says he does," Tofei stared at his companion. Asmund nodded slowly. "You're from Valkador, Asmund. You must be used to false glamour."

"That's why I'm testy."

"As am I, but we're done talking," Tofei said. "We need to get moving before light fails us."

"Which way do you suggest?" Asmund hadn't moved.

"You heard that creature," Tofei said, pointing at the boat they'd left. "We sail across the fjord and find the dock and road leading north. This Sherriff Doggan will know more."

"If he exists." Asmund looked at him and nodded. "I don't trust that spirit's words, or whatever it was. But I'm happy enough to be moving again. I've seen as much of Skarness town as I care to."

"That's settled, then." Tofei flashed him a grin, as Asmund jumped back on board and untied the stays.

"We need to find that landing before dark," Asmund said, seating himself on the bench and grabbing an oar. "You work that sail, Tofei. I'll keep rowing."

"My thoughts exactly," Tofei said, as his companion poled the craft free of the jetty. They drifted out. Tofei saw the huts and hovels of Skarness floating above the water as he took the tiller, the sail flapping and trapping breeze.

Tofei forced his mind to relax. Why ponder on events that you can't understand? Better they keep busy and get this task done. He craned his neck, turned, and glanced back at the shoreline again. Asmund's eyes were on the northern bank.

Tofei's shifting gaze was drawn to the steep cliffs above Skarness. As he looked that way, he saw a huge figure watching them from the clifftop. A giant stood there with fists on hips, staring out at them. Tofei imagined terrible eyes blazing inside his skull. He turned away, focusing on steering and the approaching jetty. *Why are we doing this? What was happening here?* Again, Tofei forced his mind to relax.

"You all right?" Asmund hadn't seen the giant.

"Fine," Tofei said. "Just thinking our options over."

"Good," Asmund said. "Let's hope we'll get food and grog in that village he mentioned."

"I wouldn't count on that," Tofei replied.

"You mean to dive into that water?" Jaran Saerk stood with the others clustered close in curiosity at the edge of the pool.

"Walk." Rafin grinned back at them, his face hardly visible in the gloom. Ahead, Unva was already wading into the black slimy water. Rafin watched as she sunk deeper and vanished below. "My turn!" He waved at the torchlit faces watching from the cave.

"Your hauberk?" Savarna called out. "You'll not swim far with that on."

"I won't need to, sweetheart. And the mail's waterproof, before you ask—so don't fret." Rafin said, and he started wading out into the lake. The Deepwater's touch was oily and cold, yet not icy. He trod carefully on the slippery, gooey stone, felt the liquid rise over him.

You coming down, dwarf? Sometime this week would be good.

Unva's sarcastic tones drifted up to him, as Rafin allowed his body to sink, stone-heavy into the silent gloom.

"On my way," he replied, gurgling bubbles. Down he sank swiftly in blackness. Deepwater proved true to its name. It seemed like long minutes had passed until Rafin splashed free of the water again and stood by the crashing spume of ocean waves.

"That's a shortcut to remember," he said, shaking off drips, adjusting the weapons on his belt, and walking over to the crouching woman. Unva's coat was soaked and dripping, but she seemed unaware and was scraping symbols on the rocks by her feet.

"Are you sure that you can do this?" Rafin leaned over.

"There's a first time for everything."

"That's not encouraging." Rafin sat down beside her and rummaged for his pipe and leaf. He spoke a drying rune and watched as his armor sizzled and smoked until all the water had evaporated. Rafin lit the pipe and tapped it, leaned back, and smiled. "It's like old times," he said.

"Shut up," the woman muttered beside him. "Go, be useful, dwarf. Watch inside the cavern mouth—lest she send anything our way."

Rafin nodded and left her to the onerous task of time tampering—a trick they had both dabbled in during their time spent in Faerie as guests of the goblin king, Greshgaran. Unlike the lofty elves and brutish trolls, the goblins were sociable and liked showing off their magic skills. There were also filthy, stinking, murderous, and obnoxious. But that was another matter. Rafin had learned a good deal during that visit, Unva considerably more.

He walked out to the cave entrance, glimpsed the sun setting beyond the shadow of dark rocks. The sea surged and sighed close by. Satisfied all was well out there, Rafin returned and passed Unva without a sound. The woman was locked in concentration, a string of rune-shells clutched in her left hand, the other one scraping symbols in the wet dirt.

She ignored him, so Rafin walked deeper into the cave, past the blowhole that had spat them out from above. He reached the twisted, multi-hued rocks that hid the murky entrance to the Faerie Gate—the portal called Cradon Iwey. Rafin felt a surge of power, a kind of magna force venting out from the crack. He stepped back and took a deep breath. Satisfied it was safe, Rafin inched closer again, peeped up the hole, and looked in.

The gateway was different this time, but Rafin knew it would be. Faerie doors were always changing. The energy had shifted, turned darker. *Angrier.* He felt giddy, like that reckless earth power was seeping through into his veins, tugging at him—a thick layer of lead sprayed on his mail, weighing him down. *Bugger this.* Rafin leaned back against a rock and puffed hard at his pipe. Restless, he spat the pipe out into his hand and grumbled, wishing he'd brought the ale kit down here.

"Steady, you old fool," Rafin muttered to himself quietly. He'd best not stray too close. You never knew who's looking out. But Rafin knew the best way to help Unva was to see what they were up to, the elves and their allies. With that thought, he stowed his pipe and took another deep breath. Mind prepared, Rafin walked into the crack mouthing a protection rune. Inside, he stopped again and listened.

What's that sound?

Feet approaching, soft and quick. Feather-feet. Elves—not the dull stomping of troll boots. Aldorian must have sent a scouting party through the World Gate, probing.

That's not good.

Rafin closed his eyes and allowed his inner sight to range out, penetrating the labyrinth beyond that crevice. He searched back and forth with his third eye, mouthing the journey charms. It seemed a long time before he saw them. Faint shapes, and a shifting shimmer of electric blue fuzzing into purple. Rafin counted a score of glinting silent figures scampering over the rocks and darting through the Lost Lanes.

Aldorian's sly people were breaking through. The World Gate must have frayed enough for a sortie. He rubbed his beard and saw a shadow creeping from somewhere much nearer. Rafin recognized Ranning the Water-Faen trotting briskly in the dark, his milky eyes filled with malice.

"Your time's coming, shithead," Rafin growled, shifting his mind gaze. He dare not break his concentration, else he lose the elves. And what was that? A shadow coming from the other side. Rafin heard a faint voice reach out to him. He saw a face emerge from the distant dark. Horns, lots of silver hair.

"Rune?" Rafin hissed. *I hope that's you.*

It is I.

"Where are you?"

On my way.

"There are elves—be careful."

Yes, and more will come. Aldorian will begin his attack soon. The war has started.

The voice was nearer.

"They are early," Rafin said. He winced as Rune's bulk emerged beside him, squeezing out from the rock like congealed muddy slime. *How does he do that?*

"That's to our advantage," his shaggy comrade said, shaking shale and barnacles from his fur. "If things go to plan, Aldorian will shortly fall out with Rumgorz. There'll be fighting in the faerie camps."

"Your doing, I assume?" Rafin couldn't get over Rune's sudden appearance through that rock. Witnessing such happenings upset the stomach.

"Yes, no ... not entirely," Rune replied. "I was merely the instigator. It's someone else's handiwork."

"Who?" Rafin had a bad feeling.

"Coristain," Rune said, mournfully.

"Not her," Rafin said, taking a long, slow pull on his pipe. "Are you out of your hairy-horned wits, Yetain?"

"Coristain will help us, dwarf. Be grateful for that." Rune sounded weary.

"How do you know? She could do the opposite out of pure spite."

"I know."

"You're bewitched, you daft-hairy-bugger. And there'll be a price. That one always wants things. Elf women are bad news, and she's the worst of them."

"I've already paid Coristain's price." Rune sounded annoyed. "Enough prevaricating, dwarf. Is Unva ready?"

"She is working on … *complicated matters.*"

"We two had best go and help her get them done."

"You can do that without me," Rafin said. "I'll stay put and have a smoke, keeping an eye on your elf friends in there."

"As you wish." Rune's golden eyes flashed with what could have been wry humor.

"Before you go, be warned," Rafin said. "That creep Ranning's on his way here. The briny-arsed maggot must have finally found a way to slither out of the lanes."

Rune didn't reply; he'd had already vanished behind the rocks.

"I'm glad you're back. Unbelievably, I've missed you," Rafin muttered and crouched low, rummaging for his pipe. He got comfy after a jiffle, loosened the axe at his side and stroked the hammerhead fondly. It had been too long since he'd had a good scrap. The elves would be here soon. Rafin glanced down at his weapons.

Which of you lovers shall I use today?

Jaran stared into the pool, the flickering torchlight revealing his face looking back up at him, hard features grim.

"Jaran." He turned and saw Savarna behind him, her fists thrust on hips. "There is food back by the waterfall. Gunard's men had the wits to bring supplies."

Jaran hardly heard her.

"Jaran!"

"I'm not hungry," he said, returning his gaze to Deepwater's dark surface. "You go."

He heard her sigh, and moments later she sat on a rock beside him.

"What are you waiting here for?" Savarna looked tired and irritable. "It's been hours. Do you honestly think Rafin and that woman will leap back out of the water?"

"Perhaps," he said, stroking his whiskers. "Or one of Sheega's creatures. Best I stay and watch—can't be too careful."

"Unva said it's a deep underwater channel leading down to the Faerie Gate." Savarna rested her hand on his arm. He shifted closer but kept his gaze on the water. "She said it's gravity-driven. You sink fast but can't come back up the same way. And I don't see Rafin floating back up with that armor on."

He turned and smiled at her, knowing she was trying to lighten his mood. "I'm glad the dwarf's here," he said eventually.

"And Unva?"

"And don't know what to say about her." His mood darkened again.

"She hates Sheega, that much is certain."

"She's conniving and sly like the Traveler, and maybe Rune. The three of them are devious and cannot be trusted."

"And yet we have to trust Rune, and Unva. What else can we do?"

"Go and kill that witch."

"It's not time."

"It's near enough, damn it. And Fin's there, Savarna. It won't help our cause if she stabs our friend in his sleep."

"He won't get much sleep with Sheega creeping around," Savarna muttered quietly. Jaran turned and saw the horror in her eyes.

"She drugged you, as I recall."

"Sheega was being playful, thinking she'd won. I doubt Finvar will receive that mirth. But he is protected. By Lofhi."

"Do you honestly believe that?"

"It makes sense, to a point. The things that have happened. We both knew Fin was different. He's part god," Gunsala said.

"Or part demon. Lofhi is an ill wight. He's the worst of the northern gods. Fin is not part of Lofhi, Savarna. I can't believe that. But the god has some hold over him. And if that trickster hurts him, I'll cut him into ribbons, be Lofhi god, demon, or fuck knows what else. It won't matter. He'll be dead."

A bubble far out across the lake became a ripple gliding toward him. Jaran watched it. Most likely an air bubble caused by falling scree. He looked down at Savarna, managing a smile.

"I'm sorry," he said.

"I know you're frustrated," she said. "We all are. But we have to wait, Jaran. Sheega is stronger than you—than *we* are. Even if we are pawns—which, like you, I suspect to be so. What choice have we, but to wait for the right moment? Unva's bringing that time closer."

"Can't see that happening." Jaran snorted derision. He stopped, hearing a soft sound, and turned swiftly. Beside him, Savarna reached for her dagger as Jaran saw a shaggy-haired figure loomed out of the dark.

"Svipdag." Jaran gave Savarna a wry look. "Another mystery."

The old warrior joined them and gazed out at the Deepwater.

"One of my grandfather's thanes," Jaran said, as Savarna's eyes glinted in distrust. He scowled "And a bear hunter."

"Did Sheega not cast her glamour over you, too?" Savarna asked the brooding figure standing beside them. Svipdag didn't respond. "How do we know you aren't her spy? That you won't creep out of some hole and fetch that giant witch-man?"

Svipdag's canny gaze showed irony. He kept his lips together.

"She hurt you, too, didn't she?" Jaran said. "Made you join the hunt that killed my father?"

Svipdag looked at him and returned his gaze to Savarna. She chewed her lower lip and fingered her dagger. Svipdag let out a long sigh and nodded.

"Aye, she did, boy," he said. "And if she had wanted me to spy on you, I would have done so. I'll not deny that. No flesh-bearing man can resist that foul woman for long. Only a fool would try." His glance shot to Jaran again. "Without the Norns' help and odds stacked high in his favor," he added, seeing Jaran's frown. "Your woman is right, Jaran Hrelgisson. We need to be patient here. After that, we'll need to act light-ning-fast."

"Why *we*?" Jaran looked hard at the grizzled old warrior.

"You could have left, Svipdag. Stolen Gunard's ship, or an island skiff. Still can. This doesn't have to be your fight."

Svipdag ignored that. "They are under the lake," he said.

"Who?" Jaran shot Savarna a questing glance. She shrugged. *More witch-men?*

"My comrades."

"Sheega drowned your friends?" Savarna paled.

"Not drowned—trapped under the ice." His eyes were sad. "She will wake their restless souls and send them here. They are her chattels and must serve the witch, else their souls be damned for eternity."

"How do you know this?" Savarna asked Svipdag as Jaran studied his eyes.

"I witnessed the punishment," Svipdag said. "I'd been away from the island and had but recently returned. Erlund, your uncle, had become her puppy. His thanes, those younger ones who had ridden with us to kill the bear." He glanced at Jaran. "To kill Hrelgi, your father, I mean."

"What of them?" Jaran felt his face grow hot, the anger rising.

"A few fled to Leeth, and some may still be alive—though I'd doubt any are sane. Those who stayed near the hall ..." He spat into the water. "They became her pets, like Erlund. Some she used as lovers, others toys for her to damage and break apart. But—as with your uncle, only much sooner—Sheega tired of them and sent the poor fools out onto the ice, her birds and dogs following, tearing and pecking at their flesh until naught but gristle and gore remained on that rime."

"You saw that?" Jaran wondered why he didn't hate this man who'd been part of what had happened to his father.

"I did," Svipdag said. "They died horribly out there on that frozen lake. But that was only the start of their anguish. She kept their souls trapped beneath that shifting ice, knowing that you would return, Jaran Hrelgisson. Promising them freedom, only if they brought you to her and trading your soul for their own."

"How do know all this?"

"Sheega told me," Svipdag said. Jaran was about to demand further when something plopped out on the water.

"What's that?" Savarna pointed, and Jaran saw a ripple moving again, faster than before. This time, he could tell it was more than just a stir caused by venting air or falling rock.

He saw bubbles, the ripples lapping closer. Savarna gripped his arm.

A wet sleek head broke free of the water, the long, silvery hair dripping. Jaran dropped his hand to Griner at his waist.

Ranning the Water-Faen grinned back at him from Deepwater's gloom

"We meet again, Jaran Saerk."

22

CASCA'S VICTORY

RASNEI WATCHED the thin dawn line of gray reveal a host larger than any she'd seen before. Casca had come. His captains were lined up alongside the bulky figure of the Ran. To her left, the fighting continued, the wall having been breached. Matax stood beside her, his fists clenching and flexing open, sweat trickling down his face.

"It's going to be a rough morning, empress," the general said.

"Can we hold?" She turned and stared hard into his face. "The truth, please."

"I don't know," Matax wiped the smear of blood from his face. "Our lads have held them off for hours, but that bastard Calgara doesn't give up. Three times we've thrown his attackers back. And now this ..." His dark eyes flicked across to the vast horde seated on horses, half a mile from the city. The entire plain was covered with riders, foot soldiers, ballistae artillery, and rammers. Casca was throwing everything at them today.

"Send someone to wake Vian," she said, watching as the distant riders started moving forward. To her left, she heard shouts and saw Calgara's men breaking off to ride back to the main force, the young Ragan at their head. "Stay here, and report on my return," Rasnei ordered Matax. "I want to see that damage, how our men fare along the wall."

"Empress, it's not safe." Matax glared back at her, chewing his lip.

"Nothing is safe," she replied, before turning and walking briskly, taking the keep stairs two at a time.

Rasnei was tempted to sprint along the walls, her mind a turmoil of anger, hatred, fear, and dread. How could they hold? Today everything would end.

I will not succumb to fear.

She slowed her pace. *I must appear calm.* As she moved, Rasnei noted the dirty, tired faces of her guards. All were exhausted, with no hope in those eyes. They bowed low as she passed. Rasnei smiled at a few.

She reached the spot where the wall had been breached, a ballistae missile having knocked part of the parapet clean away. She saw Gurtei there, leaning on a Chiang. Roile, too, and the surviving Cutters. Big Lin Gu stood like an island, a Jian blade resting on either shoulder. Rasnei saw Dorthar, and her lip twitched. He noticed her and looked ashamed. She ignored him and walked across to join Gurtei as he gazed at the approaching army.

"Empress." Gurtei bowed stiffly. "Looks like a busy day ahead."

"You've already endured a tough night." She smiled. "Your men need to rest while they can."

"We could use some," Gurtei said. "Last night was a good warmup."

Rasnei registered the bodies sprawled around the walls for the first time. Most were Cardalan, but there were plenty of

Shen corpses there, too. Blood was everywhere, and a foul stench hung in the air. She felt her gorge rising and turned away, sick to her stomach.

"How did you hold them back?" Rasnei asked after she'd recovered her posture, trying not to choke.

"It was mostly him." Gurtei hinted the huge Lin Gun, who stood watching the enemy with the sheepish Dorthar. "I've never seen a man fight like that, save perhaps your Vian."

Rasnei nodded. She walked over to the two men. Dorthar bowed awkwardly. Again, she ignored him and awarded Lin Gu her full attention. The big former slave looked embarrassed and bowed low. Rasnei stopped him with a motion from her hand.

"I hear we owe everything thing to you, Master Gu."

"I killed a few of them," he said. "Eager to kill many more soon."

"Well, good, but take what rest you can—and thank you, my hero." Rasnei turned to the men crouched and seated around her. "You are all heroes. Each and every one of you is a champion. That's why we are going to win today and save this city. They can throw everything at us, those worthless Cards. Let them try. I have you, and I know that whatever they do will not be enough.

"Stay strong and stay alive. Get what rest you can." She awarded those gathered around a brave smile. "I must return to the keep—I need to be seen up there."

Rasnei noted their smiles and the love on their faces, and she felt a flood of pride. *These are my people.* They would die for her, and she for them. Rasnei glanced at Dorthar. "You're coming with me," she told him. He nodded, shouldering his axe.

• • •

"You were drinking." Rasnei deigned not to look at the big Northman as Dorthar strode silently beside her. "In the Violet Girl."

"I was, empress," he muttered. "You were asleep, and safe —so I thought, what with Vian with you. I needed some ale. It helps me think. Then the fighting started abruptly, and I saw Gu up on the walls having all the fun."

"*Fun.* You're a Northman ... I understand," Rasnei said. "You are what you are. But don't leave me again, Dorthar."

"I won't, empress," Dorthar assured her as they reached the keep stairs and started climbing. "That I swear."

"Excellent." She flashed him a grin and almost laughed at his earnest expression.

VIAN WOKE WITH A JOLT THAT SENT HIS COLD BODY crashing to the floor. He hit his head, blinked, and struggled to his feet. His vision was blurry, and he felt sick.

An attack.

But from whom? He'd been dreaming, gliding like silk over the oceans, a smile on his face. Savarna had been there. But she'd gone, and so had the warmth and the joy he'd felt. Stolen by a cold, cruel blackness that clawed inside his heart like rusty nails and choked his breath.

Vian steadied himself, hands on the bed rail. He counted to ten, let go, and walked out onto the balcony, the welcome breeze banishing the remnants of sleep from his eyes. Rasnei was gone—he saw no one around below. The entire palace seemed empty. Deserted. He heard the distant sounds of shouting and clash of steel.

She let me sleep.

Angry, Vian dressed into clothes and mail suit. He strapped his Jian blades to his back and made for the door. He didn't get there. A sharp pain lanced inside his belly like a heated, twisting dagger. Vian gasped and buckled over, dropped to his knees.

Who attacks me ...?

For the briefest instant, Vian saw a face. Handsome and strong. Dark eyes and skin, flashing white teeth, a sense of terrible willpower and control.

The shadowy face faded, and the pain left almost as suddenly as it had come. Vian regained his feet and sat for a time on the bedside table. He was needed on the walls, but first he had to find out who this was. A Cardalan shaman? Straban was dead, and he knew of no other with the power to reach him inside the city.

Besides, that face was neither from Dunnehine or Cardalan. A Yamondon jungle-shaman stalked him or, worse, a Sangala, one of the cursed warrior-priests from Omala City. But if so—who, and why? He had to find out. Casca must have hired a new shaman from the south—a man far more terrible than Straban. He closed his eyes and focused, letting his mind reach and wander.

No one out there.

He shook himself into movement. This wouldn't do. Over at the walls, the fighting was getting louder. To Vian, it sounded like the enemy had breached the gates. He heard screams and felt a shudder inside. *Was Rasnei on the walls?*

Vian wanted to rush out there and start killing. Find her, save her. But he knew that's what his mystery attacker would want. Instead, he closed his eyes again and concentrated harder than before, mouthing the words he'd dreaded using a second time. He doubted he had the strength, but he couldn't put this off any longer.

It was time he summoned the dragon.

SEVEN SHIPS CUT CLEAN THROUGH CHOP. OCTAXA smiled at the fresh breeze and distant cliffs rising to their north. They had done well—both wind and weather had been kind. He watched as the other six ships bobbed behind his. The cliffs crumbled away, and he saw an old ruin of some ancient castle, broken and strewn along an empty beach.

The Castle of Lights.

A place of great power and sorcery from an earlier age, destroyed by the gods. Octaxa saw the lost spirits wandering on that shore and looked away. The dhow changed course as castle and strand were left behind. They reached the eastern-most point of the continent, a spear of land thrusting out from Rundali. The Sunblazey Sea dwindled behind them, and the vastness of the Great Murmuring glinted ahead. An ocean bigger than any continent, and a place of secrets and forgotten realms. All this Octaxa knew from his dark studies in Omala City.

He watched the sailors work the sheets, staring at the shoreline sliding to their west, a mile or so away. He saw long white beaches, the odd swaying palm, now and then a hint of building proving some souls still dwelt in that forgotten land.

Survey complete, Octaxa retired to his cabin. He was weary. It was no small thing, ranging and probing for such great distance. But he had done well, felt content, and—more importantly—knew what awaited them at journey's end.

An Aikashi spirit.

One still lives. An enemy worthy of Octaxa's skill and power. A man possessed by the djinn demons of the east. Octaxa suspected that was the reason why that city hadn't fallen yet. But fall it would, once he got there.

I will kill you, Aikashi.

Octaxa closed his eyes and allowed his mind to relax. They had a week's sail, no more. Chulan would meet them in the harbor. After that, the rending would start. He slept for a time, but woke suddenly as a shadow drifted across his mind. He focused on that shadow and imagined he saw a great fire-breathing beast floating above his head.

You're responding. That's good.

Octaxa opened his eyes, seeing the ghost of golden dragon eyes flicker and dwindle like fires in frosty ground. *You know I'm coming. That doesn't matter, Aikashi. Nothing can save you.*

Octaxa allowed his mind to range northward until he saw a man standing on the battlements of a city, the wind lifting his fiery red hair. Octaxa called out the red-haired warrior with his inner voice.

Free your dragon, Rundali. So I can catch its spirit and rip you both from the sky.

Rasnei chewed her lip as she looked down and saw the men scream as boiling oil drenched their faces, tearing them away. The rammers were well-protected this time. Men fell all around, but the great oak swung back and forth, each time sending a thud and shudder throughout the keep parapet. They were breaking through. The walls were crumbling in places as the ballistae took their toll. Riders whooped as they tossed high ladders, vaulted from their mounts and commenced climbing the walls.

The cannons roared to her right and left. Rasnei saw the great balls fly out and tear through that army. It made no difference. There were too many. They would need a thousand cannons to stop Casca today.

Dazed, she hardly felt the nudge at her arm. Rasnei turned. A young woman stood there trembling, her eyes showing courage and determination amid the terror. She vaguely remembered a name. *Jilanna.* The girl Vian had liked.

"You've come from the palace?" The girl nodded, tried to answer. "Where is Lord Vian?"

"He is gone, Light of—"

"What do you mean? Gone where?" She almost spat the words out, and Jilanna stepped back. "Out with it, girl. Where is he?"

"Vian said that he was needed elsewhere," Jilanna informed her. Rasnei stared at the girl and almost struck her pretty face. She clenched her fist, then slowly released it again.

"What did he tell you?" *This has to be Savarna. She's called him away from me.* Vian was leaving Ta Shen to its fate as Rasnei begged him to. She felt a mixture of relief and rage. *You've deserted me after all.*

Jilanna said nothing. Rasnei rounded on her in fury. "Speak, else I have your tongue!" Rasnei saw a score of Cardalan riders had cleared the walls a hundred yards away. Her guards were engaging with them, Gurtei among them.

"He said ..." Jilanna paused, and her mouth dropped open. Rasnei felt a shadow passing overhead as a great shout went out across the battlement.

THEY WERE IN! RAN CASCA WHEELED HIS MARE AROUND in victory circles as he watched the ram shatter the gates. His warriors clambered over the walls in groups, killing and falling upon the broken foe.

"I have won!" He yelled across to Calgara, who grinned back at him before leading a new assault on the gate. Ta Shen was broken. Let the slaughter begin.

Casca rode forward at a pace, his bodyguard of thirty riders bunching close, with shields raised to protect their Ran from any stray arrow. He ordered them make for the gates. As he rode closer, Casca saw figures on the keep, one of them a woman.

I am coming for you, Rasnei.

Casca laughed, as though drunk, as his horse thundered toward the gates gathering speed. *Father, I achieved what you couldn't.* He rode faster yet, full gallop, his men beside him and the shadow of the walls reaching over them. Those proud walls were pitted and cracked. Casca grinned—he'd pull them down stone by stone. He would slaughter every living creature, and sow salt in those famous gardens.

I have won.

A shadow blocked the sun to his right. He heard yells and shouts of fear. A horse crashed into his beast.

"What the fuck is that?" Casca shielded his eyes as the sun reappeared. He saw something beyond it, moving fast. *A bird?* Far too big.

A dragon. The rumors he'd heard had been true.

"You'll not steal my victory!" Casca saw Rasnei up there, watching the dragon's path. He pointed at her, a figure beside her holding a bow. Casca stood in his saddle and shouted again: "I'm coming for you!"

Casca swallowed a scream as an arrow punctured his eye

and he tumbled into darkness. For a moment, Casca hovered high above the city. He saw the dragon gliding toward him, a mile of glinting gold. And he saw pale Rasnei's smiling face.

It was my victory, Casca told her.

Both dragon and empress vanished as he sank into final blackness.

"It's Vian!" a voice she vaguely recognized as Gurtei shouted close by. Rasnei watched in awestruck wonder as the huge metal-winged bird—as it appeared to her eyes—swooped low over the fleeing Cards.

The enemy attack had stalled the moment the golden dragon appeared. Vian saved them again. Her beloved, the half-human killer. *That dragon out there.* She saw the beast glide like an arrow, its claws scooping up men from their horses and dropping them again.

The Cards were in full flight, their leader dead. She'd seen the arrow strike Casca's left eye and watched with dispassion as he tumbled from his horse. Her mind hardly registered the sight. They'd won the day, *Goddess be blessed.* Because of Vian. The enemy were in turmoil. No leader or shaman to control their rout. Those left on the walls had been dispatched with ruthless efficiency.

"We should follow after them," she heard another voice. Matax?

"No need." That was Gurtei again. "Empress, are you well …?"

"What …?" Rasnei tore her glance from the dragon and saw Gurtei staring hard at her face.

"You looked far away. I wondered if you were …"

"I am well." She flashed him a smile and followed the dragon's ruinous path again. Twenty minutes she watched, until most of the scampering army had fled the plain, leaving a shambles of wandering, panicking horses, running men, more dead and dying, abandoned contraptions, and ruptures and scoops in the soil, where the swooping beast had ripped up the fleeing foe.

Rasnei watched wide-eyed as the dragon turned away, flying north. She witnessed him circle, soaring high, turning again, and returning to the city from far across the hills, near that high ridge where she'd left him before arriving in the city. She watched the dragon cut the blue, high and fast, the sunlight blazing from his wings.

Oh, Vian …

Rasnei felt her heart thudding in her chest, the tears welling in her eyes.

"What's that?" Dorthar tensed beside her.

Rasnei saw something dark manifest like a storm cloud far out to sea. Unnaturally swift, the cloud mustered and swelled as it moved toward the city. The dragon saw the cloud, too, and let out a stone-ripping roar.

Arrow-swift, Vian-dragon sped across to greet the hastening cloud. That darkness took on the shape of a clenched fist. Rasnei glimpsed a face and demon eyes. She thought she heard a voice.

Dragon met cloud and vanished within.

What followed confused her. The cloud shifted and fell apart, fading into watery mist and vanishing. The sky was clear again. But there was no sign of Vian … the dragon.

At last, she saw him, twisting up in agonized spirals. Was he hurt? Arcing high, the wings shuddering, shaking, before falling back and plummeting down beneath the waves.

"Vian!"

Rasnei gripped Dorthar's hand so tight, her nails dug into his heavy leather gauntlets and marked the flesh beneath.

UZCARA DRAGGED HIS DRUGGED BODY FROM THE BED AS the women rushed outside to see what had happened. A guard emerged white-faced, then a second.

"What ...?" Uzcara stood too quickly. He spat blood and, giddy, sat back on the bed. He gripped the stump of his arm and cursed until the dizziness passed. He closed his eyes to shut out the pain until a familiar voice reached him.

"Brother."

Calgara stood at the tent entrance, his face covered in blood, some of it clearly his own. Other men were bunched behind him, all of them blood-drenched with wide staring eyes.

"Where's Casca?" Uzcara tried to stand again, but deemed it a bad idea and slunk back slowly.

"Dead," Calgara glared back at him like a man possessed by demons.

"How is that possible?"

"Arrow," the guard muttered.

"Came from the sky," another added.

"Fuck off, wankers." Uzcara bid them go, then stared hard into his youngest brother's eyes. "What happened out there?" *Had Calgara lost his sanity? Were they all mad?* "Speak, damn you."

"Dragon." Calgara chewed the word out, as though he was working on gristle. "A golden dragon fell on us."

"You're telling me that a fucking dragon killed our brother?"

Calgara shook his head. "An arrow killed him. I saw it happen. I was close by. We were both looking up at the walls where the dragon had come from. Someone shot Casca in the eye. He's gone. brother."

"Well, fuck … and where's this dragon now?" Uzcara felt the acid-anger rise, upsetting his stomach. He leaned over and spewed on the sheets.

"Gone," Calgara replied. "We fled the plain."

"Get my horse." With infinite care, Uzcara rose to his feet. He felt better having thrown up, but he was still weak and giddy as a newborn lamb.

"Brother, you can't go out there—it could come back."

"Do it."

Calgara nodded. He left Uzcara leaning on the bedpost. Minutes later, he heard a snort, and the guards reappeared. He shuffled outside and blinked in the bright afternoon sun. Uzcara glared at the sky as though it was his enemy.

"I don't see a dragon."

Calgara appeared and stood beside him. "I said it had gone."

"Help me up." Uzcara bid his brother and another steady the horse as he hoisted a foot into the saddle. He cursed, heaving his heavy body up with his remaining hand. He sat the saddle for a moment, getting his strength back. "Stay here."

Uzcara left them staring after him. He rode through the camp, witnessing the bustle of noise and anxious voices. *An army in retreat.* He didn't like what he saw. What the fuck had happened out there?

He cleared the camp and rode out onto the plain. The

fierce Shen sun made him giddy again, dressed as he was in undergarments and hose. He glanced at the distant walls, seeing how they appeared to float in the shimmer. He'd lost five brothers to that city. Ta Shen was cursed. He should leave it be. They'd inflicted enough damage on the enemy. Over the centuries, throughout the long years. This month. His father had been obsessed. Casca looked to be going the same way. Uzcara missed Cardalis and Laregoza. He hated this place like no other. Fuck the fabled riches. He'd leave it all be, had he the choice.

But Uzcara knew that there was no choice. He'd lost blood and kin, and—far worse—honor. He would get his strength back and hammer his troops until they dreaded his wrath more than any dragon. That done, Uzcara would return and sack that city.

I'M DROWNING …

Vian …

He saw Savarna swimming fish-swift toward him through the green.

I'm dead, sister. Go back to your lover.

She gripped his hand, and Vian felt himself lifted up until his head broke the surface. There he floated for a time, weak as kelp stranded on a dry beach. The dragon was gone, the Aikashi no longer inside him. The dark-faced enemy had taken its soul.

Octaxa.

He knew the name, for the cloud had echoed that word as it engulfed him. Close, but much too far away, Vian saw the distant cliffs and the huts of Ta Shen harbor. He lacked the strength to swim, so he was content to drift and float, his body carried wherever.

At least we saved your city. Rasnei would be safe. It was all that he could ask for. Vian floated as his mind wandered. He felt at peace, calm. He'd done all he could. Savarna had helped him. He'd repay that if he could, when he crossed the silvery doors to the Otherworld. He could watch both his women from there.

Vian floated, light fading around him, the warm water chilling as the long day slipped into dusk. He heard voices and shouts. His mind was wandering again. The cold would take him, or else a fish. It didn't matter. *We are autumn leaves in a gale.* Vian closed his eyes, allowing the water to seep into his soul.

The voices were nearer. Djinn demons coming for him. *The Aikashi's dead*, he told the demons, spitting bubbles, his mouth moving. He felt his limbs leaden and tire. *Not long now* ... Vian saw distorted faces, swelling and shrinking animal masks.

"Go away, djinn." Vian struck out at the closest face. A hand gripped his arm and hoisted him out of the water.

"He's alive," a rough voice said.

"But for how long?" another voice replied.

The world went black, and Vian Eltayn knew no more.

End of Part Two

PART III

THE FINAL MOON

A RIPPLE IN THE VORTEX

THE SILVERY-BLUE HARE ran through fields that tingled and chimed with musical dew, each droplet shining like a diamond and speaking to her of many things. Coristain ignored the playful grass. Ahead were the Faerie camps, the pale conical tents of her brother's men. She saw Aldorian's high banner shimmering outside the pavilion where he held war court.

She steered clear, her lean hare shape flitting into triangular violet woods and hopping over crystal streams until the brooding dark of the troll camps festered in tallow torch light below. Past these, Coristain saw the revolting round yellow hovels that the goblins had built for their temporary stations. She needed to avoid Greshgaran's folk too. Goblins were lore wise. They would see through any guise and guess her purpose.

But trolls were stupid, clumsy folk. Not interesting clumsy, like her Yetain. Trolls were ugly and stank of stale, damp bones. That said, they did have some appeal. They were lusty and enthusiastic. Elf lords were always so distant and vain, neglecting the manifold needs of their ladies.

The hare reached the camp. Coristain saw the hulking guards—huge, green-skinned, half-naked creatures, spears and clubs in their gnarly fists. She entered the maze of tents and clutter, finding more trolls seated around a great fire and roasting the flesh of some large beast. The smell reached her nostrils, and she crinkled her nose. Ugly folk indeed.

Rumgorz's tent was easy to find. A vast, square, ramshackle of timber and wattle-daub—more like a dank cave than house, as was their preference. The trolls' ancestral home was mostly underground. Outside, a huge guard leaned on a double-headed axe, his shaggy black hair tangled around his face. He appeared half-asleep, but Coristain knew better than to take the chance.

She mouthed a rune, allowed her hare-body to shift and shrink. She became a bubble, drifting and lifting, gliding across to where the guard stood inert. His head moved as she passed, as though sensing her presence. Her bubble drifted through the cracks in the door, and the guard settled back.

Inside the hut was a spacious gloom. Coristain made out odd shapes: tables, chairs, a lone bucket that stank of fresh detritus. And a bed, upon which a huge figure rested, black eyes open and staring at the thin trail of smoke rising from the only candle.

Coristain's bubble floated across, reached the candle, and popped open. It became a slime of wax, sliding down settling in the sconce tray.

"I know you're there." Rumgorz's head moved slightly. She saw his deep-set charcoal eyes flicking toward the door. "Aldorian has sent a spy, it seems." He sat up. Coristain studied the huge, naked chest, the corded arms and shifting muscle beneath his green oily skin. "Show yourself, before I call my guards to tear you open."

"That would be a waste, great king." Coristain chanted three times, and the spell returned her to her natural form. She stood before the troll king, clad in a shimmering hare-broached gown of silver and green, rubies glistened in her ears. Her scent was of violets and jasmine. She smiled, seeing the lust in his terrible eyes.

"See me as a gift from the Elf King," Coristain said, unclipping the silver hare-broach, allowing her gown to drop and settle. His eyes drank in her nakedness.

"Aldorian is generous indeed, to gift me with his sister."

"Twas not his idea," she purred, drifting over to gaze down at him. "We elf women have needs, and our men are much absorbed with their preparations. Of late, we've been neglected — forgotten, even."

"Ha—is that so? Then your husbands and lords are foolish indeed. But elves were ever a shallow folk. We trolls know how to cherish beauty, in our own way. Come to me and I will see you well served, Coristain."

"You remember me—I'm impressed."

"You were my son's lover once, I recall."

"I was, albeit far too briefly. Whatever became of Gruntzor?"

The coal eyes flared with sudden fire, and Coristain was filled with dread. She dared not upset this king. There were rumors surrounding Gruntzor. Dark tales. She smoothed her smile and took in his huge chest.

She glided close, brushed her long fingers over the coarse black hairs of his torso. The cold eyes watched her, relaxed. The danger had passed for the moment. Coristain's sly glance flicked to the lamp, soon to be dwindled to smoke. His retainers would light another. She didn't have long. *Am I a slave to time also?* she thought as she rubbed harder into his chest.

"I would fain see you properly, great king," her hand slipped down.

Rumgorz chuckled, a deep sound like gravel sliding down a wintry slope. "You are a forward woman."

"Why delay pleasure?"

"Why indeed." The king stood before her, his great height looking down upon her. She studied his body, the granite-hard face, the deep-set and terrible eyes, the latent power blazing within like storm lanterns in a gale. Her glance dropped lower, taking in his shoulders and the mighty arms, corded with golden torcs. Stolen gold from Swartzheim, by its look. Coristain allowed her hands slide up his sinewy thighs, as at last her eyes feasted on the huge column of his sex.

Coristain raised a crafty brow as she slid her nimble fingers, teasing him. The king closed his eyes. She worked her fingers faster with her right hand, while the left unclasped the hidden pin in her hair. She raised it high, gripped tightly in her deft fingers.

Rumgorz sighed, his mouth dribbling.

Die, troll!

The king roared in agony and fear as her hand stabbed down, the needle piercing deep, and the hell-spells she woven into its point mingling with the poison and seeping into his veins.

"You treacherous bitch!" Rumgorz glared at her, choking blood. He stumbled, tottered and fell tree-heavy, face first, striking the ground like a granite boulder. Coristain grabbed her gown and wrapped it around her body, mouthing the vanishing rune as the massive guard roared into the hut. He saw the king lying prone, and for the briefest instant caught

Coristain's eye before her escape-rune took hold and she faded like smoke in sunlight.

The troll swung across at her with his double-headed axe. Coristain floated up to the roof again. She became a moth and crawled through the smoke hole. Once there, she lifted high and took silent flight to the distant elf camp. Below her, the trolls woke to noise and fury.

Coristain sought her brother's pavilion. She drifted in, and she saw the king standing gazing at the flames and fury where the trolls were stirring.

She appeared before him. Aldorian's eyes glittered like ice as they studied her.

"Sister. What ill deed have you done?"

"A deed that you, brother, will thank me for one day."

"How is that? I hear troll voices. Are we under attack?"

"If not, you soon will be." Coristain flashed him an artful grin. "I stabbed Rumgorz—he's dead. I came to warn you brother. You had best rally your captains. As for myself, I'll not linger hereabouts."

She spoke a rune, became a dragonfly, and darted out into the void. Aldorian chased her in swallow form.

Coristain arrowed toward the thin veneer of the pulsing World Gate.

"Sister, wait!" She heard his bird voice as he swooped after her. "It is not yet time on the other side—the crossing will alter everything, damage our chances."

"Farewell, brother!" Coristain reached the throbbing, shifting glare of fusion and entered within. For a moment, she locked eyes with her brother. Then he was gone, as was Faerie. Everything.

"They took the bait," Rune said, sounding pleased. Rafin had grown bored and wandered over to see how the witch and Yetain were getting on. He'd lost the elves—doubtless they were traversing the Lost Lanes, as best they could. Even elves had to be careful out there. He'd check back shortly to mark their progress.

"What has happened?" Rafin puffed at his pipe and yawned. "It doesn't look like you've achieved anything special."

"That's because you have dim dwarf eyes that only see clearly in the gloom." Unva glanced up at him angrily. "Rune's right—this should work."

"They're coming," Rune told him, showing his peculiar smile. "The elves and trolls—maybe the goblins, too, if they're caught in the middle. She pulled it off."

"How can that possibly be good news?"

"Because it's *too* early," Unva said, as though addressing an obtuse child. "Go back and keep watch, dwarf. We need to be out of here before they arrive."

Rafin stared at her. Unva looked at Rune and sighed. "Explain," she said.

Rune nodded slowly. "The trolls attacked the elf camp, killing many," he said. "Aldorian's people have fled through the World Gate, and Rumgorz's will be following after. Their fragile truce is over. Coristain killed the troll king."

"What?" Rafin decided he'd make an extra-potent brew, soon as he got the chance. He strongly suspected Rune and the woman had started something they'd regret.

"Yes," Rune said. "It was our idea to sow dire discord in their camps. Coristain escaped and fled through the World Gate. Her passage wasn't noted by the Guardian. But the others will be—the violent noise caused vengeful trolls and her brother's elves. The resulting echoes will reverberate throughout the nine worlds, and it's not time yet—that's the key. Too early, as Unva says. The conjunction hasn't welded yet. The premature momentum will shatter the link-codes between worlds and enable Unva and myself to alter the moon's course. Bring it forward in time."

"You don't say." Rafin lit his pipe and sucked hard.

"When the armies of Faerie enter this realm," Rune explained, "the final moon will be in the last quarter. One week from the conjunction of spheres. The right time for Jaran Saerk to plan his attack. We'll no longer have to wait. Even better, Sheega will be caught off guard."

"What about Coristain?"

"She's … *somewhere.*"

"That's helpful," Rafin said. "Should I expect her to pop out from the caves, as well as the entire fucking Faerie army?"

"Just go keep watch while we finish up, will you?" Unva glared at him. "You don't have to understand this, dwarf. There are few of us left who can."

Rafin blew out his cheeks. "Suits me," he said. "You pair deserve each other." He awarded Rune a sharp look. "Next time you want to explain something, you had best slip inside my head again. That way I might have a notion of what the fuck you're talking about."

"He understands," Unva told Rune. "The dwarf's just angry he wasn't part of our plan."

Rafin glared at her and sucked his pipe. "Enough," he said. "I'm off."

JARAN HAD BARELY GLIMPSED THE MILKY, SMILING EYES before Ranning vanished below the murky water. He didn't hesitate, hoisting Griner high with both hands and wading into the oily drink. He reached the spot where Ranning had been and cut down hard with the axe, hewing into the brackish water. Thrashing and swiping all about. Jaran knew his action was futile, but the swinging calmed his frustration and rage.

Anger cooled, Jaran waded back to the cave shelf where Savarna stood watching him with the others. "Now she knows where we are," he said to those gathered there.

"She already knew," Svipdag said. "The caves above Cradon Iwey are the only place on this island where you could hide for more than a few days. Sheega cannot reach you here. Gronteyer's roots are outside her domain. Her spells and creatures have no effect in this place. Not even Faerie can alter things inside these caverns."

"What do you know, old man?" Jaran asked him.

"Many things," Svipdag said. "Most of them bad. I dabbled in sorcery in the southlands. Something I regret, as the nightmares have never left. Back here, I learned more. I wanted to understand why it was that Sheega stayed put on the north of the island. I needed to know the islanders were safe. The thought was driven by my guilt of what happened. Thus, I took to these caves and learnt their secrets, too. There are many."

"The Faerie gate." Savarna nodded. "It was not how we entered Valkador."

"Oh, but it was," Svipdag said. "I saw your arrival, *Aikashi*." Jaran blinked hearing that, and he saw Savarna's face redden. Svipdag ignored them. "The Yetain creature held the channels open long enough for you pair to reach the beach near the Great Hall. Rune didn't want Sheega to sense your approach. Her mind is often on the Cradon Iwey."

"You were watching from the North Seat?" Jaran said.

"I was," Svipdag nodded. "I've been expecting you, Jaran Hrelgisson. And your friends. The moon and stars have carved your names in the night sky. Bear, tiger, and falcon."

"You probably heard that from Unva," Jaran said, not wishing to believe this old wastrel.

"What did you call Rune?" Savarna asked him at the same time.

Svipdag smiled secretly. "The Yetain were of Faerie too. Another myth, they frequented the northlands long before the time of humans. Before even the High Gods first arrived from their hallowed halls. The Yetain have always been here, though most perished long ago."

"I don't know what you are talking about," Jaran said, irritated. "Rune—whatever he is—needs us as much as we do him. Has admitted as much. Let's keep things simple. Tell me how I can reach Sheega without her knowing I'm there."

"You can't," Svipdag said. "That should be obvious, boy. But I doubt you'll have to wait much longer."

"And why is that?"

An arrow struck the stone by Jaran's head. He ducked instinctively, pulling Savarna down beside him. He heard Svipdag yelling and the sound of running feet. Jaran looked up and saw Rafin and Unva emerge from a crack, Rune's bulk lumbering behind.

"Best get your running feet on, people," Rafin shouted across to them. "The elves are here."

"Where the fuck have you been?" Sheega rounded on Ranning as he stood dripping in her hall. "I've had to think fast, since you left me to do everything."

"I was hoodwinked," Ranning told her. "Stuck in the Lost Lanes, tricked by that villain Rune."

"And where has *he* gone?"

"Cradon Iwey." Ranning grinned at her. "They are all there with their hero. Jaran Hrelgisson has quite the following."

Sheega scratched her chin. "This is Unva's doing."

"She and the Yetain. They've opened the sluice gates." Ranning barked a laugh.

"What are you saying?" Sheega felt the rage returning. *Had she been outplayed?*

"I'm saying that Faerie is here, on this island."

"That cannot be," Sheega said. *Can it?* "It's not yet time."

"*Time* has been altered," Ranning said. "To draw the elves in. Before I saw Hrelgisson and the orange-cat woman in the upper caves, I spied that dwarf king we duped. Rafin was at the sea entrance watching on. Close by, Rune and your friend Unva worked the time keys, knowing that even you couldn't scry deep into that cave. Those two have more spell-craft than you gave them credit for."

"Stolen lore," Sheega said bitterly. "I taught Unva everything she knows. The elves did the same for Rune. Charlatans, the pair of them." She glared at him, as her rage shifted to a deeper emotion. Realization.

Time. They've altered time here on the island.

The moon had skipped a course. *I must prepare.* Sheega's face blanched with worry. Mind busy, she strode from the hall. There, she stood for some time, gazing up at the starry heavens. She saw the gibbous moon, noting its position in the sky. Her enemies had achieved the impossible and brought time forward, skipping a moon's full passage. An action caused by Faerie breaking through the World Gate too soon. She had one week before the moon waxed full. The final moon.

Ranning joined her, looking up. "Best we get ready," he said.

"Where's Gorvaron?" Sheega stared coldly at her lover.

"I found him wandering the hills," he replied, evasively. "Unva must have set a confusion spell on him. Gorvaron's hungry and angry. Ready to avenge the scorn."

"Good." she snapped her teeth together. "I raised the lake men, and I have summoned Garrosk and the remaining witch-men to the hall. Once Hrelgisson knows it's time, he'll be on his way here."

"I'll keep an eye out for him," Ranning said, showing a slight grin. "What about the Vulkorye girl?"

"Fled, while I was away."

"You really do need me around," Ranning said. "And Finvar?"

"Lurking hereabouts," Sheega told him. "I'm calling on his master. Lofhi needs to be told, if he doesn't know already. You'll find me at the witching pole."

THE STOCKY, RED-FACED MAN BLOCKED THE LANE, AN AXE gripped in his hands. The huts of a fishing village were barely visible in the steady veil of rain. Tofei slid from his mare, while Asmund remained seated. The stocky fellow tapped the axe haft with grubby fingernails.

Tofei walked toward him and saw the distrust on the man's face.

"Sherriff Doggan?"

"Who's asking?"

"Tofei Gunardsson, and Asmund of Valkador."

"Valkador doesn't exist."

"You obviously don't get out much these days." He turned and grinned at Asmund. "The sheriff here says your island doesn't exist."

"Perhaps we should fight him, knock some sense into the old fellow," Asmund said, grinning as sat his horse.

Doggan glowered. "You cocky pups will feel the metal of my axe if you don't mind your manners. Bugger off. The last person who mentioned that island brought something foul with him."

"That would be Jaran Saerk."

"Aye, know of him, do you?"

"He's our Jarle, and your rightful king, Doggan," Tofei said. "You should show some respect."

"Be off with you, I say. Jaran Saerk almost caused my death. Twice. And my sons once too. He and that evil-eyed woman, and the sly, talkative one. Those three brought the demons with them."

"The green men." Tofei nodded. "Yes, I fought with those, too. Sheega's witch guard. Unpleasant creatures. Most are dead. The ones that visited Skarness anyway, though some others are still around."

"Including a giant version," Asmund added helpfully.

"What do you want with me?" Doggan lowered his axe but still looked angry.

"Your help to spread the word."

"I don't know anyone."

"You're the sheriff—you must have folk to protect. Where are your sons, or the other fishers? Haven't they told you about the island out there? Why not set sail and take a look for yourself?"

"I've seen it." Doggan wiped his nose with the back of his hand. "Another of *her* tricks. An illusion. Were I to sail that way, it would vanish to mist again, or she'd summon a storm like she has before."

"My island is real, Sherriff Doggan. We have need of stout warriors there." Asmund tossed the bundle at the sheriff's feet.

"What is that?" He stared down at the fur-wrapped object.

"Open it and look." Tofei said.

"If this is a trick, some prank ..."

"The Traveler sent us here," Tofei said. "I think you've met him."

"I've met lots of travelers. Most aren't welcome these days."

"You know him as Gurn the ferryman."

Doggan's eyes widened in alarm. "He'd dead." He picked up the bundle and untied the cords. His eyes widened further when he saw the red arrow. "The War Arrow of Valkador. I thought it a myth. You are from there. It's true. Is the witch gone?"

"Not yet, but we're working on that," Tofei said. "Jaran Saerk needs your help, and that of your sons. A way to get back at the green killers—her *pets*. To avenge the atrocity at Skarness."

"You want me to take this ... arrow? It's a high honor."

"Asmund will journey with you," Tofei said, nodding. "Gather who you can, tell them Jaran Hrelgisson, who we call *Saerk,* is their rightful king and calls on them to fight the servants of the witch Sheega."

"That could take months and most likely result in us losing our heads."

"No, it won't. The Traveler has promised to help you,

though he cannot intervene directly. Take the arrow, Sherriff Doggan. Carry it through Leeth and Rethen—Hragglund, too. Spread the word. Jaran Saerk is calling on all Northmen to save us from the Ice Witch."

"I shall do as you ask," the sheriff said, looking bewildered.

24

THE BARROW

SHE'S WORRIED ABOUT YOU.

"Leave me alone." Finvar's eyes blinked open. He'd been dozing.

No, you need to listen. The voice was close.

"I'd much rather sleep." Finvar saw the shape crawling out of the fire. He was so tired—he hadn't slept much since Gunsala had left. The dread of what Sheega would do next hung heavily other him.

Forget sleep—plenty of time for that when you're dead.

"Which won't be long, unless you rein her back."

Sheega thinks you're backsliding. The lass needs some proof of your commitment. She's away at her pole, shrieking in the wind. It's getting tense, Fin, boy. There's been some kind of world-fabric fuckup.

"What are you talking about?" Finvar was struggling to keep his eyes open.

He watched the shape plop like sticky goo from the fire. Two ruby eyes glittered as Lofhi manifested before him. This time, he looked like a handsome troubadour, the golden harp in his hand. Dagda's stolen harp.

All smiles, the handsome figure addressed him with a pluck of his harp strings. "Unva and that shaggy pest have been interfering with complex Faerie matters," Lofhi said in a high singing voice. "The dubious pair have excelled themselves, removing an entire month from the island's calendar. I'm impressed by the wolf wench, truth be told."

"I don't know what you're talking about."

Deft fingers plucked strings, and lips curled cruelly. "It is complex for simpletons—I appreciate that. Suffice to say, your big, bad chum will be here to rescue you in a matter of days. A week, no more. You had best get ready."

"WHAT HAVE YOU DONE?" JARAN SHOUTED AT RAFIN, as he and Savarna fled back into the catacombs. Far behind, he'd glimpsed the shapes of pale figures rushing after them. Jaran recognized the same beings that had pursued them in Faerie, back at the dank marshes near the World's Rim.

"This way!" Svipdag emerged beside him again. "Take the second tunnel—it will lead you out to the southern entrance where that giant attacked you, and to the woods beyond. I'd lie low in those woods. No point you staying here any longer."

"What about you?" Savarna said.

Svipdag grinned at her. "I will lead them on a merry chase. Elves are canny, but they don't know these caves like I do. Best you run—they're gaining ground."

Jaran glared at Svipdag for a moment. He could see the elves flitting over rocks a hundred yards behind, as they cleared the last twist in the cavern. "Thank you," he said. "Stay alive."

"I intend to." Svipdag turned and walked back in the direction of the elves.

"Mad as toast," Rafin said, inching alongside Jaran. "But best we do as he suggests."

At the waterfall camp, they found Gunard and Gunsala deep in discussion. The islander Bjarni was there, and several others. But Ivar was missing. Jaran asked where he'd had gone, but no one knew.

"Time to move," Jaran shouted across to them. "Not that way—follow us." He and Savarna led the way through the twisting maze of cracks and tunnels for what seemed like hours. Eventually, light emerged. Jaran was surprised to recognize the same cave they had entered with Ivar. That seemed like weeks ago.

"Gronteyer must be hollow," Jaran said to Savarna. "Those caverns run for miles.

"Like goblin cheeses." Rafin sniffed the bright air. "Damp and riddled with fucking holes."

"I thought dwarves liked caves," Jaran said.

"That just shows your ignorance, big laddie. *Caves.* I live in an underground palace of shimmering golden light, amidst grandeur and beauty that surpasses anything your dim mortal brain could fathom. You, hero, have no notion of the vast glory of Swartzheim."

They clambered out into the sunshine.

"I'm sorry I mentioned it," Jaran said, glancing up, half-expecting to see the giant Gorvaron jumping down on them. But all was quiet. A bright clear afternoon, skylarks hovering and whistling high above.

Savarna stood beside him, blinking in the sunshine. Jaran studied his friends and noticed that both Unva and Rune were missing.

"Gone." Rafin said catching his train of thought.

"Where this time?"

"She'll be sealing that last cavern with spell-runes. We don't want those elf raiders finding us."

"Raiders?" Savarna stared at the dwarf. "I thought an army was coming."

"It is," Rafin said. "But that was just a raiding party. The van. Aldorian was testing the thread. Unfortunately, with Rune having stirred up all manner of shit, we can expect half of Faerie on this island shortly."

"Why would Rune do that?" Savarna asked the dwarf.

"I suggest you ask him yourself." Rafin smiled at her. "I'm too knackered to explain."

JARAN WALKED WITH SAVARNA AND BJARNI DOWN THE woods, the dense canopy closing over them and birdsong heralding their passage. Rafin shuffled behind with the others. Each time Jaran turned to check, he saw the dwarf in close conversation with Finvar's girl. They descended for half-hour, the pines mixing with oak and elm as they got lower. Ahead, a patch of sunlight showed a break in the trees.

Jaran stopped when he glimpsed movement down there.

"Wait here," he told the others, entering the sunny glade with Savarna. He hefted Griner warily, Savarna clenching her scimitar.

"Took your time getting here."

Unva sat on a rock smiling in the sun. Her yellow eyes looked triumphant, as though she had achieved something remarkable. Jaran heard a shuffle and wasn't surprised to see Rune emerge from the rock behind her.

"You two have some explaining to do," Jaran said, as they walked over to join them. He waved the rest to follow and heard Rafin snort in derision seeing who was there.

"We are safe in these woods for the moment," Unva said.

"That's not what I got from Rafin. Is it?" Jaran looked at the dwarf, who shrugged as he joined them.

"She knows best," Rafin replied.

"Shut up, dwarf," Unva said. She stared at Jaran for a long time, as though weighing his courage. Savarna shuffled awkwardly beside him. Jaran met the wolf witch's gaze evenly.

Survey completed, Unva nodded as though satisfied. She glanced over at Gunard and the others standing at the edge of two large oaks. Jaran was relieved to see that Ivar had joined them. He had no idea where the old hunter had been. He started to ask, but Unva was speaking again.

"You people don't need to hear this," she said to those gathered. "Gunard, you and your men await your son's return at your ship. Bjarni, you should return to your village and ready your people—it's about to get busy on this island." The men stared at her. "Go," she ordered, her yellow eyes narrowing. Jaran felt the feral ferocity of that stare. "Ivar can stay. The rest of you be on your way." She waited until they had faded off under the trees.

"What about me?" Gunsala stood beside Rafin again.

"You stay with us." Unva's yellow gaze flashed over her. Gunsala nodded.

"You've got some explaining to do," Jaran repeated to

Unva, as impatience inched up his spine. Finvar needed his help, and the caves were under attack. What next? They hide in a wood while Sheega comes to say hello? He was tempted to hit Unva with something hard. Instead, he gazed at Rune, who nodded slowly. *You two are testing me …*

"Well …?" Jaran held the witch's yellow stare.

"First, I'd appreciate some gratitude," she said.

"For what?" Jaran tried to keep his voice low. "Conjuring spells and buggering about welcoming the hell-hordes of Faerie onto my island?"

"That's part of it, but not most," Rune said, and Rafin snorted again.

"I'm tired of this," Jaran said to Savarna. "I'm going to finish this today. Finvar—"

"—is alive," Unva snapped at him. "He won't be the minute *she* senses your approach, fool. Either that, or Lofhi will fry his brain."

"How do you—"

"Shut up, and listen, Jaran Saerk. You too, Savarna."

Jaran stiffened, his fingers squeezing Griner's haft. Savarna flashed him a wild look. He folded his arms. "Go on … we're listening."

Unva nodded. "Thank you." She glanced around the glade. "I'm so much happier in a wood. Those caves. This is better … we are safe enough here."

"You already told us that."

Unva hardly registered his anger. Rune shuffled up beside her.

"Jaran Saerk," Unva stared intently at him, her yellow eyes demanding his full attention. "Are you ready to kill your enemy, Sheega the Ice Witch?"

"You know that I am."

"That is good." She smiled. "You have *one* week to achieve your goal."

"How is that possible?" Savarna asked. "The appointed time was over a month away."

"Unva bent the mechanics of time with cunning spell-craft, enriched and protected by the shield that is Cradon Iwey," Rune said, and Rafin nodded enthusiastically behind him. "I was able to help Unva by asking a favor from someone I knew long ago. That *individual* caused a rupture in the World Gate by killing the troll king, Rumgorz. That resulted in the trolls and elves shattering their truce. The fight that followed Coristain's actions led to the vengeful trolls crashing through the World Gate too early, as they pursued the elves."

"It's that simple," Rafin added with a dry grin.

Rune ignored that. "Aldorian had no choice but to flee as his army was under attack. So many breaking through the World Gate at once shattered the Time Laws. Unva was able to crank up the gears and pull the moon forward, skipping an entire month's passage."

"Hmm, that clears that up nicely," Rafin muttered, producing his pipe. "Well done, my friend."

"One week?" Jaran shook his head unable to take it all in.

"Seven days," Rafin nodded.

Jaran glared at Rune and the woman beside him. "It doesn't change a thing. It's still too much time, with half of Faerie, and Gorvaron, and the gods know what else she's got brewing, all coming after us. I need to kill Sheega today."

"You are not strong enough yet," Unva told him. "One task remains before you can face her with confidence. After that, a few days will change everything. In Leeth, Gunard's son passes the War Arrow. He will return inside a week. I only stole time on this island. Over a month has already passed on the mainland since he and young Asmund left."

She almost smiled seeing their blank expressions. "Don't fret about that. We need to get busy."

"Doing what," Jaran asked her. "More waiting?"

"Raising your ancestors so they can help us."

Jaran blinked.

"Yes, Jaran Saerk." Unva smiled at him. "It's time you woke the ghosts of Valkador. It's only right. Sheega has her slaves and allies, and we need to balance the scales."

"Barin's Howe is by the Great Hall," Jaran said.

"I'm not talking about the Whitebear," Unva said. "Barin will appear when he is ready. He's out there somewhere, waiting." She looked about, and Jaran followed her gaze, half-expecting to see Barin emerge guised as a huge bear crashing through the woods. He saw Unva's yellow eyes flashed to Ivar, who stood close to Gunsala—both resembled figures carved in stone. "You know the place, Ivar Ketilsson. Of that, I'm sure."

"I do," Ivar nodded, and Jaran noted the fear in his eyes.

"What's this, Ivar?" Jaran stared at the islander.

"She's means Taic's Howe," he said, shaking his head.

"Barin's nephew." Jaran stared at Savarna. "The wild one he mentioned. Barin said that I was like him."

"Your forbear," Unva nodded.

"It's a bad place," Ivar said. "Not safe."

"Where is it?" Jaran asked him.

"A barrow, not far," Ivar replied, still looking unhappy. "To the south of here, close by where the hills meet the western shore. Taic's Howe is hidden in a hill fold. There are seven great beech trees growing there—the only ones on the island, brought here from distant lands in days gone by."

"We'll go there after dark," Unva said.

"We shouldn't." Ivar's eyes were wide.

"Not you, oldster," Unva told him kindly. "Jaran must accompany me alone. Even Rune and Rafin with all their Faerie experience would not be safe from any wights we might encounter at that barrow."

"Why would my ancestor harm my friends?" Jaran asked her.

"Hmm, good question," she replied. "It's called Taic's Howe, but Ivar is right. It's a bad place. Like Cradon Iwey, the barrow lies over another gateway. But not into Faerie, alas. There are channels underneath Taic's Howe that lead down to the very gates of Yffarn. Taic himself wanted to be buried there to protect his people from the evil below. Even Sheega dare not entangle herself with that place. The power beneath that barrow is what kept her away from the southern end of the island. That and Gronteyer's secrets."

"Hadn't Jaran best stay clear too," Savarna said.

"He will be protected," Unva told her. "As will I, for a brief while only. Jaran must speak the runes I pass him carefully, and call on his ancestor. Taic will come, and hopefully others, too."

Gunsala spoke for the first time: "You might need me there." Jaran noted how bright her eyes seemed, as though she was excited, anticipating the danger.

"Jaran and myself, no one else," Unva told the girl. "The rest of you must wait here until we return."

"I will come," Savarna said.

"Not even you," Unva replied. Savarna looked at Jaran for support, but he shook his head.

"Tonight?" Jaran asked Unva, ignoring Savarna's sharp glance.

"In a few hours," she said. "Best you rest up."

"I'm ready now," Jaran told her.

Hours passed and darkness settled silent in the wood.

An owl called out, and another answered. Jaran stood waiting for the witch, his left hand gripped in Savarna's, the right resting on Griner's steel. They'd rested the best they could until dark and after, by Unva's candlelight, had walked the forest, through the lower hills to eventually reach this place.

Jaran could hear the surge and sigh of waves—the sea was scarce more than a mile below where they stood. Ahead were tall trees, their shadows swaying. Ivar was right—this place had an ominous feel. The old islander had left them after guiding them close. He'd make for Bjarni's village, he'd said. Jaran had logged the worry in his eyes.

"Where did you disappear to earlier?' Jaran had asked him.

"I was looking for Svipdag," Ivar had replied evasively. Jaran had let that go.

Rune had departed too, after mentioning that elven woman's name again. She was someone he had to find. Jaran had hardly listened. Rune's erratic behavior was just another haze in a world of false shimmers.

They'd waited half an hour. Savarna's eyes were tense, her grip on his hand tighter. She, Rafin and Gunsala had all insisted on coming as near as they could. Jaran saw the dark shapes of birds settle in the trees. Crows or rooks. They made no sound, but even from this distance, it seemed to Jaran that they were waiting for him, watching and testing.

Unva appeared from the gloom, a lantern held high. She

beckoned Jaran forward, as Rafin shuffled up and walked over to join them. "I'll watch over your lass," he told Jaran.

"I don't need your protection," Savarna told the dwarf. For once, he didn't reply, and she turned to Unva. "If Jaran dies, I'm holding you responsible."

"Hurry!" Unva ignored Savarna as she motioned Jaran to join her again. "We haven't much time."

He let go of Savarna's hand. "I'll be fine," he told her.

"You'd better be," she replied.

Jaran left her standing in silence with the dwarf, the waft of his pipe trailing above, Gunsala watching behind them. He stepped beneath the shifting shadow of the beech trees. Unva placed a finger on his lips.

"I have the warding runes, and the summoning ones. They are sealed and protected. Do exactly as I tell you, and we can be done by dawn. Are you ready?" She removed her finger and hinted at the dark shape half-hidden by the trees.

"I am," he said.

"Then follow me."

The trees were huge, their shadow casting shimmers over a broad stone ledge. Jaran saw an entrance of sorts, and three tall standing stones marked the far end. A barrow, she had called this place. But his forefather had been buried here. *There is no danger here for me.* But Jaran sensed peril everywhere. The rooks shifted in the restless perches, high above. Like tiny daggers, he felt their needle-probing eyes upon him.

Unva approached the entrance, Jaran closed in behind her. "You remember the playing cards I showed you?"

"I do."

"This one is from the same set. There is power inside." She passed him the ruffled shape of a thin piece of parchment.

Jaran glanced at the playing card. Its face was dirty, the

corners crinkled. He flicked it between his fingers. "The card is blank," he told her.

"Hold it to my lantern light." He did as she said, and shifted irritably.

"There is nothing." But as he looked, Jaran saw the faint etching of shapes appear. Some kind of writing. Runes? The script grew sharper, and he recognized archaic runes tracing lines covering both sides of the cards. "I see them," he told her.

"Good," Unva said. "They will protect you when you enter below."

"*Enter?* I'm going inside?" Jaran looked at the slab and the gaping hole beneath it. A flat crack, half the height of a man and barely wide enough to squeeze through.

"The summoning will work only from inside the barrow. You must call on your kin from beneath the stones." Jaran glared at her, wide-eyed. "Go, do what you must, Jaran Saerk," Unva told him. "I will guide you from out here."

Jaran stared at her for a moment longer. Her yellow eyes held his gaze. He nodded and turned away, walking toward the barrow's crack opening. He stooped low, and with Griner gripped tight in one hand and the rune card clutched in the other, he crawled inside the barrow.

It was noticeably colder in here. For a time, Jaran crouched low, allowing his eyes to adjust to the deep dark. Minutes passed slowly. Jaran discerned vague shapes and the ripple of stone. A shimmer of dust. He looked up in surprise, seeing nothing above but swirling, smoky air.

Jaran stood slowly. He felt a wave of panic. Perhaps Unva was working for Sheega, after all? They'd been lovers once. Had she tricked him into entering Yffarn? He felt the tiny hairs tingle at the nape of his neck. Jaran gripped the playing card tighter and pushed his fear away.

These are my ancestors—this is my home.

Jaran walked forward carefully, as the dark faded to a shifting gray. He saw shapes moving on either side. Jaran ignored them, focusing on a distant, swaying green light. The light seemed to float and drift through the air leading him on. A will o' the wisp, but guiding or luring him? Impossible to know.

Jaran followed the light but never got closer. He reached a colder spot and gazed down, seeing a yawning chasm. A blast of icy, cankerous air rushed up at him, accompanied by the stench of gallows. Jaran choked and stumbled.

Keep moving!

Jaran heard Unva's urgent voice inside his head.

Stay away from the holes and vents.

Jaran shook himself and moved on. The yawning chasm snapped shut behind him, but he saw others appear, like smoking mouths, oozing dark vapor and acrid foul stench.

Those fissures smelt bad enough to be the gateways to Yffarn. Jaran picked up his pace. The barrow seemed endless. He held the card in front of his face and gripped Griner's haft.

At last, he reached the far end. A huge column of stone stood there. Beside it was a lintel. Resting on that were three skulls with tiny candles lit in the eye sockets.

Jaran chewed his beard.

You must touch the lintel stone with your card and hold it there. Ignore the skulls! Don't let them speak to you. They are not what they seem.

Jaran moved forward and placed his left hand against the tall stone, pressing hard at the card. He could sense the skulls shuddering, moving closer. He shut them out, concentrating on the parchment and the lintel beneath.

Good! Name the runes as they form in your mind.

Those names came floating at him, and as Jaran did as she told him, he felt a strange tingle of power connecting him to the tall stone. He leaned harder, pressing down on the parchment with his elbow, allowing the runes to break free from the damaged card. He felt them circle around his head. The runes spoke to him. Jaran recognized Fethu and Teiwaz, Daigaz and Raida, and the others too as they came. Jaran spoke their names in turn as the runes appeared and vanished before him.

There is one left. Her voice sounded muffled, further away.

Jaran saw the final rune floating up. *Anzuz?* He couldn't see it properly, tried to catch it with his hands, but it drifted higher. At first, the rune was shapeless—but as Jaran watched, it took on the form of a manikin with glittering ruby eyes.

Welcome to my world, Jaran Saerk.

Jaran gasped as the Anzuz rune cracked open and an icy blast hit his face. He almost dropped Griner as the parchment-card in his hand caught fire and burnt his fingers.

"Unva," he gasped, hearing no answer.

The stone loomed over him. The ruby-eyed manikin had gone. Instead, Jaran heard the distant, peeling notes of a melancholy harp.

"Lofhi, I know you're here. What trickery is this?" Jaran choked in shock, as cold, hard fingers gripped his cloak and pulled him inside the stone. He couldn't breathe, and it felt like lead-heavy hands were pushing down on his chest.

I am dying …

A blow struck his head. Jaran fell through draughty air as a denser darkness rushed up to greet him. As he fell, he looked across and saw that something large fell with him. An animal, with fur the color of freshly settled snow. The Whitebear had come. Jaran wasn't alone. The crushing pain left him, replaced by a flood of pride and courage.

You're back.

I've been waiting for you, he heard Barin's booming voice. *It's time to wake the others.*

25

THE VISIT

THE HORSEMAN DISMOUNTED and ran for cover. He didn't get far—Gujun's tossed dagger struck his back, and the Card disappeared. Gujun slipped from his horse and ran into the brush. The man was crawling, making mewling sounds. Gujun stood on his back, crouched low and removed the dagger with a twist, before quickly slicing it across the Card's throat.

The spy had been dangerously close to Stagan's camp. Who had sent him there? The Cards were in uproar, distracted and distraught. Ran Casca was dead—another of the Ragans, too. Things hadn't gone their way.

Gujun had arrived back at the camp yesterday, after taking the river ferry and purchasing a fast steed at the north docks. He'd reached Shateke's villa to find Chulan three days gone. He'd wasted no time, changing horses and riding east to reach Ta Shen four days later.

Chulan had interviewed him on arrival. The magister was in good spirits, having arrived by carriage two days earlier. The Shen camp was making ready, the time for attack near.

By chance, Gujun had been scouting the woods, mainly to get some space from the bustle and action in the camp. Fortunate for the Shen that he had.

Gujun rode back swiftly. Goi Stagan greeted his return at the camp perimeter fence.

"Why are there no lookouts in the woods?" Gujun asked the garrison commander.

"There are, and I've men posted all along the high ridge," Stagan replied, looking puzzled. "Good fellows, lying low and well hidden."

"So well hidden they're fucking asleep," Gujun told him. "I found three Card spies creeping through the woods. And a rider who was trying to escape when I caught up with him, before returning here."

"What of my men?" Stagan demanded.

"Dead, most likely."

"I'll send out a reconnaissance troop to scour and see what happened. Thank you, Slayer." Stagan scratched his chin. "Strange is this—the Cards have never shown any interest in the countryside behind their camp. That's the reason why we've stayed safely hidden for so long. And you know about the fresh turmoil in their camp? They are preoccupied, so why send spies out this late?"

"It must be Uzcara's doing," Gujun said. "I've heard he's a thinker, unlike the other brothers."

"He's wounded—my scouts inform me."

"So long as that cur's still breathing, he's dangerous."

"I agree with you, Slayer," Stagan said. "We need those Vendeli to arrive. Chulan's presence has stirred the men up. They're agitated, edgy. Need to fight."

"Should arrive soon," Gujun told him. "They left Laregoza the same time as me."

"I hope that you're right, Slayer," Goi Stagan wiped sweat from his face. "The magister was enquiring as to your whereabouts."

Gujun cursed. He was getting weary of Chulan's meddling. "I'll go see what he wants," he said. "Best you find those 'good fellow' scouts of yours and flog their lazy hides bloody."

"It shall be done—you have my assurance of that." Goi Stagan's face turned grim.

Gujun left the garrison leader to his busy day and returned to the camp, stabling his horse and taking time to wander through the ordered lines of tents—so different to the shambles that made up the Cardalan camp.

Uzcara had sent spies into the woods. If one got back with word of Stagan's army, it would ruin everything. The Cards were in disarray, but they still outnumbered Stagan's force by several thousand—even with the leftover company from Pol Shen garrison swelling the Shen ranks.

Chulan was taking tea, seated in a wicker chair outside his tent. He was fussing his face with a fan and looked irritable, his eyes watching Gujun's approach.

"Where have you been, Slayer?"

"Killing Cards, while Stagan's lookouts slept in the woods."

Chulan looked alarmed. "Are there any more, do you think?"

"No. I scouted the woods and ridge above. But Uzcara suspects something—we have to act soon, else lose the advantage of surprise." Gujun had learned about the harrowing events of the previous week from Chulan on his arrival.

"Uzcara will be Ran by now," Chulan nodded. "Word is, he lost a hand but retains his head. More's the pity."

"Any word from the Vendeli?"

"Yes," Chulan nodded. "The shaman, Octaxa, sends word in his fashion." Chulan looked uncomfortable, and Gujun raised a questioning brow. "They'll arrive shortly," Chulan added quickly, as though wanting to change the subject. "We haven't long to wait."

"That's good," Gujun said, "because another fuckup in the woods could ruin your grand scheme, magister."

Chulan glared at him but nodded slowly. "You are right, Slayer. Uzcara must suspect something. Maybe you should pay him a visit."

"I want to live to enjoy the villa you promised me," Gujun said. "Uzcara and the other brother will get themselves killed when that city falls—if not by the defenders, then by us."

"Yes. If all goes to plan," Chulan said, sipping his tea.

"Was that all?"

"No." Chulan placed the cup down on the table. "Octaxa's man, Grodu. What happened to him?"

Gujun shrugged. "Alive and well, last I saw him."

"I received a bird from Genza the morning I left the villa. He was demanding news of Octaxa, awaiting word from Grodu, who was supposed to contact him after the meeting at the villa. Genza was more obnoxious than usual, and threatening, too. His message stated that if I didn't show proof of our support, he would contact his brothers demanding that they put every Shen to the sword, throughout this entire country."

"That's not surprising," Gujun said. "You betrayed his trust."

"Careful, Slayer—it's unwise to test me."

Gujun shrugged. "Perhaps," he said. "You are right."

Chulan sipped his tea, his dark eyes angry. "Concerning

Grodu. You're not telling me everything, are you?" he asked eventually. He steepled his fingers and stared hard at Gujun.

"Grodu doesn't work for the Vendeli."

"I suspected as much," Chulan nodded. "Who is his real master?"

"Ulani of Yamondo," Gujun said. "Grodu told me himself. He volunteered to spy on the Vendeli, and was placed in the fighting pits by the Yamondons. Though originally from Golt, he is fiercely loyal to that king. I'm not sure why."

"Curious." Chulan stroked his thin moustaches. "Why did he tell you?"

"I don't know—wondered the same thing. Grodu said he liked me." Gujun smiled wryly.

"I can't imagine why."

"Perhaps you should inform Octaxa," Gujun said.

"Perhaps I should." Chulan nodded, smiling. "But it could be sensible to watch this play out. I've heard little of the Yamondon king. Ulani might make a useful ally if the Vendeli overreach themselves. That's all I need from you for the moment. I suggest you get some rest, Slayer. It's going to be a busy few days."

"You're awake—that's good." Rasnei leaned over him.

Vian smiled up at her. "I've slept long?"

"Over a week," she replied. "You stirred on and off, had a fever. Nolenzes has ensured me you would be fine with enough rest."

"It's becoming a habit of mine." He smiled. "He told me I almost drowned."

"You were lucky," she told him. "Matax had alerted the fishers to go search instead of work on their catch. They found you floating face down."

"I thought I was dead."

"What do you remember?"

Vian thought about that for a moment. "Falling, and sinking," he said. "Changing, fading back. I saw Savarna, I think. It was peaceful. I was sad."

"Don't be sad, Vian." Rasnei gripped his hand. "You are alive and unhurt—it was all that I could ask for. You saved us yet again, my love."

"I am alive, Rasnei, yes. But only in part."

"What do you mean?" Her brows crinkled in concern.

"The dragon, my *Aikashi*. He's gone." Even saying the words left him feeling empty and alone. Drained, like water from a vessel tipped over and left forgotten in the drying sun.

"I'm sure your *Aikashi* will come back, Vian. Once you've rested enough.

"He has gone, Rasnei," Vian said bitterly. "The dragon is dead."

"How do you know that?" She wiped his brow with a brush of her hand.

Vian shook his head. "I'd sooner not talk about it."

She nodded, parting his damp hair with a finger. "You should be proud, Vian," she told him. "Your dragon bought us time. Better, by far. The enemy is in disarray. Gurtei and Lin Gu were all for leading an attack into their camp. Finishing this. Matax convinced them to hold back. The Cards still outnumber us ten times over. That said, I was tempted to let them take their chances. And Casca's dead."

"He is?" Vian sat up.

"Roile the Cutter shot him when the Ran was looking up at your golden beast."

"Roile." Vian grinned, feeling a slight return to cheer. "I never pictured that one as a hero."

"You are all heroes," she told him, and turned. Vian heard someone cough politely at the door. Rasnei nodded, and he saw Matax appear and gaze down at him with a smile.

"I'm glad you're well," the general said, moving his mouth with some difficulty. He had a fresh, ugly scar crossing his right cheek, from under the eye and cleaving through the upper lip. The stiches and swelling had badly discolored that side of his face

"Thanks to you," Vian told him, as Rasnei smiled.

"Our fishers were determined to find you," Matax said carefully. "Most saw the spot where the dragon … *you*, landed in the water."

"That's a bad slice," Vian told him. "Lucky you didn't lose an eye."

"Yes, it improves my looks, they tell me." Matax managed a lopsided grin. "Gurtei stitched it himself—he's quite proficient with needle and thread." Matax turned to Rasnei. "Uzcara is outside the gates, empress. It looks like he wants to talk."

"Uzcara?" Vian tried to stand and wished he hadn't. "He survived?" he added after the wave of dizziness passed.

"Unfortunately, yes," Matax said. "You should have dipped those Jians in poison. Uzcara leads the Cardalan army now Casca is dead. Besides Calgara, and the one in Cardalis, he's the only son left."

"Let's go see what he wants." Vian made to move again, but Rasnei placed a firm hand on his chest.

"Best you stay here and rest more," she said. "I'll sent someone back to report everything that happens."

"We don't want Uzcara seeing you," Matax added. "Better he thinks that you're dead, alongside your dragon."

"He's cleverer than Casca," Vian said, hiding the pain he felt at Matax's last words. "A canny veteran commander from the River Wars. Be careful."

"Uzcara's come alone," Matax said, "though his captains are there, in the distance." He turned for the doors.

"I'll return soon," Rasnei said, and kissed him.

Vian closed his eyes. "If Uzcara comes close enough, tell Roile to put an arrow in him," he said as she left the room.

Vian leaned back and groaned. He felt weak and broken despite what they said. His body was unhurt, but for the first time in his life, Vian was truly alone. The *Aikashi* had gone, and Savarna was far away, beyond his reach.

I am half of what I was. A broken remnant.

Vian had felt the joy of that *Aikashi* raw power blazing and surging inside and outside for those gloriously long yet fleeting moments. *Flying, swooping, killing. Saving her city.*

But foul sorcery had wrapped his dragon wings in chains, pulling Vian's *Aikashi* down and down, until the waves had swallowed them, seeping inside the beast, extinguishing his fury. The *Aikashi* had sacrificed itself for Vian, allowing him rise to the surface. For Rasnei, and Ta Shen. He closed his eyes.

Nolenzes came and attended him—the girl Jilanna, too. She'd been promoted to Nolenzes' second and had a home near the palace. After she'd left, Nolenzes told Vian that one of the soldiers was sharing the place with her. Jilanna had looked happy, younger.

When both had gone, Vian slid from the bed and dressed

quickly. He left his armor behind, but carried a Jian sloped casually over one shoulder. Vian slipped out the palace and wandered the gardens, stopping on one of the dragon bridges and gazing down at the golden fishes, as a wave of weariness and sorrow swept over him.

Savarna.

Vian closed his eyes. He focused on her face, but saw nothing and knew that she, too, was gone. *Rasnei, my love, your price was high—it has cost me my soul.*

Vian stood on that bridge for long minutes, the tears falling unnoticed from his eyes. *The greater part of me is dead. I'm like a tree struck by lightning in a storm.*

He felt heavy and weary again. A thought came to him. There was something he hadn't done for so long. Vian returned to their chambers in the palace. He found his flute where Rasnei had placed it. He took the instrument out and stared at it.

If half of me is no more, the remaining half must live as never before.

Vian placed the flute in his mouth and played long and hard.

UZCARA SAT HIS HORSE, HIS COLD GAZE ON THOSE watching from the keep. His captains had advised against this. Calgara, too. Be they hadn't deterred him. Let them shoot him like the cowards they were. It mattered not. Uzcara had suffered enough in this place. Part of him would welcome an arrow.

Go on, shoot me, you scum!

Uzcara knew they wouldn't do it. Not until he'd addressed them.

The gate creaked open slowly. The Shen had repaired the broken hinges and added fresh timber struts. But the gates had been broken once and would shatter more easily next time. Uzcara saw a lone rider emerge. He also noted the bowmen ranging along the walls. He slammed his spear butt down hard in the dirt and rode closer, his remaining hand held high, palm forward. *A gamble.* But these Shen were curious folk.

The rider trotted his horse toward him. A stocky, heavily mustached man. He looked more like a brigand than a soldier. *A fighter*, thought Uzcara. That explained why the city had held out so well. They had some solid warriors behind those walls. Casca hadn't expected that, the fool. Uzcara had heard that the man Vian was dead. The dragon had killed him. Uzcara wasn't sure what to think about that. His wrist was still a torture, but he refused to acknowledge the nagging pain.

The heavyset rider stopped a dozen feet away. A hard face stared at him from inside the conical Shen helm. *You're not used to wearing one of those*, Uzcara thought.

"Those archers up there will shoot you, should I raise my hand," the envoy said.

Uzcara smiled. "If they do, my riders will fill your fat flesh with arrows, too, before you reach the gates, Shen."

"I daresay." The stocky Shen looked past Uzcara, where his captains ranged closer, but held back beyond bowshot. He turned and grinned at Uzcara, "Ours might shoot anyway," he said. "You Cards have outstayed your welcome. That said, as it appears that you want to parley, I for one am all ears." He held out his hands wide, so those on the walls could see. "Name's Gurtei."

"Good," Uzcara said. "One thing you should know, Gurtei of Shen. I am not Casca."

"We know who you are."

"Well know this also," Uzcara said. "I won't be making my brother's mistakes, nor those of Caranax before him."

Gurtei smiled. "I wouldn't expect you to, seasoned battle captain that you are. Just you and the young one left, though. And half your army destroyed. For what? Hmm? A negotiation might be sensible, *Ran* Uzcara."

Uzcara decided he liked this Shen. The man was shrewd and brave. A leader.

"You've been lucky, Shen. Your gods have looked after you. But that's over." Uzcara looked up at the sky. "There are no more dragons, Gurtei. Your demon beast—wherever you summoned it from. It's dead. Your city will fall to me on the next attack. Those broken gates, the damaged walls—neither will hold out another day. You know this to be true."

"And yet our walls still stand," Gurtei said. "The gates are mended and reinforced. We are stronger than ever. Our resolve undented. Why waste more of your men, Uzcara? As you said—you are not your brothers."

Uzcara smiled. "Because I hate your fucking city, Gurtei. That's why," he said. "Ta Shen has divided us like nothing before and weakened the republic. We never should have come here. It was folly. But that doesn't matter. My brothers died because of you, and my father, too, albeit indirectly. I hold you Shen responsible."

Gurtei shrugged, relaxing his hands. "I understand how you feel."

"But I offer you this much," Uzcara said. "As one honorable warrior to another. Open your gates to us, tomorrow at dawn. I will spare the women and children, even the older men. It's the best I can do."

Gurtei nodded and glanced up at the sky. "I'll look for you in the morning, Card," he said. "Don't worry—my sword will be sharp. Until then." Gurtei flashed him a grin and turned his horse about. Uzcara watched him enter the gates before turning his steed and cantering back to where the captains waited.

"We attack at first light," he told them. "Their messenger was bluffing—he sounded desperate. The Shen know they can't hold for long."

Octaxa stared at the tower with fascination as they sailed close. He'd never seen anything like it before. In Omala City, there were many wonders—buildings ancient and beautiful, structures built by his ancestors who came from the desert lands after the Crystal Wars.

But this was different, stranger even than the mud towers and ancient beehive dwellings in the extreme south of his country. A mile to the west, it watched their passage, standing like a single defiant finger. A tall, glistening spire of rock that dominated the skyline. The tower stood on a promontory ranged by white cliffs. Octaxa saw dolphins diving and dipping in the blue-green waves surrounding it.

Octaxa turned to his skipper standing beside the helmsman. "Quite a sight, Corvo, is it not?"

Corvo nodded. "It's called the Spike, Holy One. They say the ancient folk built it long before the first Shen arrived." Octaxa knew Corvo had sailed these waters several times. An experienced skipper, he'd promoted the one-eyed sailor to captain and charged him with commandeering all seven ships on their voyage east.

"The Aralais." Octaxa smiled, and nodded. He liked the old stories. Didn't matter whether they were true. But whatever folk had built that white tower were no average masons. He watched the gleaming Spike pass to port as they drifted by, the red sail trapping fresh breeze.

"How long before we reach Ta Shen harbor?"

"We're in the bay area already, Holy One," Corvo said. "We should reach the harbor ere nightfall. I think it best we anchor offshore until we know it's time to attack."

"Excellent!" Octaxa slapped his shoulder. "You've done well, Captain Corvo. I will inform my Sangala—we'll prepare for a busy day tomorrow."

He left his captain and helmsman to their work and dropped through the hatch to his cabin. Once inside, Octaxa prepared his concoctions and readied his mind. He'd felt weary after the mind-fight with the dragon. During that attack, his Sangala had linked with him—as had Utuxla and the men back in Laregoza.

They'd channeled their minds together and stored the energy. Octaxa had used his third eye to track the dragon's path. He'd timed it perfectly. The Sangala had struck in unison and blasted the golden dragon from the sky.

The *Aikashi* was dead, its mortal host surely drowned. The city was theirs to take, providing the Shen Chulan did his part. It was time to ensure that he would.

Octaxa closed his eyes. He focused, knowing his Sangala were all above deck. No one would disturb him down here. He allowed the pitch and roll of the dhow to seep into his mind, his heartbeat matching that rhythmic motion. He focused harder, channeled. Let his thoughts drift up, high above deck and beyond into the blue summer skies ahead.

Octaxa became a spirit bird, gliding along the ocean, skirting the cliffs and sandy shoreline beyond. He circled once, saw the seven ships close behind. Satisfied, he summoned full speed as he winged west, until the morning sun glinted on golden roofs.

The Golden City, Ta Shen, was as beautiful as he'd heard. Octaxa bid his mind-bird fly above, hovering hawk-like as he gazed down, noting the high walls, damaged in places, as well as the mass of buildings squeezed inside—the capacious ornate gardens with their dragon bridges and tidy circular ponds.

Tempted to linger, Octaxa forced his mind across the city, passing over the great walls and skirting the siege clutter and decaying corpses strewn across the plain. He hardly noticed that broken machinery, or the week-dead corpses scattered, their bodies stripped of flesh by jackal, fox, and crow.

Octaxa skirted the Cardalan camp and settled in the woods covering the slopes of the long ridge behind. From there, he ranged out until he saw the Shen camp hidden amidst the trees. Octaxa drifted down through the foliage and waited.

CHULAN HEARD A SOFT SOUND. HE'D BEEN DOZING IN his chair, the recent journey having caught up with him. Goi Stagan was drilling his men further back in the woods. Gujun the Slayer was away scouting. Nothing but birds and tranquility left in the camp.

Chulan heard the sound again. A ruffle of tent flaps? Perhaps a bird? He opened his eyes and wished he hadn't.

A huge, black-skinned warrior stood before him, the sinewy arms folded. A blood-red cloak covered his broad shoulders, back, and part of his naked, tattooed chest. The hair on his head was shaved on one side, and his long golden earrings twisted in the sunlight. The stranger wore gold and silver serpents coiled up his arms.

"Shaman Octaxa." Chulan choked the word out like bile. "I've been expecting to *hear* from you."

"And I thought it past time we met in person, Magister Chulan." As Chulan watched him, Octaxa seemed to shimmer and fade, before returning to normal. Chulan shivered—he'd heard the stories of the Sangala's legendary power.

"Where is your fleet?" he managed to get out. This visit not beneficial for his health. "How long before it arrives?"

"This evening." Octaxa smiled. "We are in the bay, approaching fast. I cannot linger, but thought I'd drop by to make certain you are ready to play your part."

Chulan nodded quickly. "We are. Our army will attack as soon as the Cardalan tear down those gates. My master spy informs me that their new leader, Uzcara, has vowed to take the city in the morning. I believe him, though it's been said before. Once they're through the gates, we Shen will follow close behind. I'll need your people to clean the harbor area."

"We'll cast anchor offshore." Octaxa grinned, shimmered, faded, and took solid form again. "I'll expect you to send a flare up from that ridge when it is time."

"It shall be done."

Octaxa's grin widened. Chulan noted the perfect teeth. "I'll see you soon, *emperor.*"

He vanished. Chulan saw a trail of dust scatter the mud and heard the soft sound of wings departing. He yelled at a servant to bring him fresh tea, and added that he needed extra sugar this morning.

Chulan didn't mention the visit to anyone. But when Gujun returned, he made the Slayer promise he'd send out that flare himself.

"Go to the ridge at first light," Chulan told him. "Take a few good men. When the Cards start moving toward the city, get ready." Gujun nodded, looking curiously at Chulan, who for his part still didn't feel well. "Damn it, man. Are you listening to me?"

"The ridge, at dawn." Gujun nodded.

"We watch and wait," Chulan said. "I've good reason to believe the Vendeli will arrive tonight. How long before the city falls?"

"Soon," Gujun told him. He had studied the city's walls from the long ridge. "The walls are badly damaged from Casca's last attack, and the main gates are vulnerable, having been broken once. Their cannons are spent, as are the other weapons. I think a full-on attack by Uzcara will do the trick."

"Good." Chulan felt better. "We'll need to notify the Vendeli as soon as the city's defenses are breached. They can't land before that, else they will be vulnerable. Once you're certain, Slayer, ride to the cliffs and send out that flare. Launch a second this end of the ridge. They will be our signals."

Gujun looked at him for a moment.

"What now?"

"Do you mean to take your carriage through the main gates and proclaim yourself emperor?"

Chulan tolerated the impudence with a thin smile. "I'll let the dust settle first," he said. "Besides, I know another way into the city." Gujun's brow raised, and Chulan smiled again. "You don't know about the postern, do you, Slayer?"

"I don't."

"It lies on the southern flank of wall, near the harbor and ocean end. A small hidden door. I'll expect you to await me there after the flares go up."

Gujun nodded.

"A secret way into—and out of—the city should things go awry," Chulan told him. "Rasnei won't know it's there. It's not been used in years and is almost forgotten. My counterpart told me it was his private door. A secret known only to the privy council."

"I'll be there," Gujun told him. "Before that, I'd get some rest, magister. You don't look well."

Damn the man.

Chulan drained his tea as Gujun left him. He certainly didn't *feel* well. The long journey here had left him rattled and sleepless. And that ... *visitation.*

Chulan hoped he wouldn't have to deal with the Vendeli often. Octaxa's sudden appearance had aged him. He forced a smile. It would all be worth it. Uzcara would take the city for them. Gujun was right.

Ta Shen would fall tomorrow. The portents were favorable: the moon's position, Octaxa's fleet, the Cards unexpecting. The hour for Chulan's triumph was almost here. Let the Cardalan Republic have their victory. It would be a short one. Chulan would take his ease for the rest of this day and through the night. He'd be fully recovered tomorrow. And, all going well, by nightfall the Shen would have a new emperor. Chulan's enemies would be dead. The thought brought some much-needed peace to his troubled mind.

Tomorrow, I am emperor.

THE FIGHT AT THE VILLA

TRISA WAS ANXIOUS. They had ridden hard the last few days, ditched the camels as planned and purchased fresh horses at Largos. Valgarn and Dolusa had slipped into the docks at night, but found no one. A tipsy Laregozan sailor in one tavern had proved helpful, informing them that some Vendeli ships had left a couple of weeks ago.

"Stopping at Soloza—there's to be a meeting held there," he'd told Valgarn. "There's talk of an alliance with Shen. Treachery, Genza's knows about it. Vendel's top people are participating. The dockers told me."

Dolusa thanked the sailor with gold. After that, they'd moved out of Largos quickly, staying long enough to restock with food and fresh water, and Valgarn insisted they buy some grog.

They hadn't got far from Largos when Trisa spotted a lone figure on the road. A large man, walking with a pack, a stout spear serving as a staff in either hand.

She'd heard Dolusa laugh and seen him ride forward.

"Looks like we've caught up with the king's spy," Valgarn

had said to her as they waited for Dolusa to return.

The "spy," Grodu, had confirmed what the drunk mariner had said back in Largos and joined their party.

That had been four days back. They'd arrived in Laregoza's second city this morning. Again, the Tarakai and Valgarn patrolled the docks and taverns, carefully enquiring after the Vendeli. They soon discovered that both Tulomon Caze and Utuxla were staying at an expansive mansion on a cliff east of the city. It was built for Carda the Conqueror and recently gifted to Octaxa by the current Ran in Cardalis. Trisa was afraid her man was about to do something rash.

"Do you think Octaxa's there too?" Valgarn asked Tarakai Dolusa, as he handed back the spyglass.

"I hope not, for our sakes."

"He left with the ships," Grodu informed them. "The Sangala chief's vessel was to lead the other six to Ta Shen. Their plan is to help the Shen rid themselves of the Cardalan invaders."

"Who's with Caze?" Dolusa asked the former gladiator.

"Utuxla and a score of other Sangala, plus Caze's own people. Mostly servants and such. Some fighting men. I counted no more than fifty while I was there."

"You met Chulan's envoy?" Valgarn asked him.

Grodu nodded. "I did. Like me, Gujun didn't much care for the Sangala."

"Where is he now?"

"Most likely back in Shen."

"We had best attack at night," Valgarn said later as the tavern proprietor poured tea for Trisa, and Dolusa and

Valgarn discussed their options with Grodu. "Lie low until dusk, I saw a lot of Card troops in the city today. Genza must suspect foul play."

"For good reason," Dolusa said.

"Genza's waiting for news from Octaxa." Grodu smiled at some private joke. "He's not going to receive any. The Vendeli have cuckolded Genza. He'll be furious, and the road to that villa will be watched," Grodu told them. "The Sangala second, Utuxla, is a sharp one. He'll be expecting trouble from Cardalan, perhaps Talimi Garrison."

"He's about to get trouble," Valgarn muttered, and Trisa felt that shiver of worry again. She knew she couldn't stop the inevitable, so she might as well contribute.

"There's another way in," Trisa said, and they gazed at her in surprise. Valgarn's look was almost comical. She placed her teacup on the table and smiled. "I heard some women talking at the market where we bought supplies this morning."

"Please tell us more," Dolusa said, offering a side glance to Valgarn.

"There was much whispering about the goings on at that villa," Trisa told them. "The Sangala and their guests were the talk of the city. There's a dock for small craft hidden under a steep cliff. Stone stairs climb up to the villa, one of the women said. That landing stage might prove a better option than the main road."

She noted how Grodu in particular seemed impressed, as they agreed this could work.

A rough plan formed during the next hour. They stayed in the tavern, waited until dusk, and headed out quietly. Dolusa and Grodu went looking for a redundant skiff to steal, so they could check out the hidden dock and stairway. They arrived back a couple of hours later.

"It will work," Tarakai Dolusa said. "But only a few of us can go. The rest must join via the road, once we've silenced the guards."

"We'll need to wait until morning," Grodu said. "Too risky climbing those stairs in the dark, and we dare not carry torches."

As they approached the villa, spymaster Dranan bid his men dismount and await his orders. He'd left a small retainer force at Largos and ridden here with one hundred and fifty men. Each one was freshly drilled and keen for action. Dranan had ridden out of Talimi Garrison after learning Octaxa had sailed east.

"You men stay hidden in these trees, while a few of us go see what's happening at that villa," Dranan told the officers. He bid Cama, his second, choose a handful of men to ride with them. Dranan assumed Octaxa's Sangala would be expecting a visit from Genza's soldiers. They'd best not reveal their plans too early.

His group reached the main gates of the villa. Dranan recognized the brute, Utuxla, standing silhouetted beneath the arch of the doorway. The man was no less fearsome than the last time he'd seen him, leaving Largos the other month with the Northman Valgarn—who was probably long dead, and this man responsible. Utuxla smiled as he saw them arrive.

Dranan was no coward, and a veteran of the endless River Wars. But Utuxla had unnerved him almost as much as his chief, the shaman Octaxa. Dranan held his nerve and sat his horse, a hand on his sword pommel.

"Genza grows concerned, Sangala. We've received no news

from your master. And in Largos, I heard that Octaxa has sailed for Shen."

"He told your Ran he was going there," the hawk faced warrior-priest flashed his teeth. "Your people need Vendeli help breaking into that city. You Cards have proved hopeless at the task thus far."

Dranan refused to be baited. "I'm happy to interview Tulomon Caze instead." He smiled slightly, but noticed the lack of reaction on Utuxla's face.

"Tulomon Caze?"

"Your High Califez, forgotten him already? There's a rumor that Caze arrived here a week ago on board your vessel, Utuxla. Don't look so smug—you can't deny he's inside. The sailors at Largos docks are most helpful when drunk."

Utuxla shrugged. "They lied to you."

"Why would they do that?"

Utuxla shrugged again, looking bored. "Go back to Genza. Tell your master all is well here. We Sangala are looking after Octaxa's house for when he returns, after taking Ta Shen and bringing back our share of the riches."

"What of Grodu?" Dranan demanded. "Genza was expecting Octaxa's man in Cardalis. I received signal that he never arrived."

"The roads are hazardous."

"Not for Grodu." *You don't know where he is either.*

Utuxla matched his gaze, until Dranan turned away. "Best you return to Cardalis, Captain Dranan. There's nothing happening here."

"So it seems." Dranan nodded. "I bid you good evening." He urged his horse to circle and cantered back down the road.

He rejoined his men in the woods a mile from the villa. "We attack at dusk," Dranan told them. "I want Caze alive, and Utuxla. For questioning. The bastards are up to something, for sure. And be careful. We'll need to be quick. The Sangala are rumored to be adept at sorcery. Best we take them unawares."

Dranan walked over to where his lieutenant was tightening his saddle. "Cama, a word." He signaled the other man follow him into the quiet of the trees.

"We've no guarantee of success," he told Cama. "I need insurance. You'll head back to Largos. Round up our boys and go search the harbor for any Vendeli ships. If Caze or Utuxla escape our nets, they'll head that way."

Cama nodded. "As you wish, spymaster."

THE KNOCK WAS SHARP, BREAKING HIS TRAIN OF thought. Tulomon Caze leaned back in his divan. He'd been enjoying the warm breeze on the high verandah. The expansive terrace and shelter awarded wide views of the ocean. He'd spent most of his time there since Octaxa's departure last week.

"Who is there?" Caze expected some servant and was about to scold. Instead, he saw Utuxla standing in the doorway. "What do you want, Sangala?" Caze felt a flash of anger. Utuxla had no business interrupting his afternoon in such a vulgar manner.

"High Califez, forgive the intrusion, but we have visitors."

"Best you deal with them." Caze watched as Utuxla stared back at him. He sighed, summoning patience. "Who?"

"Dranan—he's the Cardalan spymaster."

"How interesting." Caze straightened. "What would their spymaster want with you?"

"He's got word you're here, High Califez. Ran Genza has been busy. This Dranan has men hidden in the woods, I suspect they'll attack after dark."

"For what reason?" Tulomon Caze stifled a yawn. This was tedious news. "Are we not allies with Cardalan, at least for the moment?"

"We were," Utuxla said. "But Grodu never arrived at Cardalis. Genza suspects foul play by Octaxa, and he's ordered Dranan confiscate the villa."

Tulomon Caze felt a quiver in his belly. Grodu had departed at the same time as the Shen messenger. Why hadn't he reported to Genza as he'd been tasked to? Grodu was fiercely loyal to Octaxa. Had that sly Shen messenger killed him? He doubted that was possible.

"What do you suggest, Sangala?"

"That you leave here, High Califez. For a short time, while we deal with these soldiers."

"Why would I do that? I like it here."

"You're in danger."

"Aren't you Sangala supposed to protect my person? I've my men too. How many Cardalan soldiers are out there?"

"Over a hundred, perhaps two," Utuxla told him. "In the woods on the city road. I followed Dranan and took stock."

"I thought a Sangala was worth ten other men," Caze snapped. He was angry, mostly about Grodu. Had he missed something here?

"We are, lord, and we will deal with these fools. But I cannot protect your person and also fight off Cardalan dogs. It's best you lie low for a while."

"Like some common brigand?" Tulomon Caze shook his head. "Even were I to consider such a woeful option, how would I slip out unnoticed, with both highway and woods full of enemies?"

"I'll send four of my best warriors with you," Utuxla said.

"You're not answering me. Where?"

Utuxla hinted below. "There's a tunnel beneath the villa that leads down to the rocks. There's a hidden cove down there, with a skiff kept ready."

Tulomon Caze nodded slowly. "Very well, what's your plan?"

"My men will sail you safely to Soloza, High Califez. Once there, you can wait in my vessel until I join you. Once I do, we'll disembark. Safely at sea, I'll mind-contact Octaxa and report on the latest situation."

TRISA SAW THE DISTANT HOUSE PERCHED ON THE EDGE of a cliff at dawn, several miles south of the city. Valgarn had raged at her to stay behind in the tavern, but she'd calmly ignored his protestations and insisted on coming.

There were six men beside Valgarn and herself. Grodu, Dolusa, and four volunteers from his troop. The rest were camped outside the city so as not to draw any attention.

Their small boat bobbed close, and she heard Grodu curse.

"What's wrong?" Valgarn asked him.

"There was a skiff tied up at that dock last night. Someone has left."

"Just as well I told some men keep a close eye out in the harbor," Dolusa chuckled. "They'll report any nocturnal activity to my watch officers."

They drifted close to the rearing cliff. Valgarn grabbed an oar, Grodu another, as Dolusa steered the boat to shore. Trisa saw the tiny cove slowly reveal itself—a stone quay and faded steps cutting up into the cliff, zig-zagging tight and vanishing above.

"Stay with the boat," Valgarn told her.

"Good try." She smiled back at him.

"I'm going to be killing people with my axe, woman."

"And I'm going to be helping you."

"Fuck." He rolled his eyes but knew he was defeated.

Grodu tied off the boat, and Valgarn leaped ashore, with Trisa following close behind. They took the stairs carefully—they were steep and worn badly in places.

Trisa saw gulls swooping above, and nests of the noisy birds were off to her right. It was hot, and a steady breeze whipped her hair.

After twenty minutes climbing, they stopped. Grodu cupped an ear and looked at Valgarn and Dolusa. "Are you hearing that, too?"

Valgarn awarded Dolusa a wild look. "Someone got here first."

Trisa heard the distant clash of steel, accompanied by angry shouts fading off. And what was that? Surely it was a man's agonized death cry?

"It must be Genza," Valgarn said. "I thought I recognized some of Dranan's people in the harbor."

"We need Tulomon Caze alive," Dolusa said, glancing at Grodu. "Are you sure he's here?"

"He was when I left," the big fighter said.

"You had better hope that Vendeli vessel's well-watched," Valgarn said to Dolusa. "We don't want our big fish swimming away."

They continued up, the sound of fighting getting closer. They reached a gateway hinting a gloomy tunnel beyond.

Again, Valgarn pleaded with her to stay put, but Trisa shook her head. "My place is with you, Northman," she told him. Again, he rolled his eyes.

The tunnel was lit by sconces. The way led to more stairs, these winding up to another door. The sound of fighting came from the other side.

Grodu stood by the door, a spear in either hand.

"Ready?" He flashed them a grin.

"Do it!" Dolusa said.

Grodu nodded and slammed his huge arm into the door, smashing through the timber and knocking it open.

A tall, red-cloaked warrior blinked at them. He gasped as Grodu's spear cut into his belly.

"Find Tulomon Caze," Dolusa said as they rushed into the villa.

Trisa felt sick to the bones. There were corpses strewn everywhere. It was apparent that most of the fighting was over. Trisa gagged at the stench, seeing men sprawled with limbs akimbo, hewed guts sliced open like rotting fruit at market. They were mostly Cardalan soldiers, but she saw the odd red-cloaked Sangala lying covered in blood.

Grodu went one way, Dolusa another, his four men close behind. Trisa stayed close behind her man.

Valgarn stepped over corpses, clearing the rooms one at a time. Trisa saw no one standing, but the sound of fighting continued outside. They entered a large hall with a central table. A dead Cardalan officer lay face-down on the cloth, another man pinned under him, the Card's dagger protruding from his eye.

Valgarn swore as he saw a figure crouched in a corner, his hands pressed on his belly, trying in vain to staunch the blood seeping out.

"Dranan!"

Valgarn rushed over to the wounded man. Trisa followed, her eyes on the double doors leading outside to where the fighting had dwindled. She guessed few survivors were left. Valgarn squatted beside the pale-faced Dranan. "He's Genza's spymaster," he said, looking up at Trisa.

"Can we help him?"

Dranan opened his eyes. "You won't stop this," he spat blood. "I'm done for."

"We can try." Trisa looked at Valgarn, who shook his head.

"Caze isn't here," Dranan said as blood bubbled from his lips. "They were ready. Good fighters. I ... underestimated ..." Dranan let out a long sigh. Valgarn reached down and closed his eyes.

Grodu appeared, his face covered in blood. "I found two of the Sangala," he said with a grin. Trisa shuddered. Dolusa and his men emerged from the other direction, one of them missing.

"We need to find that bastard Utuxla," Valgarn said.

"You go—I'm searching for Caze," Grodu said, disappearing back into the antechamber. Dolusa ordered his men accompany Valgarn out the doors leading to the verandah. They stopped abruptly.

Four Sangala stood at the far end, having dispatched the last of Dranan's men. Trisa had never witnessed so much slaughter. She couldn't count the number of dead. Her legs felt weak.

The nearest Sangala turned and smiled when he saw them. Trisa felt her heart quaver. Utuxla carried a curved sword and oval shield, his dark face and chest covered in blood, and his red cloak almost torn in two.

"You betrayed us, Northman—I was right." He turned to the other Sangala. "Kill the Yamondons, but save the girl. I'll deal with this fool." The three Sangala with him started walking slowly toward Dolusa, cruel smiles showing on their faces.

Trisa ignored them. She stayed put beside Valgarn as Utuxla approached, still smiling. He stopped a few feet away, looked at Trisa, and grinned again.

"I will use your woman well before I let her die," Utuxla said. "I knew you'd let us down, Northman. But your new friends the Yamondons' plot has failed. The High Califez has gone— Octaxa, too. We fighting Sangala killed the Cards, like so much ripe barley. Now it's your turn. At least with you, I can take my time." He leveled his tulwar, flicking it at Valgarn's face.

"Stay behind me," Valgarn told her, his axe sweeping in a wide arc and hewing down at the Sangala.

Utuxla stepped to his right and sliced across with shocking speed.

Valgarn barely blocked that thrust with his axe. He caught his balance and wildly blocked another probe. Utuxla stepped forward, sword circling.

"You are clumsy and stupid—it's what I expected." Utuxla launched a vicious series of blows at Valgarn, forcing him backward, the heavy axe struggling to counter the lightning speed of that tulwar.

Unnoticed, Trisa reached down and picked up a short sword from one of the Cardalan dead. She bit her lip, seeing Valgarn back away again as Utuxla stepped confidently toward him. The curved sword snaked back and forth, probing and stabbing, the shield blocking any counter from his axe. The Vendeli moved like a dancer—every smooth blow led to another, without him breaking a sweat.

Valgarn desperately blocked a lunge with his axe haft, the edge of the tulwar slicing across his hand above the fingers. Trisa mouthed a scream as she saw him swallow the pain and follow through, striking the Vendeli's shield, sundering it in two. The broken remnants hung from Utuxla's arm.

Utuxla cast the broken shield aside and scooped a crooked dagger from his belt. Trisa heard the fighting continuing behind her, but she dare not turn.

Utuxla advanced again, cutting close, stepping sideways. Sweeping and slicing. Every blow caused her man to retreat. Valgarn's counterstrokes got wilder, in turn forcing his enemy back.

But Utuxla calmly awaited his chance and renewed his response with equal ferocity. Valgarn made to swing at his head. He stepped forward, slipping on the blood.

Valgarn sprawled. Utuxla grinned and made to strike. He stopped in surprise, though, seeing the sword sticking in his kidney. Trisa twisted the blade with a smile as blood filled the Sangala's mouth. He looked at her with startled eyes and tried to curse. Trisa jerked the blade sideways again. Utuxla sobbed and stumbled. Valgarn, back on his feet, swung the axe down hard, and Utuxla's head rolled free of his body.

Valgarn's eyes met hers briefly before he leaped at the two remaining Sangala from behind. Dolusa was hurt. He'd killed two of them, but his men were dead. Together, he and Valgarn finished the last pair.

Dolusa collapsed, and Trisa rushed to help him. His arm was badly slashed, but he'd live. Grodu emerged covered in blood.

"I found the rest of the Sangala," he said. "The last one was helpful, told me Caze had fled to Utuxla's ship and is awaiting him there."

"Guess where we're going," Valgarn said with a grin.

"How is your hand?" Trisa asked him, as Valgarn walked toward the harbor gates. She bound it with cloth, but the blood was still seeping.

"I feel nothing, perhaps a dull ache." He grinned at her. "You saved my life."

"I told you I would help." She kissed him. "You, Northman, shouldn't have underestimated me."

"I never did." He kissed her back. They'd returned to the tavern briefly. Dolusa had notified his men and learnt to their relief that Cama, Dranan's lieutenant, had the harbor ringed with guards.

Cama greeted them at the docks. "Northman, Dranan spoke well of you," he said, after Valgarn related what had happened at the villa.

"He died well," Valgarn told him. "This is my friend Dolusa from Yamondo. He has business with the Vendeli."

"As do I," Cama replied. "We have their dhow surrounded."

"We'd better not rush them at once—they'll get wary," Valgarn said. He turned to Cama's man charged with watching the ship. "Four Sangala, you say?"

"Aye, that and the crew, sir. The passenger went below."

"Stay here," Dolusa told him. "This need not concern you, Northman, and you are hurt."

"Not as badly as you, Tarakai. And I'm invested—your

king will repay me well, of that I'm sure."

"He will," Dolusa said. "Once we have Tulomon Caze stuffed and pickled in a cage."

"Since there's no way of stopping you men, we had better get this done," Trisa said, and Valgarn hugged her.

Dolusa stared at her, shaking his head. "I'm going to miss you, lovely Trisa of Rundali. I might even mourn the departure of your lover."

"I didn't know we were leaving?" Trisa said, she looked at Valgarn. He shrugged.

Grodu met them at the harbor, where he'd been watching the ship from the quay. Together, they walked across to the red-painted dhow.

"Tulomon Caze! You cannot escape. Show your face and spare your men," Dolusa called across.

Trisa saw sailors staring back at them, and one tall Sangala leaning on a spear.

"Looks like we'll have to go onboard," Valgarn said.

"Stay here, you and your woman," Dolusa told them. "You've done your part, Northman. Leave this to Grodu and my people."

Valgarn nodded after a few moments.

"Keep those Sangala occupied," Grodu said to the score of men following him across the gangplank.

"Crossbow!" Dolusa called out, pointing to where a sailor had appeared and was aiming to shoot. One of the Yamondon archers let loose first, and the sailor pitched into the water with a grunt.

"Keep your eyes out for more," Dolusa said.

The fighting didn't last long. She saw Grodu's huge form cut a swathe through the sailors gathered on deck and disappear below. Meanwhile, the Yamondons surrounded the four

Sangala. These sold their lives dearly, until Grodu appeared and butchered three of them in as many seconds. He looked angry. The last Sangala stood, spear held ready.

She could see that Grodu was speaking to him, the man shaking his head slightly. She saw Grodu's sword slice the last enemy's throat and watched him sink to the deck. Another search followed, before Grodu returned.

"Caze has gone," he said.

"How is that possible?" both Dolusa and the Cardalan leader Cama demanded angrily.

Grodu shrugged. "Does it matter? I'm telling you that Tulomon Caze has sprung our traps."

TULOMON CAZE SWAM CAREFULLY AND QUIETLY, CUTTING clean strokes as he distanced himself from the ship. Caze had known they would come. Obviously, the Cards would be guarding this ship. When he'd seen Grodu, he'd guessed how they'd won at the villa. Utuxla would be dead, and the other Sangala, too. He'd had to act fast, sliding down the hull as the sailors watched the harbor. Slipping silently away, floating and diving underwater, then swimming hard and fast to the far side of the quay.

Caze reached the docks and buildings, then crawled out of the water. They'd be searching for him everywhere, both Cardalan and Yamondons. *Allies.* How had he missed that? It had to be Grodu. Octaxa's man had betrayed him. That meant the Sangala chief was implicit.

Tulomon Caze flitted through the harbor. He saw men working, following one as he whistled his way to the nearest tavern. Caze caught up with the man and stabbed him with his secret thumb dagger. He dressed swiftly into the docker's clothes and kept walking. By nightfall, he'd reached the city limits.

"Why not go to Yamondo? The king likes you." Trisa asked him, as they guided their horses north along the road. Behind her, the lights of Soloza twinkled and sparkled.

"Because we didn't deliver, and I'd sooner not waste time searching for a drowned rat to wash up on some beach. Genza owes me."

"He is treacherous."

"He will pay," Valgarn said. "Besides, I have you to look after me."

"That is true," she said. "I'm glad it's just us now. But I'll miss Dolusa and his men."

"As will I," Valgarn reached across and squeezed her hand as they neared the woods where they would camp for the night.

Light was fading fast. She saw an owl gliding past and gulped. A dark-haired woman had appeared from nowhere and stood on the road watching them. Trisa blinked in surprise and looked again, but she'd gone. *A trick of the light?*

"Did you see her?"

Valgarn reined in, his face pale and eyes troubled. He stared at Trisa for a moment before answering.

"She's back," he told her. "Something bad must have happened."

"Who?" Trisa knew the answer even as she spoke.

"Yes," Valgarn said nodding. "Looks like I'm needed back in the north."

THE SUMMONING

JARAN FELT his feet settle on soft ground. He gazed about at the smoky atmosphere, making out odd shapes moving slowly toward him. Beside him, the great bear stood motionless, its fur a sheen of snowy down.

"Where is this awful place?' Jaran asked, and shuddered as his voice echoed around his head.

"In the place between worlds where the dead can speak freely."

The voice came from his right. He turned slowly and saw Barin standing and smiling, the huge shadow of the White-bear fading behind him. His ancestor carried the war axe Wyrmfang across his shoulders. "You've done well, lad. But the hardest test is still to come."

"I'm hoping you'll help me with that."

"I'll be there."

Jaran watched the shapes drift nearer. Eventually, he defined them as men. He saw the outlines of sorry-looking figures with long shaggy hair, carrying weapons that glowed faintly. Among them were axes, swords and long spears, some broken. Most carried round shields slung across their backs.

"Follow me," Barin said.

"Who are those wretches?"

"The lost. Your witch, Sheega raised them from beneath the lake. She's sent them out to hunt. They are searching for your soul, Jaran. We cannot tarry here."

Head full of questions, Jaran followed his ancestor into the gloom. He walked as though in a dream, occasionally glancing back to see the trail of mournful warriors following behind, their eyes glinting like pale lanterns. *Erlund's men—she took their souls.*

Ahead, Jaran saw a long, flat stone with runes carved along the sides and on top.

"I will keep these dreary fellows at bay," Barin told him. "Take that hell-axe and smite the stone hard as you can."

"What ...?"

"Just do it, boy. And quickly!"

Jaran stared at Barin for a moment. He felt dazed and confused. What was happening here? He saw the shadowy shapes looming close. He nodded at Barin and jumped up onto the slab.

"Is this ...?" He stared down at the rune stone. Barin had his back to him.

"Damn you, boy. Strike down with your axe!" Barin's voice sounded desperate.

Jaran slid Griner free, gripped hard in both hands. He took a deep breath. "How's this?" he shouted and swung down as hard as he could, striking the rune covered stone.

What followed was an explosion of light. Jaran heard a dismal ringing of bells in his ears and the faint sound of distant laughter.

Where am I?

He must have fallen from the stone. *So dark.* He lay face down in wet mud, Griner still gripped in one hand. Barin was gone, as were Sheega's mournful dead. Instead, a rangy, scruffy-haired Northman watched him with a curious expression.

Jaran rolled to his feet and scooped up Griner, his eyes on the fair-haired warrior. "Who are you, and what just happened?"

The stranger grinned at him, revealing three good teeth. "You should know who I am, Jaran Saerk. You're the one that brought me back. Thanks for that. I was bored shitless down there."

"You are ... *Taic*?"

"Taic I am, or *was*. Hard to be sure if I'm fully back." He squeezed his nose, belched. "That did feel real. And I can smell soil. It's odd how you always miss the little things. Where is this place?"

Jaran gaped at the skinny, fair-haired man for a moment and shook his head. *You're my ancestor?* All that ... whatever he'd gone through was to raise this fellow. Hardly seemed worth the effort, never mind the horror. Jaran shook his head and looked about. He was back in the crow glade. Taic's Howe glinted ominously through the trees. Jaran chewed his stubble.

"Where is Barin?" he asked Taic, who was gazing around in wonder at the trees.

"Buggered if I know," Taic replied. "I haven't seen my uncle for ages. Last time was ... I can't remember. Probably on the Starlight."

"There are meant to be more of you," Jaran told him. "My ancestors. We've a crisis, and little time to solve it." He decided not to add how disappointed he felt.

"I expect Sven and the boys will turn up when the fighting starts," Taic said with his horrible grin. "Uncle, too, most likely. Why is there a snow bear standing behind you?"

Jaran turned, saw nothing. *Barin?* "Are you there?"

No answer.

He turned back and awarded Taic a puzzled look. "You can see a white bear?"

"Standing behind you, clear as mud. Err, snow, I mean. And look, there's a yellow-eyed woman coming to join us."

Jaran turned again and saw Unva standing, the lantern held high in her hands. "Who is that?" She hinted Taic and didn't sound pleased.

"I'm Taic," he answered. "Apparently, I've come to help."

"You are the ... Taic?" Unva shook her head. "Valkador's second Jarle. The illustrious adventurer warrior?" She shook her head. "Not quite what I expected."

She turned to Jaran, who was still feeling numb from the explosion. "You summoned him successfully. That's good, I suppose, though I'm no longer certain he'll help us much."

"I was a Jarle?" Taic stared at her with his mouth open. "My memory's addled. Sorry I'm not what you were expecting, witch," Taic asked her. "You are a witch, aren't you? You whiff like one. My nose can detect camphor and peppermint, a hint of sage? Good to smell stuff again. Don't let my big uncle Barin find you—he'll hit you with something. Doesn't like witches."

"You are talkative for a ghost," Unva said, glancing sideways at Jaran, who was lost in thought.

"It runs in our family." Taic smiled at her. "Please tell me why I'm here."

"To help me kill a witch," Jaran told him.

"Another one," Unva said quickly, licking her lips. "Not me."

Taic nodded slowly, rubbing his whiskers. He reached back, producing a spear and shield from nowhere. "Well, here I am," he said, thudding the spear butt into the soil. "Happy to help a family member. What is this place and why does it feel so unpleasant?"

"It's called *Taic's* Howe," Jaran said wryly.

"That's horrible," Taic said, looking up at the shadow of trees, the stones glinting in moonlight. "Are you telling me I was entombed inside that rock?"

"Hard to believe, but yes," Jaran said. "I had to go inside and fetch you. It wasn't pleasant. Unva here helped with the runes, spell-codes and ... other stuff."

"Hmm, yes, I could see that would prove tricky," Taic said, rubbing his chin. "Now, cousin—*can I call you cousin?* Descendant is a bit of a mouthful. "

"Fine by me."

"First things first," Taic continued with enthusiasm. "I'll need to know our plan. Where's the witch, and can I hit her first? Before that, I need food and ale, lots of ale."

Jaran stared at Unva. She chewed her lip and turned away.

"Let's get started," Jaran said, slinging Griner across his shoulder and turning his back on the stones.

GUNSALA STOOD BESIDE THE REDHEAD SAVARNA AS JARAN Saerk reemerged through the gloom, followed by Unva and a scruffy-looking stranger with long, straw-colored hair and a stubble beard. The stranger was looking around like someone who'd woken from a dream induced by potent mushrooms.

His pale blue eyes were smiling. He appeared a simpleton, but Gunsala's Vulkorye spirit sensed the strength inside him. This man had been a hero once.

The stranger saw her, and his mouth dropped open in surprise. "Vulkorye." He glanced at Jaran. "She's a ..."

"She is ..." Jaran said looking across at her with a faint smile. "We'll explain everything to you."

"I can't wait to hear it all."

Gunsala watched the newcomer curiously. He grinned at her for a moment and turned his gaze to Savarna, who stood with Ivar, her fists shoved in her hips.

"What are you staring at?" Savarna said to the stranger.

"Some fine-looking women gathered here," the straw head said.

"This is Taic," Jaran said. "A ... *relative.*"

"It's good to be here," Taic said. "When do we get started?"

"Taic ..."

The voice came from behind her. Gunsala turned and saw Ivar gripping his spear, his hands shaking. "You're *the* Taic? The same legendary Jarle who saved Valkador from the War Hounds of Leeth, after Barin the Voyager sailed off the edge of the world?"

"That's an exaggeration," the man called Taic said. "But yes, I'm he. At least, I think I am. I've been stuck in a dark hole for a very long time."

Gunsala looked at Savarna, who was frowning. "Another witless relic from the past," Savarna said, awarding Taic a sour look. She turned to Jaran. "I think you had best rely on that axe, rather than lost kinsmen. And where's Barin—wouldn't he prove more useful? No offence," she added to Taic, who didn't seem to notice, as he was staring up at the sky with a whimsical smile.

Feeling detached from the group, Gunsala followed the others back into the glade, her mind fused with tension. Valkador was vibrating with sorcery. The dead were living, Sheega's sendings, and Faerie creeping out of the caves. Her Vulkorye was stirring inside. She could feel the apprehension and excitement building. *Our time approaches.* Finvar would be most vulnerable during these next few days. She couldn't stay here any longer.

As she walked behind her new friends, Gunsala felt something trembling at her waist. She glanced down and untied the small sack she had hanging from her belt. *Elanion's gift.* The seashell was throbbing, its color altered to an iridescent green.

It is time.

Gunsala stopped and waited until the others were inside the glade, all preoccupied with the eccentric newcomer, Taic. They wouldn't notice she'd gone for a while.

The green shell throbbed and pulsed in her fist, its emerald light spilling out through her fingers.

The Goddess needs me. Finvar needs me.

Gunsala stowed her shell in the bag and started walking quickly back through the trees.

SHEEGA STRODE BRISKLY INTO THE HALL AND SAW FINVAR watching her from the seat by the fire. "You had better get ready," she told him. "There has been a shift of pace. I'll need your full cooperation, Finvar Droll—else your fiery master will grill you alive. Or failing that, I'll do worse to you myself. Understand?"

Finvar nodded, mumbling something. He looked pale and tired. Utterly defeated. Sheega scowled at him, not liking what she saw. Lofhi had better not let her down with his wretch.

"Is Jaran on his way?" Finvar muttered, as though asking himself the question.

"He will be very soon," Sheega said, changing tack, taking the other chair and smiling sympathetically at the wretched creature. Her mood had shifted—she was back in control after that initial shock. Again, Unva and that vile Yetain had stolen a march on her.

Didn't matter. It would prove their last victory. Once Hrelgisson was dealt with, she'd finish Unva and Run and seal their dooms in some delightfully extended manner. She'd have her full powers back. Even Elanion Herself wouldn't be able to stop Sheega this time. Nor her wily husband, if He cared to try.

Fuck them all. No one was going to spoil her day. That day was coming sooner than she'd expected. A month sooner— thanks to Unva and her hairy accomplice.

But they'd done her a favor. Sheega was tired of waiting, pacing about while Hrelgisson and the girl hid protected like moles in those caves. The time had dragged lately. But Faerie's impetuous intervention had altered everything.

Inadvertently, Aldorian had broken the fragile laws between worlds, by allowing his elf army to enter this realm's atmosphere before the gates were open. She'd felt the elves creeping inside her head. Aldorian was agitated, trying to reach her. Angry and vengeful. Something unexpected had happened in Faerie. *Treachery.* Sheega knew that smell. She probed deeper as she watched the fire, ignoring the miserable man seated close by. She needed to find the elf king, ensure he did what was needed. *First ...*

Sheega laughed— a merry sound. She noticed Finvar jump slightly, as he tried not to watch her.

"What is funny?" he said, avoiding her eyes.

"You are."

"Why?"

"Because you're so easily defeated. I slapped you about— so what? Since then, you've been sulking like a scolded child. No wonder the girl left you. But don't fret." Sheega laughed again. "Once you've helped us out, I'll find that wench. I might fry her Vulkorye mind, but you'll have her plump, ripe body to play with—though she might dribble, the poor little thing."

"Gunsala is stronger than you think."

"Is that a threat to my person? A defiant spark in your eye?" Sheega laughed once more, scoffing at his discomfort. "You're bright for a human, Fin. Surely you realize I cannot let the wench live. Elanion Fuckface, my greatest enemy—we go back eons. That wondrous bitch chose Gunsala for her conduit. That's a sort of *champion*, if you prefer laymen terms. Much like clumsy Tyho chose poor Hrelgisson, and Lofhi fashioned you. Pieces on a board, to be played and discarded. But not you. You're the lucky one."

He looked at her, his face torn with anguish.

"True love—was it?" Sheega smiled, enjoying herself. "Ah, so sad. Love was always a human weakness. We immortals never let emotions get in the way of self-promotion. It's the Weaver's fault. The Maker of Worlds. The Faceless One wasn't fully occupied when he fashioned your race from mud. There were distractions, mostly from our crew. Unlike us, you humans were created flawed. If you're still determined to be miserable, blame Him, not me."

Sheega looked up as Ranning walked into the hall, a silver

cloak made of seashells flowing around his broad shoulders. He glanced at her and at Finvar and smiled slightly, before standing in front of the fire and warming his hands.

"What news?" Sheega asked him.

"I sent Gorvaron to the caves again," Ranning said. "Told him to wait there. Garrosk and the other Witch-Guard are ready to defend this hall, as are your undead."

"The lake men are preoccupied in limbo," Sheega told him. "Hrelgisson went to Taic's Howe. I saw him in my mind's eye. He's raised a warrior from the past. There will be more coming. And the Whitebear is lumbering around somewhere."

She crinkled her nose, noticing the worry on Ranning's face.

"Hrelgisson's corpse friends won't save him," Sheega insisted, "because we have Finvar here to do our dirty work. Haven't we?" She flashed Finvar a beautiful smile, and he nodded, his eyes on the fire.

"I'd sooner not depend on this sorry fellow." Ranning gazed hard at the man. "He is shifty for a mortal. I sense duplication. You should let me kill him, or feed him to Gorvaron."

Finvar glared back at Ranning, and the Water Faen chuckled. "See the rage burning inside? The man is torn, Sheega. Do not trust him."

"That's because he's frustrated," she said, waving a dismissive hand. "Poor Finvar Droll has no control over his organ. Lofhi plays with it and gets all the benefit. Isn't that so, Fin? Shame …" She smiled at Finvar again.

"Leave me alone." He glared at her, his eyes showing a brief glint of firelight.

"Don't stare at me like that," Sheega told him, as Ranning

chuckled. "You know I speak the truth, Fin. Lofhi tortures you, I *feel* your pain. He's a bastard, is Lofhi—worse than any of us, and you bear the brunt of that. That's hard. Ignore Ranning. He doesn't like anyone, and he's tetchy. I know you won't let us down."

She leaned forward on her chair.

"Once you've done the nefarious deed, you will be free of Ranning and of me. Should you wish to be. Everyone will leave you alone after you've buried my rune dagger deep in Hrelgisson's heart." Sheega produced a twisted blade in her left hand and flicked it deftly through her nimble fingers. Finvar watched it with haunted eyes. "There are curses woven into this steel that run as deep as Tyho's axe. What say you, Finvar Droll? Are you ready to become an Immortal, one of us?"

"I will do as you bid," Finvar said, nodding, but still avoiding her gaze. Sheega half-noted that Ranning had left them.

Sheega nodded slowly. "I have no doubt of that."

She watched the fire, seeing the small shapes moving inside. "Lofhi has assured me," she said in a quieter voice, her playful mood having shifted elsewhere. "Relax," she told him. "Eat, and drink—I'll make something special. You're much too thin. And do cheer up. You stand to gain so much! Lose your foolish fancies and embrace this opportunity. Who knows? You might want to stay on."

Sheega shifted her legs by the fire, revealing several inches of pale, naked thigh. She saw him notice before quickly looking away.

She smiled. "I'll always need good servants around me, Fin. Gantallian's been sulking of late. And Ranning ..." She leaned closer again. "Between you and me, I grow weary of him. Perhaps, you'll kill him, too? For special favors ..."

Sheega slid a hand up his thigh and squeezed. Finvar stiffened, and she laughed.

"Think about it, will you? We've not long to wait, you and I. The elves are coming, Finvar. Trolls, too. They'll most likely be fighting each other, thanks to that meddling cow Coristain. I saw her essence floating around the ether. She's crossed already and is here somewhere. I'll catch her."

"I don't know who that is." Finvar was trying hard not to look at her legs.

"Doesn't matter." Sheega shifted again, revealing more of herself. "Do you not like what you see?" Sheega stroked his thigh, her fingernails teasing higher. Finvar's eyes looked like they were about to pop from his skull. *You look in pain.* Sheega sighed and, bored of her game, let go. Finvar slumped deeper in his chair.

"Get some rest, Finvar Droll." Sheega stood and walked to the door, her wolf-skin cloak swirling about her shoulders. "I need you to be in top form when your big, stupid friend arrives. He's going to try to save you, of course. As will Savarna, too, I suspect. Instead, you will kill Hrelgisson, and I'll deal with the redhead. If that little minx of yours shows her face, I'll cut it off and place it in a vase." She laughed at the horror in his eyes and left him to his misery.

SHEEGA WALKED OUT INTO THE BRIGHT, CLEAR MORNING. She looked up at the faint gibbous moon staring down at her.

I'm ready for you, moon.

She walked down to the lake and on to the seashore. Ranning was out there staring at the ocean, two of the Witch-Guard with him—doubtless dreaming of watery Telimantua.

She ignored them and took the curving track up to her witching pole. There, Sheega stood for a long time, as the waves danced ahead. She watched their moon-sparkle surge forward, washing her feet, before retreating in rhythmic repetition. As she gazed into those waves, Sheega's third eye saw the myriad creatures writhing beneath those chilly waters. Silently, she named each one. When she wearied of her survey, Sheega seated herself cross-legged beneath the pole.

It was time to call on certain people. She'd spotted her son Valgarn in the southlands journeying with a wench. *My only son.* She'd left him be, knowing Valgarn was lost to her. Her boys had been a disappointment. *No surprise*, tainted with weak mortal blood as they were. She would haunt Valgarn's dreams from time to time. *Later.* There were more important issues to solve.

Sheega closed her eyes, allowed her mind to travel, float and drift, like dandelion-dander lifting through the air. Creeping into the dark ethereal fabric that fluttered between the worlds.

Aldorian.

She could see them marching in their thousands, crossing through the glowing, throbbing mile-high doors that separated the nine worlds from the Otherrealm.

Aldorian!

Ahead were the horsemen, riding steeds of shimmering blue. Sheega saw him among them at the head of the host, his pale eyes shifting from left to right, searching—the long, white hair flowing behind as he rode.

Who calls?

It is I, Sheega.

Show yourself, so I can kill you! Much harm have you caused, Deyna.

Not I. That was your own sister's doing, and yet you accuse me who would be your ally, if not friend. Though I would prefer the latter.

Sheega saw him laugh as he rode through the World Gate.

The trolls attack us from behind. We will carry our conflict through to Ansu. The war will be long, as our foe are mighty and their anger great now that Rumgorz is slain.

I can help you defeat them, so we can share this world together.

Why would you do that?

An act of friendship, of course. I have small love for trolls or goblins, who sided with them against you. But I hate mortals far more. Help me take back Ansu, king! Together, you and I can defeat our enemies, the trolls, the old gods. Mortals.

You were one of the old gods, were you not?

I was betrayed, I would have vengeance. And these newcomers, Tyho and Kullaan, even Lofhi, are impostors—they have no jurisdiction here. This was your home, Aldorian, and mine. We never quarreled in those days. It was the Weaver's meddling, his filthy last born—those creatures whom he loved so much. The humans. They've ruined everything, and the new gods make it worse. Help me put things right.

I shall.

Aldorian's horse faded through the crack in the shimmering World Gate. He was through—the elf army had arrived. Sheega felt a thrill of anticipation. Once they cleared the traps of Cradon Iwey, the elves would manifest on the island. The trolls, too, but she could deal with that. Aldorian's people would protect her from Tyho and the others. Sheega knew they were waiting out there. Her other enemy, the Traveler, too. All were biding their time, counting the final hours.

Sheega glanced up at the moon again as it floated high

over the water. Six days remained. She rose like silk and walked back to the hall. Finvar still sat dreaming, as though trapped in a trance. This time, she ignored him and made for the mirror chamber. She must make ready her final preparations. Sheega would go scry the mirror for Hrelgisson's whereabouts and nudge Gantallian, threatening him with elf magic if he didn't sharpen up.

Sheega smiled as she tapped the copper mirror with her fingers.

"Wake up!" she told the cringing face inside. "We have work to do, imp."

STORM WARNING

Dawn's pale light crept through the drapes. Rasnei rolled free of the covers and walked out onto the balcony. It was already late summer. The birds sang in the gardens below, and the sky was a hazy, pinkish blue. It would be hot today—perhaps there would be a storm out to sea.

She watched for a time, allowing her mind wake fully. She heard Vian snoring in the bed. He'd slept so much, and she worried he'd never be the same. His dragon was dead, he'd told her. She'd returned from the walls and found him playing his flute. A melancholy tune, it had brought a tear to her eyes.

A knock at the door.

She walked back into the chamber, passed Vian's sleeping form and stood by the alcove.

"Who is there?" Rasnei demanded. She expected Nolenzes or the girl Jilanna. Instead, Gurtei's gruff voice came from the hallway.

"Highness—you had best get ready."

"Uzcara?"

"Here."

"I am on my way." Rasnei cursed—it wasn't fully light yet. The new leader meant business, and word was he was no fool. Uzcara would test them hard today. She dressed quickly, kissed Vian's sleeping face, and stared at him for a moment, brushing his hair.

"Stay resting, my love. We'll need your strength and wisdom later." Rasnei kissed him again and dressed quickly into her battle gear. Ta Shen needed to see its empress on the high keep. She'd been there most mornings. It would be a sorry tale to let them down on what might prove their final day.

UZCARA GRINNED AS HIS RIDERS CANTERED CLOSER TO the walls. Hidden in their midst was the ox train, each large animal bearing chains that carried the pine trunk. Not as big as the great oak rams that Casca had employed, but it didn't need to be. Casca had relied on the ballista and buggering about, but Uzcara was going for speed.

He waited until they were inside arrow range and gave the order to charge.

"Make for the gates!" Uzcara roared, bringing his horse to heel and allowing his warriors canter past, urging their mounts to gallop. He saw the Shen lined up on the walls, their spears and helmets gleaming.

"This day you die!" Uzcara made a chopping motion with his gloved, handless stump.

He'd ordered Calgara make for the damaged walls again, taking half his force. The others rode at speed for the gates, the mule train following behind.

Uzcara heard the whine of arrows, then saw men scream

and pitch from their mounts. It had started, it and would finish today.

VIAN BLINKED AWAKE. SOMETHING WAS AMISS. HE sensed peril, rolled from the bed, and ran out to the balcony. Rasnei had gone, and a fierce, hazy sun cast heat shimmer ahead. He heard the sounds of fighting. It sounded close. *Were they inside the walls?* Impossible.

Damn this sleeping. Vian dressed quickly, grabbing his armor and helmet, and made ready. He turned when a cough interrupted him. The girl Jilanna stood by the door. He hadn't heard her come in. She looked pale and afraid.

"What has happened?" Vian demanded.

"Lord Gurtei says we cannot hold," she said. "They have a new ram and are attacking the gates, and so many have brought scaling ladders. I fear that the walls are breached in several places."

"I am going out there."

"The empress gave orders for you to rest."

"I'm done fucking resting," Vian snarled at her and saw the panic in her eyes. "I'm sorry, Jilanna," he added, softening his tone. "I didn't mean to frighten you. I'm angry, but that's not your fault." He touched her arm gently and forced a smile. "Tell Nolenzes that I am fully recovered and much needed on the walls."

She nodded and made to leave.

"Where is the empress?" Vian asked her.

"At the keep, or she was—the guards reported."

Damn, you again, Rasnei. Why didn't you rouse me?

Vian held Jilanna's gaze for a moment longer. "Get every

available person in the palace ready with any weapons they can muster, in case they break through. And they might, Jilanna. We have to be ready for that. This Uzcara is worse than the other Rans. I'm sending Rasnei back here. The guards need to be ready for her return. Keep her in arm's length. Understood?"

She nodded again and fled the room.

Vian watched Jilanna depart. He seized his Jian blades, strapping them across his back. He found the Chiang spear resting against a closet wall. He grabbed it and left the chamber, his eyes blazing and head pounding like distant thunder.

GUJUN WATCHED AS THE RAM BROKE THROUGH THE gates. Two hours had passed since the dawn attack. The Cards had breached the walls in three places. And, at last, the gates had given way. The slaughter would start now. It was time he sent the signal.

Gujun vaulted onto his saddle and rode at speed along the ridge. One of his riders reached him. "Light the battle flares, and inform Chulan it's time," he yelled at the man, as he cantered past.

Gujun reached the small camp where a group of his Slayers were seated around a fire. They jumped to their feet when they saw him. He slid from his horse and gazed out over the cliff, seeing seven brightly colored ships a mile offshore. The Vendeli were awaiting his signal.

"Send the flare!" Gujun ordered, and watched. He remounted and sat his horse in silence as the rocket screamed and shrieked skyward, leaving a blazing trail of scarlet. The nearest ship replied with a violet flare.

Satisfied, Gujun ordered the men to rejoin the others, while he cantered down from the ridge taking the woods. From there, he would skirt wide and find the postern Chulan had mentioned. After months of waiting, they were running out of time.

GURTEI YELLED ORDERS AS THE ENEMY POURED IN through the broken gates. He saw Rasnei gazing down there, her face stricken with horror. The Northman Dorthar stood beside her, heavy axe in his hands.

"Empress, you must leave here," Gurtei called across to her.

"My place is with our people."

"Retire to the palace," he begged her when he'd reached her side. "We cannot hold out here, empress. Your safety is paramount. If you are hurt, the defense will crumble. Go, please."

She bit her lip, nodded. "You are right."

Gurtei ordered a troop to escort the empress along the north wall, taking the longer route back to the palace, as there was no fighting that way. He'd keep the bastards busy here for as long as possible, allowing her and Vian form a final defense in the palace.

Matax emerged, his face streaming with blood from where his face wound had reopened. He'd been with Lin Gu fighting at the breaches, but that battle was already lost.

"The empress?"

"Dorthar's with her," Gurtei told him. "They're making for the palace. Be safe there for a while."

"An hour, perhaps two." Matax wiped more blood from

his face. "We have to get her out of the city, Gurt. The harbor. I'll send a troop to ready some craft."

"Lead them yourself, Matax. Pointless both her generals dying here."

"Gurtei …"

"Go on, man!"

"I'll be back," Matax said, mopping his face with a red hand.

Gurtei nodded and was about to reply when a huge roar announced the enemy had entered the barbican and were coming their way.

"Here we go." Gurtei leaned back against the wall and waited until they appeared, a score of helmeted faces, the hatred gleaming in their eyes. The Cards yelled as they attacked, and more appeared behind them. "They think Rasnei's here," Gurtei said to Roile beside him. He saw Lin Gu emerge from the other direction.

"We need to hold as long as we can," Gurtei shouted. "Allow Rasnei to escape the city."

He glimpsed Lin Gu grinning at him and ducked instinctively when a spear flashed at his face. They were here. Gurtei answered his curved blade, knocking it aside.

Gurtei killed the man with a back-sweep. A second spearman jabbed at him, and there were warriors scaling the high keep walls with ladders behind. Gurtei was surrounded. The Cards smiled at him, taking their time. They would know him as a leader.

Gurtei could hear Lin Gu fighting close by, surrounded like he was. He heard Roile cursing in the other direction.

A young hawk-nosed warrior emerged through the enemy and glared at Gurtei. "Where's your bitch-empress, Shen?" the officer said. Gurtei vaguely recognized him as the last Ragan, Calgara.

"She isn't here," he said.

"Pox take her and your people," Calgara signaled his men resume their attack. "I'll make do with you instead. Kill him."

Gurtei closed his eyes. He smiled. *You're an old fool, Gurt. You duped yourself by believing we could win.*

OCTAXA STOOD AT THE PROW, AS SEA BIRDS FOLLOWED above their wake. It was mid-morning and already hot. Not the fierce, dry heat of his homeland, but a sultry, clammy swelter that would sap the energy of most men. But not the fighting Sangala, nor especially Octaxa, their leader. He was content. He smiled at the sunshine, as Corvo yelled for oars and his men brought the dhow to rest gently at the nearest quay. Octaxa turned and watched the other six vessels moor up alongside.

Within minutes, Octaxa and his men had vaulted onto the quayside and started racing toward the distant walls that hid the city beyond.

"Kill everyone, unless I order otherwise," Octaxa yelled, leading the hunt across the harbor.

MATAX RACED TOWARDS THE HARBOR GATES AND skidded to a halt as a loud blast shattered his eardrum and sent him flying. *An explosion.* The harbor gates had been smashed open, and the tall shapes of red-cloaked warriors rushed through.

The harbor was taken. The Cards must have breached the Sea Gate. As he blinked back bloody tears, Matax saw the swarthy knot of foreigners gather in a tight bunch, led by a very tall man cloaked in black leather. He wore a skull cap on his head with three blood-red feathers protruding. A shaman —it had to be. And these people were not Cards.

Treachery.

Matax tried to stand, but another blast sent him face-first in the dust. He blanked out.

CHULAN WAS WAITING BY THE WALL AS GUJUN EMERGED at the hidden postern. The small, sharp-eyed magister looked happy for once.

"You've exceeded yourself, Slayer. All goes to plan. Stagan is attacking the enemy's rear. Uzcara will have no idea he is under attack."

Gujun shrugged. "What next ... *emperor?*"

Chulan smiled again. "*Yes*, and soon. First, we need to find Rasnei and stay clear of the Cards until Stagan and our Vendeli friends have them trapped. Follow me inside, Slayer. The tunnel will lead out to the inner edge of the harbor wall. I expect that the shaman, Octaxa, will meet us there."

GET ON WITH IT.

Gurtei heard fighting close by, as he waited with eyes closed for the death blow. Why hadn't they killed him yet? He heard shouts and the sound of running feet. He opened an eye. Calgara and his men had gone. Instead Vian stood there, a Chiang spear dripping blood in his gloved hands.

"Happy to see you." It was all Gurtei could manage.

"Where's Rasnei?" Vian's gold-flecked eyes were wild. Gurtei had never seen him look so angry.

"With Dorthar," he replied. "I sent them back to the palace." He glanced around, seeing only corpses on the parapet and keep tower. "What happened here? Where are the Cards?"

Vian shrugged. "I'm not sure, but it looks like Uzcara is under attack."

"From whom?" Gurtei staggered to his feet. "It cannot be. Calgara was …"

"That one got away," Vian said. "I killed a dozen, maybe more. Lin Gu went after the rest. The main fighting's moved inside the city."

"We had best join."

Vian stared at him. "First, I need to know that Rasnei is safe in the palace?"

"I hope so," Gurtei said. "I sent Matax and a company to escort her there, before the attack reached us."

"Good," Vian said. "And you're right, we need to find out what's happening below." Gurtei was about to respond when he heard a familiar shout. He turned to see Roile racing toward them from the north wall.

"What's happening?" Gurtei said, as Roile almost crashed into him.

He glanced wild-eyed at Gurtei and across to Vian.

"We're fucked," Roile told them.

"What …?

"The harbor's lost. Invasion. The Vendeli."

"The Vendeli are here?" Gurtei's face blanched. "The empress is trapped in the palace?"

"Octaxa!" Vian stared at Gurtei with an intensity that made him shiver.

"You knew about this?"

Vian shook his head. "The Vendeli shaman—this has to be him. Octaxa slew my *Aikashi*. The dragon you saw. I am needed in the palace." Vian turned and vanished inside the barbican doorway.

Gurtei blinked and tried to take stock. Roile crouched low beside him. There was fresh shouting below, and the sound of steel on steel. But who was fighting whom?

Beside him, Roile fumbled for an arrow but didn't appear to have many left. He walked across to the parapet, stepping over corpses that still seeped blood.

"Gurt, you'd best take a look at this."

Gurtei staggered across to join his friend. He shielded his eyes from the glare and glanced down. What he saw left him gasping in disbelief. A Shen army was out there. Perhaps five thousand strong, clad in glittering armor and each conical-helmed warrior carrying Chiang and painted shield.

"What the ...?"

"It's Coi Stagan from the river," Lin Gu appeared. "That's his motif on the shields. They must have been holed up in the woods."

"Then we have won!" Roile grinned.

But Gurtei felt a sinking sensation in his belly.

"Who ordered a force of Imperials to hide in those woods? Why not intervene earlier and help us? And why are the fucking Vendeli here? This must be Chulan's doing—and his dog, Gujun the Slayer."

"We had best go and find out for certain," Lin Gu said.

Uzcara couldn't understand what had happened. There was fighting behind him out on the plain. He sat his horse inside the gates. All around him, his riders were whooping and shouting as they rode on through the ruin. There were dead Shen defenders sprawled everywhere.

Calgara had been in the vanguard. He'd seen his young brother up on the keep tower. It looked like the fiercest fighting had happened up there. But as he'd ridden closer, Uzcara had lost track of his brother and those fighting on the keep.

He'd watched on as his main force of riders reached the city, scaling the walls with a hundred ladders. The ram mules had reached the gates, surrounded by archers firing up at the enemy, who had struggled to shoot back against that storm. Uzcara had grinned in satisfaction when a great shout announced the gates had buckled a second time.

He'd spurred his horse forward.

Time to reap the harvest.

But as he drew close to the gates, Uzcara saw men waving him back, and he heard shouts of alarm.

"What's happening?" he yelled across to a captain who was gazing back toward their distant camps. The man pointed, his voice inaudible inside his helm.

Uzcara turned and shielded his eyes. He thought that he saw men out there. Soldiers marching in orderly file. Hard to be sure in the fog of haze and chaos surrounding him.

The camp should be empty, and Uzcara had no infantry force, bar the artillery men and rammers—most of them dead. And yet there were men out there, and getting nearer. An army. Uzcara stared for a moment, rubbing his eyes in disbelief.

"They're fucking Shen," the same captain shouted across to him, before wheeling his horse about and making for the gates.

Can it be true?

Uzcara didn't believe it possible. A trick of the light, maybe? An illusion caused by more sorcery? With the dust and heat shimmer, it was so hard to tell. But something untoward had happened. He'd thought the city taken, but as Uzcara entered the gates, the sound of fighting got louder. The Shen were rallying. This wasn't over yet. Worse, there seemed to be an army out there on the plain. Where had they come from, and who the fuck were they?

Genza? Perhaps his brother had sent more men east, sensing their victory and wanting some of the loot. But why would Genza not contact him on arrival? As he sat his horse under the arched gateway barbican entrance, a hand covering his eyes, Uzcara had the sinking feeling he'd miscalculated. That was the enemy out there. The Shen had outmaneuvered him. But how?

He saw Calgara emerge, his left arm soaked in blood and hanging limp at his side. His helmet was missing, and he looked ashen pale.

"What's happening?" Uzcara rode across to Calgara, whipping men in the face to get out of his way. The fighting had ceased around him, moved further into the city and streets beyond. A few Shen stood their ground inside the barbican courtyard. These were dispatched before he got to his brother. "Calgara, talk to me!"

He heard drums rolling a marching beat and the sound of boots approaching outside the gates. *A trap, but set by whom?*

Calgara looked at him, mumbled something, shook his head, and lurched back inside the barbican walls. Uzcara cursed and made to follow, but there were too many bodies blocking the way. He heard a man scream to his right and saw the Shen arrow sticking in his gut.

Another rider tumbled. A third. There was scant space to maneuver here. Uzcara looked outside again. This time, there was no doubting his eyes. He could see neat lines of spear-carrying, heavily armored warriors marching for the gates in drilled precision. Shen infantry from the River garrison. How had this happened without him knowing about it? Too late to worry over that. Uzcara needed a plan, and fast.

"Get inside the city," Uzcara yelled at his men. "Butcher any man, woman or living thing. We'll take their palace and hold any nobles hostage. We'll fight our way out of this disaster. Move!"

But it soon became obvious that this was well-planned. Uzcara led his men into the central square. He saw that the Shen defense had rallied around a huge warrior carrying twin Jian swords. A hundred or so, they'd taken defensive positions, blocking the streets, and were shooting arrows at any of his men who entered. It was a death trap. They were caught like bugs in a jar.

The huge fighter had seen Calgara, who was leading a troop into an alley. Uzcara watched in dismay as his younger brother was cut down and butchered by the men there. Behind Uzcara, his riders panicked as more arrows struck them, and he could hear the Shen attackers arriving and pouring like disturbed ants through the gates.

We've lost.

Uzcara vaulted from his horse and sprinted across to a street corner. As he ran, he saw them trample Calgara's body and butcher the last of his men. The Shen soldiers were inside the city. His men had nowhere to go. Uzcara picked up his pace, switching from street to street and heading deeper into the city. He would find out who arranged this and cut out their eyes.

Before that, he had to stay alive. Uzcara heard shouts and knew that he'd been seen. He ran full pelt, entered some gardens and kept running, his breath like fire burning his ribs. He turned a corner, tripped, but regained his feet swiftly. They were gaining on him.

A man blocked his path. A tall, black-skinned warrior with a naked chest, and a long cloak tossed over his broad shoulders. He carried a heavy tulwar in both hands. *Vendeli.* Genza's allies had betrayed them. Perhaps his brother had, too.

You treacherous bastards.

Uzcara was missing a hand and an army, but he wasn't finished yet. He barreled into the Vendeli warrior, catching him off guard. Uzcara got his feet under him and jumped clear as the Vendeli recovered with lightning speed and swung out with a heavy blade.

Uzcara jumped back. The Vendeli swung across with the other tulwar. Uzcara trapped the weapon with his scimitar and stabbed up under, slicing into the tall man's side. He twisted the blade. The Vendeli stared at him, shuddered, and sank to his knees. Uzcara kicked his face in and tugged the sword free. He crept back into the undergrowth, looking for somewhere to hide.

The sounds of fighting were everywhere. It was as though the entire city had erupted. He waited for several minutes. The pursuers must have been distracted. Uzcara seized his chance, gripped the sword, and crawled out through the bushes.

This wasn't over. He'd survive, recover what men he could rally and make these treacherous bastards pay.

A boot thudded down on his neck. Uzcara tried to roll, but a kick in his side sent him sprawling.

"I'm Octaxa, and you've killed one of my Sangala," a deep voice said. "Have you any idea what I'm going to do to you?"

Uzcara closed his eyes.

THE LAST AUTUMN FLOWER

GUJUN WALKED behind Chulan and his servants. They carried lanterns, the damp tunnel pressing in and down around them. How had he not known about this place? The old guard must have kept it a tight secret—a legacy of the rivalries in this ancient city. But not from Chulan. His spies knew everything. That's why he would win today. Magister Chulan always won.

Emperor Chulan. Gujun had his own opinion on that. He wouldn't voice it anytime soon.

Gujun saw light growing ahead. They'd reached the tunnel end. He emerged squinting and saw walls looming to his right, adjacent to the larger one they'd accessed via the postern. The harbor lay on the other side. Ahead, a lane curved toward gardens. Chulan entered and walked briskly with confidence. This part of the city appeared deserted, but Gujun could hear fighting—it came from the main gates, a half-mile away.

The palace roofs glinted gold in the distance. Gujun

guessed they were heading that way. He heard the sound of soft tread to his left and slid his Jian blades free.

The Vendeli emerged from the gardens, like red-cloaked specters surrounding their little party. Chulan froze, as did his servants. Gujun leveled his blades and circled slowly.

The leader was smiling. He carried a grisly trophy—a severed head stuck on his spear. As Gujun watched, the man wrenched it off and tossed the head at Chulan's feet.

"Who is this?" Chulan looked sickened.

"That belonged to your enemy, the Cardalan, Uzcara," the Vendeli said. "I found him crawling in the gardens like a grub, trying to escape your vengeance."

Chulan glared at the head for a moment. "Where is Rasnei?" he demanded, his voice shaky.

The black-skinned warrior shrugged. "Do you expect us to do everything for you, Shen?"

"She'll be inside the palace," Gujun suggested. The leader reminded him of Utuxla, but even worse. This man had real power.

Chulan nodded. He looked shaken. The tall Vendeli noticed his discomfort and smiled. He caught Gujun's glance and stared back, as though amused. Gujun almost shivered at the latent malice in that gaze.

"You're the shaman, Octaxa," Gujun said.

"And you are Gujun the Slayer," the man smiled. "My second, Utuxla, sent word I shouldn't trust you."

Gujun didn't reply. He stepped close behind Chulan, who'd started walking briskly toward the palace gates that were barely visible beyond the dragon bridges and gardens winding the way ahead.

"Looks like we're making for the palace," Gujun heard Octaxa say to his men, as they started following behind.

Gujun turned about, his twin Jians ready.

The shaman smiled. "Relax, Shen. We are friends today, remember."

"Aye, for the moment." Gujun turned again and caught up with the magister.

RASNEI GAZED OUT FROM THE BALCONY. HER EYES WERE moist, but she wouldn't weep. They had done so well. Won every battle and risen to each challenge, however terrible.

But how can you stop the inevitable? Hold out against a force so much stronger? Dam a river's flow with your cupped hands?

And yet she'd believed they could win.

Rasnei heard fighting continuing near the main gates. Some forays were closer—doubtless the Cardalan attackers had penetrated the streets. It was only a matter of time before they reached the palace, like so many rabid hyenas. There weren't many guards posted below. She had ordered most of the Palace Guard to the walls. The few who remained would be swept away like dust in a storm. After that ...

Dorthar stood resolute, like an island bastion awaiting the storm inside her chamber. He'd hardly moved, both strong hands resting on his axe. He'd smiled at Rasnei as they'd entered, telling her this wasn't over yet.

She'd smiled back. *Not quite.*

They'd arrived back at the palace half an hour ago. Rasnei hadn't been surprised to find Vian gone. The girl Jilanna had told her he'd gone back to the keep, that he was seeking her and had told the girl he would bring the Empress Rasnei back here.

Rasnei hoped that Vian would return, once he knew she was back in the palace. Unless he was ...

No. She would know if that was so.

Nolenzes appeared with two men, half-dragging a shaking figure. She hardly recognized General Matax.

"We found him in the palace grounds, unconscious," Nolenzes told her. "He'd crawled from the harbor gates. There was some kind of explosion."

Rasnei ordered strong tea and bid Matax rest on the bed. He drank, carefully at first but then downed the hot liquid in one choking gulp. "The Vendeli are here," he said, speaking louder than was needed.

"What happened to you?" Dorthar asked, looming close beside her.

"Explosion," Matax shouted, touching his ears. "The gates were blasted open. I can't hear ..."

"The Vendeli?" Rasnei was trying to grasp this latest news.

Matax made a mewling sound and slapped his head. "The harbor, yes! We went to secure ships for your departure. Instead, we encountered ..." He shook his head. "My men are dead. I got away only because the invaders were distracted."

Rasnei nodded. There was nothing to say. The Vendeli must have made a bargain with the Cards. Didn't much matter. They were done for anyway.

She saw Jilanna appear. The girl confirmed what Matax had told them. Word had spread among the palace servants that a foreign fleet had landed at the harbor docks.

It was over.

"See to our general," Rasnei ordered. Nolenzes nodded, and the two orderlies helped Matax clamber to his feet.

"I'll recover," Matax shouted as they led him away. Rasnei nodded, her mind lost to dreams.

"How many guards below?" Dorthar asked Nolenzes.

"Scarce twenty remain. Most are on the walls."

"Hopefully some will return here with Vian, when word gets out the Vendeli have joined the fun. What a fucking mess." Dorthar leaned on his axe, his eyes on the door.

Rasnei ignored the men. She walked out onto the balcony again. Such a beautiful day. Sultry and hot. Hazy and dreamy, as only southern Shen could be. She saw Vian's flute on a table where he'd left it. She picked up the instrument and tucked it inside her flared sleeve. Rasnei would use the thin blade to sever her throat before the jackals arrived.

Dorthar had followed her and seen the flute. He didn't know about the secret it held. He looked sad, yet proud.

"We're not beaten yet, empress," he told her.

Rasnei smiled at him. "Have you heard the poem called *Autumn's Last Flower*?" Dorthar shook his head. "It's one of my favorites. But it's sad, Dorthar. Because life is sad. *Life* is the flower in the poem, you see."

"I don't read much poetry, empress." Dorthar looked uncomfortable.

"No matter. Indulge me, please," Rasnei said, and he nodded. "All summer, she smiles—that flower. A bright blossom in the sunshine. She's worked so hard, pushing up through grimy winter soil, striving with urgency and need in springtime. In summer, she can smile, for a short while. But come autumn, she must fade. And die—as do all of us."

"But return again next spring," a voice said.

Rasnei turned as the tears fell from her eyes. Vian stood there, face covered in blood, a Jian blade gripped in either hand. He placed the swords aside and walked over, kissing her long and hard. Afterward, he turned to Dorthar.

"They are coming," Vian said. "The Vendeli, and the traitor Chulan."

"Chulan?" Rasnei let go of his hands. "Here?"

"He is," Vian said. "I got here as quickly as possible. It's unclear what has happened, but the city is in turmoil. The Cards have lost. Both Uzcara and Calgara are rumored dead."

"How is that possible?" Dorthar demanded.

Vian shrugged. "I'm not certain, but it concerns Chulan. I saw Shen imperials fighting Cards at the Main Gates. It got tricky there, so I ran back here via the north wall. There's an army attacking the Cards from behind. A Shen army."

"Then we have won after all," Dorthar said.

"They serve Chulan," Vian said. "I saw Roile and Gurtei, the few Cutters left. Gurt told me the Imperials had Lin Gu surrounded, along with the Cards. The fiercest fighting is by the Violet Girl."

"Chulan is making a play for emperor." Rasnei nodded. "I should have suspected he'd be involved all along. He's been far too quiet."

"Bastard!" Dorthar spat on the floor.

"Looks like we have company below." Vian pointed down. Rasnei saw red-cloaked warriors walking casually toward her palace gates. She counted a dozen, but there were many more. At their head was a very tall, hawk-faced figure, his scarlet cloak swaying, a skull cap with three red feathers on his head. She shivered seeing the man. He looked unclean, evil.

"That's the shaman, Octaxa," Vian said quietly. "I have business with him."

"Vian ..." Rasnei gripped his hand.

"You stay here, my love," he told her. "Dorthar, keep her safe until I return."

She saw Matax emerge. "I've heard the news," he said, managing to keep his voice low. "What can I do?"

"Find Lin Gu," Rasnei told him. "Or Gurtei—anyone. Tell them they're needed here."

"If they still live, I will find them," Matax nodded. He was limping, but he carried his sword confidently and left them alone on the balcony.

"Wait here," Vian told her. "I will be back soon as I can."

"Stay alive, Rundali," Dorthar growled at Vian. He nodded, flashed her a grin, and left the balcony and chamber.

"Vian!" Rasnei called after him. "There are too many, even for you."

GUJUN TAPPED THE MAGISTER'S SHOULDER AS THEY approached the gates. He could see the guards waiting there, about twenty men carrying long Chiang spears. They looked terrified, having seen Octaxa's Sangala walking slowly toward them.

Octaxa was working some kind of spell. The air felt leaden.

"Best we hold back," Gujun said. "Let these shaman-priests do the work." Chulan looked at him and nodded quickly. They watched as Octaxa approached the gates. He heard a crossbow twang and saw the bolt drop like a stone when Octaxa held up his fist.

"I don't like these Vendeli," Gujun said quietly.

Chulan smiled at him. "They are a useful weapon, Slayer," he said.

"That could prove treacherous to handle," he replied.

"We've no need to watch this fiasco," Chulan told him. "I

doubt those fools will keep Octaxa occupied for long. But why wait? There's another entrance to the palace. I wish to end this properly. That means making sure Rasnei doesn't slip away. You coming, Slayer?"

VIAN RACED DOWN THE STAIRS TO THE LOWER PALACE. A guard appeared before him, almost crashing into him with his Chiang catching on the wall.

"Easy, there," Vian said.

"They're attacking." The guard looked terrified. "He's using sorcery ... our gates ..."

"Follow me," Vian said. The man shook his head, so Vian pushed past and trotted through the rooms and corridors until the sounds of steel clashing and death screams could be heard. He reached the gates and saw the guards sprawled on their faces. A score of Vendeli stood over them, watching as one of them dispatched the last guard. He couldn't see his enemy Octaxa among them.

Vian walked forward, a slight smile on his face. "That was almost too easy, wasn't it?"

The Vendeli turned and watched him approach. "It's the *Aikashi* man," the nearest said. "Our leader thought you were dead. Drowned with your dragon. But only half of you survived, heh? The weak half. We'll happily finish what's left of you."

The Sangala surrounded him with spears. Vian smiled at them. He hoped Dorthar would keep Rasnei save, at least until she could escape. Or Lin Gu, Gurtei, or someone could save her.

They were waiting for him to move, savoring the moment.

Vian closed his eyes. He focused. *Sister.* He sent the mind blast, reaching out

Savarna. I need your help.

Vian opened his eyes, felt the Jian swords tingle in his hands. Their eyes were gleaming, his foes. Relishing the moment.

Time slowed like treacle flow.

Vian saw the nearest raise his spear and strike.

Savarna ...?

I'm here.

GUJUN FOLLOWED THE NARROW TRACK AROUND THE gardens, noticing how Chulan knew exactly where it was leading. The four servants followed the magister. They had their swords drawn. Until now, these had been hidden beneath their gray cloaks. Gujun followed silently behind.

They reached an alcove, a door showing beneath.

"The servants' forgotten entrance," Chulan said, glancing back at Gujun. "Rasnei's father showed me the blueprints of the palace during my time down here. Ta Shen has many secrets, but I am aware of most, if not all."

"And you're repaying that favor by usurping his daughter," Gujun said.

Chulan flashed him an annoyed look. "Needs must, Slayer. You of all people should understand that. I'm doing this for Shen."

Of course you are.

Gujun followed the armed orderlies inside the door. Ahead was a narrow corridor lit by sconces fixed along the walls. Damp and gloomy, it looked like no one had been

down here for years. The air smelt musty and heavy. Gujun
sniffed. There was another smell he could detect.

Gunpowder?

Chulan reached a second door. He pushed against it, but
it wouldn't give. He waved at the servants. Two of them
kicked and shoved at the door until it creaked open. They
entered, Gujun following a moment after. He saw a shadowy
hallway leading past what appeared to be a forgotten armory.
Gujun glimpsed suits of armor as well as long, odd-looking
Chiang spears and other curious weaponry.

"These date back to the Third Dynasty," Chulan informed
him. "There are more cannons and such beyond. All are rusty
and forgotten. We are directly beneath the Imperial
Chamber."

Gujun followed in silence as Chulan led his group across
the cobwebby hall, until another wall emerged. Gujun saw an
arched doorway. This one was open. It looked like the hinges
had rotted off decades ago. Careless of them, allowing such
disrepair beneath the palace. Careless and *fatal*, Gujun
thought.

Beyond the door was a narrow stairway winding up in stiff
tight, circles. Here Chulan made his servants walk ahead. He
followed, hands buried in flared sleeves. Gujun stayed back
and took the stairs two at a time.

A long, winding climb led to yet another door. One of the
servants rattled it. It was locked or barred from outside. With
three kicks, the door splintered, allowing the men to enter
with Chulan following, after they'd reported back that no one
was there.

Gujun stepped into a wide-open avenue lined with colon-
nades. He blinked. They'd passed from the tomb-like shadows
and emerged dazed into the glorious light of Ta Shen's Golden

Palace. Gujun heard fighting somewhere nearby. He slipped his Jian blades into his hands. The sounds of steel came from ahead and below. The palace seemed even bigger inside than it was on their approach. An impressive building, much like a golden egg that doesn't show the hairline crack below.

Chulan walked briskly, flanked by his men on either side. His shoes clipped across the mosaic floor. The colonnade awarded stunning views of the water fountains and inner gardens below. At its far end, the passage opened into a wide hallway. Gujun saw two guards leaning on Jian spears, looking in the other direction.

"The Royal Chambers lie through those doors," Chulan said quietly. He whispered something to his servants. Two of them rushed at the guards. Gujun saw them turn when they heard the sounds of feet. Their brief, stunned expressions were stolen from them as tossed daggers found their mark. Gujun raised a brow. Chulan's orderlies were uncommonly good with a knife.

The guards slumped. One stirred as they passed. Gujun sliced down, silencing the man. Chulan pointed at the doors, and the other two orderlies took over, opening them wide with swords drawn level. They entered within, followed by Chulan and the knife-throwers. Gujun hung back for a moment before following.

They'd entered a wide antechamber with high, arched windows, the sun's golden light filtering through. Gujun noted the priceless urns and vases along the walls, the intricate paintings, the maze of mosaic tiles resting at his feet.

And the iron-clad Northman, leaning on his heavy axe.

Gujun recognized the armor as one worn by the Sapphire Guard. Rasnei's Auxiliaries. One at least had survived, it appeared.

"I've been expecting you," the Northman said, hoisting his axe. "Time to die, Magister Chulan."

"I think not." Chulan motioned with a finger, and the four servants angled toward the big auxiliary. Gujun held back, curious as to the outcome.

THE FOUR RUSHED HIM AT ONCE. DORTHAR KNOCKED A sword aside and batted another with his axe. He rammed the butt into a third man's face and kicked out at the fourth, sending the man spinning backward.

A sword slice caught his arm. Dorthar twisted and jabbed up, catching the assailant under his chin with the axe's beard and lifting him from the floor. Dorthar let him drop. Twisting again, he sliced through air and struck the next man's neck, sending his head sailing.

He grinned. Two more. They weren't servants—these were good fighters, most likely drafted from the Pol Shen secret police. Dorthar glimpsed the magister and a small, calm-faced warrior in leather beside him. They were leaving, making for Rasnei's chamber.

The nearest swordsman stabbed low, catching Dorthar's thigh. A good strike, but the fool had gotten too close. Dorthar swung down hard with the axe, cleaving through the man's shoulder bone, following through to his groin.

The last one swung at him. Dorthar shoved the corpse at his face, knocking him backward. He stepped clear and swung again. The axe bit into the man's side and cut him clean in two.

Dorthar leaned over, gasping for breath. His leg was bleeding badly, and he felt weaker by the second.

Rasnei ...

Dorthar wiped blood from his face and staggered toward the doors leading to her chambers. A shadow passed over him —a man blocking his way. The newcomer was very tall, shirtless and sinewy. He wore a scarlet cloak and a skull cap, with three red feathers sticking up.

"I've come to take your soul, Northman," the black-skinned warrior said.

"Fuck off." Dorthar swung hard and fast with his axe. The blow went wide, and as he swung again, Dorthar felt a wrenching, ripping pain in his belly. He glanced down at the knife.

"I only wish we had more time." The tall warrior smiled at him.

Dorthar felt his body sinking. He spat bloody phlegm at the man's face before the spear reached his heart and carried him away.

RASNEI STOOD IN HER ROOM, HER ARMS FOLDED NEATLY. She was alone, Dorthar still guarding the rooms outside. She'd heard fighting nearby, and he'd appeared. Her smiling enemy, Magister Chulan. His faithful hound Gujun stood beside him

"You got the Vendeli to do your dirty work," Rasnei told Chulan, placing her hands on her sleeves, as though fidgeting and anxious.

He bowed slightly. "And the Cardalan Republic. It took careful planning and intricate timing, empress."

She switched her gaze to Gujun, noticed the doubt in his eyes. "Strike quickly, Gujun the Slayer. You haven't long. This place will be ringed with loyal Shen very soon."

Gujun looked at her but didn't respond.

"Loyal to me," Chulan said. "The first emperor of a dazzling new dynasty. Your time was always over, Rasnei. This was never personal. It was common sense. Shen could hardly regain its former glory with a woman on the throne."

Again, Rasnei noted the discomfort in Gujun's eyes—but still he said nothing. She looked past them as a third figure appeared. Rasnei recognized the leader of the Vendeli she'd seen from the balcony.

"You impostors will pay dividends of pain for this," Rasnei told the Vendeli.

The shaman smiled and stood beside Chulan, towering over the magister and his assassin. He dipped his head in a mock bow.

"So, your *Aikashi* lover survived to fight again." He smiled at her. "Shame Vian won't see you one last time. My men are killing him as we speak, Empress Rasnei. Afterward, we will empty your coffers and palace with the full support of the new emperor." He grinned at Chulan, who nodded.

Rasnei stepped back, slid her hand inside her gown and felt the flute. "Are you to be the headsman, Vendeli? These Shen traitors are too timid." Before Octaxa could respond, a new voice interrupted him.

"Your Sangala are overrated, shaman," Vian said.

"You killed my men?" Octaxa turned quickly. Rasnei twisted the flute open.

"Several," Vian said. "My friend Lin Gu and his boys are dealing with the rest. You won't be going home rich, shaman. You won't be going home at all."

Octaxa laughed. "A player to the end, Rundali. But it's you who have lost today. You've lost *everything*." He pounced across to where Rasnei stood, and with lightning speed grabbed her arm. He raised the long snake-curved knife in his hand.

Rasnei was quicker.

She twisted the flute again, so the instrument split apart. Skinny blade freed, Rasnei stabbed up and hard, the thin steel puncturing Octaxa's bare arm below the bicep, passing clean through.

He glanced at the metal sliver in shock before striking Rasnei's cheek with the back of his hand, sending her sprawling. Rasnei rose to her knees, heard a shout, and saw Vian launch himself at the Vendeli's exposed back.

"Kill the Rundali," she heard Chulan yell at his man. Gujun remained motionless.

Rasnei staggered to her feet. Vian and Octaxa were locked in combat, rolling across the floor, the flute dagger still sticking through his arm. But she noticed Vian was wounded in several places. He looked pale and weak—he couldn't last.

Vian ...

Rasnei was still looking over at her lover when the dagger entered her chest. She glanced down dreamily, saw Chulan yank the blade free, and shove her onto her back. He crouched over her, holding the knife and grinning. His breath smelt bad, she thought.

Vian ...

Rasnei couldn't see her lover anymore. Instead, Chulan leaned closer toward her with his dagger. She watched in fascination as her blood dripped from the crooked blade. Chulan raised the dagger again, appearing to savor the moment. Rasnei closed her eyes.

The blow never came. She heard a gurgle, a sob, and the sound of a body hitting the floor.

Vian had glimpsed Rasnei fall. He'd rolled onto his side, as Octaxa's knife cut into his shoulder. The armor twisted the blade, but the pain shot up his arm.

He was weakening fast, and the Vendeli shaman was a strong man. Worse, he was calling on his powers, getting stronger every moment.

"Rasnei ..."

Vian had seen Chulan standing over her, a knife in hand. He felt the anger fuel inside.

Savarna.

Was she still there?

Help me!

I am with you, brother ...

Vian felt a sudden surge of tiger-strength coming from deep inside. *Tooth and claw!* Vian-Savarna wrestled the knife from Octaxa's hand and reversed the blade, stabbing deep into the Vendeli's right eye. The twins' combined rage twisted the blade free, and Vian lurched to his feet.

Rasnei was kneeling and holding her chest. Vian crawled across to her. Savarna's strength had left him almost as swiftly as it had appeared. He hardly registered Chulan's quivering corpse seeping blood, the throat sliced wide open.

"I owed you that much, Rundali."

Vian saw Gujun the Slayer standing over by the doors.

"Farewell, my friend," Gujun said. "You were a worthy adversary. I doubt our paths will cross again." He turned and vanished through the doors. Vian hardly noticed his departure.

"Rasnei ..." He cradled her close as she slunk into his

grasp. Vian felt a shudder inside and knew Savarna had left him. Very soon, his empress would, too.

Rasnei ...

"I am dying ..." She smiled up at him. "It doesn't matter —don't be sad. We danced a wild, wonderful dream, my Vian. My dragon-prince. My sweet, darling player. What a vivid dream we danced. Tell your sister ... I ..." Rasnei closed her eyes.

No, Rasnei ... No!

She was still in his arms when Matax appeared sometime later, with Gurtei and Roile and a group of fighters.

"The city is saved," Gurtei muttered, his tired eyes rimmed with tears. "Goi Stagan joined us, after he learned of Chulan's treachery. The Cards are gone, all dead or missing. The Vendeli, too. Lin Gu killed the last of the Sangala. But I guess none of that matters anymore."

Vian hardly heard him. His mind was already lifting far away, following Rasnei's voice until it mingled with the fading chords of distant flute song.

THREE DAYS LATER, VIAN STOOD ON THE HIGH KEEP, a cool breeze lifting his hair and stinging eyes. Autumn would come early this year. He watched as a white hawk lifted and glided along the wall before dipping and swooping down. Hunting.

Vian heard footsteps behind him. Gurtei stood there, Roile was with him.

"I hear you're leaving us," Gurtei said.

"I never planned on staying this long."

"Going to find your sister?"

Vian shrugged. "Perhaps—I shall try." He felt dreamy, almost as though he wasn't here. But these were his friends, and despite everything, they had won. Vian had lost, but that was another matter. He looked up at the sky for a moment, turned, and smiled at them.

"Where will you go?" Roile asked. He'd lost an eye in the street battle, his ruined face a mess. Despite that, the dour Cutter was almost cheerful this morning.

"Up there." Vian nodded to the sky above. He held his hands out to his sides. "*Everywhere.* Until I find it."

"Your dragon …?" Gurtei looked at Roile, who shrugged.

"The bow, Kerasheva," Vian told them.

Gurtei grinned. "Another mystery, Rundali. Why am I not surprised?"

"It's out there somewhere," Vian said. "The emerald bow will bring her back."

"She's gone, Vian," Gurtei said softly. "Nothing will bring your Rasnei back. But you made her happy, my friend. Yours was the purest light in a dark, troubled world."

"I will find it." Vian looked at his friends. He noted the sorrow in their eyes and decided to change the subject. This wasn't their fault. He forced a smile. "I hear you've been promoted again," he said to Gurtei.

"Aye, and Matax—wasn't our idea."

"Magister Gurtei." Vian smiled.

"I'm using the term 'administrator,'" Gurtei said. "The word 'magister' carries a stain that won't be washed clean."

"I'm pleased for you, Gurt. What about you, Roile? Sorry about that eye."

"Still got the other one to keep track of this fat bugger," the lean archer responded. "Stop old Gurt from delusions of grandeur."

"And Matax?" Vian asked them.

"Recovered well," Gurtei said. "He's got his hearing back in one ear, and the other one should follow. His leg was a mess, but they removed the shrapnel. Matax will walk with a limp, but he can still shout orders. Gu made him high Goi over the Imperials. Stagan is his second."

"Where is the mighty Lin Gu?"

"Probably drunk," Roile said. "Hiding from his admirers."

"Emperor Gu—who'd have thought it?" Vian said.

"Not him," Gurtei replied. "Poor bugger actually looked scared when they raised him up on that plinth. Think he'd rather face another Card army."

Vian nodded. "That I can believe. Lin Gu did well. I've no doubt that he'll be a shrewd ruler—Gu has the best people supporting him." Vian looked up at the sky again. "My ship departs on the hour. Best I make for the harbor." He held out his arms, and Gurtei hugged him. Roile punched his shoulder.

"I shall miss you, Rundali," Gurtei said.

"I fucking won't," Roile added, showing a rare grin.

Vian nodded and turned away, lest they spot the tears staining his eyes.

"Best man I ever knew," he heard Roile mutter as he left them.

"I thought *I* was," Gurtei replied.

"You're just a fat tosser, Gurt."

"A fat, important tosser."

"Aye, that's true enough."

After their voices had drifted away, Vian walked the wall, gazing north at the long ridge where his dragon had seen off Goi Ban's riders, allowing Rasnei escape to this city. That seemed so long ago. He reached the harbor, dropped down from the wall, and approached the gates.

Vian stopped, seeing a bulky figure leaning on a Chiang. He had a half-filled sack of wine in his left hand and was chugging.

"I needed some peace," Lin Gu told him, as Vian approached. He offered the wine sack, but Vian shook his head.

"Too early for me. Lord emperor, I should add." He bowed "I never congratulated you."

Lin Gu winced. "Don't."

"Field slave to emperor." Vian smiled. "I doubt that's been done before."

"I owe it all to you, Rundali." Lin Gu shoved out a hand, and Vian gripped it with his own. "I wish you well, Lord Vian.

"As do I, you and your country, Emperor Gu."

Vian left the big man alone to drain his wine sack as he made for the quay. The first Yamondon trader had arrived. He would stop off in Laregoza.

End of Part Three

PART IV

STEEL AND CLAW

30

THE GATHERING

C

That day, Tofei saw the figure on the hill again—a huge giant with fist on hips. He glared down at them as they rode, silver eyes filled with lightning.

The Traveler laughed behind him. "See you, men, Kullaan the Terrible has come to join us. His brother Tyho will be close. Now to victory!"

A month had passed since he and Asmund had left Valkador. Doggan and others had spread the word, creating a tide of excitement that grew and swelled until all the Northlands stirred with the ringing of steel.

The War Arrow had reached every corner, from the smoky ruins of Grimhold Castle to the wastes of Hragglund, from the dark forests of Rethen up through to the ice lands of tundra Leeth. Men had come, and more would follow. They rode in a party of sixty warriors, all young and each one eager to fight for the hero, Jaran Saerk.

The War Arrow having done its work. They had been

making for Skarness when the tall stranger had appeared on the road. The Traveler had joined them this time.

"This fight involves everyone," he'd said. "Including Myself." Tofei never questioned who he was. A god, perhaps, or some fell being. It didn't matter. With the Traveler and mighty Kullaan aiding them, what chance did the witch stand?

Kullaan had appeared when they set sail, Sherriff Doggan having acquired a longship for the purpose. They left Skarness behind, rowing out the fjord on that clear late summer day. Ahead were the mountains of Valkador.

Tofei grinned at Asmund. "We sail to free your island," he told him.

Tyho strode through the clouds, his terrible sword Turfain trailing behind, creating lightning sparks as the tip touched the ground. Tyho saw His brother and greeted Him. Kullaan waited with fists on his massive hammer, Mjonner, as Tyho joined him to gaze down on the ship crossing the sound. Tyho mouthed a rune and saw a white bird take wing from that vessel. Tyho shrank down to mortal size, and Kullaan did the same. They stood on the cliff edge, two young men with their long golden hair streaming in the wind and brave smiles on their handsome faces.

"What of Lofhi?" Tyho asked.

"He'll be there," Kullaan replied. "No doubt well-hidden. He is using the man Finvar as a foil."

"More like a fool."

"The conduit, Gunsala, is well-placed to help with that."

Tyho shook his head. "The girl lacks experience. Our aunt should have chosen someone stronger, older."

"What Gunsala lacks in experience is made up by her vigor," Kullaan said. "I have high hopes for her."

"And I *hope* that you're not disappointed." He turned as a white bird fluttered by, settling behind them. Tyho recognized the bird as the same one that had left the ship a moment ago. "I thought you'd drop by, uncle. Hate missing anything, don't you?"

The bird stretched out its wings and became a man, leaning on a heavy spear. The single eye blazed across at them. The Traveler grinned and walked up to stand beside them. "A fine sight, is it not? Like the old days. Heroes sailing to war."

"To their deaths," Tyho said. "More souls for you to gather. I thought you'd have enough by now."

"Aye, uncle," Kullaan said. "The Shadowman, your old foe, is no more. And yet you never cease in your morbid reaping of the dead."

"Heroes only. I'm very selective."

"And what of Elanion?" Tyho asked him.

"You're asking me that?"

Tyho chuckled. "You had best get back with your new friends, uncle. The crows will be gathering on that island. Sheega won't be duped easily."

"You pups don't know the half of it," the Traveler said. "I've never underestimated Deyna. In many ways Saan's dark queen was more dangerous than He was Himself—even though Old Night got all the attention. Deyna was ever the cunning one. My youngest sister learned much from Cul-Saan before His mighty fall. Saan perished, yet Deyna survives still —even though the Weaver Himself wants her dead."

"You sound as though you admire Sheega." Tyho watched the ship, smaller now, nearing the island.

"And I do," the Traveler said. "She's like a daughter to me, albeit a troublesome one. There's only three of us left from the First Days. Originals. You second batch wouldn't understand —you weren't around during the Making. When there was only beauty. Before vain Cul-Saan became Old Night and festered in perennial loathing."

"Why not side with Sheega?" Tyho glared at His uncle, the artful wayfarer men called the Traveler.

"Perhaps I will." He smiled back, jokingly. "Ah, but you know why, Ty. She is perilous and threatens this world that I —and my wife, for all Her faults—cherish beyond any other. I have watched Undeyna throughout time. She won't quit until she destroys, either herself or everything else.

"I've long tried to protect this land from Deyna's malice," he continued. "Without interfering—we can't do that, can we? That's why I got you involved, Ty. Kull, too. Griner must strike off her head, else she uses that conjunction to manifest and rear up as She once was, fully returned to Her ancient powers. Nobody needs that to happen. An ancient and new threat to the galaxy. Sheega the witch must die, so that Undeyna's lost soul can finally be allowed to rest. And the only one who can do that is Jaran Saerk, with your axe Griner."

"You had best go join them," Kullaan said. "We will watch the outcome from these cliffs. Once Lofhi appears, we'll deal with the villain."

"He's too subtle to fall for that," Tyho said.

"What of Faerie, the elves and trolls?" Kullaan asked.

The Traveler grinned. "That will work itself out, thanks to Coristain."

"We have less than a week to wait, nephews, as mortals

measure time. What say we retire to the Hallowed Halls and sup some ale?"

"Agreed," said Tyho and His brother. "But first We should pay visit to our hero." The three lifted as birds and winged off into the upper skies.

Savarna walked back into the glade and crouched low by the fire. It was early morning, and she'd had a restless night. She'd listened to Jaran talking to his strange ancestor for most of the evening, as Unva and the others sat in a group surrounded by trees, a fire roaring, some islanders joining them. So much had happened, Savarna found it hard to keep a grip on what was real or a dream. That, and the rising dread of what was coming next.

Despite her worries, she'd been sleepy and left them to it, rolling herself in a blanket. She'd heard their voices murmur for a while before drifting off, only to awaken hours later, cold and alert.

Vian's green-gold eyes blazed inside her skull.

He'd called her. *Twice.* Savarna had never heard him sound so desperate, so *lost*. She'd risen and seen her friends were sleeping—including Jaran, who snored beside her. She'd left the glade, calling out Vian's name in her mind as she walked deeper into the owl woods. Savarna had glimpsed three figures crouching in moonlight. Rafin the Dwarf and Taic leaned close, as though listening. Unva, seeing her pass, held up a playing card painted with the face of a burning dragon.

"Vian needs you," the Wolf Witch had told her.

Eyes alert but mind cloaked by shadow, Savarna had walked deeper into the woods, calling his name. What had happened? She had seen Vian in that city, smelled the pain and death, felt his anguish. Savarna had reached out, called on her tiger, and sent her mind ranging out to join him.

Ta Shen had fallen.

Savarna had felt her *Aikashi* with her as they fought beside Vian in the palace grounds, her mind-claws rending the Sangala one by one. Tooth and claw—the savage joy of the kill. She'd faded back as her strength failed but had returned with renewed effort when sensing Vian snared by the Vendeli shaman's dark power. There, Savarna had joined him again, forcing her mind across the immeasurable distance.

She'd seen Rasnei fall. After that, the signal had faded and her *Aikashi* mind-body had crashed back, jolting into the moment. She'd woken face-first in the dew, her body sweating and cold, her mind exhausted and shredded by the shaman's twisted malice.

AND NOW IT WAS MORNING, AND AGAIN VIAN WAS LOST to her. Savarna staggered back into the camp and saw Jaran staring up at her. He looked like he'd been awake for a while. He watched her approach, his eyes large with worry.

"Where have you been?" he demanded. She shrugged and saw the concern turn to anger. "Are you hurt?"

"Tired," she told him. "Didn't sleep very well."

"What happened? Were you in trouble? Why didn't you wake me?"

Savarna sighed. "It wasn't your fight."

"Vian …"

She nodded. "My brother called me while I slept. Across the void. At first, I thought it was a dream, but he kept reappearing. His image was strong. I knew Vian was in trouble and had to help."

"Your *Aikashi*."

Savarna nodded wearily. "Vian was hurt. Rasnei ... she." Savarna shook her head. "Our contact faded before I knew for sure."

Jaran looked at her. "Get some rest," he told her. "Unva and Rafin are plotting our next move. My ancestor Taic is with them."

"What of Barin—isn't he the one you need the most?" She didn't want to add that Taic's sudden mystery appearance had underwhelmed her.

"Barin will come," Jaran said. He reached up and stroked her tangled hair. "You look cold—take my blanket. I need to walk off this stiffness and get my mind working."

Savarna nodded, taking her seat by the struggling fire and wrapping both blankets around her shoulders. "I'll be fine," she told him as he stood over her. "Don't stray far."

"That from you." Jaran glanced at the sleeping bodies in the camp. "As far as I understand any of this ... witchery, we have only a few days left to wait. I need to exercise with Griner. My shoulder is stiff—it hasn't fully healed since the changeling."

Savarna watched him leave in silence. She closed her eyes. She was ready for this witchery, as Jaran had called it, to be over. Savarna tried to picture Vian's face, but he was lost to her, and she lacked the strength to seek further. Knowing it was futile to push, she relaxed and felt a wave of sadness flooding her.

Vian, I'm so sorry.

Savarna slept late into that day.

Jaran walked for several hours, climbing up into the misty hills that clung like dew-brushed gossamer to Gronteyer's pine-clad knees. He hadn't been alone for so long. He needed to think, to stare down at the ocean, to allow his mind settle while he worked his body. So much had happened, and more to come. And yet, he understood so little.

Jaran walked briskly as the rising sun warmed his back, the mist fading quickly as though withdrawing from his path. He reached a high place that awarded panoramic views of the Leeth coast and Skarness Fjord. Jaran saw three ships sailing out into open water.

Tofei? It had to be. Warriors were coming who'd answered his call. Unva only changed the time on this island. Out there, a month has passed. He chuckled to himself. None of it made sense to his warrior mind. He fingered Griner at his waist.

I need you to hit that witch, axe, so we can get this done.

Jaran's smile ran away from his face as he watched the tiny vessels bob and sway. Those brave men had no notion of what they would face. The War Arrow hadn't been his idea, but he felt responsible.

Jaran turned away and looked south, seeing the distant villages, the strand of beach, and Gunard's ship. His men would be down there, excited to see the sails approaching. Lastly, Jaran looked up at Gronteyer's dark shoulder. The giant Gorvaron was out there somewhere. Another issue to be resolved.

What was Sheega brewing? She would know what Unva had done. She'd be ready, like him, eager to finish this.

And what of Fin? How fared his friend? The girl Gunsala

had slipped out of the camp while he was deep in discussion with Taic. Gunsala would help Finvar—she had before. A Vulkorye, they said. Another mystery he wouldn't dwell on. But against Sheega? A girl alone?

"We kill the witch and her creatures. It's all that matters," he said to the wind.

"I'm pleased that you are ready, Jaran Saerk. Much depends on your success."

Jaran turned sharply and saw the War God, Tyho, seated on a rock. He wore a wolf skin cloak over his naked, scarred torso. Gold torcs and bands glittered up his arms. He held a huge black sword in single hand.

"Torvang," Tyho spoke the name, and the sword appeared to shimmer in his grip. "This, too, is a weapon of legend and power."

"Griner will suffice," Jaran said.

Tyho's silver eyes blazed into his. "Torvang belongs to a different hero, Jaran Saerk. A tale that's not yet told."

"Why do you hate Sheega?"

"There is the darkness and the light," Tyho said. "But inside each of those are shades of gray, constantly shifting back and forth. This"—the god waved his black sword at the sky —"*dance*, we'll call it, is a vast fabric of constant motion, a rhythmic circle of events and counter-events. The past always leading to the future and circling back. A cosmic board laid out by the Norns, where pieces battle for dominance. Every player must contribute to either the dark or the light, but the shades are always shifting to and fro. Good and evil as you would understand them have no meaning. They are just words. *Concepts*. As are love and hope. Ideas that mortals create to explain their futile existence."

"And yet you need us."

"We do." Another voice. Familiar, it came from behind him.

Jaran turned slowly. He smiled as he saw the tall figure of an old man walk past and stoop over Tyho. He was wearing a wide-brimmed hat and leaned heavily on a spear whose light cast a glow the same color as Tyho's eyes. The old man smiled wryly at Jaran. He had only one eye.

"This is your real guise," Jaran told the Traveler. "You two and others have been using me since I was born, honing your hapless champion for this one purpose—to turn the game in your favor."

"DO NOT judge us so HARSHLY, mortal." A third voice. He saw Kullaan's shadow staring down from higher up the mountain. "WE are pawns to the GAME, as are you. BIGGER pieces, but still at the MERCY of the DANCE."

"Faerie punctured the World Thread," the Traveler told Jaran. "Sheega and Unva—they made that happen. Sheega wanted the elves involved, and Unva's guile taunted them across too soon. We cannot put those pieces back in the box. Aldorian and dead Rumgorz. Sheega and Ranning. Rafin, Rune and Unva—all of them are dancing to the same chords. You alone, Jaran Saerk, are free as only a warrior can be. Fulfill your destiny, hero. Serve us well this one time, and you are free."

Jaran stared at the three terrible beings gazing upon him. Strangely, he felt no awe, but rather resentment. "What of Lofhi and my friend, Finvar Droll?"

"It will play out soon," the Traveler said evasively. "Sly Lofhi cannot evade Us for long. Let Tyho and Kullaan worry about the Trickster. Focus on your one task, Jaran. Perform it well, and you will never be troubled by any of us again."

Jaran watched as a thin trail of mist rose from the grassy

hummocks, drifting over and surrounding the Traveler and Tyho, as more clung to Kullaan further up the mountain. The mist congealed. Jaran watched the three gods fade into the fret before a sudden blast of wind took it far out to sea, dispersing it like raindrops high above the waters.

"Don't worry about them, boy."

Jaran turned again. This time, Barin was standing behind him, his big hands gripping the huge double-headed battle-axe, Wyrmfang. "You are much like my friend, Corin an Fol. I miss that troublesome lad."

"So it goes," Jaran nodded. "Gods and men and witches. The *Dance*, He called it. Are you staying around this time? I'm sure Taic would like to see you."

"Look for me at the Howe by the Great Hall," Barin said somberly. "At dusk, three days hence, when the full moon rises."

"And you'll help me kill her." Jaran nodded, but instead of responding, Barin faded from view as the gods had before him. Jaran shrugged. He hauled Griner free of its loop and started swinging the blade in wide, hacking arcs.

GUNSALA WALKED ALONG THE GRAY BEACH, THE SHINGLE sighing as the ocean seeped over and surged back. The moon followed, flanking her left. She'd seen it rise over the cliffs of Leeth.

My home—will I ever go back?

She felt dreamy, almost like she was someone else. Goaded and pushed from the inside, causing her to move forward without control. The feeling was strange, and yet wonderful. *The Goddess is inside me. The Vulkorye.* Gunsala could feel the excitement rising, the anticipation of battle and glory. But when those moments faded, she felt the icy dread of pain, loss, and sorrow.

The emotions hit her in waves, as though tuned in with the tides washing her feet, as she walked beneath that gibbous moon. Elanion's abalone shimmered and sheened, flicking through deep blue-green to violet-crimson and on through yellow to gold. Fading back to silver and darkening again to blue-green. A cycle of colors, much like the universe – always shifting, yet remaining, as nothing ends. For how can there be an ending where there is no beginning? A small part of her understood, as she gripped the shell tighter.

Gunsala picked up her pace as doubt crossed her mind. Finvar was in peril, the time almost here. But what could she do? How would she confront them? The witch, her minions, the giant. *And Lofhi.* Part of her wished she'd remained with the others, allowed the hero Jaran Saerk to fulfill his destiny. *Why am I involved?* Her heart quailed at the thought of the risk she was taking. But the warrior woman lodged inside her soul laughed at that timidity.

This is our destiny. Our right. We are Vulkorye.

Gunsala shut out the timid voice. *Finvar needs me, the Goddess is with me, and you. Together, we will make this work.*

She'd been careful, watchful, spending most the day hidden in scrubs under the shadow of Gronteyer's western rise. The mountain was behind her. She could see the glitter and sparkle of Sheega's ice lake, the moon's reflection skimming the surface. It would be dawn soon—two nights had passed since she'd left the others.

How many days remained? The moon was almost full. Gunsala broke into a trot as she saw the low hills and the hall's crouching shadow cresting their ridge. She bit her lip, gripped the sword Gunard had given her on the voyage across, and made with determined legs for that distant rise. She would reach the hall by dawn.

After that …

ALDORIAN FELT THE RAGE BURNING DEEP INSIDE. THEY had played him for a fool: the Yetain, his sly sister, the witch Unva, even Ranning. All of them had tricked him, and all of them would pay. The World Thread had shimmered and throbbed like a swollen muscle as he rode through, his army of glittering warriors reaching the tunnels that led to the cave mouth some called Cradon Iwey.

Aldorian knew the island from its older name. He'd visited here in the glorious time, long before the poisonous grubs that were humans claimed the place for their own. In those days, Ansu had belonged to the elves and their cousins, the golden Aralais. The Aralais had gone mad, blasted by their own sorcery and the age-long war with their dark kin, the Urgolais.

Aldorian's people had left the realm when the gods sided with men, driving the denizens of Faerie into the dark, deep corners of the world. The elves never forgave that betrayal by the high gods. They'd had to fasten a new existence in the middle realms, alongside their ancient foes, the trolls and goblins.

Aldorian had all but forgotten his bitterness until the visit from Ranning, the creature Rune and his own sister Coristain's devious actions had fueled that ancient grudge.

And Rumgorz was dead. Killed by Coristain. What had she been thinking? Did she hate her brother that much to inflict such spite on her kin? Coristain had fled through the

World Gate and was simmering somewhere. Aldorian would track her down. And Rune. *All of them.*

But first, he had to deal with the trolls. There had been fighting at both sides of the gates. He'd left a rearguard in Faerie to stem the avenging tide. The trolls had broken through, the treacherous goblins having switched sides and joined them, making it impossible for Aldorian to return to Faerie. The way back was blocked, the way ahead full of problems.

There were trolls here, too, in Ansu. On this isle. Several hundred of the brutish folk had cleared the gates before Aldorian ordered his rune-mages seal them again. These trolls were in the tunnels surrounding Cradon Iwey—as were his men, and others. A scouting party had reported seeing humans. They'd been stopped for a time by a graybeard with a spear. A lone warrior, but he'd known the tunnels well and eluded their pursuit.

But Aldorian's memory was infinite. He knew this place of old. He led his army through the Lost Lanes, chasing trolls and killing with vengeful joy, until they reached the doorway into his old home.

Cradon Iwey—the portal leading to Ansu.

There, for a time, the elf army gathered in the forms of blowflies, lining the sea-cliff walls. The gods were abroad and would be seeking Aldorian. The moon was not yet full. He'd broken through too early because of his sister's wickedness.

That didn't matter. They would stay in the cave and await the conjunction. It was close. The moment the full moon rose high, the elf king would order his warriors to ride out onto the beaches of Valkador.

Let Tyho and Kullaan try to stop them. Those new deities were no match for the elves en masse. Ten thousand strong, Aldorian's riders would destroy their enemies, be they troll or god, sorceress or man. The time was almost here.

As he faded himself into the rockface, Aldorian watched as a butterfly entered the cave, flitting close and darting away. He reached out with his mind, knowing this to be no random insect. The butterfly expanded in his vision, turning black and melting like wet tar. He saw red glowing eyes that blazed into his own.

Lofhi, even you cannot escape this time.

The eyes were surrounded by smoke that grew and took on form, becoming a manikin. A golden figure clutching a harp.

How dare you take the Dagda's form.

I do as I please, elf.

You will pay.

Yeah, yeah—you're full of crap, Aldorian. You elves have scant imagination.

You gods betrayed us.

The ruby eyes blinked, as though surprised. *How do you work that one out? I've done nothing but support your cause. My kin don't like you. But guess what—they hate me, too. We have things in common, elf. Yes, I know you're angry, King Aldorian, and you've brought your little army across. The grouchy trolls too. But listen ... all that shining Faerie steel won't work without a nice slice of skullduggery and buggeration. That's where I can help.*

We elves do not need your help, Trickster.

Time will tell—and time is fading, timeless one. The golden manikin winked at him and disappeared. Aldorian saw the butterfly drifting out toward the dark cave water and beyond.

Let Sheega and the water Faen help Me to help you, Lofhi's voice reached him. *We all have one thing in common. We hate fucking humans.*

IVAR HAD HAD A SEED OF WORRY SWELLING INSIDE HIS belly all day. Not only the doom of what waited—Jaran's confrontation with the witch and their slim chance of survival. The visit by Kullaan on the beach had shaken him more than he'd admitted. Things were about to change—he could sense it. Not only on Valkador but throughout the world.

Ivar felt it in his bones. He wasn't worried for himself. *My days are passing swiftly, and soon I shall rest in the halls of my fathers.* Ivar was fretting for Bjarni, Myra and the girls. And Asmund and Olof and the young folk. They had no concept of the terror Sheega would unleash. *A storm that most of us won't survive.* Whatever Jaran Saerk achieved, life would never be the same for them. There would be scars both hidden and showing. And there would be death.

Ivar had seen Jaran return with the joking, rangy stranger. A smiling ghoul from the howe. A man who claimed to be Jaran's ancestor, Taic. Once a legend in Valkador, almost as illustrious as his uncle, Barin the Voyager. But the stranger made for an unlikely ghost. Ivar had kept his distance, part of him believing the man an impostor, perhaps sent by Sheega herself. Or, worse, Lofhi had sent him. Even if he were the real Taic, he and Jaran had crawled out of that barrow. Other wights might have slipped out unnoticed. The place held more dark secrets than Ivar dared fathom.

But there was another concern. It crept inside him and wouldn't let go. Cradon Iwey. The yellow-eyed woman—there were so many strangers here. *Unva.* Ivar didn't trust her.

Another witch. The dwarf Rafin. Where had he come from? And Rune the riddle master? Those three had meddled with something best left alone. They'd opened a rift in Cradon Iwey. Svipdag had disappeared there. Jaran had told Ivar the old warrior had gone to lead the elves away. He'd slipped off earlier to look for him but had returned exhausted, having spotted no sign of his friend.

Elves. Could it be true? Creatures from Faerie, a place he'd never believed existed.

Ivar had been dozing when he'd seen Savarna appear, her eyes wide with cuts and scratches on her arms and legs. Jaran had left the camp soon after. Ivar decided to follow. But when he saw Jaran make for the high cliffs, he chose another course.

Svipdag was alone in those caves. Trapped with gods-knew-what after him. Elves or malevolent spirits raised by Unva's meddling. It didn't matter—his friend needed help.

I have to go back there.

Ivar made for the caves, eventually reaching their old camp where the giant had attacked them. Days ago, or a month? Again, Ivar couldn't tell. He entered the cave and crouched his way through to the crack at the rear. Armed with fish spear and bow, Ivar walked and crawled through the dark, not daring a brand, even if he had fire.

Ivar walked for a while, his eyes getting accustomed to the gloom. He stopped when he heard the voices—strange, metallic shouts echoing from somewhere far below. He moved forward, but froze hearing the unmistakable sound of clashing steel. Someone was fighting. But where? It sounded near.

Svipdag?

Ivar slanted his spear low and moved on. He had to keep moving forward and not succumb to the rising panic swelling inside. He was beyond foolish coming back here. Svipdag was most likely dead, and whatever lurked ...

Ivar reached the Deepwater by pure chance and heard the dull thud of the waterfall where they'd set the other camp. It was there that he saw them. A veil of light filtering down from a crack above revealed their silhouettes moving slowly. Ivar saw what appeared as huge, ugly figures, stooped and walking along the far side of the lake. Their oily bodies glowed a faint, sickly green. They carried ungainly-looking weapons—clubs and axes, the odd ragged spear. He counted twelve.

Trolls.

Ivar knew the legends, the ancient stories. Didn't matter that he'd never believed in them. He'd been wrong. Those trolls came through the Faerie Door. The yellow-eyed witch had let them in, and the gods alone knew what else. They were moving further away, their dark voices booming like hollow drums. Ivar waited until they had gone and quickly made his way to the place where he'd seen them leave.

There was something else there. He saw bodies strewn by the water. These also glowed, but with a dull blue shimmer that faded as he watched. One had his eyes open, the slanted, milky orbs gazing at Ivar with a malice that almost choked him. Those eyes became smoky and their light faded too. He walked closer.

Ten bodies, further away. Small warriors, slender, covered in blue mail that gleamed like hoarfrost in winter pastures. *Elves*. That explained the fighting.

Ivar leaned down over the nearest body. He reached forward to touch the shimmering metal of the elf's helmet, but a rough hand grabbed his cloak and pulled him back.

"You cannot touch them, else a curse follows you and tears out your soul."

Ivar recognized Svipdag's gruff voice. He turned as a flood of relief made him shudder.

"I came back for you," he said.

"No need," Svipdag said. "But I'm grateful. We have to move quickly, old friend."

"What … happened here?"

"An elf raiding party," Svipdag said. "They were stalking Unva and the dwarf. But the trolls found them first. It was a brief fight—these are the remnant who fled. The trolls you saw caught up with them. The tunnels are riddled with trolls. Can you not smell them?"

Ivar wasn't sure—he'd never smelt troll before. His nose did detect an acrid, stale aroma.

"There are more elves here too," Svipdag told him. "Many, I believe, but well-hidden. They're waiting, Ivar. As are we all."

"For the full moon."

"The final moon." Svipdag's eyes flashed at him.

"We need to find Jaran Saerk," Ivar said, and made to turn.

"There's a quicker way out that even you don't know about," Svipdag said. Without further word, Ivar followed him in the other direction.

FINVAR DROLL HADN'T SLEPT IN THREE DAYS. HIS MIND was a wandering maze of worry, fear, and panic. Sheega was always there, either in his dreams or standing before him with that cold, crafty smile. She hadn't struck him since the last time, but he could see the present danger lurking in her eyes.

She'd taken to her mirror chamber often, where she'd held concourse with the copper goblin, Gantallian. He'd followed once, despite the fear. The hideous shape in the mirror had hissed when it saw Finvar and tried to vanish inside his prison.

Sheega had laughed, seeming delighted that Finvar had come. "He thinks you're Lofhi come to drain his soul. 'Tis only the Trickster's shadow, Gantallian. His scion, Finvar the Droll."

Sheega had bid her imp—as she called him—show Finvar the island through her mirror. He'd seen the caves where Jaran and Savarna had taken refuge, watched the giant horned Gorvaron striding over the mountain. And last, he'd spied Gunsala walking along the beach, a shell of shifting light pulsing in her left hand.

"She's coming to save you from me." Sheega had laughed a second time and clapped her hands together. "Poor little cunt —I'll prepare something special for her."

"Spare Gunsala, and I'll do anything you want," he'd told her. "Kill Jaran, anyone. Just don't hurt her."

"You will do what I want because your master has promised me," she'd replied, as the imp chuckled inside the copper. "The reward is your freedom. Don't wager that on a foolish girl. Gunsala must die, Finvar. I've told you that already. She is Elanion's creature."

Since then, she'd left him alone. Finvar had spent hours by the fire, rolled tight in misery and furs, the great smoky hall empty, silent, and cold as judgment. Mercifully, he hadn't seen Ranning again, nor had Lofhi paid him a visit. But the one time Finvar dared step outside the hall at night, he'd seen corpses walking - the dead warriors she raised from beneath the lake - led in chains by three witch-guards.

Finvar had glanced up briefly at the moon rising over that glazed water. *Almost full.* Lofhi would return soon. The pain would follow.

He closed his eyes. It was time he prepared for the final confrontation. Gunsala was coming, as was Jaran. The forces of light and darkness were about to clash, with him stuck neatly in the middle.

"I am the endgame," Finvar whispered to himself. "This was what I was created for."

JARAN STOOD WITH TAIC AND IVAR AS THE SHIPS DANCED through spume toward them. He'd joined Gunard and the villagers down at the harbor. Unva had mined the area with protection runes. They had two days. It was time to return to Barin's Howe.

Savarna gripped his hand tightly. He smiled at her. They watched as the three longships moored alongside Gunard's, each one filled with fighters, their spears and helms glinting in the sun. Jaran saw Tofei jump ashore and rush to hug his father. A joyful reunion, but Jaran felt little cheer.

"More warriors will come to toast your victory, Jaran Saerk," Tofei called up to him. Jaran was surprised to recognize Sherriff Doggan among the thanes gathered on board. For a brief instant, he glimpsed the Traveler standing at the prow of the furthest ship. He stared over at Jaran for a moment and raised his hand before becoming a white bird, lifting and drifting off over the water.

Heart heavy, Jaran gazed at the busy scene below. The doom of what awaited hung over him. At his waist, the axe Griner seemed heavier than usual.

You're thirsty for blood—I can sense it.

The axe hung from his belt like an anchor. Jaran brushed the steel with a finger. He was eager to get started. Ivar

Ketilsson had returned from the caves with Svipdag, confirming that both elves and trolls had entered Cradon Iwey. The island was about to be invaded. Jaran had told Savarna about his encounter with the three gods, though he'd kept it from the rest.

That evening, they built a ring of fire on the beach. Unva sat in its midst working spells. "There are two I can call on, to help me with my craft," she told Jaran and Savarna as they sat with her. "I need you to leave me be, but send Taic in here. Your ancestor can be useful for once and protect me from any night gangers when I make the calling."

Jaran and Savarna left her and joined the villagers and warriors seated outside the fire. Ivar and Svipdag stared at him as he crouched beside Savarna. "Are you ready to claim your revenge, Jaran Saerk?" Svipdag asked him.

"I am," he replied, and on a spur of impulse, he stood facing all gathered there. Jaran unsheathed Griner and held the axe high above his head, with both hands parallel.

"By this uncanny axe, I swear that by midnight tomorrow, Valkador will be free and the witch Sheega no more!"

31

THE HUNTRESS

As a white feather, Coristain lifted up through dreamy blue clouds, her sharp elf mind darting back and forth. Their ploy had worked. Her brother had broken through the World Gates. War would follow. She and the Yetain had started a movement that would alter the cosmic balance and change fate—not only in this world, Ansu, but throughout the entire multiverse. The thought was appealing to Coristain. Millennia spent doing nothing, and now …

Even so, she dared not gloat.

Her brother's wrath would be terrible. Elves had already died due to her actions in the troll camp. Many more would follow, and Coristain's mind-sight scanned back through World Gate. They were closed fast. The return to Faerie was barred. They couldn't go back. Aldorian was trapped here in Ansu, as was she.

But the thrill of change drove that ceaseless boredom far away. The elf warriors neglected their women. Not only as lovers, but they disdained their women's counsel as well—

always had. Coristain had taken lovers from any place she could find them, as much to spite the king and elf lords as to sate her many needs.

She had to keep moving. Aldorian and the vengeful trolls would stop at nothing to find her. She had no friends here and wasn't naïve, expecting no help from Rune, wrapped up as he was in the murky business with Undeyna.

There is One ... The thought was sparkle of light in her eyes.

Thought-driven, the feather drifted over dark waters. The island Valkador was lost to cloud behind her. Her brother had chosen his side, goaded by the Faerie loathing of humans. Coristain also must choose. There was One who might see things her way. A gamble. Coristain deemed it worth the try. Though she could no longer travel the wormholes, Coristain possessed the code skills to seek the one being she hoped would grant her salvation. The Emerald Queen, her rhythm echoing out from distant Galenki.

Filled with new purpose, Coristain changed her form, becoming a stone plummeting into the ocean. On impact, she became a fish and swam down deep, where her enemies wouldn't find her. She found a cave, swam inside. Lurked. She sealed the entrance with protection runes and began her various chants. The Goddess was far away, but She was always listening.

GUNSALA STOPPED SUDDENLY AS THE MORNING LIGHT shone on the roofs of the great hall. She saw Sheega standing there, arms folded and her long, dark hair flowing wild in the wind. The witch was smiling as though she could see

Gunsala, who'd been careful to keep to the trees as dawn broke.

Gunsala shivered, feeling the Ice witch's malice reach out, as though searching for her. Deep inside, Gunsala felt that other woman rising to the challenge.

"Sheega is scrying for me," Gunsala said.

Let her find us, the Vulkorye replied.

SHEEGA SENSED THE GIRL'S APPROACH. IT WAS THE LAST day, and the final hours would soon arrive. She felt so alive. She'd spent the night taking everything Ranning had to give, leaving him exhausted and burnt out. He'd slipped away to prepare the Witch-Guard and Gorvaron.

Hrelgisson and his allies would be here by dusk. Sheega had some time to finalize her reception. Fireworks and confetti, perhaps a sacrifice out on the lake. By moonrise, she would be more than ready. At the zenith, Sheega would strike, killing them all. Even Finvar, who had dared to challenge her. Perhaps Lofhi, too? Why not? With Hrelgisson dead, the last barrier would tumble. Sheega would be Undeyna again, fully restored to her former dark majesty. She trembled with excitement at the thought.

Once they were all dead, she'd seek out her arch-foe. Elanion would be defenseless, the Mistress of the Trees but a shadow of whom She'd been. Elanion would die, as would the Traveler, Oroonin. They had always treated her badly. It was time for recompense. But she'd start small and have some fun with Gunsala this morning. The miserable girl was crouched inside the woods, like a dried-up wood nymph. Sheega could almost smell her flowery scent.

First you, Gunsala. Next Savarna, and finally Jaran and the others.

It was going to be a busy day.

Sheega raised a hand and pointed at the woods. *I'll send my dogs to bring your body.* She whistled, and the huge white hounds came bounding, the blood-red ears sharp and snarling, lolling mouths dribbling and slavering in eager anticipation.

"Hunt!"

Sheega pointed at the woods again. The hounds circled, bit, and snarled. They bunched and barked. "Hunt!" She said again, and watched them scamper down from the hall, racing over the fields toward the shadow of trees, their rough canine voices filling the valley. Her hounds would shred the girl's body, leaving the Vulkorye soul for Sheega to lay bare.

She laughed.

Next, it was time for her birds. Sheega needed to know which route Hrelgisson would be taking. She snapped her fingers, and three black gulls appeared from the sky. Her favorite birds, she'd fashioned them out of gossamer and Old Night's spittle. Sheega traced the search runes and bid the gulls fly south.

She watched the birds drift through the morning cloud, her ears catching the distant sound of hounds baying. They'd have her cornered. *Hmm. Time to inform Finvar of his lover's sorry fate.*

Sheega smiled and dusted her hands. She turned and walked briskly back into the hall. Once inside, Sheega would tease her prisoner. Before that, she must attend to the final details with Gantallian.

TODAY'S THE DAY—ARE YOU EXCITED?

Finvar had wanted to keep his eyes shut, but Lofhi's voice got inside his head and pulled his lids open. The god was standing in the fire, which sizzled and crackled around his shadow. Finvar tried not to see the smiling manikin, those ruby eyes full of humor and malice. Lofhi was garbed in gaudy fashion today, as though marking a celebration. He wore a gold jacket with matching trousers, and black-and-white striped boots, the ends turned over. His hair was a rainbow of shifting colors and light. He stepped out of the fire and leered down at Finvar.

"I need to rest, so that I'm ready," Finvar muttered, avoiding Lofhi's ruby gaze.

"Yes, of course," the god said. "I empathize completely. It will be challenging for you. But … think of the rewards."

"Being free of you, and her."

"Oh, yes, there's that. But you'll be immortal, too. Like Us, only not so important, of course. It's a big promotion, Fin lad. You should be grateful. Everything I've done for you."

"I am," Finvar muttered weakly. "Just confused. It's a large adjustment."

"That will pass."

"Where is Gunsala?"

Lofhi's eyes clouded for a moment. "I'm not certain."

"You're lying," Finvar stared directly at the god for the first time. "She's on her way here, isn't she? I saw her walking the beach. I don't want Gunsala hurt, Lofhi. I'm doing everything you ask, so do this much for me in return."

"Fucking mortals." Lofhi's handsome face mocked him. "I'm giving you eternal life, and you repay that with this ceaseless whining about that dull Vulkorye wench. Gunsala works

for Her, Fin. The Emerald fucking Queen. We can't let her …
well …" Lofhi waved a dismissive hand. "It's not my decision,
and … I think it's been dealt with already. Can you not hear
those dogs?" Lofhi craned his neck as though listening. "Bad
way to go."

"What are you telling me?" Finvar felt his face redden
with fury

"That your Gunsala is most likely dead already. Torn apart
by Sheega's pups. There, I said it. Go and cry."

"You had better be lying." Finvar rose to his feet and
pointed at the gaudy figure standing by the fire.

"Or, what …?"

The red eyes turned amber and blazed into his own. Finvar
screamed as his face ripped open like shredded parchment. He
collapsed, sobbing. The pain vanished immediately and left
him shaking on his knees.

"That's a small taste of what I can do to you, Finvar
Droll. Forget Gunsala. Instead, get some rest and stop this
moping. That's an awful human trait. I need you sharp,
matey. Hrelgisson will be here ere dark, with Griner sharp-
ened nasty. You'll need to stay clear of that axe. I sowed
treacherous runes into Griner's steel." He reached for
something in the fire and tossed it at Finvar's feet. "You
can use this for the game-changer when chance allows. The
blade has been dipped in hemlock and digitalis, with a
light brush oiling of nightshade." Lofhi's smile was
beautiful.

Finvar glanced down at a black, smoking dagger. There
were dark runes carved along its serrated blade.

"I'll see you tonight." Lofhi flashed him a final grin and
jumped back into the fire. The flames licked at the manikin
greedily, until Lofhi's image exploded into dust and shooting

sparks that peppered Finvar's startled face and him left choking so violently that he coughed up blood.

Savarna stood beside Jaran and Gunard as they stared out from the prow, Gunard's longship cutting through waves on that fine, windy morning. To her left, Gronteyer's mighty shoulders bristled with pines, a green host marching up to the shroud of snow capping the summit.

A brave day. She'd watched as the ships had made ready and set sail. The four longships, packed with eager warriors, would make for the harbor, where no doubt Sheega would be waiting. All were on board aside from Unva and Taic, who had left earlier with Svipdag and Ivar and were making for Svipdag's cave, where Unva would summon her help. A few other islanders had stayed behind with Myra and the elders.

Savarna felt Jaran jostle beside her. She glanced up, hearing shrill sounds, and saw dark, triangular shapes moving at speed high above. "More of her birds," she said.

"They'll be reporting back our progress," Jaran said.

"I wonder what she'll have waiting for us," Gurnard said, nodding as Tofei joined them with Asmund. Savarna had noted how these two had become close after their travels in the mainland. She hadn't spoken to either since their return.

"Whatever—we'll be ready," Tofei said, his eyes bright.

"We know about the giant Gorvaron," Jaran said. "I expect there will be other witch-men, though I'm not sure how many are left."

"One is more than enough," Savarna observed wryly.

"And there's Ranning, and whatever hell-spawn she summons up from Yffarn."

"Unva will deal with that side of things," Savarna said, hoping she was right. "Your Taic is there to protect her," she added, as much to convince herself. "He's expecting more shade-warriors, is he not? To combat her ghosts."

"That's what Taic told me, and Barin."

"You are not convinced about Taic."

"I'm not convinced about anything," Jaran told her quietly, as Gunard was lost in conversation with his son and Asmund. "I'm trying not to think about the other night. The barrow where Taic came from. The memory makes my head hurt. Better to focus on victory tonight."

"Unva said the moon has to reach its zenith," Savarna said, gazing at the passing waves. "You cannot strike before."

"I heard her," Jaran said. He turned to the three men present. "I'll need you to keep her creatures busy on the beach. You won't be fighting men, so you'll have to be prepared for sorcery, and the gods only know what else."

"This is our island," Asmund said. "We'll fight whatever comes our way."

Savarna looked at the young man. He'd changed, hardened. Asmund's task with the War Arrow had made him a warrior.

"We will be ready for whatever that hag sends." Gunard nodded and threw his burly arms around the two younger men. "This is your destiny, Jaran Saerk. We Northmen—whether of Valkador, Leeth, or beyond—are honored to be a part of that."

"You are my thanes." Jaran grinned at them. "They will sing your names in the halls for centuries to follow."

Savarna raised a brow and gazed at the ocean again. The men left them alone, Gunard returning to the helm with Tofei and Asmund joining Bjarni, who stood beside the helmsman.

Savarna looked back past the white wake trail, seeing the three ships following. "Are you ready?" she asked Jaran.

He smiled at her. "What do you think?"

"Do we have any kind of plan?" Aside from the talk of destiny, revenge, and songs, along with Unva's wily spell schemes, Savarna wasn't aware of a strategy.

"We two stick together," Jaran said.

"Obviously."

"We find Finvar, and that girl of his—Gunsala must in trouble."

"Yep."

"You and Finvar keep Sheega occupied, while I wait for Barin."

"Are you certain he'll show up?"

"I am, yes." Jaran stared at her. "But not until the right moment—as you keep saying to me. I need to be at Barin's Howe with Sheega distracted. Everyone has to push at the same moment: Unva, Rune and Rafin, you and Fin, his Vulkorye, me and … well, bugger it. All of us must do this."

"And the Whitebear will come?"

He nodded. "Whatever happens to me, save Finvar and his girl. And save yourself—I'm sure Vian will be looking for you. That witch is going to be focusing most if not all of her energies on me."

"Sometimes you say the stupidest things."

"I know—I'm a Northman."

Gronteyer's shadow slipped behind. Savarna glanced back, half-expecting to see the giant Gorvaron glaring down from the snowy heights. She saw nothing—only a solitary eagle gliding high above the broken clouds.

"Not much further," she said. They'd rounded a corner

and she could see low hills, a lake that sparkled like silver, and behind that the great wooden hall.

Jaran saw where she looked and nodded. "I'm proud to have you by my side," he told her.

"Where else would I be?" Savarna replied, a tear welling at the corner of her eyes.

GUNSALA HEARD THE HOUNDS BAYING AS THEY RACED through the woods. She ran to the top of a hill and waited for them to break through the trees. Terror pulsed in her veins, but she willed it down and gripped the shell as slowly the Vulkorye spirit rose up inside her.

She slowed her breath as she saw them emerge. Huge, pale hounds, a sickly white hue covering their coats, their ears blood red, and their yellow jaws dripped slaver. They circled, pawed, jumped, and snapped, sensing she was close. Gunsala stood on the rise, her hands pressing harder on the shell. The hounds started baying.

"Help me."

I'm here—close your eyes and trust in us.

"They are coming!" She looked down. The hounds clambered up the hill, scenting and sniveling. The biggest approached, saw her standing there and let out a howl.

Close your eyes!

"What?"

Do it!

Gunsala obeyed the voice inside her. She heard the other hounds roar and howl, the largest scraping his claws in the ground. They weren't attacking and seemed confused. Gunsala opened an eye. The leader, a huge white hound, stood on its hind legs and sniffed her face.

Keep them shut.

She blinked her eyes closed, feeling the dog's hot tongue slither over her cheeks.

"They'll eat me." She shuddered the words.

They have no power over you. Trust me. Join with me, Gunsala. You are flesh and I am spirit. Together we are stronger than any creature she has.

Gunsala heard the hounds snarl and scrape the dirt, as though disturbed. The tongue had left her face. She heard snuffling and the sound of paws padding away. The snarls were fading off as the dogs left.

Open your eyes.

She obeyed and saw the ghostly pack gathered at the bottom of the rise. Sheega's hounds glared up at her beneath the rime-glinting pines. Her Vulkorye was right. Gunsala smiled as she felt that familiar alien strength charge through her veins, like lightning bolts. She gazed down at her body and laughed. Where had these garments come from? Gunsala was dressed in fur and gold. There were heavy torcs and bracelets on her arms. Her head was covered by a winged helmet, and her bare feet tingled as if on fire.

"The Goddess speaks inside us," Gunsala had felt her mouth move, but the words hadn't come from her voice. "We are Vulkorye—it is time."

"It is indeed," she replied with her own voice. "I am ready."

Gunsala laughed as the hounds circled and sniffed the air. It was their turn to be nervous. She felt something in her hands and glanced at her left. That hand gripped a spear, while her right held a great bone horn.

The Goddess is with me.

Gunsala placed the horn to her mouth. She blew three long notes. The dogs turned and ran. Gunsala and her Vulkorye spirit gave eager chase. The quickening had come. Time to turn the tide. She yelled and held the spear high over her head. Gunsala ran, her fleet bare feet dancing, hardly brushing the soil as she sped after Sheega's pack.

A HARVESTING OF SOULS

UNVA HEARD THE NOISES. First the dogs baying, and then the eerie wailing coming from the woods near Sheega's hall. She smiled. "Those hounds have met their match, judging by their agitated voices."

"That wail sounded like a woman," Ivar said, looking shaken. Beside him, the grim-faced Svipdag shook his head.

"That was no woman I'd like to meet, in this world or the others," Taic replied, looming close. "And I've met some rough ones."

"One of your comrades, perhaps?" The shrewd-eyed Ivar was watching Unva carefully.

"Shut up, you stupid men," she told them. "You're worse than Rafin. You're here solely to keep a visual on those woods, in case that giant, Gorvaron, or any other sending comes our way. Leave me to do the thinking, and keep your lips together."

They took the hint and let her be.

Unva smiled. She knew Gunsala had found her Vulkorye again. That had been a challenge scream. Sheega would have heard it, of course. The Vulkorye were strong, but Gunsala was an innocent. If she acted too soon, or rashly, she could ruin their chances.

Unva gazed back inside the cave. Ivar stood staring out, off to her right. Svipdag had retired inside, most likely rummaging through his stuff again. She'd sensed that one's knowledge right away. That was the reason why she brought him and not Rafin. The dwarf would be more useful guarding Jaran's flank from Faerie, or whatever Sheega sent out.

"Taic, come here." The rangy throwback strolled over and leaned on his spear. "Make yourself useful. Scour those woods below us. I need to concentrate hard and cannot be interrupted. This next phase will take some time."

Taic nodded, slinging the spear over a shoulder and disappearing into the undergrowth.

"No speaking," she said to the other two behind her, after seeing Svipdag emerge. "You must be silent as mice." They nodded. Unva closed her eyes, commencing the summoning spells and chanting, picturing their faces and Rune's.

Are you near? This to Rune

Close enough, I slipped inside Cradon Iwey again. Faerie is here—the elves are being harangued by the trolls. We won't have to worry about Aldorian for an hour or so.

Coristain?

Seeking help, I believe.

Good.

Jaran will arrive at the hall shortly—I'll need to be down there.

Keep me informed.

She let Rune's shaggy image slip away and focused on the others. They were far off, but their visages became stronger as she chanted. Two shadowy figures, flickering and fading out of her inner vision.

Do you see me?

We do, Blue Culmeni said, her ashy voice drifting through the ether like wood smoke crumbling winter leaves.

Kigva?

I'm here, too. We are coming, Unva.

Hurry! It's about to start.

SHEEGA STOOD OUTSIDE THE HALL, HER WITCHING STICK and a crooked dagger clutched in either hand. She'd heard the woman's defiant challenge. Gunsala was coming and had found her secret weapon. She must have activated the abalone shell.

I should have taken that toy away from the child.

Sheega contemplated telling Finvar that his Vulkorye was coming. Instead, she gazed at the woods and saw her hounds spilling out, yapping and jumping about.

You dogs failed me.

Sheega narrowed her gaze. The pack leader howled and circled, its tail catching fire. That sizzle turned to a blaze. The pack leader whined and snapped his jaws before exploding into a ball of flame. The others came running back to her, tails between their legs.

Try harder next time.

Her birds had already returned. Hrelgisson was close, the four ships visible several miles away, clipping through blue chop.

Sheega felt the challenge coming from the lead vessel. She

sensed Griner's malice, and she smiled. *You'll not use that cursed axe on me.*

She turned to see Ranning beside her.

"Are you ready?"

"All done as you requested," he replied, looking at the dogs. "The woman is coming to save her man." His milky eyes hinted the edge of the forest, where a tall, helmeted, silvery, glowing figure had appeared, a round shield slung behind her back, and a spear and horn in either hand.

"Keep that Vulkorye occupied," Sheega told Ranning. "I need to focus on those ships. Are Garrosk and the others ready?"

"The Witch-Guard will greet Hrelgisson's warriors on the beach when they arrive," Ranning told her. "Your loyal dead thanes too. That should prove a good reception."

"What about Gorvaron?"

"He's hungry." Ranning grinned. "I'll send him to deal with Gunsala."

"Good." Sheega's smile was viscous. "That works."

"What about the elves?"

"I haven't heard from Aldorian yet. He's delayed. The trolls are giving him trouble, I expect. Thanks to that minx Coristain and the festering furbag Yetain."

Sheega envisioned a very special punishment for Rune this time.

"The elf king needs to deal with them swiftly and get here," Ranning said. "We need Faerie in case the big crew drop by." He looked up at the sky hesitantly, as though half-expecting to see Kullaan gazing back down at him.

"Aldorian will be here," Sheega said irritably. "Don't spoil my moment. The gods, too. No one's missing this show. Even your Grandfather will be quaking in his watery halls by the end of the night. Everyone is going to witness my return to glory. Gods, humans, Faerie, all of them!"

"Hmm, best I get busy, too." Ranning glanced sideways at her and vanished back inside the hall.

"Keep an eye on Finvar Droll," she shouted after him.

"Two," he replied. "One for Lofhi, the other for the man."

Sheega turned away and watched the distant shieldmaiden sprinting free of the woods.

"Poor Gunsala." She smiled. "You've peaked way too early, my dear."

Moments later, Sheega saw the huge shadow of Gorvaron lurching toward the trees, his hands dragging what looked like the bottom half of a tree. The giant's club would keep the Vulkorye spirit occupied until he got close enough to eat her host.

All is well, Sheega said to herself, starting the brisk walk to the shore and on to her pole. The wind was whipping harder than before. It was bitterly cold. She'd arranged that nicely. Those warriors were in for a shock—they'd sailed from summer into the ice. She'd sprinkled fresh rime in her lake this morning. The surface glittered with blue-silver as Sheega walked past, noting the runes she'd carved there herself.

Sheega reached her witching pole. This was where it would happen.

The conjunction.

She gazed up at the horsehead skull. Three of her birds settled on the bone and pecked the hollow sockets with black greedy beaks. Sheega smiled at them. She held her hands out wide, the ragged sleeves draping dark, her hair wild and tendril-free.

Unva was sending mind bolts her way. Sheega brushed them aside like drifting moths, but she noticed others who had joined her. Those pathetic warlocks who'd survived Dunnehine.

They wouldn't survive much longer.

Sheega closed her eyes and called in her power. She sensed the moon rising from the crust far away. She raked her fingernails down her cheeks until they dripped tears of blood.

Giddy with excitement, Sheega opened her eyes and stared up at the clouds racing past. There were faces in the clouds, shifting and frowning down at her. Among them, she saw Tyho, His brother Kullaan, the Traveler. Finally, her arch-foe, hated Elanion. Mistress of the Trees. She flicked her bloody fingers at their faces.

"I'm coming for you next!" Sheega yelled as the wind buffeted her face, and the storm she'd summoned whisked and howled around her body.

GUNSALA LAUGHED AS SHE SAW THE GIANT STORMING toward her.

We'll start with you, Hell-spawn.

She stowed her horn and unslung the shield from her back. Next, she readied the spear and hurled it across.

The giant paused as he saw the spear arc high and fall toward his face, stepping aside at the last moment. He glared at her and started moving again.

Gunsala laughed again. A new spear appeared in her hand. She tossed that, and the giant dodged. She threw a third. Again, he jumped aside, lightning-quick for so bulky a being.

Gunsala gripped a sword. Long and slender, the leaf-shaped blade was rune-traced and sparkled as she held it ready.

The giant was yards away, his monstrous features glaring at her and his single curled horn thrust out from his forehead.

Gunsala leveled her sword, adjusted the shield at her arm and started walking down to greet him.

Finvar rolled free as faggots exploded in his face. Lofhi stood before him. His red eyes burnt into Finvar's skull.

"It's started," the god said. "Are you awake?" He wore flames for garments, his face and body shimmering with an orange glow.

"I'm getting there," Finvar muttered. "Where's Gunsala?"

"Occupied." Lofhi blurred to smoke and circled around his head. "Ranning sent his giant weed-spawn to eat your wench. Shame. But this love affair of yours was never going to end well."

"Damn you!" Finvar leaped to his feet, but Lofhi's mind-blast sent him sprawling.

"It's not my fault," the god told him. "Get over it. I sense my miserable kin out there looking for us. I need to lie low for a while, Fin. Make sure you're ready. Let me down, and I'll torch you from your insides out."

Fuck off …

Lofhi vanished from his mind and eyes. Finvar shook the faggots off his skin and rolled to his feet. The hall was empty. Lofhi had gone, at least for the moment. And Gunsala was in trouble. He wrapped a heavy cloak around his shoulders and stepped outside the hall.

Jaran leaped onto the stone quay, Savarna jumping behind him. He could see the witch's creatures half a mile away, approaching the harbor in a shambolic line. Witch-men and shadowy warriors. Off to the north, he heard fighting. Looking that way, Jaran saw a shiny figure with a sword and shield being attacked by the giant Gorvaron.

Fin's Vulkorye.

"Rafin?"

The dwarf appeared beside him. He'd spent the voyage supping ale on the last ship.

"Can you and our boys keep that lot busy, while I help Gunsala kill that giant?"

"Aye, but be quick about it, lad," Rafin said. "She's most likes sent him out as a distraction."

Jaran nodded. "You coming?" he said to Savarna.

"What do you think?"

"We need to save that girl, so she can find Finvar. You'll need to help her, while I lure that troll away."

"I'll kill him with you."

"No, I've a better idea. Go to the hall and find Fin," Jaran told her. "Let him help you destroy her mirror. Rune spoke about it. It's her power source, and there's a demon inside. We need to neutralize that goblin."

"I'm not leaving you to fight that monster on your own."

"I won't be on my own." Jaran grinned at her. "As I said, I've a plan."

It is time.

Aldorian motioned the runes with his fingers and squeezed his body out of the rock. Joining him, the husks of a thousand flies cracked open and dropped into the dark water. His warriors were ready. Outside the cave mouth, Aldorian saw the white moon rising above the ocean. Afternoon had dwindled to evening, a pale gray shade of twilight.

Twilight belonged to Faerie.

"It is time," Aldorian told his captains, and bid them unfurl their silver banners. The trolls who'd followed them here were all dead. Greshgaran's goblins, too. He'd deal with the main enemy hosts when they returned to Faerie, after unlocking the sealing codes barring the World Gate. Before that glorious return to the Otherworld would come the reaping. A harvesting of souls. The age of humans would soon be over.

Aldorian gave the command. His blue-silver warriors mounted their glittering steeds and, as light fell to dusk, urged their mounts gallop free of Cradon Iwey. The setting sun shrank before them as though in flight of the elves' fury, and the moon rose triumphant, casting its glimmer on the ocean ahead. The elves turned north, a glittering storm of silver and blue.

LOFHI WATCHED THE ELVES RIDE OUT. AN IMPRESSIVE sight, if you liked that sort of thing. Lofhi didn't. All show, and no substance, the elves. He'd been inside Cradon Iwey, seen the dead scattered in those tunnels. *Messy.* Many were elves, the trolls trapped this side having sold their lives dearly. Lofhi had a soft spot for trolls, but the goblins were his favorite. He found a score of Greshgaran's folk dead and vowed a silent recompense with the elf king once this business was over.

Aldorian was over-hasty, having waited so long at the door. Lofhi wouldn't rush things. The moon was rising, but it needed to be fully dark outside before he'd journey back to that hall. Let everyone else do the hard work.

I'll rest easy here for a time.

CORISTAIN WALKED THE PEARL-WHITE BEACH, THE sentient shells cracking and glistening beneath her feather-light touch. *Her shells—she'll know I'm here.* Coristain slowed her walk, noticing the tall woman poised at the edge of vision, a white slender needle of stone shimmering in haze behind her. Beyond that tower were two lozenge-shaped suns, their rays casting a vibrant orange glow.

The woman watched her approach with large, cold eyes that flickered green through gold. Her hair was a fusion of copper and silver, long and flowing in the warm breeze. She reached out and grasped something from the sky. Coristain felt a stab of dread, recognizing the emerald bow clutched in the goddess's hand. The other hand held aloft a single golden arrow.

"The hunt has begun," the Goddess said as Coristain approached. The elf maiden was tall, but this woman towered over her.

"I need your help," Coristain said.

"Why would I help the elves who deserted their cousins, my beloved Faen?" The gold-green gaze penetrated her skin like tiny hot darts of burning metal.

Coristain held her ground. "That was my brother's doing, queen. Long have I struggled against the elf king's will."

"We know this, Coristain. Yet you are as treacherous as Aldorian. Why should I trust you this late in the day?"

"Because we want the same thing, queen. My people, the elves, broke the Final Law. Inadvertently, my brother has broken through the World Gate before the conjunction. That calamity will send a ripple out across the void. *He* will be made aware."

"*He* is already aware," Elanion said. "I cannot intervene directly, as well you know. But I offer you this chance. Take Kerasheva, Coristain. The Emerald Bow belongs in Ansu. It will be needed. This current thread will end soon, but the main Dance continues. I will protect your person, elf, in exchange for an obligation."

"What would you have me do?" Coristain trembled at the smile curling the Goddess's lips.

"Seek the lost ship, *Arabella*, and its captain, Carlo Sarfe."

"Where should I start my search?" Coristain asked.

"In the past," Elanion said, as her image faded, replaced by a noisy darkness and the rush of icy air. "Take the bow, elf. Find Carlo's ship. We will meet again in time ..." The voice faded as Coristain tumbled through electric clouds, shifting from realm to realm, swiftly crossing the dimensions of time and space.

WE WILL MEET AGAIN IN TIME ...

The faint words drifted through Gunsala's head like liquid fire. She felt the Vulkorye's joy surging through her veins. Gunsala knew the Goddess was watching them from afar, aiding the outcome. That had been Elanion's voice—the dream-woman she'd met on that beach.

She is with me. You, giant, are no match for us.

Gorvaron hefted his massive club, his brutish arms held high and ready to crush her. Gunsala laughed. She stabbed and lunged, dancing aside as the tree club struck the ground, was wrenched free and swung back at her face.

Gorvaron was astonishingly quick for a giant. She'd got a few strikes in, scoring dark lines along his calves. He'd hardly seemed to notice.

They'd battled for several minutes. Gorvaron hadn't got near her with the club, but it seemed like he wasn't trying that hard and, like her, was enjoying this contest.

"You can't escape, woman. I am Gorvaron."

"You are hell-spawn seaweed, and I'm sending you back from whence you came." She stabbed up with the sword, aiming for his hairy thighs.

A mistake. Gunsala realized it too late.

The club swung across like a pendulum and batted her sideways. She'd gotten in too close. *Amateur*, she heard the Vulkorye grumble. The blow sent Gunsala flying through the trees. Unswayed, she landed poised and ready, feet on toes, the shield and sword facing forward.

Gorvaron roared, seeing her tumble. He charged at her, hoisting the club, but he stopped when a shout turned his head.

"Who's there?" Gorvaron stared back at the trees. Gunsala saw two figures approaching and recognized Jaran Saerk and the woman, Savarna. The redhead was signaling for her to run toward them.

Gunsala shook her head. *I'm in control of this game.*

The two ran toward her. Gorvaron must have recognized Jaran. He ignored her and started crunching down toward the newcomers.

Don't you turn your back on me.

Gunsala ran after the giant, shouting, and with sword held high she swiped up at his legs. She missed. Gorvaron had picked up his pace and got ahead of her. He was roaring obscenities, eager to face Jaran Saerk. The Northman was waiting, swinging his axe Griner in spinning circles. Beside him, Savarna was calling her name. She started running toward Gunsala.

"Finvar needs you." Savarna rushed up beside her. "Let Jaran deal with this witch-man."

"I can kill him and rescue Finvar." She felt annoyance.

"Why risk the chance?" Savarna said. "Together, we can seek Fin and help him, before the witch and her people return to the hall. Jaran will lure Gorvaron away from here."

Gunsala glared at her for a moment and nodded. "That makes sense," she said. Together the women ran from under the trees, making for the distant shadow of the hall. As she ran, Gunsala noticed a dark shape flit out from the pines' shadow. Lofhi watched her with those coaly eyes.

"You're next," Gunsala said, running past.

JARAN MADE SURE HE KEPT AHEAD AS GORVARON pursued him across the rime-covered fields. It was evening. He'd hardly noticed the light fading. The sound of fighting intensified toward the beach. He'd seen Savarna and Gunsala running for the hall.

Where was Sheega hiding?

Jaran would know soon enough. First, he would deal with Ranning's creature and anything else in his way.

Jaran ran faster, picking up his pace, zig-zagging toward

the back of the hall. Gorvaron almost caught up with him twice, the massive club renting holes in the rimy soil as it sailed past Jaran's head.

He turned and traded blows, launching Griner at the hairy legs. Gorvaron seemed nervous of his axe and retreated back, allowing Jaran get ahead again.

The hall loomed close. Jaran turned a corner and made for the dark buildings behind. He reached Barin's Howe. Was it dark enough? *Am I too early?* Gorvaron came crashing up behind him.

Jaran shoved Griner up onto the stone and clambered after the axe, narrowly avoiding getting crushed by Gorvaron's club. He rolled over, making for the center of the slab.

"I need you!" Jaran yelled down into the murky tunnel at the Howe's northern end. "Barin!"

Gorvaron grunted as he heaved his vast bulk up onto the stone. He hefted the tree-trunk club and started walking toward Jaran, his terrible eyes glittering gleeful malice.

"Ancestor, where are you?"

I'm here.

"I don't see you!" Jaran glanced around in desperation. It was almost fully dark, and the moon had risen high above. Gorvaron was nearly upon him. Hard to get a good swing here. Jaran readied Griner.

Brace yourself.

The voice was a rumble inside his belly.

"That you?" Jaran stared at Gorvaron who was looming over him, the tree trunk ready to drop on his head.

"Barin?"

Instead of an answer, Jaran felt his body shudder and shake until he worried that he'd explode. Gorvaron had stopped and looked puzzled.

"What's happening?" Jaran's stomach cramped violently and his head throbbed like iron balls hitting a tin roof. Gorvaron stood gawping as though thunderstruck.

Jaran lurched forward. He tried to scream as the pain ruptured inside him. He looked down at his hands.

They weren't there. Neither was Griner.

Instead, Jaran saw massive paws with curled black claws.

We are one.

He was dimly aware of Barin's voice inside him.

We are the Whitebear.

RAFIN HACKED AT THE FEET OF THE HONEY-GREEN warrior. The creature fought with savage skill but was no match for the dwarf. He hued again, cutting a leg from under the witch-man and slicing down a third time as he fell.

Rafin glanced up from his work. The dead warriors were ranging out from the frozen lake like floating ghouls. He could see more of the witch-men, and something else coming from the beaches. Hard to make out because the light was almost done and the moon not yet fully risen.

But as Rafin stared hard, his keen dwarf gaze penetrated their disguise. An elf army rode toward them. He saw countless horsemen on smoky blue steeds, the horses with the pointed tapered heads and ears of Faerie beasts.

"We need to seek higher ground," Rafin yelled at Tofei, who had been fighting close by his side. "Those are elves fresh out of Faerie. We'll be swept apart like winter dry leaves if we linger here."

"The hills!" Tofei shouted at the fighters gathered close. "Make for the hall! Jaran will need us there." At Tofei's command, the Northmen broke free from the enemy and started running up from the beach, toward the dark line of woods and the smoky haze of hall and hills surrounding.

Rafin trailed behind, his short legs struggling to keep up with Tofei, Bjarni and the younger warriors. "Go on!" he yelled. "I'll join you presently."

Sherriff Doggan caught up with Rafin. He had a slice under one eye but was grinning. "It's good to be fighting again," he told Rafin. "What's that?"

Rafin turned and squinted through the dark. He heard unsettling noises coming from behind the hall. One had to be the giant, Gorvaron—a series of curses and thuds and shouts. The other sound was worse. A scraping, ominous roaring.

"What's making that other racket?" Rafin exchanged a quizzical look with Doggan.

"Let's go see," the sheriff said. Rafin saw that Tofei and Gunard had almost reached the hall. The corpse warriors were drifting that way, as were the surviving witch-men. A look back to the beach told them that the elves arriving like a silver storm cloud in the gloom.

Rafin glanced up at the moon. They had an hour, perhaps less. He heard deep horns and saw more figures had appeared further down on the beach.

Trolls. Some more must have got through. *Good.* They would keep Aldorian busy for a while. Rafin shouldered his axe and gripped the hammer in the other hand. The awful sounds were getting louder. Sherriff Doggan loped beside him, his axe gripped in both fists.

They'd almost reached the yawning blackness behind the hall when another figure emerged from the gloom.

"I thought you boys would need some help," Taic said.

"You're meant to be with Unva," Rafin told him. He

wasn't sure how to take this shade. Dead mortals could be as dangerous as Faerie folk.

"Nah, I'm needed here," Taic told him, shouldering an axe. "Nor would I miss this." He pointed his chin at the gloom ahead.

The three reached the darkness framing Barin's Howe. "Stay here." Rafin motioned Doggan keep an eye out on the hall where fresh fighting had started. "Me and this gawky spook will go see what the noise is all about."

Rafin walked into the dark with axe and hammer in hand. He blinked as Gorvaron's huge shadow loomed into view. The giant had his back to them and swung a blurry shape at something large and white.

"Is that what I think it is …?" Rafin stared at the shaggy snarling, distorted shape.

"It's Uncle!" Taic was grinning beside him. "Let's go help."

"Are you fucking mad?"

Rafin stood his ground and watched as the giant swung his tree club out at what appeared to be a huge white bear, a ghostly creature almost as big as Gorvaron.

Doggan appeared, his round face white when he saw what they were watching. "Our men are surrounded," he yelled. "We've got to help them."

Rafin looked at the shadows circling each other upon the stone slab. "You stay here," he told Taic. "I'm needed at the hall."

"I'm coming too," Taic said. "Uncle's got things covered here."

Sheega shuddered as the three witches sent bolts at her face. She reached out with her mind and blasted back. She laughed as she glimpsed Blue Culmeni screaming, her violet hair on fire. Unva's attack was broken for the moment.

High above, the gods' faces were swelling and shifting as moonlight merged with cloud. Sheega heard their dark heavy voices. She raked her fingers down the pole.

Ranning!

He wasn't around.

Gantallian. No response from that quarter. Something was amiss.

Sheega sensed a force working against her. She saw the elf army attacked by trolls and sent her mind back to the hall. Her dead and the witch-men were surrounding Hrelgisson's fighters. All good there. Sheega's mind-gaze drifted past them to the howe. And she saw him. The shadow of the Whitebear. A monstrous snow bear locked in combat with Gorvaron.

Even as she watched them, Sheega witnessed the huge bear catch the giant's horn with a massive claw and rip off his face. Gorvaron hit the stone like thunder. The Whitebear turned its snout toward her, sniffing the air as though scenting her blood.

"I'm here!" Sheega yelled at the wind. "Come and fucking get me!"

She saw the bear snuffle the giant's corpse with its maw. Moments later, it was gone.

Gantallian, Ranning—I need help!

Gunsala entered the hall and swept her Vulkorye gaze around. She saw shadows drifting away and heard distant laughter. Savarna was searching the far corners for the mirror chamber.

"Lofhi?"

"I'm glad you made it, Gunsala. I've missed your sweet embrace."

Finvar stood beside her. She hadn't seen him appear and knew this wasn't her lover. He had Finvar's face, but the eyes were ruby red and cruel. They mocked her.

"Free him," Gunsala stabbed her sword toward Lofhi's face. He faded and melted like liquid, appearing again to her right.

Gunsala.

She heard Finvar's struggling voice, before Lofhi quenched it with his own.

"Finvar is part of me, Gunsala. More so than before. I have claimed his soul. I shall release it once he performs his final task. First, Vulkorye—I'm going to deal with you."

SAVARNA COULD HEAR GUNSALA SPEAKING TO SOMEONE close by. She couldn't be distracted and kept searching. Jaran had asked her to find the mirror chamber—Sheega's knowledge source. Eventually, she stumbled upon a room of shadows and light. She saw a copper face leering out at her from the dark.

Who are you? The voice was a rusty metallic squeak, and the bug-eyes and ugly distorted features stared at her with loathing. Savarna's *Aikashi* growled inside her belly. *A djinn,* the goblin said. *We hate the djinn.*

"You must be Gantallian." Savarna stood before the mirror, gazing in. The goblin shrunk back, as though afraid.

Aikashi, Gantallian's metallic voice reached her. *Be kind—none of this was my idea.*

"Kindness is not our nature." Savarna felt the tiger roar inside her. Next, she was jumping forward, leaping into the mirror with arms outstretched. They became claws, rending and ripping. Gantallian gurgled as the tiger ripped him into tiny pieces. Time to shatter the mirror.

JARAN YELLED IN PAIN AS A BLOW LIKE A BOULDER HIT his face, knocking him prone. He felt a wrenching tear, as he and Barin were forced apart. Jaran rolled to his knees and looked back. For a fleeting moment, he saw the shadow of the Whitebear staring at him from beneath the sheen of moonlit trees.

"Thank you," Jaran said, as he staggered to his feet. Barin had gone to join the others fighting outside the hall. Jaran left them and entered the building from the rear. He saw two figures facing each other by the fire. Jaran recognized Finvar and Gunsala—but Finvar's eyes were glowing red, and he was smiling.

"I knew that you'd come, old friend," Finvar said. "I've been waiting for you."

"As have I."

Jaran turned sharply and saw Sheega standing in the hall, the smiling Ranning beside her with a long, slim blade in his hand.

Jaran strode toward her, but Finvar blocked his way, pulling out a dagger and stabbing.

"Fin? What is this?"

Kill him! A voice shrieked up from the fire trench.

Finvar smiled at Jaran. "Here's the thing." He winked. The knife twisted in Finvar's grip. Deftly, he turned the blade upon himself, stabbing hard into his chest. The ruby eyes popped wide in alarm, as Finvar Droll slid to the ground.

You tricked me ... The voice whined from the fire

Gunsala crouched low by Finvar's side. Jaran saw Savarna emerge from the gloom, her eyes wide with disbelief. Sheega and Ranning stood watching motionless. To Jaran, it seemed, time itself had frozen.

"Finvar?" Gunsala cradled Finvar's head as Jaran stooped beside his dying friend.

"I killed Lofhi with his own dagger," Finvar's brown eyes smiled back at her. Jaran loomed over the two. "It was the only way to outfox the Trickster. Sorry, girl—even a Vulkorye couldn't prevent that."

"Finvar, you can't leave me," Gunsala said. As she spoke Jaran noticed her face changing, becoming softer. A girl, no longer a Vulkorye. Unable to speak, Jaran saw Gunsala sob, as she kneeled and gripped his friend's hands with her own.

"Let's finish this, Hrelgisson," Sheega said, fading like dust shimmer from the hall.

Jaran nodded, "I'm ready." He hoisted Griner and walked out into the icy dark, the moon glowing full and casting silver over the lake.

Forgotten, Ranning stepped toward Gunsala, a dagger in his fingers. Jaran hardly noticed as she leapt to her feet and rammed the sword in the Water Faen's gut. Ranning made a mewling sound. Jaran glimpsed his body implode and seep like spilled treacle through the cracks in the floor.

Jaran walked outside.

She's at her pole." He saw Rafin shouting and pointing north along the beach. "Waiting for you there."

"Good." Jaran waved at him. "This won't take long." He turned away and walked the trail, the moon high and huge, a silver blazing ball above his head.

Jaran reached the horsehead pole by the shore. He saw the dark-haired woman standing there, her hands hidden beneath the rune staff. Sheega was smiling, the moon appearing directly above her head. She shifted and held out her arms. One hand clutched a crooked knife, the other a rune staff—a short stave capped with a weasel's skull.

Jaran could make out distant figures watching them in silence. Luminous faces flashed like torchlight above the surge of waves. The gods had come to witness the conjunction.

"You've done well, Jaran Hrelgisson," Sheega told him. "But now it's time to die."

Unva rolled as the blast struck the cave, blowing a hole in the roof. She saw Ivar diving for cover. Svipdag had vanished behind a pile of fallen rock. Beside her, Blue Culmeni was weeping, her beautiful violet coils still smoking and half her scalp burnt to scaly crust.

"Shut up," Unva told her. "It will grow back."

"It hurts," Culmeni sobbed.

Unva ignored her. "This is our big chance. Jaran is there. We mustn't delay." She looked up at Kigva and blinked as two other figures blurred into view. Unva saw the Vagrant and his lover the Siren merge through mist and stand beside Kigva.

"We're here to help, if you'll have us," Rasgalan said.

Unva glared at them for a moment, then nodded. "Let's do this," she said.

RAFIN HEWED THE HEAD FROM THE LEADER. HE watched as Garrosk's torso quivered, and green slime slid from the severed neck.

"Ugly fucking things."

Down by the lake, Jaran's two ancestors were surrounded by the dead Sheega had raised. He watched as Barin held out his massive war axe, and the dead thanes vanished one by one.

Tofei loomed beside him, his face bloody and eyes wild.

"We've won," he said.

"Not yet. There's still a witch to kill," Rafin told him, and they made for the hall. He walked inside, seeing the liquid slime resembling the remnants of a body splattered on the floor. Even as he watched, the body was solidifying and forming anew. Milky eyes winked at him. Rafin peered closer. A finger moved.

"Still alive, eh, Ranning?" Rafin asked.

The milky eyes narrowed.

"Remember me?" Rafin slammed his boot down hard, snapping Ranning's neck like a dry twig. The oily body twitched once, then stilled. "This time you'll stay dead."

Rafin carved the vengeance rune, and the remains of Ranning's watery corpse hissed and evaporated like steam up through the holes in the roof.

Rafin walked across to find the girl Gunsala, her armor scarlet and weapons placed aside. In her arms was a man he didn't recognize but knew must be Finvar Droll.

Gunsala held a shell to his wound. The abalone pulsed red through green.

"Finvar is dead," Gunsala looked up at Rafin with faraway

eyes. "But the shell will bring him back, if I use all my strength."

Rafin nodded sadly. He moved on, seeing another figure emerge from a room at the far end of the smoky hall. He recognized Savarna, her features covered in blood.

"What happened to you?"

"The mirror exploded in my face." She smiled grimly. "Gantallian's parting shot. He'd set snares inside his prison. "Where is Jaran?"

"With the witch. It is finally time."

"I must join him, Rafin. Finvar, too."

"Alas, but it's too late for that."

"What?" Savarna glared at him and followed Rafin back to where the girl sat with dry eyes over the dead body.

"Fin! No, this cannot be!" Savarna rushed and gazed down in despair. She turned to Rafin. "We need him to help kill the witch."

"It's too late, Savarna," Rafin said. He blinked when the dead man opened an eye.

"It's so nice being surrounded by optimists." Finvar Droll winked at Savarna.

"You were dead!" Rafin exclaimed.

"You're Rafin the dwarf," the man said. "Charmed to make your acquaintance. Yes, dead I was. I had to die to fool Lofhi. He'd have seen through anything else. By stabbing my own heart, I also took his."

A new voice spoke up. "My shell and this girl's love saved you, Finvar Droll. Payment for all that you have done."

Rafin and Savarna turned. A tall, willowy woman smiled at them. She had eyes of green and gold and hair of copper spirals. Her beauty was not of this world.

Rafin swallowed a curse. "Your ... Her ..."

The woman smiled at him before turning to the other man. "Stand, Finvar Droll," the Goddess said. "Let your poor Gunsala rest. She sacrificed her Vulkorye to bring you back. Gunsala is weakened and must sleep for a time. The shell I gave her is no more, but your woman will recover. My gift to you."

Rafin saw Finvar gaze at the sleeping figure in his arms. He kissed Gunsala's face and stood, joining Savarna and Rafin.

"One last favor—please watch over her," he said. "Until we're back."

"Go help Jaran Saerk," Elanion replied. As Rafin watched, the Goddess faded like mist over summer water. "The moment is upon you."

JARAN FELT AS THOUGH HE WAS TRUDGING THROUGH boiling mud. His limbs were heavy and stiff, the axe dragging in his fingers. He tried to raise Griner, but the weapon slipped and fell.

Sheega stood with the weasel staff in left hand. She poked that at him. Jaran tried to move, but the ground formed claws that wrapped around his boots, holding him trapped. The staff swung across at him, its weasel eyes glowing with tiny fires. Sheega stepped forward, the dagger raised high.

A silver blast of light struck the witching pole, knocking her off-balance. The invisible claws left his feet, and Jaran jumped clear.

Sheega spat blood from her mouth. She jabbed the rune staff viciously into the air and he heard distant screams. Sheega smiled at Jaran and tossed the staff aside. "I won't be needing that anymore," she said. "Come try your luck with this blade." She offered the dagger out with palms held flat.

Instead, Jaran reached down for Griner.

Quicker than his blink, Sheega struck, lashing out cobra-swift with the crooked knife to stab at his eyes.

Caught unawares, Jaran rolled free. He grabbed Griner and jumped back.

Again, she struck out at his face with inhuman speed.

Jaran leaped back a second time, the knife barely missing an eye. He tripped and swung wild with the axe, almost dropping it again.

Sheega laughed. "Be careful with Griner. It's a most treacherous weapon."

Jaran braced his feet, gripped Griner tighter.

Sheega returned to her witching pole, still shaking from the blast. She pointed up at the faces in the sky.

"See them watching up there? You're their champion, Jaran Hrelgisson. Those cowards haven't the appetite to confront me themselves. It was always that way. Take heed, because They are as much your foe as am I."

Jaran gripped Griner in both hands and moved slowly toward her. The witch's dark eyes followed his every move.

He got close and started to swing.

She slid out from the pole and jabbed at his eyes, knife questing, fingers scraping air.

Jaran jumped clear again. He circled to her right and swung across hard with the axe, catching the horsehead pole and slicing it in two.

Sheega screamed in rage as her earthing-channel faded. "Gantallian!" She yelled. "Ranning?"

"They are both dead."

Jaran heard a familiar voice. He saw Finvar emerge and stand beside him on his right.

"Lofhi?" the witch looked around, her face ashen.

"He's gone, too." Savarna appeared to his left.

"That is not possible," Sheega said, her eyes narrowing to icy slits. "It cannot end this way."

"It already has," Jaran leaped at her and swung out with Griner in a wide savage arc. The axe struck Sheega's white neck and sliced through. For the briefest moment, he saw her eyes staring back at him, the hatred nearly blinding him with icy pain.

Then Sheega's head rolled free and dropped to the dirt.

"Burn that body, and cover the head."

A new voice. Rune had returned. Jaran turned slowly, half-dazed. He saw Barin and Taic standing with Savarna, their faces filled with pride.

To his left, Rune gazed down at the smoking, sizzling body of the Ice Witch. "Savarna, you must destroy her body, and Finvar deal with the head. That way the witch stays dead. Quickly now, she's reforming!"

Even as he watched in horror, Jaran saw Sheega's head sliding toward the oozing torso. The head spurted tiny dripping fingers, creeping and tugging up to the body: joining, twisting and welding together, with a squeaky grinding, scraping noise.

Enough.

Jaran swung down again, splitting her face apart. This time, Savarna hewed at the body, and Finvar knelt down to stab out her eyes.

Barin threw a sack his way. Jaran grabbed the head from Finvar, seizing it by the smoky hair and jamming down firm inside the sack, while Finvar deftly tied the cords.

Taic passed a blazing brand across to Savarna. "Burn that body," he said. "We learned the hard way how to kill witches, here on Valkador."

Savarna shoved the brand down. Jaran and his companions watched as Sheega's corpse blazed into sudden flame.

"It is over," Jaran said, as the full moon vanished behind silvered cloud.

EPILOGUE
THE SKERRY

THAT LAST MIND bolt had ripped her body from her soul.
Unva drifted like a cloud, gazing down as she floated, her
mind at peace.

We won—I have my vengeance.

She saw the others lying far below, their bodies broken
and scattered like discarded dolls. Culmeni, Kigva, The Siren,
and The Vagrant: the last of the warlocks. Their souls were out
here somewhere. She'd heard Sheega's last vanishing wail as her
dark spirit screamed back down to Yffarn.

Unva rose higher, drifting into the clouds. Looking down
again, she saw the four ships. Men gathered around the
wooden hall, the ice melting swiftly on the lake surrounding.
A bright, warm, late-summer morning.

Ahead, like a shifting, rotating aura, the World Gate shimmered and shut fast. Unva saw the fleeing elves and trolls
trapped and, one by one, extinguished like bugs in lava flow.
The way was closed forever, and Faerie could never seep
through again.

Up higher, in the clouds, she saw the others—Tyho and His brother The Traveler, who waved at her as she floated past.

Our work is done here, Unva. She heard him say.

You did nothing.

Unva floated up further and out. The sky darkened. She drifted and faded. Dream-Unva became a wolf again. She felt the savage joy as she ran through the forest, joining the other wolves, her old friends, as the moon was swallowed by starlight.

Her mind mingled with dust sparkles and finally disappeared.

ONE WEEK LATER

Gunard readied his ship as the people gathered close. Jaran stood with his friends on the quayside. Savarna smiled sadly, and Gunsala gripped Finvar's hand.

"Why must you go?" Jaran asked Finvar, feeling sorry for this parting.

Finvar grinned at him. "This lass and I once flew all the way to Wynais. We've decided that we want to see that city again."

"You're sailing—why not fly again?"

Finvar looked rueful. "I lost the knack. Even Lofhi wasn't all bad. He taught me so much."

"I'm sailing west," Gunard told them from the ship. "Svipdag and Barin inspired me with their bold tales. Tofei's coming, and young Asmund, too. We'll drop this daft pair off somewhere along the way."

Finvar thrust out his hand, and Jaran squeezed it hard.

"Shit, that hurts—let go!" Finvar shook his hand in the

air. "Take care, Northman, and you, tiger lassie. I will miss you both."

"Steer clear of trouble, Candle," Jaran said, as he gripped Savarna's warm hand.

Savarna broke free of his grasp and hugged Gunsala. "Look after that fool," she told her.

"She always does." Finvar smiled, jumping onboard, as Gunard's men cast off from the quay.

"Think we'll ever see them again?" Savarna wiped a tear, from her eye as she leaned against him.

"I'd wager gold coin on it," Jaran said, smiling. But his heart was sad and he doubted he'd ever see his friends again.

THREE MONTHS LATER

The skiff beached on the shingle, and Valgarn leaped ashore.

"Are you sure you want to do this?" Trisa asked him.

"I have to," Valgarn replied.

She nodded. "You wait over on the skerry. I'll go."

JARAN SAT IN THE HALL, THE FIRES BLAZING. WINTER had come early, but he welcomed its embrace. They'd spent the last months working on the hall and cleaning both Barin and Taic's Howes, their shades having departed soon after the witch's fall.

It was early afternoon, and he'd returned from hunting. Ivar Ketilsson had shown him his favorite spots, Svipdag having departed with the others.

Savarna sat beside him as the new thanes drank and boasted, and their women—led by Myra—laughed and joked at their antics. The villagers had built new huts beside the hall. Rune had cleansed the building of Sheega's stain, before he, too, left them, departing to the ice realms to seek word of any survivors of his lost kin, the Yetain.

Jaran filled a horn with ale and sighed as he warmed his feet by the fire. He saw one of the thanes approaching and recognized Bjarni, his new sheriff.

"There's a stranger at the door," Bjarni said. "A woman. Sounds foreign."

"Let her in," Jaran said. "Poor lass must be frozen out there." He exchanged a curious glance with Savarna as the woman approached their high seats through the crowded hall, led by Bjarni. She wore a hood, and her features were covered by the heavy shawl.

"You are welcome here," Savarna said beside him.

The woman shook off her hood and stared at them. She was dark-skinned and handsome, though her face was lined, and the eyes echoed sorrow. She looked like she'd endured much in her time.

"She's Rundali," Savarna whispered in his ear.

"What news do you bring, lady?" Jaran bid her speak.

"News of your cousin," the woman told him.

"I have no cousin."

"Have you forgotten Valgarn Erlundsson?" The stranger stared hard at his face. "My man's mother's drow came to him in a dream. Sheega bid Valgarn avenge her."

Jaran stood, and the hall went silent. One of those brothers had survived after all.

"Where is Valgarn?"

"He'll meet you for holmgang at a skerry close by," the woman said. "I'll lead you there."

Valgarn leaned on his spear as the boat bobbed across the narrow channel to his right. He'd found this tiny islet while sailing around Valkador. It lay in the shadow of the mountain, south of his mother's hall. The water was shallow enough to wade across. He'd never explored this part of the island as a boy. Sheega hadn't let them.

Valgarn saw Trisa walking hunched beside another woman, a shrouded figure following close behind. The two women would witness the outcome. Hrelgisson wore no helmet, his hair trailed long and pale. Valgarn saw the axe and shield hanging from his belt.

Hrelgisson waded across to the skerry. Trisa stood close together with the other woman by their skiff on the shore, as though talking. The girl had flame-red hair. Valgarn recalled the stories he'd heard in Cardalis, about another woman from Rundali—a redhead connected to Jaran Saerk.

He waited with folded arms as Hrelgisson jumped free of the brine and walked toward him.

"I had assumed you dead." Jaran Hrelgisson stared at him for long moments.

"Not yet," Valgarn said, casting the spear aside and reaching for his axe. "I promised Mother I'd kill you first."

Hrelgisson nodded. "Let's get on with it."

Valgarn didn't move.

"Why are you hesitating, *cousin*?"

Valgarn dropped the axe in the dirt. He stared hard into Jaran's face. "I've decided not to obey my mother's last wish," he said. "Now that I've looked upon your face, I feel no hatred. Only sorrow for what we two have lost."

Jaran lowered his axe. Valgarn could see the women's anxious faces.

"Is it over—the Blood Feud?" Jaran Saerk asked him.

"For my part, it is," Valgarn told him.

Jaran smiled. "Come back to the hall. You and your woman. Stay with us as honored guests. As … kin."

Valgarn shook his head. "My hypocrisy only runs so deep," he said. "But I wish you well, Jaran Saerk. I would have liked to have fought beside you. Alas, mine was a darker road." He picked up his axe and spear, and he started trudging through the chilled water, back to the boat where their women waited with puzzled expressions.

"What happened?" Trisa asked wide-eyed, as Valgarn rowed their skiff out into the channel, Hrelgisson and the redhead watching them from the shore.

"We talked, briefly," Valgarn told her, and she kissed him. "I decided not to kill him. Where would you like us to go next?"

"Anywhere, as long as I'm with you."

"I liked her," Savarna said later that evening as the wind howled outside. "I still don't understand why he didn't fight you. We always heard her sons were monsters."

"The others were—perhaps Valgarn, too, once. I'm glad I didn't have to kill him," he added after a moment's thought. "Valgarn's changed, I reckon. Must be that Rundali woman's influence."

"Yep, has to be." She smiled. "Rundali women are—"

"—trouble."

She cuffed him, and Jaran laughed.

ONE MONTH LATER

The island lay draped in snow. At first, Savarna hadn't wanted to see the white powder settle, as it brought memories of Sheega. But this was different—a healing whiteness that rested, silent and soulful. They'd fished on the lake that day. Tired, she'd retired early, and Jaran had joined her. Most of the villagers had returned to their homes at the south of the island. The hall was quieter these days, though some of Jaran's thanes stayed in the new huts. Savarna had been dozing when a voice reached her from afar, waking her at once.

I need to see you.

Jaran was playing dice with Ivar, Bjarni, and a few others who'd remained at this end of the island.

"I'm stepping outside to get some air," Savarna told him, wrapping a woolen cloak around her shoulders.

"Don't tarry, 'tis chilly out there," Jaran said, looking up as she passed.

Savarna walked down past the lake and on to the beach. She saw the tiny boat and the hooded figure standing beside it. She felt her heart surge as she ran toward him.

Vian tossed the hood back and held out his arms.

"Oh, brother, is it really you?"

"I've come to say goodbye, Savarna," he told her.

She noted the sadness in his eyes. "Rasnei ... I'm so sorry, Vian."

He looked up at the stars. "She's out there somewhere.

Everyone is. Nothing ends, Savarna. Because there is no beginning. The Dance just ... dances forever."

"What will you do?"

"Find Rasnei."

"She's gone, Vian." Savarna felt the tears gather at her eyes.

"Kerasheva will bring her back."

"What ... I don't understand?"

"Elanion's Emerald Bow." Vian smiled at Savarna and
cupped her chin with a cold wet hand. "I dreamed of it in Ta
Shen. I'm going to find Kerasheva, Savarna, and use the
Emerald Bow to free my Rasnei."

JARAN LOOKED UP SHARPLY AS SAVARNA ENTERED THE
hall, her face lost to shadows. He caught her eye and crossed
over to where she sat. There, Jaran watched her in silence for a
time.

She looked at him, then turned away.

"That was Vian—wasn't it? Your brother was here." Jaran
gripped her hand and noted the loneliness in her eyes.

"He was." She nodded, fresh tears forming on her cheeks.
"Vian told me that he'd come to say goodbye. That he was
going to free Rasnei, find the bow called Kerasheva." She
shook her head.

Jaran nodded and clutched her hand tighter. "From what I
know about your brother, I'd expect Vian Eltayn to do exactly
that."

She smiled at him, her eyes grateful. "You're right, my
Northman," Savarna said. "With Vian Eltayn, anything is
possible."

"I'll raise a toast," Jaran stood, holding his drinking horn.

"To Vian of House Eltayn in Rundali. May Vian find the bow he seeks and free the woman he loves." The thanes cheered and swallowed and shouted. "To Vian of House Eltayn!

Savarna smiled as the tears brushed her cheeks, and Jaran stooped to kiss them away.

THE LONE CRAFT CUT THROUGH CHOP TOWARD THE distant lights of New Skarness. Vian hopped ashore. The next morning, he traded gold for a horse. He'd ride west and south to seek the fabled city of Wynais. Once he'd learned the secrets of that place, Vian would search for news of the sailor called Carlo Sarfe.

A new journey lay ahead. Vian smiled as he saddled his horse.

"Nothing is forgotten," Vian told the mare, as he urged her canter through the town, making for the steep hills framing the fjord and wild open country beyond. "We are but wind-blown leaves, scattered beneath the heavens."

THE TRAVELER WALKED THE BEACH, AS THE TWO ORANGE suns shone high above.

"My boy did well," He told the woman staring coldly at him from Her tower.

"He had scant help from you."

"Like You, wife, I couldn't risk getting involved," Oroonin said. "I had to keep Tyho and his thug brother in check. Fortunately, Finvar got to Lofhi first, outfoxing the fox. Ironic —I liked that."

"Why are you here, husband?"

"We've averted a disaster in the cosmos, sister. I thought perhaps We two should celebrate."

"I want nothing to do with you … brother."

"You don't mean that, Elanion," the Traveler replied with a sigh. Would She ever let that business go? "We've been through so much, You and I."

"Go away, Oroonin."

"Undeyna is dead," He said, smiling up a Her. "The Shadowman and His dark queen are no more. We can rest, at last."

"You know that isn't true, Oroonin." Elanion's gold-green gaze mocked him. "The Dance is never over. The eternal dragon must eat his tail."

"You're right," the Traveler said, and made to turn away.

"Hmm, come on up," Elanion said. "Perhaps it's finally time I forgave You."

"Time," the Traveler chuckled as he sprinted up the winding stairs of Her tower. "And to think that I used to consider that a purely mortal concept.

Here ends the Saga of Jaran Saerk the Berserker, Savarna and Vian of House Eltayn, and Finvar Droll, formerly a member of the Midnight Cutting Crew.

The legends of Ansu will continue …

MAP OF TASHEN

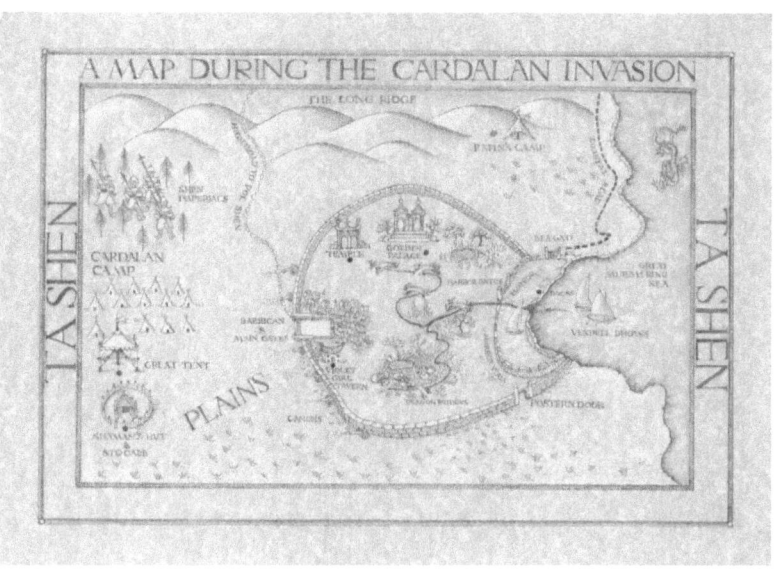

READ ON FOR AN EXCERPT FROM
LEGENDS OF THE LONGSWORD

"Got your attention?" The poniard quivered on the table top, and twenty pairs of eyes looked his way - including the proprietor, who'd been ignoring him these last ten minutes. "Good. Hate to think you were avoiding me." Hagan smiled, removed the dagger and thrust it back in his sheath.

"We are busy today," the innkeep looked worried. For good reason. Rough tavern, wrong side of town. And some local gang members already well into their cups.

Hagan glanced casually over to the corner table where four big swarthy individuals turned their heads away and continued with their dice game. "Not sensible, drawing attention to yourself, stranger," the innkeep said, his worried glance on the mark left by Hagan's dagger.

"I think you're worried enough for both of us," Hagan yawned snatched the ale from the proprietor's sweaty hands and downed three-quarters. "That's better." Thanks. Been a long week." He managed a rare smile.

The man nodded and turned to another customer, but Hagan grabbed his collar checking him. "Name?"

"Rezala," the innkeep mumbled. Hagan let go and the man dusted down his collar. He looked alarmed – stressed.

"And this place?"

"*The Crimson Moon*. Did you not see the sign above the door?"

"No," Hagan said draining his tankard and shoving it on the table. "Another. *Please*." He smiled again—rare that. *I must be in a good mood. Won't last—never does.*

"You can go now," Hagan winked at innkeep Rezala. "Customers waiting," he pointed to the far side of the room where three large men had just appeared. They looked as thirsty as Hagan had been. They also looked violent and angry—ready for trouble.

Hagan loosened the sword by his side. He'd greased the scabbard this morning, the sort of thing that's saved a man's life. Hagan sipped this second ale. Strange life. *I'm an exile. A…renegade.*

It hadn't sunk in. His departure from Morwella had been rushed. No time to dwell on niceties. Too busy dodging arrows, stealing boats, stowing away on merchantmen. *And here I am…*

Permio. A tavern, in the worst corner of a very bad city, Cappel Cormac. Hive of every cutthroat, cutpurse, and murderous whore imaginable. A place where, he, Hagan felt quite at home.

But he was angry. He felt wronged—they'd exiled him. The Duke, his people. *And for what?* A bit of raiding and robbing. Hagan the Highwayman. Hagan liked the thought of that. But it was the principle. The word *exile* tasted bad. Lacked honor. *I didn't deserve that.*

Others had done far worse and they hadn't suffered such a punishment. They'd been hanged, a few hung, drawn and quartered. But he'd been *exiled*—the dishonor was a stain on his family's name. Not that that mattered as they were all fucking dead. But the Delmorier family had once been wealthy merchants, before Hagan's grandfather had squandered every penny, except the few his only surviving son lost in the vice dens. Father choked on his ale one night—selfish bastard, served him right. Didn't leave much for the skinny boy he'd abandoned, Hagan's mother having left them years earlier.

He'd grown up poor—survived the streets of Vangaris. Had nothing except his family's name.

But a name was important. A name meant—*everything*. Until now. Way down here he was just another villain, another killer with a grudge.

Hagan sipped his second ale, his mood darkening as he thought about how they'd wronged him back there in the north. A thousand miles away. *I can never go back—see home again.*

Didn't matter, Morwella was a shithole anyway. Taxed and squeezed not only by lofty Duke Tomais, but by the High King over in Kella City.

At least he was free now. Almost spent of coin, no horse, no home—*but free.* Hagan smiled a third time. *It's becoming a habit.* Then turned his head as fighting broke out near the door.

The newcomers had rounded on those gang members at the table. Old score by the look of it, Hagan wasn't interested. Just glanced over, saw the bottle broken and rammed into the fat one's eye. *Messy, that.* Hagan, mood shifting again, chugged down his drink and stood up. He needed somewhere to sleep out the afternoon, and food. That too.

The fight settled almost as soon as it had started. Two dead on the floor, the fat one screaming as blood streamed from his ruined face. The gang had fled, the three big lads were seated at their table. They wore broadswords, Hagan noted. Northerners like him.

Mercenaries.

One glanced his way as Hagan waded through the crowd, smoke, and perfume of whores as he aimed for the door. That swung open again, creaking, the hot afternoon sun blinding Hagan for a moment.

A man stood there. Tall, long shaggy hair, and a huge sword swung across his shoulder. He barreled in, clearing a space through to the taproom where Rezala still sweated and grumbled.

"You're banned," Hagan heard Rezala say. Glancing back, he saw Shaggy-Hair reach over and grab Rezala's collar. Not the innkeep's day.

"Shut up, and pour me a large one." The accent was odd but familiar. Another northerner. Hagan was intrigued, and he noted how the three big men at the table were also staring at this longswordsman. They looked angrier than before. And one reached for his blade. The tall fellow didn't notice; he was watching Rezala fill a tankard.

"Better enjoy that," Rezala said. "Last one you're getting."

Hagan saw the innkeep nod to the nearest mercenary.

"That him?" The sellsword asked. Rezala nodded. The longswordsman seemed oblivious, cradled his ale and sighed, as though he was sharing a tender moment with his lover, no one else around. Hagan wondered if he were soft in the head.

All three were on their feet. Big, angry, and well balanced. Confident. *Professionals.* They shoved sweaty bodies aside heading for the place where Shaggy-Hair was making love to his beer. Men grumbled and swore, the odd one spat. But they parted like palm leaves in summer storm letting the three large figures through.

Hagan scratched his face where a mosquito had bitten him. He hadn't cared about the earlier fracas, but was interested now. Why were these northerners here? And who did they work for? He needed to know, could be useful later.

"Outside." Hagan saw Rezala hint the door as the nearest mercenary stormed up behind Shaggy-hair. "Don't want another mess in here."

The man ignored him, and slowly slid his broadsword free for maximum effect, men parting either side to allow him room to swing.

"Put that back or I'll shove it up your arse," the accent was almost Morwellan. The lead mercenary paused, sword half out of scabbard, his fellows hustled close behind.

A mistake.

Shaggy-hair turned, and with a speed Hagan had seldom witnessed, slammed an open palm hard into the leading mercenary's face, cracking the small bone in his nose. He crumpled, sunk from view. The other two leaped forward.

And were knocked back.

Elbow to face, fist on balls, boot stamping on ankle. Shaggy-hair grinned as he grabbed the pair by their ears and slammed their heads together. They slid to join their comrade on the floor.

Shaggy-hair turned away and started on his ale again, ignoring the swarm of eyes and hostile glances.

"And you said *I* was drawing attention to myself," Hagan muttered to Rezala, who had glanced his way briefly before crouching low, whispering to a boy. Hagan watched the lad vanish out a back exit, the bright glare dazzling him a second time.

"Off to get the Watch I should imagine," Hagan said, as men resumed their seats, apart from the three sprawled on the floor. They showed no sign of moving any time soon.

"Expect so," Shaggy-Hair turned slowly and noticed Hagan for the first time. "Don't know you."

"Just arrived," Hagan said. "Think I'm going to like it here."

"No one likes it here," Shaggy-Hair said.

"Friends of yours?" Hagan hinted the three on the floor.

"Not really. They work for his boss," Shaggy-hair leaned over the counter, grabbed an empty tankard and hurled it at Rezala - catching him on the back of the head and knocking him from his feet.

He turned and grinned at Hagan. "I was banned anyway," he said, draining his tankard and striding from the room, a wave of bodies parting to let him through. Hagan suspected most had hands on daggers, and some would be following.

He chose to tag along.

"Wait," Hagan said, and the longsword stopped, turning slowly to stare hard at Hagan. *A man like me—a killer.* Someone with a grudge.

Steely eyes, the hue of northern oceans. Lean face, long bones, wicked scar above right brow. Black leather tunic and trousers. Silver studded belt, and battered mail shirt showing beneath.

"Name's Hagan Delmorier."

"Corin."

"From where—I can't grasp that accent."

"Fol—I'm Corin an Fol," he replied as though that were significant.

"Isn't that a province of Kelthaine?"

"Fuck off—it's a free country," the man called Corin said. "Nothing to do with Kelthaine, or the fucking High King."

"Sorry," Hagan shrugged. "Just curious."

"So are they," Corin said. Hagan turned and saw at least a dozen men had followed them out into the swelter of a Cappel Cormac afternoon. They stood in a circle surrounding Hagan and his new friend.

"I would leave if I were you," Corin said. "Me they want."

"I've only just arrived," Hagan yawned—past time for his afternoon nap. The stomp and scrape of boots in the distance, getting nearer. Shouting too. "Sounds like the Watch."

"Time I left," Corin said, and whirled around planting a fist neatly on the jaw of a bystander who'd got too near. He stepped sideways, slid the huge sword from its scabbard and shoved it point-first into the hot dry mud that served as a street in this shithole of a city.

The watch filed in looking nervous, tense, and very angry. "Your move," Corin said, flashing them a grin. They shuffled, glanced sideways at each other. A captain of sorts pushed his way through. Rezala yelled at him, holding a wet cloth to his bleeding skull.

"I barred him," Rezala said. "He's a troublemaker."

"All your punters are troublemakers," the captain looked pained, not wanting any of this. He pointed to Hagan. "And who is this?"

"I'm Hagan—just arrived."

"Well you'd better bugger off," the captain of the watch said. "Else we nab you for collusion."

"I only stepped out to enjoy the sunshine," Hagan said. No one was moving: captain, innkeep, the watch, tenants from the inn, and now bystanders and street vendors and even the odd, scarf covered whore—everyone had eyes on that two-yard sword, and the wild-eyed northerner leaning on it.

The captain approached Hagan, while staring at the other northerner. "I said go," the watch's leader hissed in Hagan's ear, then turned and yelled at his men. "Get him!"

Three spears levelled and poking, their owners thrust forward without too much enthusiasm. Bad mistake. *You have to do something properly, or not at all.* Hagan stepped away from the captain and blinked as metal glinted, there was a whoosh and a meaty thud. He saw a man's head rolling in the mud. A second joined it, then an arm.

"Time to run!" Corin shouted across to him.

Past time. Hagan turned on his toes, cat-graceful he pounced at the captain and kicked him in the groin, following up with an elbow to the face as the watch leader crumpled. Hagan grabbed an arm, swung the captain around into the next man attacking him. Both sprawled. Hagan saw Corin was loping down the street with that huge sword whirling like a windmill.

For fuck's sake... Thanks for waiting. Hagan stepped back, slid his rapier free and cut left and right. Swift clean strokes. They backed away. A gap appeared. He ran through just in time to see Corin vanish into a side street.

GLOSSARY

Valkador
 Ivar Ketilsson: a hunter
 Bjarni Orlsson: a villager
 Myra: his wife, Ivar's daughter
 Geda and Silfi: their daughters
 Torund: a village elder
 Haning: a village elder
 Asmund: a villager
 Olof: a villager
 Gorstein: a stranger
 Svipdag: a vagabond cave dweller
 Jaran Saerk: a returning hero
 Savarna: a Rundali shapeshifter
 Finvar Droll, their friend
Leeth
 Doggan: a district Sherriff
 Gunsala: A girl from Grimhold Village
 Tomsag: a thane
 Halfti: a thane

Helga Kregat: a legendary witch

Gunard: an outlaw thane

Tofei: his son

Cralf: an outlaw

Dustan: an outlaw

Shen

Rasnei Cai Ti-Shen: The Sapphire Empress

Magister Chulan: once her enforcer, now a traitor

Gujun: an assassin in Chulan's pay, leader of the Silent Slayers

Dorthar: a veteran auxiliary serving under Hranic Finehair

Gurtei: Former MCC leader, now a general in Ta Shen

Roile: a former robber in the MCC

Truggan: a former robber in the MCC

Lin Gu: a former slave

Goi Stagan: leader of the Shen River garrison

Captain Matax: general in charge of Ta Shen defense

Nolenzes: a physician

Jilanna: a Laregozan servant girl

Vian of Rundali, the empress's lover

Cardalan (West)

Ran Genza

Dranan: Genza's spymaster

Cama: his second

Dupacris: Genza's seneschal

Nuando: a bodyguard

Valgarn Erlundsson: a Northman mercenary

Trisa: a Rundali slave

Cardalan (East)

Ran Casca: leader of the attack on Ta Shen

Ragan Uzcara

Ragan Racara

Ragan Casla
Ragan Calgara
Vendel
The Yanturi: Vendeli ruler in Omala City
Tulomon Caze: his spymaster and enforcer
Octaxa: a shaman-warrior, leader of the Sangala
Utuxla: his second
Grodu: a former gladiator working as a spy for Octaxa
Yamondo
King Ulani Baha III: Yamondon ruler in Cantacari
Dolusa: Ulani's nephew and Third Tarakai
Jelagi Gur: a steward
Storgo: the king's bodyguard
Bagelzei: a soldier and member of the Baha royal family

Others

The Traveler: a mysterious warlock
Unva: a witch from Dunnehine. Enemy of Sheega
Carlo Sarfe: a sailor
Warlords in league with Unva:
Blue Culmeni
Big Kigva
The Siren
The Dream Scraper
Rasgalan the Vagrant
Deities and Creatures from Otherrealm
Tyho: The War God
Kullaan: The Wind God
Lofhi: The Trickster
The Emerald Queen: A mysterious deity
Undeyna: Former goddess/sorceress, now known as Sheega
Aldorian: Faerie Elf King

Coristain: An Elf Maiden

Rumgorz: Faerie Troll King

Gruntzor: His son

Greshgaran: Faerie Goblin King

Rann: A daughter of Sensuata, The Sea God

Ranning: A banished Faen from Sensuata's Realm

Gorvaron: formerly a giant Cragga from Fol, now serving Ranning

Gantallian: a goblin imprisoned inside a mirror, forced to serve Sheega

Rune: A Yetain from the frozen wastelands

Garrosk: A Witch-Guard

Rafin the Smith: a dwarf king from Swartzheim

Gamalene: his wife

Drini: his youngest daughter

Would you trade your soul to save your life?

The Crimson Lady knows that her soul may be the price she has to pay to get revenge.

If you enjoyed *Blood Feud*, you will love this new tale, *The Crimson Lady*. It's available free for newsletter members only. Don't miss out! Join our fun newsletter the JW Webb VIP Lounge. *Subscribe today!*

ENJOY THIS BOOK? THEN HELP SPREAD THE WORD!

Reviews are one the most powerful tools in my arsenal when it comes to getting readers for my books. Much as I'd like to, I don't have the financial muscle of a New York publisher. I can't take out full-page ads in the newspaper or put posters on the subway.

(Not yet, anyway.)

But I do have something much more powerful and effective than that, and it's something that those publishers would kill to get their hands on:

A committed and loyal bunch of readers.

If you have enjoyed this book, I would be so grateful if you could spend just a few minutes leaving a review, wherever you bought it. And I'd love if if you'd like to email me a link to the review! ansureviews@gmail.com

Thank you so very much!

ABOUT THE AUTHOR

J. W. Webb is an English writer living in Georgia. Mostly he writes fantasy, though sometimes diverts in even stranger directions. His epic saga , The Legends of Ansu, blends the mystic grandeur of JRR Tolkien with the gritty realism of GRR Martin. Webb's characters are three dimensional and flawed, their world a tapestry of vivid color and constant motion. All the books feature beautiful bespoke sketches by the late Tolkien illustrator, Roger Garland.

www.ingramcontent.com/pod-product-compliance
Lightning Source LLC
Chambersburg PA
CBHW032254020726
47495CB00001B/104